Tor Books by Ed Greenwood

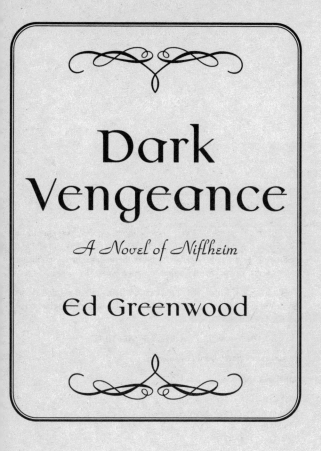

Dark
Vengeance

A Novel of Niflheim

Ed Greenwood

TOR®
fantasy

A TOM DOHERTY ASSOCIATES BOOK

New York

DARK VENGEANCE: A NOVEL OF NIFLHEIM

Copyright © 2008 by Ed Greenwood

A Tor Book
Published by Tom Doherty Associates, LLC
175 Fifth Avenue
New York, NY 10010

www.tor-forge.com

Tor® is a registered trademark of Tom Doherty Associates, LLC.

ISBN 978-0-7653-5695-6

First Edition: August 2008
First Mass Market Edition: September 2009

Printed in the United States of America

0 9 8 7 6 5 4 3 2 1

To Brian,

Who deserves much, much more than this

From the slave pits of the Dark Below, spoken in hushed tones:

"He fought back!"

"He slew his overseers!"

"He escaped!"

"Maybe he will return. Maybe he will lead us all to freedom!"

For the first time there is a new companion for the oppressed of the slave pits of the Dark Below.

That companion is hope.

From the bedrooms of young princesses and priestesses of the Dark Below, said breathlessly:

"The Hairy One dared to escape!"

"Our warriors could not defeat him!"

"One of our own aided him!"

"She was mangled and grotesque. She allowed herself to be crippled in combat—yet suffered herself to live."

"She allowed herself to become a monster!"

"She used to be one of us . . . and she still lurks in the shadows."

"We are not safe. None of us! Not from our slaves, or our own kind—or even ourselves."

"Remember, she used to be one of us!"

For the first time a blemish on Dark Below society has managed to survive, and its taint is felt by all.

A taint, and fear!

Dark
Vengeance

Prologue

Fair words should be first spoken,
but are no more than false, weak noise
if backed by no skilled and ready sword
and alert, firm resolve.

   —*saying of the priests of Thorar*

S ister," Jalandral Evendoom purred, "I've been
hunting you for a long time."

Taerune stared at him, her mouth dropping open in
astonishment.

Jalandral?

Here?

In this small, damp cavern so close to the Blindingbright, the realm of the Hairy Ones?

Her brother took a slow, smiling step toward her. Behind him, Old Bloodblade stepped silently out of a dark
side-cleft, sword and dagger raised.

Tall, dark, and lithe, Jalandral smiled confidently, a
smile that told all eyes he knew he was as deadly, fear-
less, and handsome as Olone ever made any Niflghar
rampant. His sword looked as long and whisper-sharp as
he did.

To any eye, Taerune and Jalandral Evendoom looked
like blood-kin; she was as tall as he, and—even in her
weariness—every whit as fluid in her movements. Yet
her left forearm ended not in an elegant long-fingered

hand, but in a wickedly curved sword blade. Her other hand was now moving along her belt, seeking a dagger.

Jalandral's smile widened, and grew wry. "You think you've any hope of keeping your life, sister, if I want to take it?"

"Do you want to take it, Dral?" the maimed, outcast Evendoom asked, her whispered words a challenge.

"Why should I not? You are an outcast, your life forfeit. Your maiming shames us before Holy Olone, and you are *insane*—besotted with love for the Hairy One, the forgefist who is the valuable property of our House, and whom you helped to escape."

"You are wrong," Taerune told her brother coldly. "As ever, brother, you conceal or ignore your misjudgments with style and loud overconfidence. I *am* outcast, so it matters not to you or any Nifl of Talonnorn *what* I am—when I am far from Talonnorn, in lands Talonar don't control. No one rules these caves but the Ravagers, who rightly care nothing for the laws—and opinions—of Talonnorn."

"Yet behold," Jalandral purred, taking a step closer. "Talonnorn reaches out for you, even here."

"Talonnorn? Or just you? Brother, does our House survive in Talonnorn?"

"Evidently," Jalandral sneered, taking another step and hefting his long spellblade menacingly.

Then, swift as any striking cave-snake, he spun around, a second, shorter sword thrusting point-first out of one of his sleeves to menace Old Bloodblade, who'd been creeping up behind him.

"*Yes*, fat old half-gorkul, I knew you were there," the Evendoom lord said softly.

Old Bloodblade snorted. "And so? You used the time that gave you to think up a clumsy insult and offer me warsteel so woefully slowly? No wonder we Ravagers slay proud Talonar lords with such ease!"

Despite that "we," the longtime Ravager war captain led no one, now; his band had perished to the last Nifl. He was fat—*very* fat, for a Niflghar—and wore a none-too-clean patchwork of belted-together scraps of old, salvaged armor that bristled all over with the hilts and grips of heavy, well-worn weapons. He bore a broad, well-used sword in one hand, and a dagger in the other. Jalandral's spellblade flared with awakened magic, and the dagger in the Ravager's hand glowed in magical answer.

"You are what you always were, buffoon," Jalandral told him coldly. "Beneath my notice."

The old Ravager shrugged and strode right past the Evendoom lord, turning so as to stand between Jalandral and his sister, facing Jalandral.

"So much is my gain," he said gruffly. "Sadly for you, would-be kinslayers are not beneath mine."

Jalandral's reply was a sneer as he stalked purposefully forward, sword gleaming.

Bloodblade rolled his eyes, contorted his face in a broadly exaggerated imitation of Jalandral's sneer—and struck aside the Evendoom lord's sudden thrust.

Jalandral hissed and slashed at the fat Niflghar, their swords clanging together. Sparks flew as both blades sang off each other in sudden blurred haste—intricate thrusts, parries, and lunges that skirled very briefly before Bloodblade flicked Jalandral's sword up and out of his hand, disarming the young Evendoom lord with seemingly effortless ease.

The long, slender Evendoom spellblade rang off the cavern ceiling—and fell with a crash to bounce on the stones in front of the old Ravager's worn, scuffed boots.

Snarling, Jalandral reached for one of the long daggers sheathed at his belt—only to flinch back as Bloodblade kicked his sword back to him.

He hesitated, fearing the Ravager would strike at him if he bent to take it up, but Bloodblade yawned and stepped back with a bow, waving his hands at the fallen spellblade with a flourish, like a Talonar servant presenting a flamboyant feast dish. Behind him, Taerune watched in silence, her arms crossed—for all Talonnorn like a House crone watching rampants spar with practice swords.

With a hiss of rage Jalandral ducked down, plucked up his sword, and sprang to the attack again, calling up the fire the spellblade could spit, to cook his foe.

It boiled up, warm and raging.

The dagger in the fat Ravager's hand pulsed again, and an astonished Jalandral found the spellblade's fire . . . contained!

Snarling in its imprisonment, nigh-numbing his arm in its restless hunger . . . yet he could not unleash it.

Hundreds of times he'd willed these flames to lash out at a foe, just as he was seeking to unleash them now, but this time, nothing happened.

He strained, jaw clenched.

Nothing at all.

Humming a jaunty tune, Old Bloodblade stepped forward and crossed swords with Jalandral as if they were two House younglings being taught the first basics of blade-work.

With a snarl of rage Jalandral struck at his foe, seeking to bind the Ravager's blade with his own and thrust his point home, at the same time abandoning its inner fire in favor of the lightning it could also spit.

Which awakened obediently, sending the usual thrumming numbness up his arm as he danced to one side, parrying and counterthrusting as swiftly and deftly as he could. The lightning reached its height and then roiled, caged just as the fire had been.

Some magic in that damned dagger must be—

Jalandral found his hand empty, and heard his spellblade clang off stone somewhere behind him.

The Ravager had disarmed him again, just as casually as before.

"You—" Rage making him grope for an insult florid enough, Jalandral plucked out one of his knives as he stepped back.

"Stop posing," Bloodblade growled at him, "and start

treating other Nifl as equals. Then, perhaps, you'll live. Perhaps."

Jalandral stared silently at the older, shorter, and fatter Nifl for a long time. Then he sighed, sheathed his knife, and asked, "And if I do?"

Taerune stepped forward.

"Then you'll have time to listen, while we all talk," she said calmly. "As there is much to talk about."

1

A Face in the Fire

Nightskins come and nightskins creep
Keep your sword right sharp
Nightskins catch and nightskins keep
So may your sword drink deep
                    —Orlkettle firesong

*G*ood hinges," Harmund the weaver said happily,
moving them in his hands.

Not so long ago he'd have said that grudgingly, if
he'd have admitted it at all. Yet with the passing days
upon days, Orlkettle had warmed to the terse giant who
worked tirelessly at the village forge.

Old Bryard the Smith might have been more than
grudging, for the giant who called himself Firefist did better work than Orlkettle had ever seen—hinges and door-
strapping and handles, not just picks and axes and
war-blades. Instead, Bryard trusted this Orivon Firefist.

By night and by day the muscled giant stood at the
anvil or the forge, saying little but nodding and smiling
often as he worked. More and more, Bryard sat on his
own guests' benches and talked with the men of Orlkettle, as they all watched the man of lost Ashenuld—the
man who had been taken as a boy by the nightskins and
enslaved in the Dark Below, only to escape alive all these

years later—craft better work than Bryard had ever managed.

And that was saying something.

Orlkettle had been proud of Bryard, and peddlers came often to buy his forge-wares. Yet this Orivon was two clear strides ahead of the old smith in skill, and more, doing work of such strength and finish and sweeping-curves beauty that word of it had spread far.

There had come a day when a long-bearded priest of Thorar had climbed down stiff and sore from six days on a mule to bring Firefist an old, crumbling Holy Helm in need of mending . . . and gone home beaming after his tears of joy were done. And he could bring himself to stop constantly running marveling hands over the gleaming thing of beauty that Orivon had gently set before him.

Gently, that was the way of Orivon.

Not thrusting aside old Bryard or anyone else, not loudly declaiming his views or his will to all Orlkettle. He chased no lasses, and calmly stepped aside from fights and provocations as though they had never been offered, answering them only with a calm, reproachful look. He dwelt at the forge, and ate with Bryard's family or at the board of the Tranneths, who made the best kegs and barrels this side of Orlpur and rejoiced at the iron bands he made for them (and who had lost their own daughter Aumril to raiding nightskins just as Orivon had been lost, a season before he'd first stalked into Orlkettle with fearsome sword in hand and a bundle of other fine swords, all of his own making, under his other arm).

Orivon paid for all that went into his mouth with field-work and repairs, like any village man.

The village of Orlkettle had slowly lost its fear of him, and men now nodded to him in the street, and no longer tugged their children back from his reach.

For his part, Orivon Firefist was flourishing. Arms and shoulders of corded muscle, a torso that should have been white but that was browned all down the front by forge flames and the mottled scars of many small burns, he was usually to be found stripped to the waist, poking his beak of a nose and scowling brows close to the forge to peer at red-hot metal without regard for its fierce heat.

His height, obvious rugged strength, and oft-bare torso proclaimed who he was from afar. Closer eyes saw flowing brown hair, beard, and mustache, and a gaze that could pierce when it wanted to, and held no fear. His wardrobe seemed to consist of scorched-in-many-places leather breeches, broad belts, leather boots, a weather-cloak, and little else.

Harmund the weaver looked across the forge now, in the time of long shadows ere sunset. Orivon was patiently raking coals together to receive more wood, to make the fire hotter. When he was done, Harmund knew, he'd look up, and could then be asked the price of six hinges like the one in his hand, and how soon they could be ready.

Then they both heard the bells, and that unasked question was forgotten in an instant.

Many fine bells all jingling in rhythm meant a peddler signaling his arrival in Orlkettle, bringing wares and news.

An excited murmur arose all over the village as Orl-folk came out of their houses; Harmund the weaver was at the forge-door staring out in an instant.

"'Tis Ringil!" he called back over his shoulder, forgetting that Orivon hadn't been in Orlkettle for many seasons. "Years, it's been—and no wonder. He goes to Orlpur, and ports on the sea beyond, too!"

Orivon nodded, unhooked a chain above his head to let the great lid down on the coals to smother them, and stalked to the door.

In the long golden light of the dying day, the village square was crowded. Many Orl-folk were converging on it from all directions, calling greetings and questions as they came to a small, hunched man who was busy with his mules at the water-trough. As they watched, he swept off his feather-adorned cap and set it on the signal-fire dome with a flourish. When he straightened up again, Orivon got a good look at him. The peddler had a weathered, wise-eyed face and a pepper-and-salt beard. He wore a smart black jerkin with scarlet piping; it looked like the uniform of a courtier or a ceremonial guard—which is just what it was, though Ringil had never actually been a member of that court guard. Not that either guard nor court existed anymore.

So much Harmund told Orivon ere they joined the crowd. Ringil had hung his strip of bells and was now hobbling his train of a dozen mules. He'd already reached down a folding table from among their bulging saddlebags, and set a lantern on it to be lit when dusk drew down. "People of Orlkettle, I bring you treasures from afar! Fine things," he said jovially. "Wondrous things!"

"Flashy dross," Dorran the miller called out, just as pleasantly.

Ringil reeled in mock horror, clutching at his heart and flinging his arms up wildly. "Strike me deep!" he gasped. "Wound me sore!"

Then he winked and added, "*Fine* flashy dross."

The rasping voice of Old Authra cut through the ripple of chuckles that followed. "What news?"

The peddler nodded. "Plenty to tell, plenty to tell. There's a new king in Rond . . . the Silent Stone split apart and the witch Harresse stepped up out of the grave she's lain in underneath it these seven-score years; she's none too pleased, and most folk are fleeing Duncrown right now . . . and the nightskins are raiding again: they hit Tlustal and then Ormyn not so many nights back."

"Then they'll come here, as sure as the sun rises," Authra snapped, glaring all around as if nightskin raids were the fault of all her neighbors.

There were many murmurings of dismayed agreement—that stopped in an instant when Orivon Firefist's deep, level voice floated across the crowd.

"How many nightskins? Did they use any magic? Swords, or spells?"

Ringil blinked at the source of those questions. "Ho, you're a big one, aren't you? Thinking of fighting them?"

"Yes," Orivon said firmly.

Orl-folk stared at him in the darkening square as if he'd turned to a nightskin himself, right before their eyes.

The peddler shook his head doubtfully. "Not sure as anyone knows how many ran through Tlustal, but in Ormyn they were ten-and-seven strong, and waved swords. They had those capture-hoods that make the poor hooded ones obey them instead of running off, but that's all the magic I heard about." He peered thoughtfully at Orivon's burn-scarred torso and leather breeches. "You *really* thinking of fighting them?"

Orivon nodded.

Their eyes met for a long, silent moment ere the peddler said, "You're not from Orlkettle. Where, then?"

"Ashenuld," was the flat reply.

Ringil's eyes narrowed. "Ashenuld's lost, a ruin—because of the nightskins. How is it Ashenuld fell, but you stand here alive?"

"I was taken by nightskins," Orivon replied, "and spent years in the Dark Below. A slave."

Frowning, Ringil took a step closer to the half-naked giant, and the crowd parted silently to let him. "I knew Ashenuld well," he said quietly. "Who are you?"

"Orivon. Orivon Ralla's son."

Ringil's face changed, and everyone who saw it knew that he had known Ralla well, too.

"Well, now," he said roughly. "Well, now . . ."

"If the nightskins come," Orivon said firmly, "I will take up my sword and fight them." He looked around at the Orl-folk silently staring at him, and added, "If you'll let me, I will make swords and spears and daggers for every last one of you, and we will string chime-strings,

and practice gathering to fight in the dark; where to
stand, which doors to guard, where to watch from. *No
one* should ever be taken by any nightskin, ever again."

"You had a sister," Ringil said softly. "She was born
after you were . . . snatched. Kalamae."

Orivon took a step forward of his own. "You knew
her?"

"I sired her," the peddler whispered. "I . . . your mother
and I . . ." He shook his head. "She was never the same,
after they took our little Kala."

He held up his hand for silence, but the Orl-folk were
already giving it, hardly breathing as they watched the
peddler and the forge-giant standing, silently regarding
each other.

"I knew your father," Ringil said slowly. "He was a
good man."

He turned abruptly and strode through their mutely
parting ranks to the stone dome beside the village
water-trough. Plucking it and his cap up to lay bare the
signal-fire laid ready beneath it, he struck steel from his
wrist-bracer and blew the dry tinder into a little blaze.
Then he beckoned Orivon with a wave of his hand.

As Firefist walked closer, he heard the peddler chanting something that made the nearest Orl-folk draw back
in awe. A charm, a tiny magic that made the flames rise
up like a swiftly sprouting plant.

Ringil's chant changed; he was now repeating "Kalamae" often and insistently . . . and as Orivon came to a
stop beside the peddler, a face formed in the fire.

"Kalamae," Ringil whispered one last time, bringing
his chant to an end. He looked at Orivon and murmured,
"This is how I remember her. She'll be older now . . . if
she lives still."

Orivon stared. Dark-eyed and long-tressed, it might
have been his mother. A younger Ralla, without scars
and lines of pain and worry . . .

The beautiful face swam away, lost back into rushing
flames, and those flames started to die. The exhausted

peddler wiped sudden sweat from his nose, and abruptly became aware that the villagers were backing away, some of them shivering, and staring at the forge-giant beside him.

He turned, looked, and saw why.

Orivon Firefist's calm face might have been carved from stone, but his eyes were blazing brighter than the flames of the Orl signal-fire had ever been.

The elder Watcher of Ouvahlor shrugged. "Something happened in that cavern that none of us saw. We cannot watch everything, everywhere, and who would think to search so close to the Blindingbright? Probably he killed them; certainly there is no trace of them in Talon-norn now."

"I am not concerned with your past failings," the Daughter of the Ever-Ice said curtly. "What matters is that Blessed of the Ice Lolonmae desires to know— *know,* beyond doubt or speculation on anyone's part— the fates of the Ravager leader who calls himself Old Bloodblade, and the Lady Taerune Evendoom."

"And your own spells have told you nothing, Semmeira? Or is it easier, rather than casting them, to just trot down here and seek to lord it over the Ever-Ice-anointed Watchers of Ouvahlor? To try to bully us into doing *your* work?"

Old Luelldar's voice had deepened, and his eyes were glowing blue-white with the chill of the Ever-Ice.

Standing on the far side of the glowing watch-whorl, the junior Watcher, Aloun, fought to keep a smile off his face as he saw the priestess flinch back from his superior, awed by the holy power manifest in the elder Watcher despite her fury.

"You *dare* to defy—"

"I *dare* nothing. I *expect* a polite request for assistance, which I will of course render. Semmeira, your hunger for power and delight in misusing it—like a whip, or bludgeon, to batter those around you—is an affront to the Sacred Ice around us. Cease in this behavior, for the sake of Coldheart—and of Ouvahlor."

"You presume to lecture *me* on what affronts the Holy Ever-Ice?"

"I 'presume' nothing. I lecture you because someone must. Your holy sisters of Coldheart are far too tolerant; your ambitions have time and again weakened our victories and soured our diplomatic successes. Hear me now, if you listen to nothing else I say at all: we have no need for tyrants among us; we have the fools of Talonnorn for that."

Her eyes blazing with rage, the tall priestess sprang forward in a swirling of black robes, both hands clawing at Luelldar.

Who stood like a stone statue and endured one ringing slap, then moved with the speed of a striking tombsnake to snare both of Semmeira's wrists.

She shrieked—in fury, not fear—and struggled, spitting full in his face and jerking and arching her body wildly to try to tug free. To no avail.

"Let—me—*go!* " she hissed into the Watcher's face. He stared silently into her eyes, the blue glow in his own seeming to grow brighter.

She screamed at him, but still he stood unmoving, eyes boring into hers. His eyes *were* brighter.

Abruptly she looked away, snarled—and turned her head sharply away, twisting it back and down, to bite him.

Her teeth sank deep and drew blood, but his grip held. After more thrashings, she spat Luelldar's own blood into his face and snapped, "Set me free, Watcher of Ouvahlor. Please."

A long breath later, she tried more gently to pull free, found herself still in a stony grip, and sighed.

"Luelldar, *please.* I . . . Consider me tamed. I . . . I hear your words. I will heed them."

"Truly? Or only for as long as it takes for you to convince me to let go of you?"

Bosom heaving, the Exalted Daughter of the Ice stared

into the now-bright blue glow of the elder Nifl's eyes for what seemed to Aloun to be a very long time. Slowly, as Semmeira stared at the risen power of the Ice, her face changed.

Then Aloun heard her whisper, "Truly. If I again seem . . . overly ambitious, send word to me, and I shall return here. For more taming."

Despite himself, Aloun's jaw dropped open; he couldn't help but stare in amazement.

Mustn't! This could mean my death!

He fought to look away, but saw . . .

The elder Watcher let go of her slowly and carefully, as if he were handling a sculpture of fine and delicate glass. Nodding once, Luelldar murmured, "Exalted Daughter of the Ice, we are always honored by your presence."

That "we" made Semmeira's eyes dart to Aloun, but by then he had wisely—*just*—bent his head, and busied himself with shaping the watch-whorl to hunt another place the Watchers had been ordered to observe.

Nodding to Luelldar, she turned in silence, sleek and shapely in her robes, and departed. She looked back, just for a moment, at the door.

The elder Watcher was still standing as still as any statue, watching her, the risen power of the Ever-Ice glowing deep blue and awful in his eyes.

It was some time before Aloun dared to ask, "Luell? Am I to peer at other caverns near the one that leads to the Blindingbright for the bones of the Talonar noble and the Ravager? Or go on to Dlanathur's reques—"

"Seek the Lady Evendoom and Bloodblade, and so shall I. Blessed Lolonmae shall have every assistance we can give."

"And Semmeira?" Aloun knew he was being too daring, but it was a teasing he just couldn't resist.

The elder Watcher turned slowly to face him, his eyes still blue with dimming Ever-Ice power, and his face like cold stone.

He took a menacing step closer, and Aloun felt the first cold stirrings of fear.

Then, very suddenly, the elder Watcher of Ouvahlor grinned. "Well, now," he asked the watch-whorl between them, "who would have thought Exalted Daughter of the Ice Semmeira so hungrily craves punishment?"

Then his glee fell off his face as quickly as it had come, and he looked up warningly at Aloun and said, "You, junior Watcher of Ouvahlor, had best be *very* careful. Go nowhere alone, and tell *no one at all* anything of what you just saw. That particular priestess will murder you in an instant if she thinks anyone will learn what she just revealed. Go and lock yon door. *Now.* Before we gaze again into any whorls, I think it's time I taught you the spell that lets you plunge through one, and be taken away. Your neck may soon thank you for it."

"The Araed is quiet," the Nifl spore-trader Taerel commented, turning from the doors of the Waiting Warm Dark to stroll back to his seat. He was one of only three patrons in the place just now.

The dancer to whom he'd thrown a thumb-gem, to dance just for him, broke her provocative pose on his table in a fluid rippling of her body that made him stare and smile in admiration.

Yaressa was worth it.

Yaressa was always worth it.

"The Araed is ever quiet, these days," she replied, shifting into a slow, eye-catchingly supple dance, "since Ouvahlor attacked us, and priestesses slaughtered each other at the temple, and House-lords fell. And no wonder; so much of it lies in ruin, with cave-rats and longfang-vipers gnawing the buried bones of the unclaimed dead! Not even counting all the fled or dead slaves, I doubt the Araed now holds a tenth the Nifl it used to. Truly, Olone has turned her face from us."

Taerel snorted. "Olone doesn't naethyng know there *is* a place called Talonnorn. Talonar may like to think our city stands at the center of all Nifl thought, society, and attention, but we are just one city among many, and a damaged, wayward city at that. Here, Olone is a name for priestesses and crones to use to justify their latest cruelty, and no more. If we're lucky, no more. If ever the Goddess bends her interest full upon us, we'll all be too terrified—and doomed—to worry about how populous the Araed is. Or the vaunted greatness of Talonnorn, either."

Yaressa had frozen in her dancing, but smoothly began to move again. "For a moment," she said softly, "I thought you blasphemed, denying Olone, but . . ."

Taerel shook his head. "Oh, no, mistake me not! Olone exists and is mighty in her power. It is her priestesses, at least those here in Talonnorn, who I sometimes deny. I deny that they have the faintest real idea what Olone wants for us, and expects of us. I think, all too often, they and the crones think of what *they* want the rest of us to do, and command us in Olone's name to do it."

"This same complaint has been heard for a long, long time, in Talonnorn and elsewhere," the dancer replied. "Yet have you any evidence for thinking so—beyond your evident dislike of the Holy of Olone?"

"Ouvahlor attacked us, Talonnorn was plunged into strife and chaos—and the priestesses and crones were as astonished and unprepared as all the rest of us," Taerel pointed out. "Olone had warned them not at all. And why? Surely not because she did not know. Which means they themselves don't believe in her—or that she should govern them—enough to often, and wholly, consult with her. They mouth empty prayers and turn their interest elsewhere. Listening to Olone is no longer something they fervently do, if they do it at all. If they seek Olone's counsel only in the very jaws of doom, she will not deem them devout, or worthy of saving. And behold, Talonnorn was not saved."

Yaressa nodded, her eyes intent upon him. "So tell me, wise trader," she asked in a low voice, leaning close to him. "What is Talonnorn's way out of this? Jalandral's call for one lord over us all, to rule with the Holy of Olone as mere advisers?"

Taerel shook his head. "His grasping for power is bolder than the worst excesses of the crones. Its only virtue is that even the most stone-witted Talonar can see it for what it is, and judge accordingly. Yet he may be the cleansing flood, that the city will embrace and then turn away from, back to the Goddess."

"And if he is not? Or we cleave to him and turn not away?" Yaressa asked softly, her lips almost touching his.

Taerel drew her forward, from the table down into his lap. "Then we are doomed," he said quietly.

"So, tell me now: how much will it cost me for us to share our own little doom, together?"

2

A High Lord for Talonnorn

Let Ravager quake and Ouvahlan flee forlorn
For fear of bright and mighty Talonnorn
Let sneering end and terror dark be born
Riseth one lone lord o'er all Talonnorn!
　　　　　　　—**Talonar chant**

W hose head is it this time?" Clazlathor asked grimly, not bothering to rise from behind his desk.

The giant Nifl at the window shrugged. One forever-staring severed head being paraded through the streets on a longlance looked very much like another to him.

"Does it matter?" he grunted. "The lord of some House or other; high and mighty Jalandral will reap them all before he's done."

The spellrobe at the desk made a sour face. "*That's* true," he granted. "I wonder if he started reaping with his father?"

Munthur shrugged to indicate he knew nothing of Erlingar Evendoom's fate, could do nothing to uncover it, and he dared not make it his business anyway, and peered out the window again. Then, slowly, he turned back to Clazlathor with a dark frown deepening on his face. "I liked Erlingar Evendoom," he growled.

"A proper Lord of Talonnorn, to be sure. Knew where you stood with him."

The spellrobe sighed. "And now the city knows not his fate—nor that of Faunhorn Evendoom, or Jalandral's brother and sister, either. They've all just . . . vanished."

"A lot of foes of Jalandral Evendoom seem to have vanished," Munthur said slowly. "I'm thinking we'd best get used to it."

"As it's the new way of things in Talonnorn?" Clazlathor asked. "I have a problem with that. Not only do I not want to have to be Jalandral Evendoom's eager, bright-eyed friend with my every waking breath, I can see a day when Jalandral rules a Talonnorn that holds only a handful of living Niflghar: the few eager friends he hasn't yet quarreled with."

"Most of the Araed has sided with him."

"Most of the Araed will side with anyone who promises to humble the Houses and so treat we 'common' Nifl better. They just haven't realized yet that they're trading six lords who fought each other more than they fought anyone else, for *one* lord who will lavish all his brutal attention on his citizens: the very same 'most of the Araed.' "

"Many of the younger crones are praising and aiding Evendoom, too."

"Of *course* they are. Ambitious malcontents always want to see those in power over them thrown down. They'll find things will get rather warmer for them when that's happened—leaving *them* as the most powerful. And again, our so-sly Jalandral having no one to lord it over but them. Then they'll start enjoying the same treatment he gave those they so gloatingly watched destroyed."

Munthur grinned wryly. "For you, life is an unending series of cruel treacheries and deceptions, isn't it? So should we be doing our utmost, just now, to slay Jalandral Evendoom?"

Clazlathor shook his head. "Let him rebuild Talonnorn first, and do battle with the Holy of Olone. They'll probably manage his slaying, but he should be able to bring them down to the level of we mere mortal Nifl, first. Even Jalandral Evendoom has his uses."

Munthur's grin widened. "You don't much care what you say, do you?"

The spellrobe shrugged. "I don't much care if I live or die, now. The Talonnorn I loved has been smashed, hurled down, and lost forever, and most of our friends with it. To say nothing of the Nifl-she I loved."

"Oh? One of the dancers at the Dark? Or the lasses at the—"

Clazlathor's coldly murderous look brought Munthur's words to a halt in an instant. "Draurathra, the Eldest of Raskshaula," he snapped. "If you *must* know."

"A ruling House *crone?* I—I mean . . . Forgive me, Claz, I never knew more of her than her name, and for you to set your heart in *that* direction she must have been special indeed, but . . ."

"But a crone? And twice my age at that?" The spellrobe smiled bitterly. "Of course you're forgiven, old friend. Not all the crones are tyrants made gleeful by practicing their cruelties on the rest of us. Just most of them. She was different. She saw a Nameless of the Araed as something more than a night's pleasure among the dangerous downtrodden. A Niflghar whose mind and wants were as worthy as anyone else's . . ." His hand had been closing into a fist, but Clazlathor flung it open in a dismissive wave as violent as any sword thrust. "But she is with Olone and . . . and fading in my memories already, curse it."

He produced a belt-flask, and took a long sip from it that made his eyes tear and his thin nose flare visibly. "When Niflghar say they'll never forget, they lie. We all forget. Except the things we want to forget; they stick. So I can't forget what I saw done by young Jalandral Evendoom as he grew to be the flippant thrusting blade in collective Talonar sides, nor the streets of Talonnorn ankle-deep in Nifl blood, or for that matter the sneering maliciousness of all our nobles in the days before Ouvahlor attacked. I *want* them to suffer. All of them. Wherefore I sit and watch Jalandral butcher lordling after lordling, harvesting the heads of the Houses almost as fast as they proclaim themselves, and gather to him all the Talonar who want one ruler over the city—Jalandral, of *course*—and not the decadent, ever-feuding noble Houses. And I watch the nobles bluster and mutter, and seek to rally what's left of the priestesses to their side."

Whatever Munthur was going to say in reply to that was lost in the sudden blare of horns echoing over the city.

"What by Olone's fury—?" he growled instead, turning again to the window.

"Jalandral," the spellrobe said, raising his flask again. "Summoning us all to the forecourt of House Evendoom. He's ready to do whatever his next clever deed is, and wants an audience."

"So, shall we—?"

Clazlathor shrugged.

"I'm staying here. I'll work a spell to show us what befalls. Unless you want to walk all that way just to stand and gawk, on hand to be slaughtered if Jalandral happens to need an example or two to make the rest of us cower."

"You think it'll come to that?"

"I'll lay a good glittering handful on it," the spellrobe replied, lifting his belt-pouch of gems meaningfully. "Watch, and be made wiser—and sadder. He'll be getting tired of just lopping the heads of Houses; now the *real* slaughter is going to begin."

The junior Watcher of Ouvahlor blinked.

He was, yes, standing in his own bedchamber!

Here, not in the Watch chamber where he'd been a moment ago!

He found himself shuddering with excitement. Wetness pattered down onto the smooth stone underfoot, all around him. He was sweating—so hard and fast that it was running from his nose—and, by the Ice, from his naethyng *fingertips!*

"By the Ever-Ice," he whispered, shaking his head. "That's—that's—"

"It is not considered good form," Luelldar informed him gravely from the doorway, "to be amazed that a whorl-spell worked. Watchers are *supposed* to be masters of whorl-magic, as confident in its working as are the priestesses of Coldheart when invoking the Ice."

Aloun nodded, chuckling in mingled relief and delight as he strode aimlessly and gleefully across the room. "One moment in the Watch chamber, striding into the whorl and feeling as if it's scores of daggers, all of ice, streaming through me . . . and the next, here! Just like that!" He grinned at Luelldar. "That's . . . ah, certainly something."

The elder Watcher of Ouvahlor did not quite smile, but Aloun could hear clear amusement in his voice as he replied. "Indeed. Moreover, it is good to hear prudence return to your tongue. Cast it again."

"Here?"

Luelldar nodded. "Without my assistance, this time."

"My destination?"

"The Watch chamber. Of course." Luelldar disappeared back into the passage beyond the door, leaving Aloun alone and momentarily uncertain.

He let out an explosive sigh, shook himself to drive off more sweat, drew in a deep breath, and cast a whorl.

Its glow flooded out across the room; he let it spin, growing and deepening, as he carefully strode through the working of the translocational spell in his memory. This, and then that, and *thus* . . .

So he did those things, stepped boldly into the icy grip of the whorl, and let it take him.

He was back in the Watch chamber, with an unsmiling Luelldar watching from the doorway.

"Hah! *That's* not so hard!"

"Indeed." The elder Watcher strode across the room to embrace him, and as Aloun's relieved and triumphant laughter raged around them both, murmured, "So now learn from me the next vital thing. *Keep laughing*; assume we are being spied upon. *Always* assume we are being spied upon, from this moment on."

"Whaaat?" Aloun replied, struggling to keep up laughter and form words at the same time. "Are we?"

"Of course. Yes, I'm sure your whorl-spyings on pretty Nifl-shes have provided sour entertainment for more than one priestess. Wise of you not to dare pry in the direction of Coldheart."

Aloun's laughter died in a shocked instant, but Luelldar filled both their ears with the roaring of his own whorl-casting, wilder and larger than he was wont to conjure.

"Watch!" he snapped, tapping Aloun's wrist, and then muttering and gesturing through a brief, deft casting Aloun had always assumed was just an old Nifl's flourish.

"You saw?"

Aloun nodded, and Luelldar let his whorl collapse in ear-clawing chaos around them; its chill washed over their boots as it died, rocking the chamber. "Chill of the Ice!" he cursed, feigning anger. "They do that, every so often! You try!"

Aloun stared hard at the elder Watcher of Ouvahlor, caught the barely perceptible nod, and carefully conjured his own whorl, carefully adding the extra casting. As the whorl expanded, he could feel a tugging, a counterspin racing around its edge. Luelldar leaned close, running his arms under Aloun's as if steadying the whorl, and muttered in the younger Watcher's ear, "Creates a second whorl, hidden from most who don't work whorl-magic often, if you take care to keep it hidden. Use it to spy on something else, aside from what your main whorl is watching."

He murmured something that made Aloun's main whorl rise suddenly up around them both, englobing them in its keening, rushing power. "Can only hold this a *very* short time," Luelldar snapped, "to speak to you unheard. So heed: *always* cast a second whorl, hidden by your main one—and you must take care to keep it so—to do its own task . . . under your bidding, of course."

"So this'll let me spy on anyone I please?" Aloun's grin was gleeful. "Even here in Ouvahlor?"

The elder Watcher wasn't smiling. "Yes. Though there are many who have the means to detect your scrutiny, and if they also have the suspicion to use it . . ."

"Such a whorl can betray me," Aloun replied, nodding as his grin faded. "Still, this is a formidable tool, a weapon where I had none before. Have my thanks, Luell. For trusting me with this, too."

The elder Watcher bowed. "As I said, it is time for you to have it. *Not* as a plaything, to entertain you by your peerings-from-afar at unclad shes or the pratfalls of foes, but as something that just might let you save your own skin. Not from the foes of Ouvahlor, but from those of our city who wish us ill."

"The Anointed of Coldheart."

"And others."

"There are others?"

Luelldar sighed, shook his head wearily, and told the whirling whorl around them, "I have considerably more work to do, I see."

Before Ouvahlor's armies had attacked Talonnorn, House Evendoom had stood apart from the rest of the city, behind its own high walls and forbiddingly magnificent gates, gardens that Nifl of the Araed could only glimpse from afar and dream of treading rising in gentle, slave-shaped slopes up to the soaring walls and towers of the Eventowers itself.

Yet those armies had come, and their dung-worms with them, and much had been hurled down and despoiled. Now the space between the crowded, winding streets of the Araed and the doors of the shattered and hastily patched Eventowers was a vast, uneven forecourt of trodden dirt, bare cavern stone, and broken-stone paving, the largest open space within the city except for the jagged rock fringes around the edges of the vast cavern that held Talonnorn.

Usually that forecourt was empty of all but a few wandering Nifl—and an ever-vigilant guard of Evendoom warblades, who advanced threateningly on anyone they deemed to not have a good reason for approaching the Eventowers; House Evendoom had no intention of allowing the Araed to expand to reach their very front doorstep.

Just now, however, in the wake of the horn-calls, the forecourt was filling up with Niflghar, with more converging on it from all over Talonnorn. In front of the Eventowers, warblades and servants wearing the Black Flame of Evendoom were standing seven or more deep, wearing weapons and looking sternly ready to use them. The guard that customarily swept unwanted arrivals back out of the forecourt seemed to have melted away, or receded back into this unprecedented wall of Evendoom livery.

Their departure left the forecourt to a milling, ever-thickening crowd of Nifl who'd come to stare up at the podium House Evendoom slaves had recently erected at the Eventowers end of the forecourt: a towering, upswept stone staircase to nothing, which ended in a platform high above the forecourt. Jalandral Evendoom was wont to declaim thunderous speeches from it, denouncing all who disagreed with his dream of one lord to rule over all Talonnorn, and restore the city's vaunted great-

ness. Though no one stood atop it now—and grim Evendoom warriors and spellrobes on its stairs kept matters
that way—no one doubted that the horns meant Jalandral Evendoom intended to proclaim something important from it shortly.

Tongues were busy speculating as to just what that
announcement would be, but the owner of every last one
of them knew what the eloquent Lord Evendoom was
striving toward: establishing himself as ruler of Talonnorn, to rule the city as the fabled Yaundril had once
lorded it over the lost Nifl city of Murkalandorn, or as
Devaurre the Darkqueen had ruled the distant Niflghar
city of Aumrael, in the time before her six daughters
had turned to Olone, together slain her, and founded the
six ruling Houses that so many other cities—including
Talonnorn—now echoed.

Would it be a bold announcement, here and now, or
was this only the next stride toward the throne for Jalandral, a pretext for seizing more power or gems or a title?
Or would he seek to goad the priestesses or the five
other Houses of Talonnorn into swords-out dispute with
him?

If the latter scheme was what he intended, it seemed
his rivals were both ready for such trouble, and expecting it. Bands of Nifl were approaching the forecourt
now with House banners fluttering at their fore: the
Grim Skull of Dounlar, the Talon of Oondaunt, and a
little way behind the Glowgem of Oszrim, with Raskshaula and Maulstryke still far off down distant streets.
The spellrobe Clazlathor and his friend Munthur,
watching magically from afar, did not have to peer hard
at the Nifl already gathered in the forecourt, or the
groups striding to join them under House banners, to
know that everyone was well armed and probably armored beneath cloaks and robes, though not a war-
helm nor doorguard's heavy metal plating could be
seen. The wary way the gathering Nifl kept hands near
their belts, the sharp glances they shot this way and

that, the general air of grim readiness . . . Talonnorn was expecting trouble.

The head adorning the longlance, earlier, had belonged to Oszrim, which—if Clazlathor wasn't mistaken—now left Raskshaula as the only House whose lord survived from before Ouvahlor had attacked. He peered hard at those walking under the many-eyed Raskshaula banner, but could see no one that might be Lord Morluar Raskshaula. Not that noble lords didn't have magic aplenty to disguise themselves, if they wished.

Horns rang forth again, startlingly loud, from the black turrets of the Eventowers—and the small Evendoom army parted at its center like two curtains being drawn smoothly apart, to let a far larger stream of gleaming Evendoom warblades out into the forecourt, flowing forward in menacing numbers and haste to surround the soaring stone podium. Clazlathor smiled tightly and bent his attention to the podium stairs, grimly curious to see if his hunch was right: that Jalandral Evendoom would use a spell or a hidden inner stairs to appear atop the podium, and never appear on the outer stairs at all.

The Evendoom timing was perfect: the banners of Raskshaula and Maulstryke were just now advancing into the forecourt, arriving on carefully separated approaches.

"And now it comes," Clazlathor murmured aloud as a sudden hush fell over the forecourt, and a tension as heavy as a statue's stone fist descended.

There were suddenly three Nifl atop the podium, on the platform that had been bare and empty stone half a breath before.

Clazlathor's eyes narrowed.

So Jalandral Evendoom had magic to carelessly spend on whims, did he? Or did he just want all watching Talonnorn to think so?

The tallest, foremost Nifl of the three now looking down on the forecourt was Jalandral Evendoom, of course; the other two looked to be priestesses or crones;

all three wore dark cloaks that covered them from throat to ankle. The horns all blared at once, now, a long and deafening cacophony that drowned out all other sounds and made even Munthur wince.

When it died away, silence fell—for as long as it took Jalandral Evendoom to draw in a dramatic breath, step to the front of the podium, and cry, "Talonnorn crumbles!"

Magic made his voice carry clearly to every ear without need for shouting. Every word came clear and hard, to every staring Talonar Nifl.

The figure atop the podium waited for applause or cries of denial, but his words echoed around a silent forecourt. The crowd of Niflghar were standing still, now, looking up at him and waiting to hear whatever he'd prepared to say.

Thus far, their silence said, they were unimpressed.

"Our city is yet great," Jalandral told them, "but not long ago was peerless, the mightiest city in all Niflheim! You remember, I remember, a time before nobles were hated! A time when they were great darklion leaders over us all, not feuding, lazy, *unworthy* preeners!"

That awakened a rumble of muttered acknowledgments. Jalandral didn't wait for it to die.

"And I remember—surely you remember—a time when the Consecrated of Olone were wise, just, and admired by all, holy Nifl-shes whom all Talonar willingly obeyed and looked to for guidance! A time before our temple became a blood-drenched battleground of priestess slaying priestess and crone clawing at crone, all of them so lost and fallen from the grace of Olone that they fought each other in nakedly self-serving ambition! A time when the very approach of a priestess awakened awe in us all, not wary fear!"

The rumble was louder, this time, and held a note of gruff agreement. Jalandral flung his arms wide and bellowed, "*I want that greatness back!* I want a Talonnorn brighter than everywhere else in Niflheim, a Talonnorn that Ouvahlor will never *dare* attack!"

The crowd was with him, now, but wary, their cries of agreement muted.

They were still listening more than they were roaring along with Jalandral.

"I want a Talonnorn where Nifl can feel *safe,* and dwell drenched in gems, as befit the citizens of the greatest city of all! I want a Talonnorn cleansed of decadence and sneering laziness and the powerful being casually cruel to all the rest of us!"

The crowd agreed, loudly but still warily.

"And I only know one way to *get* that Talonnorn!" Jalandral roared. "*I* will have to do the work to build it! I *ache* to get to work on building it! I weep that I cannot reach out and grasp that bright, great Talonnorn right now! *I must have that Talonnorn!*"

This brought heartfelt shouts of approval at last; not many, but they were there, amid a rising din of excited talk and anticipation.

"Talonar, I will bring you that Talonnorn!"

The crowd roared their eagerness.

"I will bring you that Talonnorn if you let me, proud people of Talonnorn! Yet I cannot do it if I must fight selfish, grasping-after-power crones and House lords and priestesses at my every stride! I must be Lord of Talonnorn, not just Lord Evendoom fighting against five other Houses and the priestesses of the temple, all of whom will want the city ordered *their* way—the corrupt, self-serving way that brought our city to this! Make me Lord, and I will serve you all!"

Down in the forecourt, beneath the flapping Grim Skull banner, Paerelor Dounlar—who had been Lord Dounlar for so short a time he yet failed to turn his head and heed when one of his own warblades called, "Lord!"—looked grimly past a sea of Nifl warblade noses to catch the eye of Lord Klasrar Oszrim.

They exchanged curt nods.

"I have heard enough," Paerelor snapped as he turned to look behind him, and thrust aside a tall Dounlar warblade standing in his way, "and more than enough."

His eyes sought and found the face they were seeking: Lord Morluar Raskshaula. The senior House Lord of Talonnorn wasn't standing under his banner—and was wearing full and gleaming black battle-armor. Paerelor gave him a slow, firm nod, and saw it returned.

He also saw Lord Raskshaula turn his head to a Raskshaula spellrobe, standing next to him, and saw that Nifl's eyes glow with the power of a suddenly unleashed magic.

Smiling, he turned his attention back to Jalandral Evendoom.

This should be fun.

"If I am proclaimed Lord in Talonnorn—*if* you want me as your Lord, citizens of Talonnorn—I shall prepare a guard for our city without delay, and pay them well. They will keep our cavern safe, and be ready for foes seeking to strike at us from the deeper Dark. Then I shall found—and pay well!—work gangs, to direct slaves in the rebuilding of every shattered street and building in our city, shaping larger, brighter dwellings for all! Talonar who desire to found their own new businesses shall find me generous in sponsoring them and ordering affairs in our city so they can flourish, for—"

Gasps and startled cries among the Talonar below warned Jalandral Evendoom then, even before the crones standing with him did.

Those two Nifl-shes flung off their robes to reveal black leather garb hung about with battle-scepters that could blast more of Talonnorn, to make those work gangs ever more needful. Snatching those blasting wands into their hands, they hissed words that awakened the scepters to almost blindingly glowing power.

Nifl murmured in alarm and sought to draw back

from around the podium, recognizing that they might imminently face the full-risen might of Nifl magic, the wildest fury that consumed its source, and so was unleashed only in dire moments, when all must be sacrificed.

Yet the crones weren't looking down at the crowd.

They were gazing high across the cavern, at the swift-approaching menace—a flying force that some in the crowd had seen bursting out of the spell-glow of a great translocation that had snatched it from afar.

The Hunt of Talonnorn! Whipswords and longlances gleaming, their spell-armor glowing like gems of all hues caught by firelight, the surviving Nifl of the flying Hunt of Talonnorn swept across the cavern on their long-necked, many-clawed darkwings.

Like fell dark arrows they came racing, right at the high podium. The crones standing with the Lord of House Evendoom hurled bright blasting-spells at them in swiftly hissing frenzy, but Jalandral Evendoom merely glanced at the Hunt once, smiled, and turned again to the Talonar crowded into his forecourt below him.

"Citizens, have no fear! I will stand for Talonnorn against even this treachery! *I will save Talonnorn, and I will rule Talonnorn!*"

The foremost darkwings loomed up over the podium, jaws parting eagerly—before a bright burst of fiery magic tore it apart.

Writhing black scaled fragments hurtled wetly in all directions, spattering those on the podium and the pushing, shoving-to-flee Nifl below. With them tumbled all that was left of its rider: a severed hand clutching a whipsword crawling with dying lightnings.

"People of Talonnorn, I am your Lord!" Jalandral Evendoom bellowed, his spell-augmented voice like the deep roar of the fabled Ghodal Below.

"I shall prevail!"

And he smiled a broad and crooked smile as the air behind him flared with a new spell-glow, so bright and terrible that it made even the great Eventowers seem no more than a few black, vainly reaching fingers.

"Tears of Olone!" Clazlathor whispered. "*Now* what?"

3

A Vow of Vengeance

> *Will you stand waiting*
> *When the nightskins come up?*
> *Is your sword sharp enough*
> *Dark blood to sup?*
> *Will you be ready*
> *To fight and to die?*
> *Or hide, run, or cower*
> *And when dawn comes, to cry?*
> —Orlkettle firesong

Something moved in the night, a darker shape amid the deep shadows—a shape as softly supple as any serpent.

Grammoth's eyes narrowed. Was it just Kellurt creeping over to tap on Naraya's back door again? Or heading down to the back fences, to seek the shuttered window of the widow Tayevur right down the far end of Orlkettle?

What any woman saw in the sour-faced jeweler was beyond Grammoth. Aye, Kellurt the Grand took them food and left them coins, but still . . .

The shadow advanced with sudden purpose, and Grammoth smelled a faint whiff of something that prickled in his nose, something he'd never smelt before.

Something . . . *other.*

The swiftest lad in all Orlkettle rolled away, as far and as fast as he could, coming to his feet with a shout. He flung the little bell he'd been holding the clapper of as hard as he could one way, to clang and clatter along the street, even as he hurled himself in the other direction.

Answering shouts arose, near at hand and then farther off, and lanterns flared as they were unhooded. By then Grammoth was running as fast as he'd ever run in his life, whimpering in fear with his dagger half-drawn and the lean, furious-faced dark thing right behind him and reaching for him with fingers that were long and taloned.

It can run faster than I can!

Desperately he ducked around the corner of a shed, slipped and stumbled his frantic way up and over a midden-heap, shrieked as he smelled that smell again and his pursuer's long arm came down—and then gasped, breath snatched out of his lungs in terror, as a steel sword longer than he was sliced out of the night to hack that reaching arm away.

Behind Grammoth, the nightskin sobbed in astonished pain. Through his sweating, shivering fear the scrambling youth saw teeth just above that sword; teeth that flashed in a smile that wasn't at all nice.

The sword came slicing again. As he swung it, Orivon Firefist stopped smiling long enough to hiss something sharp and triumphantly challenging in a fluid, bubbling tongue that Grammoth didn't understand—as the nightskin screamed, loud and agonized, right beside Grammoth . . . a horrible scream that turned into a wet choking and then a weaker bubbling.

The forge-giant's sword bit into jet-hued flesh again.

The long-limbed dark elf reeled, whimpering, and fell.

Orivon's blade thrust down ruthlessly, and the nightskin stopped making noises.

The forge-giant reached out a long arm, dug fingers bruisingly into Grammoth's shoulder, hauled the frightened lad to his feet, and growled, "Stay by my side. There'll be all too many others!"

Grammoth was only too happy to obey. Shouts and screams rang all around them, now, and torches were flaring, spitting brightness into a night that seemed full of running men with axes and hay-forks—and swift-darting shadows.

Orivon Firefist hadn't waited for Grammoth's reply. He was racing back out into the street, that fearsome sword gleaming as he swung it. Another nightskin shrieked, staggered, and fell. The sword thrust down brutally again, a black body spasmed—and Grammoth's gut heaved.

As he spewed his supper into the dirt, another two shadows ran past, moving like a storm wind yet making no more sound than a night breeze. Firefist heard them, though, and turned with that hard, nasty smile on his face, sword sweeping up.

The dark elves promptly veered apart, waving swords that looked like black fingers of darkness, and then ran toward each other again, trapping the forgefist between them. They meant to . . .

Grammoth threw his dagger desperately, right at one nightskin face.

The dark elf calmly turned his head aside and tilted his head away, to let the hurled knife whirl harmlessly past—but Firefist had already spun to face the other nightskin, smashed that dark sword aside, buried his own blade in the dark elf's other forearm, and sat himself down, jerking at his sword as he did so.

Helplessly, the spitted elf was hurled over him and forward, keening in pain, to crash headfirst into the nightskin Grammoth had distracted. The two raiders stumbled together, entangled, and the forge-giant sprang up to hew at the backs of their knees. They fell heavily, and suddenly men of Orlkettle were all around them, shouting in fear and rage, and stabbing down with hay-forks like madmen.

The heads of those two dark elves started to vanish messily under all the thrusting Orl steel, and Firefist turned away to seek more nightskins. Still retching, Grammoth staggered after him.

A cottage thatch was burning, and by its leaping flames the lad saw the glint of his dagger, lying where it had fallen in the street. Plucking it up, he looked down the row of houses and saw distant bobbing lanterns—and, nearer at hand, bodies sprawled in the street. There were a few huddled, motionless heaps of village homespun, but more than a few black, long-limbed, somehow *sleek* bodies, too.

Nightskins!

Amid a sudden jangling of chimes, something pitched abruptly out of the darkness between two porches, and Orl-folk on one of those porches raced to it and started hacking and stabbing with their forks at the nightskin who'd tripped and was struggling to rise.

The chime-strings!

They worked!

Orivon Firefist had found another pair of nightskins, and his sword was ringing and clanging as they tangled with him, blade to blade. Orl-folk were throwing stools, churns, and even hoes at the two dark elves from behind, seemingly without effect—and beyond it all, Grammoth saw a lantern crash and fall with the village man who was clutching it. The dark shadow who'd killed him stooped, snatched up the still-burning lantern, and hurled it up onto another roof.

Even as Grammoth shouted and pointed, the thatch smoked and then flared up, the nightskin darting away into the darkness.

Behind Grammoth, someone screamed loudly, and he spun around in time to see *four* nightskins gathering, hissing things at each other and pointing with their swords—at Grammoth, amid other things.

Another scream, right behind Grammoth, drove him to whirl frantically around again. He was in time to see a nightskin topple toward him, spewing a great froth of blood from its mouth, its head at an odd angle.

As it fell, Orivon Firefist's fearsome sword came free of its neck and was left waving bloodily in the air as the forge-giant stared past Grammoth at the four nightskins. He barked a bubbling string of words at them that sounded very much like orders, in that strange, flowing, wet-sounding language.

The tongue of the nightskins sounded . . . *exciting*.

The nightskins were hesitating, peering around as if seeking another of their kind. Evidently they couldn't quite believe anyone of Orlkettle could speak their tongue.

Orivon Firefist didn't wait for them to think such matters over.

He sprang right over Grammoth and charged the four, blood-wet sword shining in the firelight. At least three houses were afire now, and all Orlkettle was awake and shouting, rushing about on every side. Grammoth saw the four nightskins draw back, shifting to all face outward with their swords at the ready, as a fifth dark elf darted out of the night to join them.

Which was when the forge-giant who'd been a nightskin slave reached them and gave a great bellow, his sword sweeping through the night air like the largest scythe in the world.

At their faces Orivon hewed, and when they reared back and brought their blades up against his, he ducked and brought his slicing steel down in the air to reap their ankles, spilling and tumbling them in all directions as his rush carried him on into the backs of the two facing away from him. Those he trampled down, and broke the neck of one with his hand as he turned and hacked open the face of the other. Then he was bounding among the three that were left like a child pouncing on prized fruit, hacking and slashing and kicking in a frenzy that made Grammoth shiver all over again, even though it was nightskins who were dying messily in front of his eyes.

The hated dark elves moaned and thrashed in pain and sprayed blood from slit throats just like slaughtered boar . . . or humans.

And then a war-horn sounded, a horn that *hissed* more than any human horn—and suddenly the dark shadows of nightskins were racing away. All over Orlkettle, they streamed past the bright blazes of the burning homes in swift, eerie silence, vanishing back into the night.

And Orivon Firefist was running with them, faster than Grammoth could have run, his sword reaching and reaping. Biting into this dark elf and that, sending them staggering and crying out, or arching in wild thrashings of agony.

Grammoth ran after him as far as he dared, to where the leaping light of the burning homes faded into deeper night-gloom, and stood staring. Something moved, and he drew back in fear . . . only to swallow, whisper "But the Firefist ran after them all," and dare to go forward far enough to see that a blood-drenched nightskin was trying to feebly crawl away from Orlkettle. Grammoth swallowed again, raised his dagger in hands he knew were trembling—and then rushed forward, snarling in silent distaste, and plunged it into a nightskin neck, leaping away again wildly when the stricken dark elf jerked around to face him, blood bursting forth from its mouth in a horrible, helpless choking flood. Then it fell forward into its own spew, clawing the ground feebly, and died.

Grammoth backed away, suddenly cold and afraid, and found himself peering fearfully into the night with every swift step back toward the leaping flames.

"There's one!" old Mrickon snapped as Grammoth came up into the baker's garden. Men of Orlkettle trotted forward, hefting clubs and axes, and seemed almost disappointed when Grammoth blurted out his name and insisted loudly that he was no nightskin.

"More than that," the deep voice of Orivon Firefist came out of the night behind him, seeming to hold a grim smile in its tones. "Grammoth Gheskryn is a slayer-of-nightskins. I saw him kill one, and he helped me down another. Fine knife-work."

Grammoth flushed and stood taller as he saw Orl-folk peering at him, as they came hurrying with lanterns and torches in their hands.

He wasn't as tall as Firefist, though; the forge-giant strode past just then, a head above everyone else in Orlkettle. Orivon Firefist was dark and sticky with blood that was not his own, but smiled fiercely as he came out into the full firelight—and the people of Orlkettle raised a ragged cheer.

"Good folk!" he called as he came. "How many of us died, this night?"

"One, at least," someone called. "Harglin."

"I saw Toskur the Elder," someone else said. "He's lying in the street back there. There's not much left of his head."

"Dorl, and his brother Thammon, too," another man put in.

"And Kellurt Bane-of-Husbands!" Mrickon added gleefully, news that raised some chuckles.

"Two–three more are hurt bad," a younger man offered.

"And how many children are taken?" Firefist asked.

Silence fell as if he'd slain all noise with his sword, and in its heart could be heard a faint, distant weeping.

"Larane the dyer's little ones," old Bryard said grimly, waving his hand toward the sounds of grief. "Brith and his sister Reldaera. She was the prettiest we had."

The forge-giant's smile went away as he strode toward the weeping.

In the village square, a little knot of women were hugging the sobbing Larane to themselves, their backs forming a wall around her to keep the world at bay.

In silence Orivon Firefist bore down on them. All Orlkettle seemed to be following him, or have gathered in the square already. They gazed in silence as the forge-giant stopped at the nearest dark elf corpse, and rolled it over with his foot.

"We never killed a nightskin before, though," a man said triumphantly in the crowd. "And there's seven or more, just here!"

"And a lot more, where *he* went after them," another man added, nodding at the forge-giant.

Who looked around at them all, gathering their attention to him, and then pointed down at a badge on the throat-armor of the dead dark elf.

"Towers rising from darkwings," Orivon said. "Mark it well."

Some of the men—and Grammoth, too—dared to come close enough to peer.

"These Niflghar came from the city of Talonnorn."

Firefist's pointing finger moved to indicate a smaller symbol graven into the cuff above one limp Nifl hand. "The Talon of Oondaunt."

"What's that?" Mrickon dared to ask.

"A noble House of that city. A rich family." The forge-giant took two steps toward the water-trough, to where the light of the hanging lanterns was strongest, and raised his voice to add, "I know where these raiders came from."

"And this consoles our Larane *how?*" one of the women—old beak-nosed Meljarra, wife to Osmur the carpenter—almost spat at him. "Her children are still taken!"

Orivon Firefist took a step toward that angry goodwife, and the silence became an utter, hard-edged thing that seemed to sing with the tension of coming battle. (Even the weeping woman who'd lost her children fell silent, staring in frozen, white-faced stillness at the hulking man with the sword.)

Who turned, took a step toward that bereft mother, and said to her gently, "Hear me, Larane. I will go after the nightskins, and try to get Brith and Reldaera back."

She stared at him, trembling, but found no words to

say. As her mouth worked and fresh tears streamed down her face, the forge-giant looked around at the watching villagers, and raised his voice again.

"More than that: I will go after the Dark Ones and kill as many as I can, to humble them. To make them fear Orlkettle forevermore, so that they dare not come again."

The villagers stared at him in disbelief, or awe, and fear stirred in their faces. Orivon saw it and said swiftly, "You have seen how easily nightskins can die, this night. You can defend yourselves right well, friends. For behold, they have fled—though more than a score of them will never run anywhere, ever again."

There were a few yells of agreement that might have become a feeble cheer if the villagers hadn't looked so lost. "Only a few of us died, and they snatched only two to be slaves. I have heard Mrickon and old Aunjae and Thurtha talk of raids that carried off dozens, almost every child in the village. Folk of Orlkettle, you have fought the proudest Niflghar *and won!*"

That did raise a ragged cheer.

It didn't last long, but Orivon didn't need it to. Raising his hands as it died away, he roared, "Hunters, to me! Gather at the forge!"

He turned a little, and shouted, "Mrickon! Grammoth! I need you to get everyone who can swing a weapon into a ring all around Orlkettle! Standing in threes, each trio with two lit lanterns and some weapons! Stand where you can see the next group on either side. *Haste!*"

Even back-country villages like Orlkettle had heard royal proclamations a time or two; Orl-folk understood the imperious roar of command. Suddenly everyone was moving, rushing about and chattering excitedly, afire with their own victory.

The forge-giant reached out a long arm through the bustling chaos, took Larane by the shoulders, and pulled her along as he strode toward the forge, the women who'd shielded her clucking all around him like so many disapproving hens.

Bryard was there waiting for him, and Harmund, too. The old smith and the weaver held Orivon's armor ready in their hands, and the rest of the swords and daggers he'd brought from the Rift in Talonnorn were laid out like a bright swordsmith's wares along the smithy counter.

Orivon stopped at the sight of them, smiled, and then went forward again, walking slowly because he had to: the crowd of women were all tending to him, now, scrambling to help lace this on and heave that into place.

"We're here," came the deep voice of Harkon, the best hunter in Orlkettle, from the smithy door behind Orivon. "What's your will?"

The forge-giant turned to face the hunters. "You must patrol and guard Orlkettle of nights, from now on. Don't grow lax if days upon days pass with no nightskin raid—they'll be watching you, and waiting for that. Yet I need you to help me now, too: to track the Nifl who fled, back to whatever caves they came from."

Orivon settled his two best swords in their scabbards, made sure his favorite daggers were sheathed where he wanted them, smilingly accepted a skin of water and a hastily proffered haunch of roast boar, rolled them into the blanket he used when sleeping beside the forge, and looked at the door.

Then he turned back to the softly weeping Larane, and gave her a firm handclasp and the words, "I will do my best to bring your lost ones home. This I swear."

Before she could choke aside her grief to reply, he was striding away, back out into the night, the hunters closing in around him.

"I . . . I wish I was going with him," Larane whispered at last, tremulously.

Old beak-nosed Meljarra looked at her sternly. "No, you don't. You'd not last ten breaths before fear froze your heart. Since when did you learn how to see in the dark, anyway? The nightskins have some sort of spell they put on their slaves, but the rest of us'd be fair blind.

Even Harkon would come running back mewling, if you tried to take him down into the caves."

She plucked at Larane's sleeve, got a good grip, and started towing the forlorn cloth-dyer across the smithy by main force, her beak of a nose parting the crowd of women as if by magic. "Now stop talking such foolishness and come and help me make soup. He'll have your little ones back as soon as he can, and it'll help them none if you've pined away for lack of them, and left them motherless!"

Harmund the weaver was careful to make sure Meljarra was a good few hurrying strides outside the smithy before he told its ceiling thoughtfully, "Now if you could *nag* nightskins to death, you'd want Meljarra Sharptongue at your side, to be sure. I can't see Orivon Firefist or anyone else managing to creep past anything with ears if they have Meljarra along."

Bryard and a few of the older men chuckled at that— but only after they'd peered swiftly about to see if any women of the village were listening.

The hunters said little, which was just as Orivon wanted it.

If the Niflghar raiders were going to attack the human who'd just slain so many of their fellows, he wanted enough warning to get himself set, with sword and dagger ready.

They were well into the higher ground, now, where the rocks were many and the trees gnarled, many-rooted things. Harkon came back to him, pointing repeatedly and silently into the night until he nodded to show he'd understood. They'd found the cave mouth.

Orivon went forward until he could see the hunters standing uneasily on either side of it, and then turned, clasped Harkon's hand, and waved him back toward Orlkettle.

Thankfully the hunters slipped away, most of them clasping his hand on their way.

They were happy to be leaving him, and Orivon was happy to see them go. Even if they all turned out to be braver and quieter than he'd judged them to be, they'd be as useless as witless men, blinded by their lack of darksight. If every one of them groaned along under more than his own weight in prepared torches, they'd not have light enough to reach Talonnorn—to say nothing of the fatal foolhardiness of striding through the Wild Dark bearing bright light to signal your presence to everything that lurked and watched . . . or carrying torches when you should be carrying food.

Oondaunt raiders could be waiting inside the gaping darkness in the rock, but Orivon doubted it. Once they fled, they'd move far and fast, either hurrying deep into the Dark, seeking Talonnorn as swiftly as they could, or moving well away, to raid for Hairy Ones elsewhere.

Hairy Ones . . . well, beware *this* Hairy One.

Orivon watched the last of the hunters slip around the rocky shoulder of a hillside, heading back home. Then he gazed up at the starry sky, to fix its awesome array in his mind to revisit later.

A sudden movement brought him back to the rocks around him, sword out. It was Harkon, with a sack.

"From Larane. The meat left over from this night, and all the cheese in her larder. Meljarra came all this way with it cooking; can you believe it?"

Orivon smiled. "Meljarra can do anything. She just lacks enough very deaf and very patient folk to lord it over. Don't tell her that last part."

Harkon's teeth flashed suddenly in the darkness. "I won't, fear not. If you're safely down fighting night-skins where she can't get at you, 'tis *me* she'll savage."

Orivon nodded, looking at the faint beginnings of coming dawn on the horizon. "Tell Larane thanks, and I'll bring back her lost ones *and* kill a score of night-skins for each. It may take me some time."

Harkon said quietly, "Orlkettle thanks you, Orivon Firefist. You have given us hope."

"That's a great thing," Orivon replied, "but I intend to return with more than that. Brith. Reldaera."

He turned and stepped into the cave.

A few paces in, Harkon heard him mutter, "Aumril."

Then Harkon heard the forge-giant's quiet voice again, coming from a little farther off. "Kalamae."

Harkon stood listening a long time at the cleft where the deeper darkness had swallowed Orivon Firefist, but if the onetime slave of the nightskins said anything more, he didn't hear it.

4

Scheming, Bloodletting, and Endless Spite

Six houses rule Talonnorn
That knows no end to their spite
The Holy of Olone the deadly seventh
So revere the Ice
The Ever-Ice that endures
And be free of such foolishness
And self-serving venom
At least until Talonnorn seeks to conquer here.
  —old saying of Ouvahlor

Searing magical fire spat from the crones' scepters in great stabbing lances of bright light, needles of blinding brilliance that thrust at the wheeling, swooping darkwings of the Hunt.

Transfixed and aflame, one of those fearsome beasts tumbled out of the air, shredded black wings curled up and flapping. Another screamed, scorched and riderless, and fled wildly away across the cavern.

Yet the flying Hunt wasn't toothless. One rider had a scepter of his own; its first strike blasted one of the two crones standing with Jalandral Evendoom right off the podium. She made not a sound on her fall into the Nifl-crowded forecourt below, but that was probably because she fell in several tumbling pieces.

The other crone shrieked in fearful rage—and then in pain, as a second scepter-bolt lashed along her arm, baring it not only of garments, but of skin.

Then another scepter flashed, and the scepter-wielding Hunt rider spun headless from his saddle, his weapon spinning harmlessly down to land somewhere amid the turrets of the Eventowers.

Jalandral Evendoom smiled, hefted the scepter no one knew he'd had, and slid it back into his sleeve again.

"Klaerra," he told the empty air pleasantly, watching another Hunt rider lean down with a long, barbed whip and lay open the face of the last burned crone, *"Now."*

As if in reply, the air above the Eventowers blossomed into a vast, eerie blue glow, so vivid and splendid that the crowd of assembled Nifl gasped in almost perfect unison.

From out of that thrilling blue cloud more darkwings came flying fast—every one ridden by an armored Niflghar with a longlance glittering under his arm!

A second Hunt, swooping out of the heart of the spell that had brought them there, fell upon the flying Hunt in savage battle, spearing Hunt riders out of their saddles and slamming their darkwings head-on into anyone swooping too close to Jalandral Evendoom.

Who stood watching with a triumphant smile on his face, as his own hitherto-secret Hunt, which he'd trained in hiding for precisely this task, butchered the famous flying Hunt of Talonnorn. Beside him, the last crone gasped his name through bleeding lips, begging him for aid, but he ignored her.

What cared he if one more crone lived or died?

By the time the last darkwings of the original Hunt were torn bloodily apart in midair by five eager darkwings from among his own replacements, and Jalandral Evendoom turned again to face the forecourt full of shocked, struggling-to-flee Talonar Nifl, the crone was dead.

He planted a boot on her body to make himself that much taller, to tower just a little more over his new subjects, sneered at the swaying, gingerly retreating banners of the rival noble Houses, and gently cast the little spell that ensured his next words would be heard by every Talonar Nifl—even in the minds of those asleep— from end to end of the City of the Spires.

"Talonar, hear me, and have my thanks," he told them all. "I, Jalandral Evendoom, am pleased and proud to begin my duties as High Lord of Talonnorn."

He carefully ended the spell before adding, to himself alone, "And do just as I please, slaughtering you all if the whim takes me."

Aloun blinked in astonishment, his face lit by the shifting glows of the whorl. "Was he *really* that blunt? Does he think they're so afraid of him that he can get away with that? Or do Talonar expect their nobles to speak thus, by now?"

Luelldar was careful not to sigh. "Did you not notice that little lift and unfolding of his hands, after announcing the title he was bestowing upon himself? That was him ending his 'great proclaiming' spell. Evendoom fondly believes that only he—and perhaps a few spellrobes standing with his rival nobles, and he'd be amused if they conveyed his every last word to their masters— heard his last sentence."

He waved at the open expanse of floor in front of the junior Watcher, and ordered, "Cast your whorl. Revered Mothers seldom like to be kept waiting."

Aloun did as he was bid, showing no surprise at all when Luelldar worked a small second whorl tucked under the edge of his larger one, spinning around itself in the opposite direction as it scudded along under the slowly turning edge of his great eye.

At first, all the great whorl showed them was a restless sea of deep, rich violet that gaped from time to time in menacing but momentary fanged black mouths. The Anointed of the Ever-Ice did not welcome watchers upon their doings, and Coldheart's defensive wards were powerful indeed.

It was not long, however, ere the purple parted in a whorl of its own, a swiftly expanding iris whose inner edges were black and seemed to burn with little tongues of ravaging flame. Luelldar stepped forward, and Aloun was only too eager to obey his waving hand to stand well back.

Ever-more-accomplished Watcher of Ouvahlor he might be, but he was frankly terrified of the new Revered Mother of Coldheart, and did not welcome the thought of being questioned by Lolonmae at all.

Wherefore it was Luelldar who bowed gravely to the three priestesses that the shadows behind the spreading flames soon revealed, and Luelldar who murmured, "Revered Mother, we Watchers obey your outstanding command, to be informed immediately of what befalls over the rule of Talonnorn. We have news to report."

"Speak, Senior Watcher," Lolonmae replied, almost gently. Barefoot, bare-armed, and in plain robes, she looked like a young Nifl lass of low station. Seated on a throne shaped of clear ice, she was bared to it, her robes laid atop her body like unfitted cloth and gathered to her only at her waist, with a simple cord. She looked neither cold nor ill at ease.

In contrast, the two priestesses who stood flanking her had drawn themselves up tall and terrible to glare at the intrusion. They wore gleaming black hide robes and matching gloves and boots, all a-crawl with blue runes of the Ever-Ice that shifted shape and pulsed with restless power. Cold-faced and cold-eyed, Ithmeira and Semmeira stood with their arms folded across their breasts as if in disapproving judgment. Aloun found himself very glad to be back in the shadows, as Luelldar stood forth under the weight of their unfriendly gazes.

"Talonnorn has a new High Lord," the Senior Watcher

said calmly, his quiet, carefully spaced words falling into a vast and cold silence, as if they were stones falling into a bottomless well.

"Jalandral Evendoom has just proclaimed himself, at a gathering of Talonar whereat some of the few nobles to survive his purges sent the flying Hunt to publicly slay him—and he surprised everyone by destroying that force with a similar one of his own, created in secret and magically brought to the confrontation in an instant. So the City of Spires is remade, under one commander who has none of the scruples—nor obedience to law or tradition—of the Talonar rulers of old."

"*Your* opinions mean less than nothing—" Exalted Daughter of the Ice Semmeira began cuttingly, almost strutting forward.

She halted both stride and speech in the next instant, stiffening into frozen silence, when the eyes of the seated Lolonmae suddenly blazed with the vivid deep blue of the Ever-Ice.

"Our thanks, Luelldar," the young Revered Mother said calmly, as if Semmeira hadn't spoken. "Keep watching this Jalandral Evendoom; there will be strife in Talonnorn, and we should miss nothing." She lifted a finger without waiting for the Senior Watcher to begin to agree—and the great whorl vanished in an instant, leaving only a brief stirring of torn air behind.

Luelldar's smaller whorl shot away from that turbulence like the head of an arrow sent streaking from a bow, to turn in a swift arc and glide to a smooth stop, intact and spinning slowly, under Aloun's nose.

Even before the Senior Watcher bent over the far side of the small whorl, Aloun found himself swallowing—as he stared fearfully at the same temple chamber they had just been seeing in the large whorl.

"Revered Mother," Semmeira was saying excitedly, "we cannot wait longer! The time to strike is now!"

Lolonmae seemed amused.

Shifting on her melting throne of ice to a lounging

pose, she replied, "Semmeira, to those who share your character, the time to strike is always 'now.' Convince me—with a reason rather better than 'we have the might, so it should be used,' please."

"Klarandarr has said that we should—"

"The great spellrobe Klarandarr says many things, and it was he, working with *you,* Semmeira, who so fervently urged Ouvahlor to muster this new army. Of *course* you both want to use the force you have built, and win more praise—and real power, in Ouvahlor—thereby. Yet I am not disposed, just now, and without him standing here himself to give us his words in person, to be swayed by your report as to what Klarandarr may have said to you."

"Forgive me, Revered Mother Lolonmae, but I intend to give you no such thing," Semmeira replied, contriving to sound contrite, wounded, and scandalized all at the same time. "Klarandarr spoke to all the elders of our city—the Revered Mother who came before you among them—and convinced them that this army should be assembled despite our then-fresh victory over Talonnorn . . . assembled for one purpose: attacking our rival again, at the very moment when Talonnorn is weakest. That moment is *now!* "

Lolonmae shook her head, not bothering to hide the utter dismissal in her expression.

"Your recollection of Klarandarr's purpose and Ouvahlor's acceptance of it are correct, but your identification of the 'moment of weakness' is your own opinion—one which I consider both unsupported and wrong," she replied. "Jalandral has named himself High Lord, and thereby done the unthinkable. Now the rest of Talonnorn has been forced to start to think. The bloodletting the Watchers just reported is nothing to the bloodletting that will now come."

"Forgive me, Revered Mother, but the Watchers of Ouvahlor aren't the only ones who have been watching over Jalandral Evendoom. You charged me with this same duty yourself, and I have been attentive to it. I have watched this Lord Evendoom, and he is clever, and energetic, and cunning—*very* cunning. Most of his foes are already dead, and although it can be argued that slaying a Talonar noble just transforms his blood-kin into your next deadly foe, Evendoom has already eliminated most of the capable and influential Talonar nobles, and subverted the Holy of Olone who might have stood against him. His hands are already around Talonnorn's neck; any who dare to oppose him now will have to flee smartly, or be dead even more swiftly. Talonnorn's time of greatest weakness is right now."

Excited by her own unfolding words, Semmeira started to stride about the chamber, waving her hands dramatically. "If we give Jalandral Evendoom the time he needs to get Talonar defenders into the habit of obeying his orders without dispute or delay, and those defenders better ordered and deployed, Talonnorn will soon become even more formidable than it was when we defeated it. Far weaker in spellrobes and sheer numbers of fighting sword, yes, but with the internal dissension that so sapped them then—infighting that mattered more to Talonar even than our invading forces striding their very *streets!*—banished. Smaller swords than Talonnorn could once assemble, yes, but swords that obey one command, not fighting each other with a dozen masters more interested in settling Talonar disputes than the intrusions of Ouvahlor or anyone else."

"And if this Evendoom is already arming Talonnorn for war, and our attack on him becomes the very flame that forges the Talonar into one blade against us? What price your bright scheming *then*?"

"Why, then we will at least strike at them before they are ready and have taken their forces out into the Dark, so the fighting will again be at the very doors of Talonar houses, bruising their pride and shaking their loyalty to this new High Lord to whom they have given so much authority, in exchange for . . . what? No protection that they can credit! We may well doom Evendoom to face new knives at his back, new traitors in 'his' streets who otherwise would dare not challenge him!"

"You are persuasive, Semmeira. Yet ears are all too often bent by loud and oft-winded war-horns, where softer warnings should perhaps be better heeded. Ithmeira, what say you?"

The other dark-clad priestess spread her hands and said mildly, "Revered Mother, you know that I have long clung to another view. I cleave to it still. That if ever we truly humble Talonnorn, we make our greatest mistake."

Semmeira shook her head in exasperation, but Ithmeira raised her voice a trifle and continued. "So long as Talonnorn proclaims its peerless and 'rightful' greatness, and in its prideful folly presumes to publicly hold opinions as to what all other Nifl should do—and lashes out at other cities at will, with their Flying Hunt raids and by various Talonar noble Houses sponsoring their own attacks on merchants and slave-bands just as they please, they are seen as the great evil."

Ithmeira turned to face Semmeira directly, and added, "Against the great and ever-restless peril of Talonnorn, other Niflghar see Ouvahlor as a lesser evil, and a useful bulwark against Talonnorn's ambitions. We are the traditional foe of the City of Spires, the rival who feels its armed might most frequently and heavily, and who strives ever to 'get even.' Is this not so?"

Semmeira shrugged. "It is so, yes, but—"

Revered Mother Lolonmae held up a hand to silence her, and then inclined that hand toward Ithmeira, bidding her to say on.

She obeyed. "Wipe Talonnorn away, however, or reduce it to a few Talonar huddling in ruins, and all the other cities across the Wild Dark, far and near, of Olone or the Holy Ice, will begin to see Ouvahlor as a greater threat than boastful Talonnorn ever was. For do we not have the great Klarandarr, and mighty Coldheart, and apparent peace between both?"

"Oh, *come!*" Semmeira burst out, unable to contain herself longer. "You raise the prospect that city after city will send their armies far, across great stretches of dangerous Wild Dark, against us? Or even ally, combining their forces against us? These are the fears of drunken younglings, who babble endlessly of the Hairy Ones coming down from the Blindingbright with sword and fury, unless we cease taking slaves! Or warn that taming darkwings will awaken the wrath of the dragons, who will claw aside the very Rock itself to tear the Dark asunder and let in the Brightness that they may devour us! You raise wild tales told to children, that have never befallen and never will! We cannot flourish—cannot even *live,* as free Niflghar know 'life'—if we fear such impossible 'mayhaps'! Aside from long-ago legends, have you *ever* known Niflghar cities to muster together, against another city?"

Ithmeira shrugged. "And if Nifl only ever did just and only what they have done before, why are we not wearing the robes Ouvahlans wore when our city was founded? And still eating only guth-worms, that turn our stomachs today? How could our city have been founded at all, if Nifl had not dared to venture far through the monster-haunted Dark, to reaches never seen by Niflghar before? Semmeira, you seek not to assail your desired plans and beliefs with the same swords you thrust at mine!"

"I would be delighted never again to thrust a sword at anyone's *plan,*" Exalted Daughter of the Ice Semmeira said bitingly. "*I* want to be thrusting swords at the foes of Ouvahlor—before they put *their* swords through us! While we stand about doing nothing, but talking and talking and *talking!*"

"So before we all become truly enfeebled crones," Lolonmae asked her mildly, "talking until our teeth fall out and you become utterly deranged through drowning in the seething spittle of your own impatience, what do *you* want to do right now, Semmeira? If you could do anything at all, what would it be?"

"Command our army—and attack Talonnorn just as fast as we can get there!"

Lolonmae nodded.

"Every third or fourth rampant in that army thinks he should be leading it," she pointed out. "So with so many commanders to choose from, why you?"

"I—I—" Semmeira struggled for a reason, seeming for a moment like a trapped beast in a cage, looking around wildly, her hair swirling. Then her eyes flashed fire, and she said triumphantly, "On your orders, Holy Lolonmae, I have watched Jalandral Evendoom more closely than anyone else in all Ouvahlor! I know him and his preparations! Even more than the Watchers, I know exactly where and how to strike!"

"More than the Watchers?" the Revered Mother repeated, in gentle disbelief.

"More than the Watchers!" Semmeira thundered, striking her fist against the nearest pillar. "May the Ever-Ice bear witness!"

"Oh, it does," Lolonmae said mildly. "It always does. Well, then, Exalted Daughter Semmeira, hear my will. I have no power to command the army nor name its commander, for there are those in Ouvahlor who respect Coldheart but fall short of trusting us. Wisely."

She rose from her throne of ice, releasing a small flood of water, and added, "I have, however, been entrusted with a few of the most untried swords of Ouvahlor—the younglings, who have never fought before—who are intended to serve as a guard for we Anointed, when we venture into battle. A way, I doubt not, to free the most capable warriors of our city from having to wait upon priestesses they fear rather than do their best work, in battle—and to give them some chance of surviving, by putting them beyond reach of any truly foolish orders we may give. These untried few, Semmeira, I can put under your command."

"To lead into death and disaster, when I need so many more to bring down Talonnorn?" The most ambitious priestess of Coldheart did not trouble to keep the bitterness out of her voice.

"To lead in a *successful* attack, bold-for-blood Anointed," the Revered Mother replied reprovingly, "on the Ravager trademoot of Glowstone. Wherein you and our untried swords can taste battle and learn, and do Ouvahlor great service thereby. It is agreed by all of us who debate and decide what swords our city shall swing, and against whom, that Glowstone must be retaken before we assault the City of Spires."

"Yes?" Semmeira was afire with excitement now, but wary of a snare in this bright offer. "Retaken why?"

"To serve as a way-base for attacking Talonnorn, so our forces can advance on the Talonar cavern from Ouvahlor in one direction and Glowstone in the other. Anyone trying to flee Talonnorn will be caught between us, and slaughtered."

"Yes!" Semmeira agreed excitedly, and then cocked her head in open suspicion and asked, "But why does it need 'retaking' at all? Didn't we conquer it with ease when last we struck at Talonnorn? Is some sort of peril hiding in Glowstone?"

Lolonmae tossed aside her robes and gestured to Ithmeira, who caught up a dipper of water from the icy pool and delicately drenched the Revered Mother from her throat downward.

"N-no," Lolonmae told Semmeira, starting to shiver. "When we took Glowstone, most of the Ravagers there knew its tunnels much better than our rampants, and fought their ways out into the Wild Dark and escaped— only to creep right back to Glowstone the moment our forces returned home. As to why they returned: unlike

Talonnorn, Ouvahlor has no interest in conquering cavern after monster-roamed cavern of the Wild Dark, and making ourselves known targets for all in doing so."

Whatever else she might have been going to say was lost in a sharp gasp of pain as Ithmeira finished casting the spell that turned the water still running down Lolonmae abruptly into a hard casing of ice.

A deep blue glow in the ice under their feet brightened and started to rise; the Ever-Ice was responding to Lolonmae's yielding of herself.

Semmeira stood watching it impatiently, almost dancing in her eagerness. "When can I make ready?" she snapped, courtesy forgotten in her excitement.

"Now," the Revered Mother replied, managing a smile. "Yet mind you return here, to me, before you depart Coldheart. The Ice desires your surrender."

"Of course!" Exalted Daughter Semmeira almost shouted, ere she darted from the chamber. "The Ever-Ice be with me, in everything I do!"

"Indeed," Lolonmae murmured. "For all our sakes."

"Revered Mother," Ithmeira murmured, running reverent hands up the slick, cold ice she had caused to coat the body of her superior, "is this wise?"

"Of course not," the ranking priestess of Coldheart replied, stiffening as the cold blue light of the Ice reached her ice-locked feet and started to ascend through her body, causing it to glow. "Semmeira and wisdom never consort together in comfort. Yet better she be out heroically roaming the Dark than skulking around Ouvahlor stirring up dissent with her impatient mutterings about the Revered Mother being an indecisive coward unworthy of the Ever-Ice, and Coldheart a fraud that has fallen away from the holiness that she—of course—alone embodies. Let her cause trouble outside our walls, for once."

Ithmeira winced. "It only has to be once, if she causes trouble enough."

Lolonmae's smile was as bright as it was sudden. "Semmeira said those very words, once. About me."

* * *

"The Anointed," Aloun said carefully, "never fail to surprise me. To us, they're all cold superiority and orders not to be questioned, but within their walls, they're—"

"Just as Nifl as the rest of us," Luelldar replied softly. "Thank the Ever-Ice."

He turned his head suddenly, to give Aloun the same sort of bright grin favored by reckless Niflghar younglings, and added, "Yet to speak of the passing entertainment they afford us, what think you thus far? *I* think Semmeira is almost certainly overeager in rushing to her own doom."

5

To Fall in a Duel in Talonnorn

If life you spurn and pain you scorn
Seek out a duel in Talonnorn.
No cause too great nor too forlorn
To be worth a duel in Talonnorn.
Better yet you'd never been born
Than to fall in a duel in Talonnorn.
—Talonar tavern song

*N*ew arrivals?" Vaeyemue murmured, settling her whip onto her shoulder.

Children of Hairy Ones were always large-eyed with fear, and either mute or weeping.

Not that it lasted long.

They went mad and went to the stewpots, or found a way to kill themselves, or grew up fast.

Their snivelings were muted in the soft, damp warmth of the yeldeth caverns.

Everything was muted in the soft, damp warmth of the yeldeth caverns.

The rampants who'd brought the new slaves in hadn't bothered to answer her.

They seldom did.

Perhaps they considered a Nifl-she who oversaw mere yeldeth slaves was beneath answering.

Vaeyemue smiled a crooked smile, and lashed out to

crack her whip around the ankles of the largest, surliest-looking rampant. Time to teach this lot of rampants a thing or two—and terrify the new Hairy Ones while she was at it.

Besides, she was bored, and she hadn't enjoyed a big, strong rampant on his knees weepingly begging her forgiveness in too long a time.

Last shift, at least.

To the tune of the rampant's startled yell, her crooked smile widened.

"The proverbial stench of magic fills the air," Opaelra murmured, not caring if the nearest warblades heard her. "Pity it smells like ashes—and strong oldworms cheese."

The old crone managed a smile, wondering idly if she'd live to see another feast in House Evendoom. The shaking fits took her often, now, and without warning—and as far as she knew, she'd lived longer than any of the Evendoom blood in all the long history of Talonnorn.

Warblades of the house in full battle-armor, standing rigidly at their guardposts, stared at her stonily as she shuffled past them. Opaelra gave them a disapproving look and a snort of dismissal. New ways were well enough, but a little respect for elder kin, *please.*

Or House Evendoom would be no better than all the rest, much as that would annoy young Jalandral.

Ah, pardon: young *High Lord* Jalandral.

Opaelra wondered briefly what Klaerra thought of him, under the insistent velvet assault of his lovemaking. Or did they couple, anymore? After all, Jalandral could have his pick of all the shes in Talonnorn—though if he didn't tie them down and have a spellrobe or three cast spells over each and every one, that would be a swift way into the jaws of treachery, and his own death. Yet perhaps he dared not taste Klaerra unless she was tied down, either . . .

These idle thoughts took her along the mirror-polished

tiles of the new passage and into the gigantic new hall
that had been built onto the battle-ravaged front of the
Eventowers. His "throne room," Highest and Mightiest
Jalandral had presumed to call it.

Hmmph.

When *she* was his age, being Lord of Evendoom and
having an audience room was grand enough. Back then,
everyone knew the Lord of the Doomhouse was the true
lord of all Talonnorn, anyway; there was no need to
loudly proclaim it and waste a lot of slaves on too-large
and tasteless rooms to prove to everyone what they already knew.

Someone she knew was standing in the vast, gleaming expanse of tiles inside the throne room, waiting for
her.

Someone not nearly as old and bent and huddled into
her robes as she was: Baerone, a crone of House Raskshaula who was barely older than Jalandral.

Which probably meant that Lord Morluar Raskshaula
was in attendance at the High Lord's first Court.

"Ho *ho*," Opaelra said, a little too loudly. "*This* ought
to be good."

How would these glossy new tiles look, she wondered,
with blood all over them?

"I thought I had more sense than to let you talk me into
coming here," Naersarra of House Dounlar murmured.
"This is no safe place for Consecrated of Olone."

"True," Auree agreed, "but if Jalandral dares make a
move against us, we have a surprise ready for him. One
that's apt to be fatal."

"For us, or for him?"

"For us all," Quaera murmured. "Which at least will
mean he perishes, spectacularly, and so Talonnorn is delivered from the sin—the utter folly—that he has offered it. No High Lord should ever rule the City of
Spires; it is the very tension between temple and House

crones, and between House and House, that keeps the city strong and alert and ever-striving."

"I wish—" Naersarra hissed, unshed tears gleaming in her eyes. "I just *wish* you were right. For my part, I fear that particular sin is not so easily eluded. Now that he has built the door and shown it to us all—and we Consecrated remain in disarray—stone-headed rampant after stone-headed rampant will set himself up as High Lord, no matter how swiftly and surely we fell or humble all previous High Lords. All will see themselves as stronger, or more cunning, or at least less foolish and more worthy than their failed predecessors. *All* of them. They have seen their chance, now, and will not be denied it."

Huddled in their dark robes, shrouded in their cloaks up to their chins, the four priestesses stared back at her grimly. None welcomed her words, but not one denied them.

Auree, Quaera, Zarele, and Drayele had rarely been parted from each other in all the time since Ouvahlor bloodshed had come to the temple, and they all openly wore scars from that battle; none of them had prayed to Olone to be made unblemished again.

Naersarra knew it was because they did not want to forget how violently life in Talonnorn had changed, and how wrong or mistaken Talonar worship of Olone must have become. Yet she also knew how blindly many Talonar saw matters; many of the surviving older crones of all Houses regarded the four as "gone-oriad," and as blasphemous to the Goddess in their madness as any priestess-butchering House warblade.

Most Talonar saw not Olone, but only the rules and customs of Olone, to be clung to blindly no matter what befell.

Even if dangerously mad young House heirs reached higher, and styled themselves High Lord of all the city, and slaughtered every true and loyal Talonar who stood in their way.

She sighed, then lifted her chin and said, "We should go in. He won't wait to begin the butchering if we're not standing there to witness it; he wants to show everyone he's *not* beholden to Consecrated of Olone, remember? He'll start without us."

"He started some time ago," Drayele murmured bitterly as they started forward in smooth unison, Zarele working the spell that silently moved the doors wide at their approach, when the gleaming battle-armored Evendoom warblades rigidly flanking it made no move to open them.

Quaera felt a glare from one of the guards, and returned it as coldly as only a Consecrated of Olone knew how, flinging the stinging mind-message at him: *The Goddess marks you. See that you please her, if you want her dark regard to fade.*

Jalandral Evendoom was the rampant she should have been delivering that threat to—but Jalandral was one of those it would have been wasted on. He obviously believed in Olone not at all.

And, the Ghodal take him, Quaera Thrice-Consecrated was beginning to believe the very same thing.

The vast and gleaming new throne room was silent—but it was a silence so singing with tension that a shriek would have been lost in it.

Talonnorn was tense with infighting, and every Talonar stared at fellow citizens, keeping their own faces as much like expressionless masks as they knew how. Everyone sought to know just which side everyone else stood on. Though some Nifl would have heatedly proclaimed their own ignorance of just what any "side" stood for, they all knew the underlying truth: the city was being torn asunder between those who sided with Jalandral Evendoom, and those who dared to stand against him. Fear over what he'd do to them, or someone else would do to thwart him, or what would befall all Talonnorn, crawled untrammeled through the darkness inside every mind.

The darkly handsome Lord Evendoom rose from his throne, then, to stand on the broad dais before it looking slowly around at the many Niflghar ranged along the walls. No one had quite dared to stand in the open space before the throne; its gleaming tiles stretched empty.

"Citizens of Talonnorn," Jalandral said calmly, the quiet thunder of his tones making it evident magic was carrying his voice clearly to every ear, "be welcome in the *new* Talonnorn. The cleansed, renewed city that will regain the greatness we have lost, in large measure through your willing participation in a shared new vision. A vision we will forge together, ignoring tradition in favor of doing what is *right*. We have found folly in the past largely because everyone did as they pleased, defying all other Talonar as they sought to practice their own supremacy. So that shall not continue; *I* shall be the ultimate authority, and to defy my decree shall be to die or cease to be of Talonnorn. Yet I do not intend that this—"

He turned to wave leisurely at the throne behind him.

"—shall become a tyrant's throne. My decrees shall be rooted in what we decide here together, after all Talonar who desire to be heard have been heard. What my word shall exterminate is the never-ending dissent of the past, the habits we all fell into of denying and working against policies, stances, and even laws we did not personally like. When a matter is settled, it is settled, and we shall move on. We can revisit matters in debate, but outside this hall, we act without hesitation or defiance in accordance with my standing decrees. Holy Olone speaks to me personally, often and with great clarity, so I shall accept disobedience, defiance, or empty corrections from no priestess of the Talonar temple of the Goddess or any other. In this place, we shall use no magic—"

Half a dozen priestesses exerted their wills upon the spells already awake around them; magics that thrust gently at the High Lord of Talonnorn, revealing his glowing personal shieldings for every eye to see.

"—except the magics *I* employ," Jalandral added calmly, sounding completely unperturbed. "Our only weapons here shall be our voices, our reasoning, and the laws of Talonnorn. Laws that shall be amended as we commonly see fit, henceforth. I am not going to begin any nonsense of asking every Talonar or visitor to discard every last dagger at the doors, but hear me: except as weapons are drawn at *my* bidding or with my express permission, to wield any weapon in this hall is to forfeit one's life."

"This decree is unlawful," a voice interrupted calmly, "and thus as empty as the prohibition on magic you uttered just previously. Not a good beginning, Jalandral, unless you mean to be a tyrant over us all the while you loudly insist you are no tyrant. Talonar are not *fools*, Lord Evendoom."

"Stand forth!" Jalandral snapped.

"My words have already accomplished that," Lord Morluar Raskshaula replied, lifting a hand to indicate the swift movements of Talonar standing around him to take themselves hurriedly elsewhere and leave him standing alone on the tiles. "Orders are precious things, Jalandral. Use them more sparingly. Bluster less. With every blustered order you hurl, a little of your respect goes with it."

"I thank Lord Raskshaula for his wise advice," Jalandral replied silkily, "even if it comes from the only lord of a House of Talonnorn to have retained his life and title through all the bloodshed that so humbled our city. Tell me, my Lord of Raskshaula, how exactly were you defending Talonnorn then?"

The old noble smiled.

"I was fighting at your father's side against treachery within our own Houses, inside the temple, and in the streets. And wondering, as we did so, the same thing your father was wondering: where were *you* then, Jalandral?"

"I very much doubt that is any of your business, Raskshaula," the High Lord snapped, "and I—"

"Have just made *another* mistake, young Jalandral," the noble drawled, the same magic that Jalandral was using carrying his calm voice to every ear. "On the one hand you promise Talonnorn you'll be no tyrant, and make decrees only after debate here in your bright new throne room—and it *is* a very nice room, mistake me not—and on the other hand you immediately presume to decide what is, and what is not, the rightful business of a citizen of Talonnorn, the moment such a citizen tries to engage in debate. You sound very much like a tyrant to me, Jalandral—and although I may be as old and decadent and foolish as you're about to try to portray me, my own follies don't matter. My perceptions *do,* just because I am a citizen. It matters not what you do or how you do it; what matters is what citizens *perceive* of your deeds and ways. I believe that the very *least* you can do, as High Lord of Talonnorn, is to let citizens of Talonnorn decide for themselves what is, and what is not, their business."

The air around Lord Raskshaula flared and crackled in a sudden swirling of sparks and stillborn flames, then . . . that fell away to leave the old noble smiling. "Attacking me with magic for *disagreeing* with you, Jalandral? Oh, tyranny indeed! Your father would be more than disappointed in you. He would be disgust—"

"Enough!" Jalandral Evendoom roared, loudly enough that the ongoing farspeech magic made his shout deafen every suddenly ringing ear, and even caused dust to swirl down from the vaulted ceiling and drift through the air. "You seek to prevent matters of governance from even being discussed, sly traitor, and falsely accuse me of—"

"Nothing," the old lord replied grimly. "I accuse you

of nothing falsely. Every eye here saw your spells rage against my shields. You seek to slay me in front of everyone and then prate of treason, without even bothering to gain the approval of all these gathered priestesses and nobility first. You are worse than a tyrant, young Evendoom; you are a hot-tempered, *impatient* tyrant. Who will bring woe to Talonnorn, not greatness, if—"

"Enough, I say!" Jalandral snapped. "I *will* have order! Lord Raskshaula, your falsehoods demean and frustrate the lawful governance of Talonnorn, and I demand you withdraw them! Or depart this place and this city, forevermore!"

"And if I neither withdraw nor depart?" the old noble asked calmly, drawing his sword and glancing along the glimmering length of its blade. "What then?"

"I shall have you put to death," Jalandral snapped. "No longer will any decadent noble frustrate matters in this city, nor work treachery among us!"

"Behold," Lord Raskshaula observed. "Something worse than hot-tempered, impatient tyranny, folk of Talonnorn. Look, all, upon bold and reckless tyranny!"

"The folk of Talonnorn cannot hear you," Jalandral sneered.

"Ah, but they can," the old noble replied, through grimly smiling lips. "That is what *my* magic has been doing, since my arrival. Having named you High Lord, the folk of Talonnorn at least deserve to see and hear you ruling their city for them. You are their servant, Lord; how can you rightfully have any secrets from them?"

"Are you going to prevent all debate and decrees, Lord Raskshaula? Even as you stand in this chamber of ruling doubly condemned: of breaking the law against the use of magic here, and the law against the wielding of weapons here?"

"Not at all, too-impatient-for-debate inventor-of-laws," Lord Morluar Raskshaula replied. "I stand here expecting that very same law of Talonnorn to be abided by. The law that holds—among many other things—

that disputes between nobles be settled by duels. You have attacked me, Jalandral Evendoom. So as the law permits me to do, I challenge you to a duel. Sword against sword, here and now, to the death."

He struck a stance, arms flung wide—and then dropped them to his hips, and frowned as if puzzled. "Or are laws mere empty words to you, to be twisted at will or flung aside if they suit not your purpose of the moment?"

"I am High Lord of Talonnorn," Jalandral snapped. "I need not entertain duels from House lords."

"Another new law of your own devising, this instant? Very well. Yet I am not challenging the High Lord of Talonnorn, Jalandral *Evendoom*. I am challenging the Lord of House Evendoom, one Jalandral by name. Perhaps you know him?"

"You mock me, old lord."

"I do indeed. But then, I believe you mock us all, Jalandral Evendoom." The Rraskshaula spellblade pulsed in its wielder's hands. "So, as Lord of House Evendoom, are you going to answer my challenge? Or break the very laws you insist you shall uphold?"

High Lord Jalandral Evendoom threw wide his hands in an exaggerated pantomime of defeat, threw back his head to look around the throne room, and announced, "Citizens of Talonnorn, I wanted a new beginning. I wanted no more of such wrangling, such *unnecessary* bloodshed. A cleansing of the old, old ways that so diminish us all. Yet it seems that one noble, at least, is stubborn enough to—"

"Ah, I see," a priestess said, using her own magic to conceal from Jalandral and everyone else just which Consecrated of Olone, from those standing crowded together on her side of the throne room, was speaking. "You're going to *talk* him to death. Just like every other Lord of a House. Such bright reform heartens us all. Answer the challenge, High Lord, or step down from your throne and depart this city. Forever."

"—to cleave to the old ways," Jalandral snapped, turning to glare at the cluster of expressionless faces on that side of the throne room. He drew his sword, the most powerful spellblade of House Evendoom crawling from end to end with dark fire, so terrible that a murmuring of awe arose among the Nifl gathered in the chamber.

"Very well. Answer it I shall."

He stepped slowly down from the throne-dais, his sword afire in his hand, and said calmly, "Klaerra."

In response, a great oval of fire suddenly appeared in the air of the throne room, surrounding the throne, the High Lord, and his challenger—and settled toward the tiles, forcing back everyone else in the room.

The doors boomed open, then, and Evendoom guards in full battle-armor rushed in, weapons drawn—only to come to uncertain halts as lords and priestesses turned to face them, and they saw, beyond, the raging ring of flames.

"What befalls?" one warblade snapped. "Stand aside!"

Obediently the crones in front of him moved away, to leave him facing the flames directly.

"The duel," one crone murmured, as he stood staring, "is lawful."

"But go ahead and rush into the flames," a younger priestess standing beside her added sharply, "if you feel your orders demand it. Just don't expect your loyalty to the High Lord to win you any special treatment from the flames."

The warblade snarled at her in wordless rage, and then pointedly looked away, grounding his sword to watch what was unfolding inside the ring.

All over Talonnorn, thanks to the magic blazing inside Lord Raskshaula's armor, Talonar were at that moment doing the same thing.

The sudden roar was like the bellow of a deep, distant war-horn. Even as a startled Aloun turned his head to try to see its source, a hitherto-hidden whorl underneath the sidetable bearing Luelldar's domed meal-platter flashed with urgent fury as it spun up into view.

"What by the Ice—?!" Aloun snapped, striding toward it.

Luelldar shrugged.

"I obey the Revered Mother. We are, as you'll recall, under orders to observe this new High Lord of Talonnorn and report on his doings. He and others have just awakened various strong magics about his person, and someone else in Talonnorn has a farscrying awake and showing Talonar what is befalling—and *that* magic triggered one of my 'waiting whorls.'"

Aloun gave the Senior Watcher of Ouvahlor a dark look. "'Waiting whorls'? What *else* relating to our offices have you neglected to tell me, yet?"

"Neglected? Nothing. Not telling you yet? Much."

"*How* much?"

"Even more than you suspect."

Aloun sighed in exasperation. "Now you're even managing to sound sinister!"

Luelldar's face was expressionless. "I prefer to see it another way, Junior Watcher. Now, you're even managing to notice how I'm sounding. At last."

The Evendoom spellblade made a sound that set the Consecrated to shivering, all over the throne room. It *moaned,* like a lover in need, and its dark fires raced up and down its length with wild and frantic speed.

Lord Morluar Raskshaula did something to the spellblade in his hands. It erupted in hungry green flames—and moaned right back at the Evendoom blade.

Someone in the vast chamber chuckled at that, and the High Lord of Talonnorn's face tightened in anger. He stalked forward, raising his sword—and it spat long black tongues of flame at the old noble facing him.

Whose robes flared, blazing up in a swift fury. In their heart, Lord Raskshaula seemed calmly unconcerned, betraying no pain at all—and when the ash that had been his robes fell away from him, he stood revealed, clad from boots to throat in gleaming battle-armor of olden make.

"So!" Jalandral spat. "You *planned* for this!"

"Not at all," came the mild reply. "I did as any prudent Lord of Talonnorn should always do: I planned for all likely needs and conditions I might face ere next seeing my armory, and garbed myself accordingly."

"There will be no 'next seeing' for you, traitor Lord!"

Raskshaula shrugged. "You're going to duel me with boasts and sneering threats? You would be wiser to save your breath for *true* traitors, Jalandral Evendoom."

Jalandral waved those words away. "My patience is at an end for your glib mouthings. Let our duel decide who is right and just." He strode forward, brandishing his spellblade.

"Oh, I've never yet heard of a duel that can do that," his foe replied calmly. "They tend to decide who has more blood to lose, and is the better blade in battle—and who gets lucky."

"'Lucky'?" Jalandral Evendoom spat. "You would hazard the future of Talonnorn on 'lucky'?"

"No," the old lord replied lightly. "Just yours."

And their blades met, flames howling against flames in a great racing circle around them. Steel clanged on steel at the heart of those flames, the two Niflghar started to glide and dance amid their swordplay—and one spellblade spewed forth a sudden rosy glow.

As that radiance settled over Lord Raskshaula, the High Lord of Talonnorn laughed in triumph.

"So passes *this* treasonous threat to my throne," he announced. "Vanquished *so* easily, too, before even—"

The radiance burst, in a spectacular spewing of rose-red, dwindling stars—and from out of their heart Lord Morluar Raskshaula sprang, striking aside the Evendoom spellblade in a shrieking dispute of warsteel that sent sparks flying—and drove his point home in Jalandral's shoulder.

The High Lord of Evendoom howled and staggered back. As he reeled, using both hands to swing his blade up in a desperate parry, he caught a glimpse of the Talonar peering at him over the ring of flames.

They were all leaning forward eagerly, peering at him. Their eyes were excited, and decidedly less than friendly.

6

Fighting, Dying, and Other Diversions

Orthael the Warblade a-hunting he went
Cave-sleeth and dung-worms in plenty he rent
Warm gore a-drenching his helm to his toe
As he stalked onward, to foe after foe
The fighting and dying were all that he knew
No singing, no dancing, no shes to make coo
When he woke the Ghodal his bold heart sang
But, laughing, it scorned him until his head rang
Hurled him afar with sword and heart broke
His glory all fled like fire gone to smoke
But other diversions not a one did he know
No family, friends, nor refuge where old hunters go
So Orthael the Warblade a-hunting he went . . .
  —*Calonar tavern song*

Seething in the heart of a rage greater than he could ever remember feeling, Jalandral tried his best attack—and found it anticipated and easily blocked.

The Raskshaula spellblade seemed to be waiting for him.

How *could* this old fool—?!

He hadn't even realized he'd snarled that aloud until his smiling foe replied, "With ease and enthusiasm, young Evendoom. You snatch up spells and use them as handy tools, not bothering to learn all their powers or experiment with them overmuch. For you, it's easier to coerce—or seduce—someone else who can work the magic for you. In *my* youth, we valued magic and Talonar more highly; spells and servants—to say nothing of kin—were too valuable to be casually used. Or thrown away."

Their blades crashed against each other and sang away, spitting sparks, but Lord Raskshaula added as if they were strolling in casual converse rather than seeking to slay each other, "Your shieldings betray your thoughts to mine, and so to me, so I can tell what you're *about* to do."

Those words made Jalandral go icy with crawling fear; he backed hastily away, hacking wildly with his spellblade. A thought came to him, and he pounced on it triumphantly. "Aha! Yet you reveal this to me, weakening yourself! You *are* a fool, Lord Raskshaula, and you are going to die here!"

"Yes," the old lord replied calmly, lunging after him so swiftly that Jalandral had to hurl himself away again to avoid being spitted as his two outermost shieldings failed, their glows going black. "I expect to die. You're younger, stronger, faster, and more vicious than I ever was. Yet even in death, I shall win, Evendoom."

Jalandral felt his jaw drop in astonishment, and struggled to find words as Raskshaula pressed him hard. He gave way, parrying desperately. "How—" He panted, astonished at the old lord's speed and skill. "How so?"

Lord Morluar Raskshaula shrugged. "Spare me, and you'll be seen as weak; in Talonnorn, that means your doom. Slay me, and you'll be seen as the tyrant I have called you—and again, you shall be doomed, though your end may be longer in coming. I cannot lose, son of Erlingar. All, mind you, because of your own deeds, and your own overproud and careless tongue."

Jalandral heard bitterness in the old lord's voice for the first time—and then, with a shock, realized Raskshaula was starting to weep. "*You could have been so great,*" the old lord whispered furiously.

"I *will be* great!" he shouted in Morluar's face, locking their blades together and using his fury and his height to lean forward, driving his foe a step back. "I'll be the greatest lord Talonnorn has ever known! All the Dark shall fear me, and Nifl-shes everywhere will swoon at the very thought of my touch! D'you hear me, old failure?"

"Unfortunately, yes," the old lord sighed, ducking away suddenly to spin and bring his blade around at Jalandral's back.

The High Lord of Talonnorn turned and struck it aside just in time, the Raskshaula spellblade sliding past his ribs so closely that his strongest, innermost shielding spell boiled away under its slicing, magically augmented steel.

Jalandral hastily backed away, almost as far as the steps leading up to his throne, and heard the eager murmurings of the crowd. They were hungry for his blood . . .

He'd won himself time to call forth another shielding spell from the Evendoom spellblade. Raskshaula, Olone spew on him, was standing politely waiting for him to resume battle, blade grounded.

Well, to Olone with bygone courtesy and all the decadent posturing that went with it, too!

"Let justice, right, and the favor of Olone prevail!" he cried loudly, and charged.

"Oh, yes!" Lord Raskshaula called back, in precise mimicry of Jalandral's ringing voice. "Let justice, right, and the favor of Olone prevail!"

Their blades crashed together with all the clanging, ringing force Jalandral could manage, as he put all his strength behind the sweeping blow, seeking to smash his foe's sword right out of numbed old hands.

It was like hacking a stone pillar.

His own hands were numbed, the shrieking protest of

his own spellblade half deafened him . . . and he heard scattered laughter in the throne room.

Lord Morluar Raskshaula was standing with blade grounded again, patiently awaiting him.

Jalandral reeled upright again, fresh fury like a bubbling flame in his ears. This motherless old Olone-forsaken lord was going *down,* yes he was, and—

Jalandral swallowed and backed away again, feeling the riser of the bottom-most throne step, cold and hard, right behind his heel.

Why was he so angry?

He, who for years had mocked and preened and laughed at—at *everything* in Talonnorn, his father, the malicious Evendoom crones, the idiotic rival Houses, the coldly sneering Consecrated of the temple . . . what had happened to him?

He frowned at Raskshaula.

"You're doing this, aren't you? You're working on my spells somehow, to drive me into a rage . . ."

The old lord bowed.

"Yes," he admitted calmly. "I am."

"I thought this was a duel!"

"It is. And I'm showing you just as much *fairness* and *honor* as you are wont to show other Talonar in your dealings with them, young Evendoom."

"Ah. So your *principles,* Raskshaula, are just as false and twisted as those of all the rest of us."

"Not at all. *I* am fighting for Talonnorn. And for the sake of my city, I will do anything, Jalandral. Anything. I'm throwing my *life* away, remember?"

"So you are," Jalandral drawled, with an air of amused calm he did not feel, as he fought to find his usual sardonic mood and settle into it. "So you are . . ."

He strode forward, spellblade gleaming as he hefted it.

Lord Raskshaula stood his ground.

Steel met steel, and they fenced, blades singing,

clashing, and rebounding again, the two of them leaping, twisting, and dancing about faster and faster.

If I am younger, stronger, and have the greater reach, Jalandral thought savagely, then so be it.

Live by the sword, old fool, and die by it!

Yet when Jalandral found himself breathing hard and arm-weary, Morluar Raskshaula was still smiling calmly, unruffled and apparently rather less than tired.

Jalandral felt the rage rising in him again, dark and warm. He backed away once more, threw back his head, and drew in a deep, slow breath—knowing by now that the old lord would courteously wait for him to do so—and . . . found calm.

Again.

Yet when he then strode back into that deadly fray of steel on steel, Jalandral found anger rising again inside him. Olone *damn* Raskshaula!

This time, instead of stepping back, he caught the old lord's spellblade on his, leaned forward until the two swords locked, guard to guard, and into his foe's face hissed, "Why are you doing this, Morluar? You were the one lord whose advice I wanted, whose word I *thought* I could trust!"

Lord Raskshaula's face, looking back into his, seemed more sad than anything else. "Then you should have behaved in a manner that could let me trust you, Dral. I wanted to. I kept *on* wanting to, as your tyrannies mounted. I started warning you—as many did—and you sneered and dismissed us, and kept right on. To bring us here."

"Yes, here!" Jalandral snarled, trying to shove the old, shorter Nifl back by means of their locked blades. "You're going to lose, Raskshaula! You're going to die here!"

It was working.

He gained a step, and then another, forcing his challenger slowly back toward the ring of flames.

"And what of it?" Raskshaula might have been calmly

assessing a trading deal with visiting merchants. "All of my friends—and foes—are dead and gone, the Talonnorn *I* knew and loved gone with them. I like nothing of what I see of this new Talonnorn you offer. Nothing at all. You've taken from me all I had left that I cared about."

"I? I barely *know* you, Lord Raskshaula! How could I have taken what you hold most dear?"

Jalandral suddenly broke their clinch, stepping back and slashing viciously at Raskshaula's legs. The old lord turned his attack aside with almost casual ease—and launched a mirrorlike strike of his own, so swiftly and smoothly that Jalandral actually had to hurl himself backward to save his own knees.

This time, Lord Raskshaula strolled after him, pressing his attack with casual elegance.

"There is something you just may live long enough to learn for yourself," he answered Jalandral, still speaking as calmly as if they sat at ease at a table, rather than seeking to kill each other in a ring of dueling flames. "And it is this: it is never easy for lords of rival Talonar Houses to befriend each other. Erlingar Evendoom was my friend, and when I see his eldest son swaggering around the Eventowers proclaiming himself Lord of Evendoom, and I no longer see the face of Erlingar Evendoom in Talonnorn, I know who to blame. Not all dead are dismissed, unavenged."

"I have *not*," Jalandral snarled, "slain my father. I don't even know where he is!"

"Then you are a lawbreaker and a disloyal son beyond match," the old lord told him coldly, "to claim the lordship of your House, when your every waking moment should be spent finding your sire and restoring him to his rightful place—or recovering his bones and avenging his death, if he has perished at the hands of another."

Lord Raskshaula let Jalandral hear his contempt for the first time. "To do otherwise—as you have done—is to leave me regarding your protestations of innocence as to the fate of your father with disbelief. Jalandral Evendoom, I believe you *not*."

The Evendoom spellblade cut at him with all Jalandral's strength behind it, but this time the old lord met and parried it with his own sword, standing unmoved amid the shriek of tortured steel.

"And if you care nothing for my opinion," he continued calmly, as if they were holding goblets full of wine rather than spellblades whose warring had numbed both their hands, "considering it will be swept away when I am dead, then listen to other Talonar, and learn this well: all Talonnorn believes your father dead, and you the cause."

"You *dare* to accuse me of this?" Jalandral snarled, at first seeking to appear righteous before Olone in the eyes of the watching crowd but finding himself losing his temper before his question was half out. "Do you truly insult me this much?"

Raskshaula shrugged. "Evidently," he replied—and parried in a manner Jalandral had never seen before, that let his blade rebound and *bend* momentarily, so that its tip darted in to slash open Jalandral's cheek, just below his left eye.

"Olone!" the High Lord of Talonnorn cried, both as an oath to pour out his feelings, and to make any devout Goddess-worshippers in the crowd think Olone was with him, healing him, as he awakened the healing powers of his spellblade.

Again, the old lord did him the mock courtesy of stepping back and halting his attack while Jalandral healed himself.

Leaving the High Lord regarding him balefully, anger gnawing steadily in his throat now.

This dangerous old lord was going to greet death here, even if it cost Jalandral Evendoom's life in the bringing of it to him.

As it was starting to seem it just might.

* * *

Aloun chuckled and bent closer to the whorl. "This is splendid!" he said with a grin, lacing and interlacing his fingers excitedly. "You think the old Nifl has a chance?"

Luelldar shrugged, did something with his will and two of his fingers that made the whorl grow larger and brighter, and said nothing.

"He's the better blade, this Raskshaula," the younger Watcher of Ouvahlor added. "But then, he would be, wouldn't he? Yet he's shorter and older, and can't be as strong. And for all his talk of doing 'anything,' he's letting Evendoom catch his breath and heal himself! And we haven't seen any sly magics out of Jalandral Evendoom yet, but he *must* have some! How soon before he gets really angry—or hurt—and unleashes one of them?"

"How soon, indeed?" Luelldar echoed quietly. "What matters is *how* the newly established High Lord of Talonnorn, Lord Jalandral Evendoom, deals with this very public defiance of his rule by the most respected surviving head of a Talonar noble House, Lord Morluar Raskshaula. Or rather, what all watching Talonnorn *thinks* of how he handles it. In that sense, however horribly he dies, Raskshaula may have won already."

Aloun looked sidelong up at the Senior Watcher. "So now the real question: who do you *want* to win? The old-blood veteran humbling the haughty upstart, no matter how entertaining his prancing has been to us? Or is the entertainment afforded us by the flamboyant Jalandral worth more than any amount of tradition, old wisdom, and morals?"

Luelldar's face betrayed nothing. "I am a Watcher of Ouvahlor," he said calmly. "In matters I observe, I do not have 'wants.' I may predict what will befall, or expect certain things to happen—in certain ways, even—but I shun all preferences. To do otherwise is to color my observations, and make them worthless to our superiors. More than that: if I cling to mistaken beliefs and judgings, I taint what I see and any conclusions I dare to reach, henceforth. It is my duty to avoid such things."

Aloun sighed. "And let this be another lesson to me, yes?"

"Of course. And the sooner you lose the habit of secretly wagering on outcomes, the better."

The junior Watcher's face went pale.

"How is it you know about that?" he whispered.

Luelldar rolled his eyes. "I am a *Watcher* of Ouvahlor, remember?" He waved his hand, and yet *another* whorl rose into view, behind him. It was right across the room, small, and dim—but grew in brightness as it came to him.

"Unless one of those you have been unwise enough to wager against has talked about your dealings—and they all do, look you, sooner or later—no one else yet knows," he added calmly. "No Anointed, to be sure."

"Sure? How can you be sure?"

Luelldar rotated one of his hands almost lazily, and the new whorl turned in the air to face Aloun, showing him the scene in its depths.

"This little whorl of mine—and no, it's *not* my only little background eye, before you ask—has been keeping its eye on the Anointed of Coldheart for quite some time."

Aloun drew in his breath sharply. "You dare to do *that?*"

Luelldar shrugged again. "My duty to my office, fellow Watcher, demands no less." He leaned closer and added in a murmur, "As it happens, I've been growing very suspicious of what Semmeira might very soon do."

"Lady," the Evendoom maid murmured, looking up from where she knelt before Taerune with eyes that were wide with admiration and love, "you are the most beautiful Nifl-she I have ever seen. Truly Olone smiles upon House Evendoom."

The other maids all nodded and smiled in enthusiastic agreement as they glided forward with her new gowns held high.

"We are *so* favored to serve Lady Taerune Evendoom," one said, sounding close to tears. They all nodded happily.

Taerune smiled back at them, though a small, dark worm of foreboding was rising in her, she knew not why.

They were bending toward her before their faces changed, this time, admiration and love melting to shock and fear, then revulsion and hatred, as they went pale and started to scream.

Shrieking and hissing, her maids shrank back—and then charged at her, faces contorted and hands raised to claw her, in a spitting, keening chorus that rose to ear-splitting terror as Taerune flung up her arms to ward them off—and saw that the left one was gone, ending in a stump that spurted blood, pumping and spluttering . . .

The last Ouvahlan Nifl is smiling ruthlessly as he twists his way through the fray that rages in the Long Hall of the Eventowers every bit as adroitly as Taerune has ever done. Avoiding both the lumbering gorkuls and the blades of his fellows, he finds room enough to thrust his blade at her spine.

Desperately Taerune twists around, seeking to strike his blade away with her left arm no matter how badly she gets cut, hoping the now-toppling gorkul she's just slain will both knock his blade down and shield her in its helpless, roaring toppling of tusked flesh.

The gorkul obliges, so the blade meant for her vitals cuts deep into her arm, driven by the entire weight of the gorkul falling past, shearing muscle and sinew and bone alike, in a pain so coldly intense that the breath is forced out of her, in a shriek like a sword point slicing down a metal shield.

She's never felt such pain before . . .

"Monster!" the maid who loves her most of all shrieks, crying tears of terror as she stares at the spurting stump of Taerune's severed arm. *"Monster!"*

Then she is alone in the darkness, choking on her own bitter tears, bitterness like blood in her mouth.

Maharla wouldn't heal me.

My father's only daughter, Thirdblood of Evendoom, and she refused to do her duty, out of sheer spite. And cast me out, with the battle still raging, to hide her crime.

Treachery forgotten in the rush to deem me the greater offender.

Blasphemer, outcast . . . *less than Nifl.*

Because I wouldn't kill myself, they think I'm a monster.

Suddenly Taerune was awake and panting in the darkness, staring up at the rough ceiling of the cavern overhead.

A cave out in the Wild Dark.

Where she was lying alone, on her back, fully clad and wrapped in a blanket, some distance from the other Ravagers who snored or sleep-sighed gently around her.

Far enough away that her sobbing awakenings wouldn't rouse them.

Out here where hungry monsters slithered or stalked. Where she was safer, among the lawless Ravagers—almost every one of them a dirty, ruthless rampant who'd not seen a willing, yielding Nifl-she in too long a time to rightly remember—than she'd be in Talonnorn.

Yes, she was safer out in the Wild Dark, sleeping with the Ravagers, than in her own palatial bedchamber in the tall, spired heart of the Eventowers.

She lifted her left arm and gazed at the blade the human Orivon Firefist—the best slave she'd ever had, tall and strong Hairy One that he was—had fashioned and fitted to the stump of her arm.

She was safer because of this, too.

She turned it, sharp and deadly. Part of her, now.

The Consecrated say this makes me a monster. So all Talonar call me "monster."

And so I am.

I *am* a monster. Yet we Niflghar—we're *all* monsters.

* * *

Black flames swirled up around him as Jalandral Evendoom strode grandly away from the steps that ascended to his throne, and started putting on a show. The spellblade in his hands moaned again, and spat more black flames. Pity they did so little against the defenses of the spellblade being wielded against him.

Olone *damn* Morluar Raskshaula for defying him and starting this—but he, Jalandral, was damned if he was going to let old Raskshaula go on making him angrier and angrier.

No. If he had to die, he was going to do it his way. Jaunty, smiling, with a jest or two and a sneer or six. Just as that grinning old highnose on the other side of yonder spellblade had been doing to *him*.

"Well, now, bright bauble of House Raskshaula," he drawled, lifting his chin as he advanced, Lord Morluar's calm old face quite close now, "have at you again. Olone has just whispered to me that she's quite pleased with me, so—"

"Indeed. She said those very words to me, too," Raskshaula replied with a smile. "And followed them with some more: I thought he was going to whimper and wet himself before your blades have even struck a handful of sparks off each other. Yet it seems he *can* stand up unaided, Lord Raskshaula, if you just give him a little, ah, aid. From time to time."

"Blasphemer!" Jalandral snapped triumphantly, making his eyes flash and the fire of his sword flare up in a perfect echo. "You—"

"No, Evendoom," another Consecrated said loudly, using magic to make her older, dagger-sharp voice carry. *"You* are the blasphemer, to claim Olone spoke with you personally when She did no such thing. We Her priestesses are attuned to Her; we can see, hear, and feel Her every nearby manifestation. None of us did, High Lord. Which means you are a liar."

"And Lord Raskshaula is not?" Jalandral snarled,

feeling anger surge in him again, almost chokingly this
time.

"Morluar Raskshaula has been Lord of House Raskshaula for a long time. We *know* he is a liar, and he
confirms—not disappoints—our expectations. He did
not name himself High Lord of Talonnorn, Evendoom.
You did."

Jalandral stared at the priestesses beyond the flames,
and they looked back at him. Eyes gleaming.

Then he turned and looked at Lord Raskshaula. Who
stood courteously awaiting him again, blade grounded.

The bastard.

Jalandral did not spare a glance for the Nifl on his
other flank. They would be waiting just as eagerly. Hoping for his blood.

He was all alone in this.

Or not.

Damn, he should have done this the moment Raskshaula had challenged him, before all the hurling of
grand words. So he could have painted it as just and fit-
ting treatment for a lawbreaker.

"Klaerra!" he called sharply.

Silence. Nothing happened.

He put a smile onto his face, took a slow and showy
step toward his challenger, and flourished his spellblade, turning the black flames roiling up and down it to
a bright ring of little flames around its tip.

A tip that he moved sharply, dragging the little sput-
tering ring through the air. Did his signal have to be so
obvious? Or was Klaerra deserting him, too?

"Klaerra," he snapped, in a clear command, flicking
his sword again. Raskshaula took a slow, deliberate, and
showy step of his own, bringing himself that much closer
to Jalandral.

Nothing happened. Again.

Bitch. Disloyal, gloating old bitch.

With a snarl the High Lord bounded forward and

tried to strike Raskshaula's blade aside, the spellblades ringing merrily off each other as the old lord parried with ease, fluid and graceful in his shiftings as Jalandral started battering him from all sides, leaping and thrusting like a Nifl gone oriad, surrounding him with a ring of thirsty, leaping steel.

That Raskshaula, smiling faintly, turned away as calmly as if the ever-darting Evendoom spellblade's assaults were so many showers of yeldeth drift-spores.

"Klaerra," Jalandral snapped again, through clenched teeth, as he felt his wind and his strength sagging once more.

He stepped back, to draw in a shuddering breath— and saw the ring of flames obey at last, racing across the throne room amid a mewling of alarmed Nifl cries, to engulf Lord Morluar Raskshaula before he could do more than half turn to see his peril.

The old lord staggered, tried to run—the ring of flames moving with him, which meant Klaerra was directing it personally—and then started to reel and darken, his hair flaring up and his spellblade spitting sparks as he fought to try to call up shieldings that would drink the flames.

Unable to keep a widening grin off his face and not caring, Jalandral pointed the Evendoom spellblade at Raskshaula and fed him dark, ravening flames, trying to batter the shieldings the old lord did have active, and hamper him in—

I, Olone, am displeased. With these flames I aid Jalandral. Hail, Jalandral, High Lord of Talonnorn!

That whisper was a thing of flame, and so both vast and gusty, swirling heavy upon every ear. Jalandral recognized Klaerra's voice, but then, he knew who was behind this; how many of these young Consecrated of rival Houses could hope to do so? To them, this *would be* Olone, and—damn!

In winning the moment for him, Klaerra was weakening him from now on. When the priestesses—and the damned crones, too!—came crying to the High Lord with "Olone says this" and "Olone has always decreed that," it would be hard indeed to thwart their wishes, and—

Then, in an instant, all the flames were gone, and Jalandral found himself cowering in a dark corner of his own mind, staring into the horrified face of Klaerra, even as she stared back at him.

Together, they were both aware of one thing: neither Klaerra nor anything any Nifl in the throne room had done had snatched away the ring of flames.

Leaving behind a repeating, swiftly fading echo of just four of Klaerra's words: *I, Olone, am displeased.*

Staring at the crisped, slowly toppling thing of bones that had been Lord Raskshaula—and then over at the Consecrated on his right, all toppled senseless, strewn about like so many discarded shes' playdolls—Jalandral Evendoom, High Lord of Talonnorn, raised his spellblade dazedly in front of his face and stared at its naked steel, the black flames quite gone.

He had no idea how to bring them back. His eyes—and his unscathed hand, passed down the flat of the blade—were telling him they were no more, yet the sword was insisting to him that they were raging.

Jalandral blinked, fought back sudden tears, and wet himself.

7

Talon and Fang

Out in the Dark the jests they are few
Proud boastings and darings a Nifl may rue
Of Olone's holy power priestesses sang
No power there but talon and fang
So Talonnorn stays and Talonar ways
Our Hateful shelter all of our days
Out in the Dark amid promises cold
No Nifl alone has a chance to grow old
　　　　　　—Talonar tavern song

Terror passed, leaving him feeling empty and sick. Jalandral found himself on his knees in a puddle of his own shame, with Talonar advancing in an uncertain arc in front of him and to his left.

Their weapons were out, gleaming and glittering, and some had smiles above them that were less than nice. Hastily he found his feet, risking a glance to the right as he moved in that direction. Thankfully, no one stood menacing him there; the Consecrated were still strewn senseless.

He was alone, all contact with Klaerra lost. He had no feeling that Olone—if it *had* been Olone, and not a trick of Klaerra or some unseen crones or priestesses seeking to make the High Lord their cowering puppet—was still watching.

Leaving Jalandral like all other Nifl: knowing that there was no one to care for his skin, nor guard it, save himself.

Well, then . . .

"Olone has touched me deeply," he snarled, finding himself hoarse and unsteady of voice, both at once. "We spoke together in my mind, and she has confirmed me as rightful High Lord of Talonnorn. Away steel, all of you, or be cast out as blasphemers!"

He drew himself upright, spread his arms wide to flourish his ruined spellblade and seem tall and grandly confident, and added, "All who gainsay me, scheme against me, or seek to harm me in any way incur the divine displeasure of Olone, and are accursed everywhere even before I banish them from our city!"

Malicious triumph was fading fast in Talonar faces before him, and everyone was lowering their blades and stepping back. Jalandral fought down a sigh of relief and raised his voice again, feeling it gather strength and regain more of his usual faintly mocking tone with each word.

"I, Jalandral, High Lord of Talonnorn, hereby declare *all* of House Raskshaula outlaws and traitors. All that they own, even to the buildings where they dwell and the garments now clothing them, are forfeit to Talonnorn. Any who aid or shelter them will share their fate."

Swinging the spellblade almost lazily, he added, "Olone's holy blessing shatters Talonar tradition. I will fight no more duels of this sort. Henceforth, all who dare to defy me will be hounded out of the city, and hunted down and slain like cave-rats. Their homes and coins become Talonnorn's, and their kin become slaves or—if they manage to reach the Wild Dark—outcast. Dispute amongst us wounded us and was barely noticed, even when we grew so weak that lowly Ouvahlor could storm our cavern and wound us sorely. Wherefore Olone has raised me, enthroned, over you."

He strode along the line of chastened Niflghar, pre-

tending not to see blades being hastily sheathed and
scepters lowered, until he reached the last dark elf.
Whereupon he spun around to regard them all with his
best cruel smile and said with soft, menacing promise:
"*Try* not to disappoint me."

Orivon Firefist trudged on warily into endless gloom,
rough walls of rock curving close at hand. He'd forgotten the damp, spicy many-molds smell of the Wild Dark,
but it was all around him now, along with the droppings
and old bloodstains and even cracked and gnawed bones
of the little scuttling things that dwelt where the sunlit
lands of the Above met the uppermost dark vastnesses of
Below.

And died, under the jaws of things he'd thankfully
not yet seen . . . though that did not mean—he whirled
around for perhaps the hundredth time, his favorite
sword out as he shot a glance at the rock ceiling above
first, but saw nothing following him.

Nothing but a brief, gleaming movement that might
have been a body hastily sinking down behind rocks, or
a peering eye hastily shut against his scrutiny.

Orivon let silence fall and then deepen, but heard no
breathing or movement except his own. Which was
worth a shrug, ere he turned back the way he'd been
heading.

He was lost, of course.

He'd never had any maps—Old Bloodblade had been
map enough for them all—and knew only that he had to
descend, and head in *this* direction (more or less, not
that the winding, rough-walled caverns and passages allowed anything more precise) to reach Glowstone.

Eventually.

If something didn't eat him first.

Not that his reception in the Ravager-moot—if it still
was a Ravager-moot, and there were any Ravagers left to
meet anywhere—bid fair to be any more welcoming than
the treatment accorded any human slave on the loose.

Though *this* Hairy One had swords and daggers to spare, and knew how to use them. To make them, too, if it came to that, and—

Something hooted, faint and far-off in the endless caves. Orivon knew sounds carried strangely across the Wild Dark, but knew he'd never heard such a call before, and was fairly certain whatever was making it was a good distance away.

Which meant it wasn't a pressing problem for him yet. He wasn't making much noise of his own, for one thing. Many beasts of the Dark hunted by scent, but had to blunder into it, or into the creature making it, to "nose" prey; amid all the reek of molds and dung, yeldeth and softly drifting spores, nothing could sniff out a particular beast-smell from a cavern away.

And for all Nifl sneerings to the contrary, unwashed human-reek was among the milder stinks of the Dark.

Thrusting his fingers into his nostrils as he shouldered through the latest clinging cloud of spores, to keep from breathing them in, Orivon shouldered his way into another cavern.

The fuzzy, purple-gray spores brushed along his arms and shoulders, tumbling in velvet silence, before they almost reluctantly drifted on past. Orivon paid them no heed; he was too intent on peering warily everywhere for foes. He found nothing worse than a long-legged spider, black and barbed, that his approach had scared into urgently wanting to be elsewhere. It scuttled through a cleft on the far side of the cavern, toward a faint glow beyond.

Orivon regarded that steady radiance thoughtfully. His darksight was as strong as ever; though there was no light near that was anything like the brightness of the cavern that held Talonnorn, he could see clearly enough in this gloom.

More than clearly enough, as he crossed the spider-vacated cavern, to see that the glow was coming from markings painted on the rock walls of a passage beyond his cavern, that curved across his intended path and intersected the narrow way the spider had taken . . . a cross-passage that ran past the markings into a greater darkness. Another cavern.

Orivon halted and stood watching and listening for what seemed a long time. Silence reigned. When time began to seem to stretch, and remained unbroken by any movements or sounds, he advanced again, approaching the two markings cautiously.

They were Nifl blazons, all right, drawn in an enspelled paint that had eaten into the rock to leave behind a symbol deeply etched as well as glowing.

Not that he could read them.

Orivon smiled wryly. They were intricate marks, differing from each other, and seemed to be meaningful symbols rather than actual writing, but that meaning could be anything. "Kiss me, Olone," as he whispered aloud, or on the other hand: drop your dung here.

They shared the glow common to all dark elven writings; he was certain these were Niflghar markings, and not all that recent. Yet not defaced or altered, either. One of them he'd seen, just once, beside a door somewhere in a back passage of the Eventowers. So was it a guide mark, a warning to "stay away," or something else?

Orivon shrugged. The two runes, if that's what they were, had been painted side by side next to a break in the curving passage: an entrance to another cavern, beyond, in just the direction he wanted to go, if he was ever to find Glowstone.

He shrugged again and strode purposefully forward, across the curving passage and along the narrower way, into the waiting cavern beyond.

It was darker than the rest of the Dark he'd traversed thus far, as if some magic lurking within it was waging silent war against his darksight. Darker, and having its own peculiar, unfamiliar smell, as if . . . as if . . .

Something moved, just behind Orivon.

He flung himself to one side without waiting to see

what it was, turning to slash in that direction with his sword.

The "something" looked like a great curved slab of rock, swinging down at him from the cavern ceiling to loom in front of his nose!

It looked as gray and hard as stone, able to break any number of swords of his crafting—and humans swinging them, too!

The forgefist ducked away—as something else that felt just as large and hard as the swinging stone slammed into his shoulder and spun him wildly aside, his own sword clattering from his numbed hand.

Diving after it to scoop it up with his other hand, Orivon caught up his steel, rolled onward as far as he could roll until he fetched up against stone—and found himself staring up at the strangest creature he'd ever seen.

Spiderlike, it clung to the ceiling above him on six long, jointed legs that seemed to stick firmly to stone, freeing its other two legs—or rather pincers; the great stonelike slabs that had swung at him—to reach down for him. They were shaped like the claws of the Ashenul-dar crayfish of his youth, but those had been a waxy whitish-brown and the size of his smallest finger—and these were each as gray as rock, and larger than the door of the grandest cottage of Ashenuld!

Eyes opened above those pincers. Six of them.

"Thorar's rough mothering . . ." Orivon whispered that curse in deepening fear, as he stared at the monster's three needle-jawed, hungry mouths, and the baleful glares above each of them. Three heads, all of them bigger than his, with necks thicker and more corded with rippling, bulging-vein-laced muscles than the strongest man he'd ever seen.

It was a cave-sleeth, but far larger than any he'd ever seen before, a sleeth of the monstrous size the slaves of the Rift had sometimes whispered gory tales about, in snatched moments when their overseers had gathered elsewhere to confer about something.

It moved like lightning, darting a short distance the way many hunting spiders did, and those huge pincers reached down in smooth unison to pluck up a rock—a boulder larger than Orivon—and fling it back the way the forgefist had come, to crash and roll in a booming and clacking of rock upon rock, blocking his way out.

In the hollow where the rock had been, shattered Nifl bones shifted and slid, a deep pile of death.

Orivon muttered another curse as he backed away. Three rows of ruthless fangs grinned at him, as the cave-sleeth followed him, advancing leisurely across the ceiling, those great pincers flexing almost playfully.

Aside from those eyes and the throats beyond those bristling fangs—and there were three of them; there was no telling if cutting one even to blood-dripping ribbons would have any effect on the others, or slow the sleeth at all—Orivon could see nowhere that his swords could pierce and harm. Most of the legs and body were armored in the same stony casings that covered the pincers.

He was going to die here. Soon, and not pleasantly, by the looks of his foe.

The junior Watcher of Ouvahlor's face was sickly pale, and he tried twice to speak through trembling lips before he managed to frame the words, "W-was that *Olone*? The Goddess? Or did some of the crones or Consecrated of Talonar work spells to trick Jalandral Evendoom, so that he just thought Olone was—"

Luelldar waved a dismissive hand. "Unless she manifests rather more forcefully, it matters not. Listen to the High Lord; he has already convinced himself it was the latter, or that if it was the former, Olone won't act against him. If he's right in that, he has won this test. For it seems the watching Talonar believe him, and are now obeying him where they were thinking of butchering him mere moments ago."

Aloun was still pale. "Do *you* think it was Olone?"

The Senior Watcher of Ouvahlor regarded Aloun expressionlessly and for a long time before he nodded.

"Yes, as it happens," he said quietly. "I have served as a Watcher for a long time, and seen Olone's work before. Yet my opinion, too, matters not. What does is what the Anointed of Coldheart—and the Consecrated of Olone, in Talonnorn—believe."

"Oh? How so?"

Luelldar's face went on betraying nothing as he subjected Aloun to another long stare. At his gesture, in the uncomfortable heart of that stare, the whorl between them spun itself smoothly apart, into half a dozen smaller whorls, that drifted smoothly to orbit the Senior Watcher.

Scooping one of them into his hand, Luelldar regarded it for a moment and then looked at Aloun harder than ever. "You've never seen a holy war, have you?"

Orivon tried to hurry across the cavern, seeking something high and solid he could stand on, to give battle where the cave-sleeth would have no room to hang above him. Hurrying was no easy matter; bones snapped and crumbled like tinder-dry fallen twigs around his boots, and beneath his hurrying feet coins and gems slid and slithered.

Nifl must have died here in their dozens, been devoured, and their treasure hoarded. Not that he had much to contribute. Orivon's right foot slipped down the length of a sword blade, plunging deep through what felt like brittle-as-eggs Nifl skulls, into more coins. The sleeth was right behind him, moving slowly with its pincers held up like a wall in front of it, almost as if it was herding him.

Or toying with him.

He found solid stone with one foot, stone that rose

under his boots as he moved. Orivon clambered hastily up out of the shifting hoard, shedding bones. He was climbing along a rising shoulder of rock that thrust high up into the cavern; as he went, he shot glances over his shoulder at the sleeth, and tried to peer everywhere else the rest of the time. Surely there were other ways out of this cave; would the sleeth have taken as its lair something it could be trapped—or walled up—in?

And did the cavern—which was still damnably dark, as if some lurking enchantment here, or even the sleeth itself, was clawing at his darksight—hold any other monsters or perils? Traps he might plunge into, or get caught in?

A pincer slammed into the stone right beside him, clawing at his leg. Orivon hurled himself frantically aside, off the shoulder of rock, rolling over to crash down into more bones and clattering metal as the pincer swung past just above him. The other pincer, as gray and large as a wall of stone, reached for him, slamming into the rock he'd been trying to climb and running out of reach just shy of where he was wallowing in a great disintegrating heap of Nifl bones, trying to regain his footing. The sleeth, it seemed, was growing impatient.

He daren't seek cover and hole up under rocks where the huge old spider-thing couldn't go; it would just wait Orivon out, or wall him in with rocks and wait for him to die. Emerging from anywhere with those boulder-sized pincers waiting for him would be greeting death with eager impatience.

He had to get out of the cavern and flee where it couldn't follow, or kill it. And it certainly wasn't going to give him time to choose where to fight it, or climb up high, or—

Three heads with fangs, six spider legs, bony plates all over its body like armor, and those gigantic stony pincers.

Not good, by Thorar.

Not good at all.

No signs that it had poison or spun webs, at least. Nor could he recall any slaves' tales about such perils. Just that the sleeth was a patient hunter, stalking prey and ferociously fighting anyone who stood up to it.

Could he try to blind some of those eyes by hurling armfuls of these old blades and bones? Not that he'd have more than one good chance, once it realized what he was trying . . .

The necks and throats were unarmored . . . but no; peering now, he could see a row of small bony plates running up to the chin of each mouth. The throats *were* armored, and the necks around that armor so thick that he'd have to hack and saw at their marbled meat for far more time than any living beast would give him. He'd helped Orl-folk butcher oxen that had slimmer haunches!

That left the mouths as its weak spot. Could his armor keep him alive inside those jaws long enough to hack and stab enough to slay? Or would the fangs crush it, and the pincers rend him, the moment it felt pain?

There was one proverbial way to find out, as the old Ashenuldar saying put it.

Orivon snarled as his boots found solid ground again and he started to climb another rocky slope, this one much lower. Any smith knows there are many ways to fashion something, but only one "best" way out of them all.

Seeing only one way forward—and one as risky as this one seemed—did not please the forge-giant at all. Nor did his size and strength mean much against a foe that was larger, heavier, and clinging to a stone ceiling he couldn't reach, let alone stand on . . .

A pincer came at him again, and this time he dodged, swayed, and then hacked with his sword, two-handed, into the joint where the thumb met the larger, slab-of-stone rest of the hand.

It was like hacking a fire-hardened steelbark tree. His blade went in a finger-width or two, stuck, and then came free as the pincer opened, the sleeth squalled in angry pain—and the great stony limb started to flail and smash, dashing shards of stone off the rock slope an instant behind Orivon's frantic leap. The sleeth surged forward, driving its other pincer through a cloud of bone fragments and tumbling old weapons in its murderous haste, to hammer this rock and that, trying to smash a bounding, scrambling Orivon to bloody pulp.

"Ho, the coolly conquering hero comes!" Orivon shouted at it, dodging around another blunt old tooth of rock. The sleeth sprang, abandoning the ceiling to get at him. *Yes!*

The forgefist ducked under that tooth of rock and then flung himself on, under the low-hanging edge of a great horn of stone that jutted out sideways into the very heart of the cavern. Landing amid snapping bones, he slid along easily in the greasy filth of deeply heaped, rotting sleeth-dung.

The sleeth swarmed after him, hissing in anger—and Orivon came charging up over the horn and right back at it, in a leap that struck two of its heads hard with his boots, and slammed his armored crotch full into the face of its central head. He let fall his sword, snatched out his daggers, and stabbed, furiously and desperately, blinding all the eyes he could reach, through snarling forests of fangs, in a frantic frenzy that ended *just* in time.

As both pincers came slamming down to smash him to the cavern floor and batter him to pulp there, Orivon kicked out hard, hurling himself back toward the horn of stone far enough that one pincer caught his foot and spun him helplessly away—and the other missed him entirely.

The sleeth was shrieking now, several of its eyes gone into yellow-green rivers of ruin and another flapping loosely well clear of its weeping socket, like the bright necklace baubles Orl women liked to wear. Yet it could still see well enough with the two surviving eyes of its central head, and they were giving Orivon a burning glare of rage as the beast lurched forward, beating its pincers on the cavern floor in pain as it came . . . but coming far more warily than before.

Sheathing his daggers, Orivon struggled to sit up in slippery sleeth-dung. It was nigh as deep as his arm, here, in a hollow where the stone of the floor fell away, which meant . . .

With a wry smile, the former Rift-slave of Talonnorn caught up a heaping fistful of dung and flung it at the sleeth's remaining eyes. It splattered across the head a little too high, but he had plenty to hurl.

Most of his second throw ended up in its mouth and fangs, leaving it spitting and even angrier—but the third struck both eyes, just as he'd wanted. He carried a fourth and fifth as he slipped and stumbled forward, and as it shook its head furiously and clawed at its blindness with two of its spider-legs, he blinded it again. And again.

By which time he was around behind the pincers, with his other sword in hand, and reaching in to slash and stab at those last two eyes.

As he got them, it whirled and smashed at him, of course—but he'd been expecting that, and sprang away fast enough that the pincer slamming into him only gave Orivon's leap a height and speed he'd never have managed on his own, lofting him far up onto high rocks with a clatter of armor.

The sleeth came after that sound, swarming as swiftly as ever, and Orivon caught up some old bones and flung them to the stones on one side. Thankfully there was some old armor clinging to the bones that clinked on stone and gave the blinded beast something to lunge at.

Which in turn gave Orivon time enough to gather his feet underneath himself and spring onto it, landing hard on its nearest end head. He clamped his legs around that head, ignoring its gnashing fangs, and drove his sword hilt-deep down its throat.

This time, he didn't get clear quickly enough; a pincer slammed into him like a hurled boulder, spinning him far across empty darkness into a clanging meeting with unyielding stones that cost him his other sword and some ribs.

The sleeth's swarming charge across the cavern after him seemed sluggish, though, and its pincers hung lower, as if it felt their ponderous weight for the first time.

Orivon welcomed that; he was gasping for air, wincing in pain at every gasp, and wondering just what harm he could do to the sleeth with just two daggers. The eye sockets were holes he could stab through, yes, but those pincers couldn't help but find him . . .

His swords were both fallen somewhere in the cavern—different somewheres, but he knew where neither of them were, which meant his blades could just as well have been in Talonnorn, or lying in tall grass in the most bramble-tangled fields of Orlkettle, for all the good they could do him now.

The sleeth was mounting the uneven rock slope that rose to the height where it had flung him, now, its pincers spread wide to try to trap him between them if he tried to leap aside. If he jumped on top of a pincer—and *didn't* get a leg caught in its grip, mind—it would fling him far, again, as it tried to get him. Yet it might also fling him high, and the rough stone ceiling was uncomfortably close, now; that stone could crush his skull or shatter his neck just as easily as the cavern floor . . .

Or he could jump right down its throats, so to speak, and trust to his speed to get down its body and on across the cavern—where, by Thorar, there *must* be a sword or spear or *something* he could use, among all these fallen weapons—before it turned. Those pincers couldn't reach him once he was well behind its heads; its own body plates prevented it arching and turning enough to let those oversized arms get at him.

The sleeth was close enough, now, that he just might be able to make its back in one leap, if he threw aside all caution and just dived forward . . .

He sprang. A pincer slammed blindly into the stone

where the sleeth guessed he'd be, grazing his leg in midair and turning him sideways.

So Orivon landed on one hip, squarely on the sleeth's back, bounced, and was on down the bumpy road where its back-plates met, all along what he presumed was its spine, to land gracefully on his feet and start a limping run across the cavern even before it started to turn.

Thorar, but it could still turn quickly! Pincers-first it spun, those great stony blocks slamming through the air like forgehammers, straight at where it thought he was.

And there was nothing at all wrong with its thinking.

8
To Bring Death to You

Forth I went, sharp sword in hand
Slaying my intent, death my command
Much blood was shed, both the old and the new
And now I have returned, to bring death to you.
—**Calonar chant**

Running hard, Orivon gasped, found the spot he was looking for, and flung himself sideways. A moment later, he was sliding helplessly, the sleeth's sudden, triumphant roar loud in his ears.

The beast knew its prey would flee—and it was right behind the forgefist, running him down.

It missed Orivon with a smashing pincer only because he'd abruptly flung himself sideways and deliberately slid in old sleeth-dung, to where he knew there was a tangle of fallen metal: Nifl swords, nigh a dozen of them, most pitted with rust and probably too brittle for more than one thrust.

Righting himself, he scooped them up hastily.

He'd not be doing more than scratching sleeth hideplates with these, but—

A pincer grazed his heel as it slammed down, and Orivon shouted in alarm and sprang away, twisting in the air to fling all the swords in his hands wildly back into the ruined faces of the sleeth.

The beast bit at and pincer-flailed the air as that brief storm of steel rang and bounced off it.

Landing in a crouch not far away, Orivon caught sight of his first and favorite sword. It was lying bright and unbattered where it had fallen, only a stride away from his right boot.

He sprang at it, snatched it up, leaped onward for a few paces before a pincer could come slamming down, and then spun around to face his foe.

The blinded sleeth was coming after him cautiously, pincers spread wide again and spider-legs darting to prod the rocks underfoot, feeling for his crawling body. The head he'd fed the length of his warsteel to was hanging limply, drooling yellow-green gore, and . . . *yes,* that side of the beast was dragging a little, its pincer, too.

Orivon smiled a grim smile.

He could slay this sleeth, after all!

Two long boar-spears would come in right handy about now, to save him from the pincers that would smash and tear at him if he tried to ride a sleeth head again, to thrust his sword down its throat.

He backed away, trying to move as quietly as possible, and peered at the rocks all around. No handy spears, of course.

The sleeth would know every cranny and handspan of this cavern, of course; he couldn't hope to shelter behind handy rocks and strike at it without it knowing just where he must be, and what he was up to. Which meant he'd have to slay it in some inevitable situation, where what it knew would avail it nothing.

He needed a boulder or upthrusting fang of stone large enough to withstand—and partly foil the reach of, so it couldn't smash or grasp him from both sides at once—those deadly pincers. He needed—

There! *That* lofty spear of rock!

Hurling away stealth in favor of haste, Orivon got himself to the rock with only a panting breath to spare. The angry sleeth was reaching out with both pincers when its prey tapped his sword against the high shoulder of rock that its right pincer could just reach.

Obligingly, it flailed away, seeking to smash anything atop that rock. When it felt nothing, the sleeth decided its tormentor must be sheltering behind the horn of rock, and reached around the other side of the pinnacle with its left pincer.

Whereupon Orivon rushed forward, down from where he'd perched on a high ledge above and beyond the horn. He landed on that left pincer running hard, and was along it and slamming into one of the sleeth's throats before it could do more than roar in startled rage and start to hastily back away.

His sword was deep down that throat, and he was stabbing with it furiously, before the beast reared back and then slammed him forward against the rock, squalling in pain—and then vomiting up a great rushing gout of blood.

Stinging, foul-smelling yellow-green gore drenched Orivon.

He was dashed into the rock with bone-shaking, dazing force, driven against solid stone so hard his armor shrieked and buckled, thrusting sharp edges into him—and then fangs were gnawing at him, squealing along the metal plates encasing him as he fought dazedly to reach the last neck and the darting, biting maw above it.

Fangs gnashed and snapped at air repeatedly, their jaws thrusting this way and that, trying to find and remove Orivon's sword arm before he could thrust his sword anywhere.

The forgefist ducked his head and kept that arm low, struggling to keep hold of his blade and to draw breath in the tightening grip of his battered armor, as the sleeth blindly rammed him against the rocks, and rained pincer-blows down on those parts of him that the solid stone behind him didn't prevent it from reaching.

Dust rose in a choking cloud, and the very rock shuddered and thundered under the sleeth's fury. Coughing,

Orivon slid down it, trying to crouch in armor that would no longer flex and slide to let him bend. He clawed at the one strap his fingers could reach, under a bent, flared-out edge of the armor he'd so carefully forged, and eventually—as he staggered sideways along rough rock, his armor shrieking in protest, those huge, stony pincers crashing into him ceaselessly and furiously— the strap slipped, and the buckle slid along it to arrive under his scrabbling fingers.

A pincer-blow finally shattered the stone behind him, spilling Orivon abruptly over and down.

Amid his wincingly hard landing and the rolling in dust and fresh gravel that followed, the strap parted and that piece of armor swung free. The sleeth's next pincer-blow caught it, tore it right off, and tumbled the forgefist over and over in its wake, his found sword clanging away again—but Orivon found himself with space enough to roll away from its attack and dazedly claw off the worst of his crushed-into-him armor.

The discarded plates made handy distractions. Scaled away across the cavern to clang and clatter on the rocks, they sent the sleeth scuttling away from Orivon long enough for him to find his feet and his breath, and cut away the last plates of his nigh-useless armor. It had served well, protecting him from swift death against the full force of those pincers and repeated gnawings by the thing's wickedly long fangs, but was now so crushed and twisted that it was hurting him to keep it on, and was best abandoned.

Orivon kept just one forearm bracer, so as to have something to thrust unscathed into jaws. Otherwise, he now wore only his bloodstained, padded under-leathers above his belt, and breeches and boots below it. Behold the Hairy One, Creatures of the Dark. Come again among you . . . hopefully not to die this easily, this soon.

"Brith," he whispered. "Reldaera. Aumril. Kalamae."

It was too late for stealth; the sleeth had heard the sounds of his armor-discardings, and was heading back in his direction, angrily but falteringly.

Orivon gave the lurching beast a cold smile, and carefully threw a trio of armor plates to land in such a way that their successive clangings seemed to mark a path of travel away across the rocks. His ruse sent the slowing, weakening sleeth off on another errant charge.

This time Orivon stalked after it, finding and picking up his second sword along the way. The beast was leaving ribbons of gore on the rocks as it went, two heads hanging down limply and its armored belly now scraping and dragging.

If feeding that last throat the length of his sword didn't slay the sleeth, he wasn't sure what he'd do—but at last the beast now looked as if sharp warsteel thrust down its throat would manage to bring it death.

And about time, by Thorar!

If the Wild Dark held many more of these, he'd never see Talonnorn or even get anywhere near it.

So, how to reach that last throat . . .

The sleeth *knew* this cavern. Even now it was turning back toward him, having heard the faint scrape of his boots or scented him in the drifting air currents it knew and he didn't . . .

Orivon stopped, turned, and looked back.

A heap of his discarded armor, yonder the bright fresh face of rock shattered by the sleeth . . . his other sword!

He couldn't trick the sleeth twice with the horn of rock, and didn't dare rush into its pincers without armor. Which meant he had to get behind it, to where he could leap onto its back or neck, close to that central head, and do his slaughtering *very* quickly. If he couldn't manage that, he wouldn't be the one doing the slaughtering.

Back beyond where his armor lay was a rising, rugged slope of broken rocks. If he could trick the sleeth into climbing it *there,* while he waited higher up, off to the side over *there* . . .

Not a good battleground, but then he couldn't choose caverns—and if he somehow managed to outrun the spiderlike monster and get out into the passages, he would be fleeing into the unknown with no place to hide, and no way to trick the sleeth into missing where he was.

Orivon started to run, not worrying about silence. He needed that other sword, and a few of the smaller pieces of armor—and he needed to get them before the sleeth got *him.*

It was charging again, rushing forward with surprising speed. Both pincers were held aloft and back, ready to slam down on him, and it was snarling now, a wet, burbling snarl of bloody spittle and pain-driven, burning rage. Orivon reached the first piece of fallen armor, plucked it up without slowing, and heaved it to one side. He didn't want the beast to blunder into the heap of armor and realize his tricks.

It clanged, bounced, and then clattered to a halt—and the sleeth slowed, suspiciously.

Damn!

Curses of Olone!

It heard Orivon, as he skidded to a hasty stop and caught up some armor plates from the little heap, and came after him.

He swore aloud, and snarled to Thorar, "Must I be my own foe-distraction, too?"

The sleeth answered him with a roar, and launched itself forward. As it came, it brought its pincers crashing down on the rocks, let them rebound, and slammed them down again.

And again.

Amid their deafening crashings, Orivon snatched up all the armor he needed, retrieved the second sword, and scrambled up the rocks to his chosen spot.

Still furiously smiting bare rock, the cave-sleeth

charged up the rocky slope. When it was past him, Orivon launched his own charge, running and then leaping high.

He came down jarringly on that last neck, got an arm around the head—and then had to fight to turn the sword and drive it through the forest of clashing fangs. The moment it was in, he kicked and twisted, keeping hold of the neck but hurling himself around and down.

One of the pincers slammed into him anyway, numbing his hip and tumbling him helplessly away through the air, sword torn from his grasp. The other pincer crashed down on the rocks, hammering them repeatedly in agony as the sleeth thrashed about, shuddering and shrieking.

He'd wounded it sorely, but was it dying?

The forgefist watched the pain-wracked beast writhe and hit out blindly.

It seemed to be growing more feeble, but that could just be weariness, not death coming on.

Orivon glanced quickly around to make sure no *other* beasts of the Wild Dark had heard all this and come running, but saw nothing but rocks and heaped bones and treasure. Plus plates of his own discarded armor.

He hefted one of those plates and threw it at the sleeth's snarling, gore-drooling mouth—the hilt of his blade was still protruding from it—but the plate struck some of the fangs and glanced off; the creature didn't seem to even notice it.

It *was* growing weaker, though.

The pincers were coming to rest on the cavern floor, the spiderlike legs rising and falling more slowly as it turned in one direction, and then, almost aimlessly, turned back.

Orivon drew his favorite sword and took a few steps closer to the monster. He should just walk away and go on, while he still had only bruises and a few cuts and broken ribs, but he'd heard tales of beasts that could heal as they slept, and then go forth as good as new to hunt their foes—and not just the folk of Ashenuld and Orlkettle had told such stories; Ravagers who knew the Dark well had told a few.

He had to—

The sleeth reared up, shuddering all over, gave a great roaring bellow that echoed around the cavern walls, and then sank into a long, raw groan. A groan that ended when the monster slumped down, its spider-legs tilting at odd angles, to sprawl belly-down on the cavern floor.

Cautiously Orivon stepped nearer, sword held ready.

Was this a ruse?

Another piece of armor, bounced off that last head, elicited a brief muttering growl and a great shudder, but no rise off the stones. Orivon took a deep breath, stepped in between the pincers, and jumped onto the central neck with both boots, coming down hard.

The beast pitched under him, giving forth a wet, bubbling roar, and one pincer lifted a little—before it slumped down into silence again.

Orivon put the point of his sword in under the lowest of the sleeth's overlapping bony neck-plates, and then leaned on it.

The warsteel sank in, the beast quivered—and then the head vomited out a huge rush of gore and sank down into it.

Orivon hastily scrambled back along the neck to keep from falling, and then sighed, turned, and started carving.

He wanted his second sword back.

One of the eldest warblades of Ouvahlor came back to her, bowed low, and made the gesture of Reverence to the Ice. "The battle-din has ceased."

"I am not," Exalted Daughter of the Ice Semmeira replied icily, "*quite* deaf yet. Have you anything *useful* to report?"

The veteran—one of only four, among all the untried

younglings she'd been given—went a little pale around his mouth, but otherwise showed no sign of anger. "We have found warning sigils—heralding the lair of a strong dangerous beast—by the entrance to the cavern where the fighting was befalling."

"So we go around that cavern, without delay," the priestess told him airily, "and on to Glowstone. Our fighting and slaying shall be done there."

The warblade bowed again, turned, and hastened away to give the orders.

Semmeira watched him go, idly lashing the palm of her hand with the whip she'd brought along to use.

At last.

She let the smile she felt inside slowly show on her face.

Ah, but she enjoyed command. *Doing* things in the name of the Ever-Ice, reaching out with power to take ever more power. *This* was what she was made for.

And should have been doing long ago.

Kryree's hands trembled as she fitted the last of the interlocking plates into place, rose from her knees, and held out the spherical map to Erlingar Evendoom.

"Thank you, *lesheel*," the Lord of Evendoom told her gently, to calm her; her large and dark eyes were full of fear, and her face pale for the same reason. Kryree and Varaeme had been his pleasure-shes for a very long time, and were not unfamiliar with either his moods or Evendoom matters—but they were not used to wearing armor and walking the Wild Dark.

He touched the intricate spherical map with both fingers, and murmured the word that would make it float and glow. It was one of the oldest Evendoom family treasures. Rare and irreplaceable, of course, but then so were loyal living Niflghar, it now seemed . . .

"We should be close to Glowstone's nearest watchpost by now," Faunhorn murmured, coming up to stand at his shoulder and point. "We must be *here,* yes?"

"Yes," Erlingar agreed. "Pity the thing doesn't show the way to Nrauluskh, to let us go *around* Glowstone and on, seeking no one."

"Pity it doesn't show the way to a huge store of weapons, loyal-to-Evendoom Niflghar to wield them, and endless food and shes, too," Faunhorn said dryly. "If only we had one of the more expensive maps."

Those words didn't strike Lord Evendoom as all that amusing, but then Faunhorn *never* made jests, and so couldn't be expected to proffer good ones.

Not that he had need to.

Lord Evendoom was under no illusions as to why such a large handful of Evendoom warblades had accompanied them out into the Wild Dark. Perhaps a dozen admired Erlingar, and were loyal to him because of that or because he was the reigning Lord of House Evendoom.

All the rest were here because of the one Evendoom even rival nobles admired: Faunhorn. Principled, merciful, dignified, and somehow *stylish* in everything he did, or had ever done.

If Faunhorn stood shoulder to shoulder with Erlingar Evendoom, then so did they; if Faunhorn turned on Erlingar, so would they, without an instant's hesitation.

Right now—armed with the old family map that showed the caverns of the Dark in a sphere immediately around Talonnorn—they were all out in the Wild Dark rather grimly heading for Glowstone.

Where Erlingar hoped to find and hire the Ravager leader Bloodblade, to keep them all alive as he guided them somewhere well away from Talonnorn. To distant Olone-worshipping Nrauluskh, or perhaps even more distant Olone-venerating Oundrel; cities where nobles were many and weak, and merchants almost as numerous and as strong. Yet cities that had no love at all for murderers who hunted victims inside their gates.

With Bloodblade as their guide, Erlingar's handful just might manage to reach the relative safety of one of

those cities before Jalandral's forces—or his private flying Hunt, or spellrobes working for Jalandral—found
them.

Jalandral's agents were out there hunting for them
right now.

"Make for that cavern, to stand guard and rest?" Faunhorn asked, pointing. Erlingar nodded, and reached out
to take the sphere and quell its magic.

Kryree and Varaeme were on either side of him in an
instant, murmuring wordless comfort and reaching to
take and disassemble the map-sphere.

"You are so *troubled,* Lord," Kryree whispered, her
eyes now more full of concern for him than fear.

Lord Evendoom managed a crooked smile. "My son
wants us all dead," he murmured, shaking his head in
disgust. "The last of my children . . ."

He spun around to look at Faunhorn, and asked,
"Were *we* ever this inexplicable to our elders? I can't
bring myself to believe so, no matter how I try."

"Our elders never knew Talonnorn invaded, or its temple torn asunder by Consecrated fighting Consecrated,"
Faunhorn said gently. "What they thought of us pri-
vately, I cannot say. Other than to observe that some of
the elder crones of our House thought of us not at all."

"If scant comfort can warm me, I bask in your words,"
Erlingar said wryly, and held out his arms.

His brother gave him a wry smile to match his own,
and they embraced. Faunhorn had always been true, the
Evendoom everyone could trust.

Just as Jalandral had always mocked and given inso-
lence.

It was out of respect for Faunhorn, who had sug-
gested that Kryree and Varaeme remain untouched, that
none of the warblades had done so much as kiss either
pleasure-she, after they had tremblingly offered themselves to all the rampants.

Everyone knew that they were not along to bed with
Erlingar at every rest, but because Lord Evendoom knew

no other way to safeguard their lives. Six of their fellow pleasure-shes lay sprawled in their blood back in Talonnorn, casualties of one of Jalandral's latest attempts to have his father slain.

Latest, but not last. They had fled Talonnorn with Jalandral's hunters closing in. At their first stop to rest, out in the Dark, Faunhorn had told the warblades that he had not come along merely to save his own skin, but because it was imperative they all survive for a time to come, when Talonnorn would need them. Probably to refound it, for the Talonnorn they all knew was lost; Jalandral was dragging it down into bloody doom, and House Evendoom with it.

Now, with Kryree and Varaeme on their knees disassembling the map-sphere into its separate metal plates, the two Evendoom brothers walked slowly across the cavern, into the heart of their silent, listening warblades.

"I do not know my son any longer," Erlingar told Faunhorn grimly. "I thought his purring indolence, his love of shes and pranks and posing, all leaned for support on Talonnorn unchanged around him; a Talonnorn strong and proud and prosperous. And now Jalandral seems hungry to twist, remake, or hurl down all; he's become the sort of Nifl who would awaken That Which Sleeps Below just to work change."

Faunhorn nodded gravely, but said nothing at all.

"I thought Klarandarr of Ouvahlor was Talonnorn's worst foe," Erlingar told his brother, "but I was wrong. Jalandral of Evendoom is the one who will destroy us all."

9

To Glowstone

If you must to Glowstone away
Guard well behind you
As sleepless you stay
For Glowstone blades keen
And Glowstone blades fast
Spill blood in rivers
that run but don't last
For Glowstone throats await
Thirsty but not few
　　　　　—Ravager saying

The dead sleeth stank—and glowed.

As Orivon stared at it, the monster's cooling flesh kindled into an eerie, sickly yellow radiance.

Silently it pulsed once or twice, light bubbling up from it, and then started to fade. The forgefist backed away warily.

Nothing happened.

Eventually, Orivon shrugged and strode to the carcass again, to cut free his second sword.

It was easily—if messily—done, and nothing odd happened.

The beast was dead.

Orivon turned his back on it and started exploring the cavern.

In his frantic scramblings during the fray, he'd seen—
or thought he'd seen—many dark cave mouths in the far
walls of the cavern. He knew he'd seen, rushed past, or
stumbled through bones and the tattered remnants of
Nifl clothing and weapons. The lowest parts of its rugged
floor were choked with bones and leavings. Which just
might hide *real* treasure.

Orivon bent, raked heaped bones aside with his sword,
and peered.

Then he did it again.

And again.

And, with a sigh, once more.

Bones and leavings, indeed. Either the Wild Dark
was full of large bands of blindly marching oriad-heads
using maps that led them straight to this cavern, or the
sleeth had hunted down prey, pounced, and dragged its
victims back here to devour. In their thousands. Mostly
Niflghar, judging by the skulls, though perhaps the
smaller ones had just fallen down among the bones to
crack unnoticed under his boots along with everything
else. There were skulls of sorts Orivon had never seen
before, some of them jutting with bony spurs, or long
and thin like the heads of gigantic needle-billed birds.
More than one skull looked frightening even in its broken, empty state.

Wading in crumbling, cracking bones, most of them
green with cave mold, Orivon sought to pluck useful
things from in and under their disintegrating tangles.

There were belts and straps of rotting hide, and
pouches and scabbards wrought of the linked scales of
various snakes and lizards of the Dark . . . and a few of
these still held contents of interest.

He found many daggers, and gathered the better ones
into a heap; something to trade with, in Glowstone.
Coins were harder to spot amid the crevices and bone-
dust, but were plentiful, most of them stamped olden-
day ovals of the cities that venerated Olone; these, too,
the forgefist gathered. Eventually he found a battered

metal carry-box that had been bolted onto the shoulder-plates of armor too small for him . . . but if he broke those plates, *thus,* and bent the result, he had a shoulder-pack that he could swing free and drop in an instant, to free both of his arms for swinging swords. It would do to carry the coins and most of the daggers in.

More coins, and weariness, as his bruises started to ache and stiffen.

Not to mention the insistent aches of his broken in-nards.

He felt hunger, too, and thirst . . .

But not strongly enough to stay awake.

And what safer place was there in the Dark for a lone Hairy One to sleep than in a sleeth's lair?

Orivon recalled a smooth, tilted shoulder of stone in one of the higher, more rugged corners of the cavern. He went and laid himself down on it, sword in one hand—and fell asleep in a seeming instant, plunging down into endless darkness.

As he fell into oblivion, he only just had time to wonder:

What did raw sleeth taste like?

"Most holy Exalted Daughter?"

The deferential murmur was very close to her ear; it was only by some miracle of the Ever-Ice that Semmeira managed not to flinch.

Arothral, the eldest warblade of the raiding band she'd been given, was at her side again, sword in hand. He'd approached in utter silence.

"Glowstone's first watchpost is just ahead of us," he added, his voice barely more than a whisper. "Shall we attack?"

Semmeira gave the veteran warrior the coldest incredulous look she could manage. "And have them warned and ready to meet us?"

"Ah, *no,* Most Holy One. I have slain the two Nifl who were on watch here, and sent two of my fellow battle-tested warblades to the other two watchposts, to serve them the same way. Helbram has just now returned; I expect Lorrel in the next breath or so."

"And you saw fit to neglect to consult with me on this beforehand *why,* exactly?"

"Revered Mother Lolonmae swore by the Everlasting Ice that we could trust your judgment," Arothral replied solemnly, "so I knew you'd approve of this unquestioningly, being as it is the only prudent tactic."

The *bastard!* The stone-faced, grinning-within, right rich-in-tongue-dung bastard!

Knowing her eyes were blazing with fury, Semmeira let her grudging, twisted grin of admiration rise to her lips so he could see it, and replied, "You pass a test, *loyal* warblade Arothral. And thereby win *my* trust of *your* judgment. Order and launch our assault on Glowstone just as you see fit."

The veteran warblade nodded, face carefully expressionless, and then bowed, backed away, and was gone, as silently as he had come.

The screams had begun, somewhere in the caverns well ahead of her, before Semmeira realized why Arothral had carried a sword ready in his hand.

And that as he'd vanished into the dark distance on her left, the slightest of metallic sounds to her right probably hadn't been an Ouvahlan warblade drawing steel and hurrying forward to slaughter unsuspecting Nifl in Glowstone. It was far more likely that she'd heard Lorrel, whom she hadn't even realized was there, sheathing *his* ready sword and turning away.

The same Lorrel who was now standing, arms folded across his chest, a careful distance behind her right shoulder, regarding her with the faintest of smiles on his face as he murmured a steady stream of orders to young warblades who hurried up to receive them, and then hastened on toward Glowstone.

Ouvahlor, it seemed, spawned no shortage of deadly bastards.

* * *

"Seek healing stones."

That whisper was fluid and lilting Niflghar, and female . . .

"Seek—"

Sudden pain stabbed through him.

Thorar, yes! He was wounded!

And had fought and slain a cave-sleeth . . .

Orivon blinked and winced, worked his stiff and crusted mouth until he could feel his tongue again, tried to roll over and gain his feet—and stopped abruptly, wincing. He *hurt.*

Ribs gone, for sure, and probably worse. He clawed himself over onto his belly and slid down the rock a little way, drawn sword dinging a faint trail as it bounced along uncaring stone in his wake.

Feeling the need to relieve himself, the forgefist peered down rather grimly at the steaming stream of blood he was producing, and wondered just how sorely he was hurt.

That whisper, in his dreams . . . healing stones.

What if, by Thorar's smiling luck, one of the sleeth's gnawed-to-bones victims had been carrying healing stones? Most Nifl who ventured out into the Dark did, if they weren't forced to flee a city as an outlaw, and become a desperate Ravager, that is.

He knew how to use those stones, thanks to keeping his eyes open when shifting furniture in the Eventowers. Though they were enspelled by priestesses of Olone for use on Niflghar—or so Talonar Nifl had said in his hearing, more than once, at least—the stones worked fine on humans; he remembered one of the oldest Evendoom crones healing her favorite pleasure-slave, a Hairy One.

Humans could even use the stones more easily than Nifl. A dark elf needed a spell to "melt" them into their injuries, or had to dissolve them in certain acids, drink the result, and undergo agonies. The stones didn't dissolve in Nifl blood, but did in the blood of Hairy Ones—

and the resulting mix was nauseous for Nifl to drink and
healed them not at all, but a human quaffing it gained
the full benefits of the healing magic.

Sleeth, now . . . he had no idea if the magic of such
stones healed beasts at all, or if sleeth had wits enough
to know what they were and try to use them, hide them,
or bargain them away.

If there were no healing stones to be had amid the remains strewn around this cavern, he'd just have to go on
to Glowstone. If the Ravagers there had even a few
glowstones to sell, though, they'd guard them very well,
demand the treasures of a city in exchange for one, and
press their advantage when bargaining with a Hairy
One . . . and a wounded Hairy One at that.

Which meant "pressing their advantage" might well
mean just gang-attacking Orivon Firefist, to slaughter
him and get for free whatever he offered in exchange for
a stone. Or poisoning or drugging food and drink he
bought, wresting what he had from him, and then slaying him at will or chaining him as a cut-price slave, to
sell to someone who'd work him to death.

Of course, all of this assumed he found something
here worth offering in trade for a healing stone. A few
daggers and even a heavy sack full of coins wouldn't do
it.

The alternative would be skulking and fighting his way
into Talonnorn, and then into the Eventowers, to find and
seize healing stones. There was a chest of them in the armory, he knew, and every crone no doubt had some hidden away, but none of them would be unguarded, and
he'd not exactly pass unnoticed as he searched for them.
And who was to say the armory was still stocked the
same way, or that it was even in the same chamber as he
remembered it being?

Moreover, there was only one Orivon Firefist, and
Talonnorn held thousands of Niflghar who'd try to slay
him—or any unchained Hairy One—on sight.

Something rattled as he thrust aside thickly heaped bones with his sword. Metal of some sort, dark . . .

A bony arm, wearing a bracer that now hung on it limply, a chased and worked metal bracer of finer make than anything he'd ever seen in Talonnorn, all metal . . .

Orivon's eyes narrowed, and he plucked it up out of the crumbling decay. Magic tingled under his fingers.

Take me and wear me, Hairy One.

The voice startled him so much he almost flung the armlet away. He managed merely to juggle it awkwardly instead, pinning it against his chest.

It was the voice in his dream, but it was whispering inside his head!

Slave, obey and know no fear, the voice hissed, sounding amused. *YOU have nothing to fear from me. So long as you obey Yathla. I have waited a long time for someone to wear me, and work my revenge.*

"Who—who are you?" Orivon snarled, hardly daring to look down at the silken-smooth, somehow *warm* metal against his chest.

Yathla of Evendoom, crone of Talonnorn, I am—or was.

"Evendoom," the forgefist sighed.

You know us, I see. Dark, bitter amusement surged in Orivon's head. *Unmatched in House Evendoom, and much feared, I was. Until I was betrayed by my younger sisters. Poisoned, helpless, I was tormented by spells, my power torn from me to enstar items of power for House Evendoom. My body died, but I lived, aware still, trapped in this war-brace, that gouts searing flame in battle. They had not expected that, and feared me greatly. Wherefore I was put upon the body of another poisoned one, and taken forth into the Wild Dark by the Hunt, to be hurled down and lost far from Talonnorn.*

"I—"

You will wear me, and bring me to Talonnorn, and I will have my vengeance upon my kin for what they did to

*me. You will see House Evendoom humbled, Hairy One.
Take some satisfaction in that, slave of Evendoom.*

"I am no slave of anyone, and never will be again!"
Orivon spat fiercely. "Speak so to me again, and I'll hurl
you where you will never be found!"

*Then wear me, free human, and heed my guidance to
find means of healing, and live. Or hurl me away—and
die of your wounds. You are dying now.*

"I . . . I'll live, with no help from you!"

For a short time. A VERY short time.

The forgefist sighed—and then grimaced and dou-
bled over, as pain surged inside him again. "I returned
to the Dark on a task of my own," he snarled. "To try to
free four children, enslaved by Talonar Niflghar. I will
not be thrust aside from this rescue!"

*You need not be. I have no quarrel with any Hairy
One. Just with those of the Blood Evendoom. Why should
any of them live and flourish, when I was betrayed and
my life stolen from me? Wear me, man! I'll aid you as
much as I can; remember, at any time you can snatch me
off and toss me aside! Right now, you need healing
stones sorely—and I know where they are.*

Orivon gasped as fresh spasms of pain wracked him.
On his knees, he shuddered, snarled in frustration—and
slapped the bracer onto his left forearm, clawing at its
buckles. "W-where are they?"

*Don't try to get up. Leave your sword for now; you'll
need both hands, and you still have your other blade.
Crawl THAT way.*

Orivon crawled.

Up along the sloping reach of stone, to the highest
rocks in the cavern. To a cleft between them, and a
headless, armless, sleeth-gnawed Nifl skeleton twisted
between the rocks there.

*Beneath it. Pouches on a ruined belt. Trust not the
hide to hold up under handling.*

Hissing in fresh agony, his mouth now full of his
blood, the forgefist thrust an arm through the brittle rib

cage and groped beneath. Spiders and tiny cave-snakes hastened away from his probing fingers—and he touched something solid, smooth, and rectangular.

He drew it forth and stared at it wearily. A healing stone.

Put it in your mouth. Spit out no blood, but swallow the liquid as it melts. Hold it in with your fingers, and choke not.

Orivon almost choked with mirth; the motherly tone that had crept into the mind-voice sounded like old beak-nosed Meljarra, back up in Orlkettle.

Choke not, I said.

MEN.

That scornful dismissal sounded even more like Meljarra, but the stone was almost gone, little weight left on his tongue, and something that was warm and cool at the same time, and soothing all of the time, was welling up in him, and the pain fading . . .

You need another, and should thereafter find all the rest and take them for the NEXT time you do something as foolish as taking on a cave-sleeth alone.

Orivon sighed, shook his head until his wry grin faded, and obeyed.

Gladrar heard the clatter of pots behind him and spun around more weary than angry. Outlaws were certainly becoming more *clumsy* than when he'd started trading at Glowstone. Why—

The Nifl who'd upset his display shelf of cookware crashed heavily to the cavern floor at Gladrar's feet, bouncing limply as his lifeblood spattered in all directions.

Gladrar snatched out his belt-knife with a snarl. Pots were pots, but yon cloth had come all the way from—

Then the old trader saw the two warblades leaping at him, blood-wet swords thrusting his way.

He died spitting out the nastiest curse he could re-member, as the hilt of the sword that had plunged right through him slammed into his ribs and snatched his breath away.

He died smiling around that oath, though, or trying to. He'd managed to put his dagger into the warblade's left eye, just as neatly as he'd managed that same trick long, long ago.

So old and limping Nifl could still surprise sneering young warblades! *Hah!* As Glowstone erupted in shouts, screams, and the clang of snarlingly swung warsteel around him, Gladrar smiled in satisfaction.

The look of utter astonishment in the dying warblade's remaining eye was the last thing he ever saw, but it was a sight worth seeing.

Orivon Firefist was completely healed, and there were six precious healing stones in the battered old carrybox, wrapped in a scrap of his under-leathers to keep the coins that were packed around them from scratching them.

He'd found a baldric and pouch that should last for a little while, to carry most of the daggers, and now—

You're not done looking yet. There's one thing more you must not leave this place without finding.

"Oh?" Orivon snarled, as his healed but yawningly empty stomach rumbled. "Food, perhaps?"

No. Something far more useful than that.

Well, he'd never overheard an Evendoom crone appreciate any sarcasm except her own; he shouldn't expect this one to be different than the rest. "Guide me, Yathla of Evendoom," he said politely.

As promised. The mind-voice was tart. *Turn to your right.*

The forgefist obeyed, and found himself following a series of short commands that led him swiftly across the chamber to a tangle of bones near one of the cave mouths. Among them was something old, metal, and decidely odd-looking.

He held it up. Three horizontal metal plates bolted together along a vertical spindle that held them stacked but apart. The plates were engraved with lines . . .

Orivon turned the spindle, eyes narrowing, and abruptly knew what he was holding.

A map!

A simple, crude drawing of some part of the Wild Dark, with caverns and passages on the plates. He saw wisps of what might once have been threads, or spell-treated strands of *something,* that had formerly joined points on the plates, to indicate where passages ascended and descended from what was drawn on one plate, to an adjacent plate above or below.

The small, starlike spot on the uppermost plate is this cavern, Yathla said gently. *Turn to your left a bit, and hold the map straight out in front of you. When you look out of the exits from this place, you'll find they line up with what you're holding.*

"Ah," Orivon agreed appreciatively, and then frowned, studying the plates more closely. "Is this Glowstone, here?"

It is. And Talonnorn is the large cavern down on the bottom plate.

Orivon shook his head. Thorar, if he'd had this—

Ah, so Hairy Ones play the "if" game just as we Niflghar do. THAT'S interesting.

A chill ran through Orivon. He hadn't known the spirit-crone could read his thoughts.

Of course. The mind-voice sounded fondly amused. *It's what we spirit-crones do.*

"What *else* do you do?" the forgefist asked grimly.

Ah, man, where's the fun in knowing beforehand? Don't you want your life to be an adventure?

"Tried that," Orivon replied grimly. "Can't seem to try anything much else, yet."

Many Nifl have said that, too.

"And?"

Died, most of them.

* * *

"All over but the butchery, now," Oronkh growled as they stopped to catch their breaths on the high gallery, three caverns east of Glowstone. The faint clash of arms could still be heard, back behind them. "We got out just in time."

The sharren nodded, too winded to voice a reply. Oronkh watched her take hold of some of the toothlike horns of rock that caverns hereabouts bristled with, cling to them while she gasped, and then turn as calmly and smoothly as if they'd merely been out for a stroll.

Ghodal Below, but she was beautiful. Slender, graceful . . . sharren were called "Olone's Curse," and shunned because they were born with fanged mouths in their palms, and sucked blood through them from unwitting humans and Nifl they seduced. The few who weren't strangled at birth tended to grow up decidely pleasant to look upon, but Nurnra was . . . stunning. Even with her gloves off, and fresh Nifl blood dripping from her hands.

She caught the gleam in his eye, gave him a look of disgust, and then ignored him to lick her hands clean, plucking the gloves she customarily covered them with from her belt.

Oronkh watched, grinning. He'd willingly yielded his gore to her a time or two, when she'd been hungry enough to surrender to his blandishments, and would happily do it again if ever she asked. However, there hadn't seemed to be any shortage of pure Nifl blood in Nurnra's recent life, and his own blood, he knew, tasted foul to her.

Part of his being half-Nifl and half-gorkul, no doubt.

Ah, well.

'Twasn't as if he'd had any choice what he was born as, either. He'd grown into a fat, tusked pessimist of a knife-seller, and that *was* his achievement.

One of them.

Another was being the deadliest knife-hurler in all the Dark, but then, the trouble with such titles was that someone else was always well on the way to replacing you. Sometimes personally and very permanently.

"Any idea who attacked Glowstone, Manyfangs?" Gloves on, Nurnra was strolling languidly forward, hand on hip, as if the deserted cavern was crowded with Nifl rampants interested in slaking their ardor, who just might catch sight of her.

"Ouvahlan raiders," Oronkh said, with utter certainty. "Accents as strong, most of them, as if they'd never been outside their cavern before."

"They *were* young," the sharren agreed.

"*Are* young, most of them. Glowstone's overrun and taken, and I think they did more killing than getting killed."

Nurnra shrugged. "Aside from those I slew, I wasn't counting. Yet here I stand, one sharren, and I left twelve-and-five dead behind me, plus another who'll die if he doesn't get healing right swiftly. Saw you any priestesses?"

"Not a one," Oronkh growled, starting to trudge along the ledge. "Come. Darkfirefall's a long way from here."

"Oh? You've decided where *both* of us are headed?"

The knife-seller stopped dead, reflected on the tone of the sharren's voice when uttering that last sentence, and decided it was more sardonic than dangerous. Nevertheless . . .

"Far from it, Softfingers. I'd never dare presume so far. I merely meant that I've lost my wares, back there, and the nearest store of knives I can call my own is hidden near Darkfirefall."

"Ah. I *do* so appreciate practical rampants. And how many did you slay?"

It was Oronkh's turn to shrug. "I didn't count, either. I'm down four throwing-blades, though, and every one of them took a life. Shall we go back for them? Or anything else?"

The sharren shook her head. "Not now. If they're still infesting Glowstone when I want to use it again . . . well, then it'll be *my* turn to launch a raid on our uninvited visitors from Ouvahlor."

"All by yourself?" the half-gorkul teased.

"No. I'll need you along, to bind and mind the few I leave alive. I do so like *fresh* blood."

Oronkh leered at her suggestively, and pulled open his leather vest to reveal his hairy, sagging paunch.

Nurnra scowled.

"Start walking, Manyfangs."

Orivon strode along through the Dark, his swords in their scabbards, the map in the crook of his arm, and his hands busy with a knife and a huge, dripping slab of raw sleeth. Thankfully, its death-glow was gone.

MUST you? You're leaving a trail of blood even a snoutless cave-rat could follow. Hardly wise in the Dark, hmm?

"The objections of Yathla of Evendoom are heard," he told her, between gnawings on the bloody sleeth in his hands, "and swept aside. If the blood draws hunting things of the Dark to me, good. I very much feel like killing something else, about now."

The mind-voice sniffed, inside his head.

Ignoring it, Orivon Firefist strode on, chewing hard. When at last he could swallow—sleeth tasted not bad— he lifted his head and told the darkness around him grimly, "Brith, Reldaera, Aumril, and Kalamae, I come. Stay alive until I find you."

10

Vipers Out in the Dark

There are vipers out in the Dark
Your worst nightmares can't imagine
So drink deep and drink often
And try not to dream.
          —Ravager saying

Klaerra Evendoom entwined herself provocatively around the soaring black bedpost, but the High Lord of Talonnorn shook his head.

"I didn't come here for that," he muttered, striding to the most comfortable chair. "I'm in need of some plain and truthful talk."

Klaerra smiled fondly, and sought the chair facing his. "Speak, Dral. What most burdens you?"

Jalandral gave her a sharp look.

What scheming was going on behind that smiling face? She knew quite well that he intended to kill her—had started to do so, twice—and suffered her to live now only because of her continued usefulness. So just when, and how, was she planning to betray him?

She was being the most willing of slaves, lovers, and mentors, seemed truly to love him and to be eager to serve him, but . . . he was not the most lovable of Niflghar, and Niflghar in general were hardly lovable or trustworthy.

"Jalandral," she said quietly, leaning forward and extending an entreating hand to him before he could say anything, "you *can* trust me. I live at your pleasure, and am quite content to do so. I am yours, loyal only to you, and will remain so. You need have no fear that I'm plotting anything against you. Truly."

Jalandral managed a smile. "I do trust you—as much as I dare trust anyone. Thanks, Klaerra. I need *someone* to trust in."

He sighed. "As usual, I'm unsure of what best to do next in any number of matters, large and small. As I sit here acutely aware that all Talonnorn is watching me, awaiting my slightest misstep, I believe I have learned or anticipated all that the rival Houses can do against me, right now, and have managed to blunt their daring. So long as I don't break down their doors and come for them, they'll plot and arm and let their hatred of me fester for a time. A foray from Ouvahlor is only to be expected, seeking to take advantage of the turmoil of my coming to power. Even Klarandarr I'm prepared for, thanks to the Consecrated fearing him more than they do me, and crafting their manyspells-trap. It's whatever *else* might come against me, unlooked-for, that I worry over. Some surprise foe out of the Dark, Ravager survivors or fallen raised to undeath by some scheming spellrobe or other or even . . ."

"Absent kin," Klaerra said softly.

Jalandral reared back as if she'd slapped him, and then sprang from his chair to tower over her. "Hey? *What do you know that you're not telling me?*"

Klaerra rose, forcing her way into his arms, and stood eye to eye as she said firmly, "*Nothing,* Lord Jalandral. Nothing. I merely know what truly matters to you, and that is House Evendoom. Of *course* you would think of your sist—"

Jalandral tore free of her, toppling her back into her chair, and strode away across the bedchamber like a black, scowling storm. "*Yes,* Olone take her! She and the Ravager Bloodblade managed to catch me between them, up near the Blindingbright, and escaped without my being able to slay either one of them. They're somewhere out there in the Dark right now."

He whirled and strode back, teeth clenched. "I should have had them hunted down the moment I got back to Talonnorn, but needed the loyal crones here, to guard my own skin, as I sought the lordship. I dare not delay longer; they must be hunted down and slain as swiftly as possible, before they can do anything against me!"

Klaerra nodded, not smiling. "And yet—"

"And yet my father and Faunhorn are by far the greater threat. Some Talonar will turn to them, where none but the lust-ridden—and the lust-ridden who dare blasphemy and can stomach deformity, at that—will fight alongside Taerune. Oh, 'tis clear Faunhorn and my father are the more important danger . . . but can they be left unhindered longer? They'll do nothing overly reckless, that endangers Talonnorn, whereas Taerune and her Ravagers . . ."

He growled, threw wide his hands in dramatic bafflement as he turned, and then strode across the room again.

"Dral," Klaerra said gently, "you can send whomever you trust—"

Jalandral's bark of laughter was as sudden as it was bitter. After a moment, Klaerra joined in his mirthless laughter, and then held up a hand and amended her words: "Whoever can best be spared, to go after Taerune and her agents, or Erlingar and Faunhorn—or both groups, or neither. What matters is that *your* place and full attention must be kept on unfolding events here in Talonnorn."

Jalandral had halted and spun around to face her, standing in silence, hands clasped behind his back, eyes glittering as he stared at her.

"You gathered malcontent merchant commoners from the Araed and ambitious younger crones to your

side, in your bid to become High Lord," Klaerra reminded him calmly. "They have expectations. They also
have discontent, restlessness, and daring. You *must* keep
firm control over them or they'll turn on you, in a whirlwind of different cabals and assassination attempts that
will almost certainly fail and frustrate each other—but
may well claim your life just because they're so numerous and are all centered on you."

Jalandral nodded, and took a step nearer.

"In short, Dral, you must *rule* Talonnorn. 'High Lord'
must not be an empty title, must not be seen by Talonar
to belong to someone whose attention is elsewhere,
whose energies are spent on other things than what is
talked of in the streets and taverns. You have claimed
the herd of wild-eyed slaves, and must now whip-tame
it and watch over it—or lose it all. Crises will be served
up to you just as fast as Talonnorn can make the platters
to proffer them; you must be seen to be ready for them."

"Crises such as—?"

Klaerra didn't hesitate for an instant. "We hear many
reports of various Talonar fleeing the city, stealing away
to places they deem safer. If enough of them leave,
those other places *will* be safer; you'll be left lording
over the most desperate and dangerous, in numbers too
few to hold this cavern against the next Ouvahlan
foray—even if Klarandarr and even his weakest appren-
tices stay home! This is but one of the crises you must
stay and deal with—and be *seen* to deal with—as swiftly
and firmly as possible."

Jalandral started to pace across the room again. "As
for those fleeing fools, best we were rid of them," he
sneered. "Better vipers out in the Dark than vipers right
here in our beds! Those who remain are more likely to
be loyal—or too scared or weak to do anything against
my rule."

"True," Klaerra agreed, "but they're departing in such
numbers that the perils of the Dark won't claim them
all. Your foes may gather, out in the Immur, and prove

deadly indeed. Remember, they know the secret ways in, how the wards work, the—"

Jalandral spat a heartfelt curse, and then snarled, "So who shall we find to hunt them all down?"

Klaerra shrugged. "Offer rewards. Use the wealth of Raskshaula and Maulstryke—both yours, now—as bait to the ambitious of the Araed. Let them be rich beyond their dreams, so long as they bring you the Nifl heads you demand. Their lazier neighbors in the Araed will thank you for sending them away for a time and removing their ploys and energetic competition from the alleys."

"*Yes*"—Jalandral smiled, brightening—"and slaves can be flogged harder, to make up the lost work. Talonnorn was humbled at the hands of Ouvahlor because we have slowly come to coddle our slaves, treating too many of them as precious skilled workers, and too few of them as expendable, stupid brawn. They spring up as endlessly and abundantly as yeldeth, and should be treated as such."

Then he frowned again.

"But with everyone out hunting traitors, who shall raid the Blindingbright for slaves?"

Klaerra smiled.

"The last House-lord left who really knew the old Talonnorn: Randreth Oondaunt. Too witless and lazy to turn traitor, and certainly cruel enough to be a good slave-taker. He'll be so glad to be out from under your close regard—have you not seen him cowering, when you thunder?—that he'll leap in his eagerness to serve you."

Jalandral smiled.

"The perfect Talonar. May they all behave the same way. Soon."

"Rub yeldeth into them," hollow-eyed Lareldra said wearily, crawling through the soft, damp, golden brown spores to get a better look at the ribbons of blood crisscrossing Brith's back.

Vaeyemue had used her whip ruthlessly, knowing just how hard she could flog without killing a slave or—quite—cutting right through the muscles of their backs and shoulders.

Brith's shoulders still heaved, and his body still spasmed and shuddered with agony from time to time, but his screams had ended long ago, and the warm, damp yeldeth muffled his weeping.

Two of the girls clung to him as much for their own comfort as for his, crying as freely as he'd been. Kalamae, as usual, had kept silent, even when Vaeyemue's whip had cut right across her face.

It was she who now bent to take up handfuls of the clinging fungus and rub it into the blood-filled scars. Brith howled, but the yeldeth muffled his frantic noise, and Kalamae didn't even pause.

"That's it," a Niflghar said from on down the tunnel, coming toward them and clawing away great threads of the swift-growing yeldeth as he came. "Rub it in well. He'll scar, but heal as fast as this filth grows."

The dark elf was a slave, not a Talonar, and the Hairy Ones didn't shrink from him or turn their backs in sullen silence. No doubt he'd come crawling just to see why the yeldeth in this stretch of tunnel was now growing faster than its harvesting, not to gloat or make trouble.

Almost gently he shouldered past them all, and went on down the tunnel, dragging a growing heap of yeldeth as he went.

Reldaera watched him dwindle into the distance, then whispered something so softly that even Aumril, just across Brith's body from her, could hardly hear.

"I hate them. I hate them all."

"That'll do you no good," Lareldra told her. "They'll—"

"Ah, but it *will*," Kalamae hissed, turning to glare. "If we cling to our hatred, it becomes a shield—and the heavier and darker it gets, the stronger we become, by dragging it around with us. *We* are going to get out of here, somehow."

Lareldra stared at her, not even bothering to shake her head. What did it matter? Let them scheme and snarl, if it kept them sane longer. They hadn't been here long enough to break, yet.

After Urmreth had died, it'd been, her first sight of the four. They'd all been brought here at various times by Talonar slavers working for House Oondaunt.

How long since the most recent arrivals, she was not quite sure. Time passed in endless, unmeasured work in the yeldeth caverns. If you harvested too slowly, the filth overwhelmed you and buried you. So you ate, and slept, and worked, and did those things again, over and over again, taking care only not to eat yeldeth you'd just relieved yourself into, or that had eaten the flesh of a slave who'd died.

Never knowing that, the Nifl in the city above ate it all, whatever gods there be take them.

She remembered the coming of these four, though, the boy and the girls, one of them a little older.

Darksight had been cast on them, and they'd been examined.

Not that the choice of what to do with them had been difficult. Too young for strong-work or to be attractive to any Nifl rapist, they were best suited for yeldeth harvesting . . . and so here they were.

With the smallest, quietest lass—Aumril, her name was—turning now to ask Lareldra fearfully what she thought would happen to them.

Wearily—she was always weary, these days, for what did anything matter?—Lareldra tried to give them her best smile.

Then she listened hard for any sounds of Vaeyemue and her whip approaching; both were greatly feared for good reason.

Nothing.

So she shrugged, there in the soft, damp warmth of the yeldeth caverns, and replied, "You will pick until you die."

Scooping up a handful of the warm, wet fungus, she let it fall back to rejoin what had already grown to cover her knees, in just this brief time of watching yeldeth being rubbed into the boy's wounds, and added, "No one ever gets out."

"And this is . . . *everything?*"

Semmeira kept that question silken-soft, but there was no mistaking the calm menace in her voice.

Arothral, Helbram, and Lorrel were veteran warblades, and had heard superiors quietly promising them death before; not one of them paled, swallowed, or stumbled over their words.

"This is everything," they replied, more or less in unison, spreading their hands to indicate the dozen-some opened chests and coffers they'd placed before her.

"Everything magical, or that we *suspect* might be magical," Arothral added carefully, "as you commanded."

Hmmph.

The most glittering loot of Glowstone was paltry enough.

Semmeira pointed at one of the chests, and Helbram bent, retrieved the item she'd indicated—some sort of slender metallic scepter, set with many tiny, winking white gems—and held it before her for inspection.

The Exalted Daughter of the Ice peered at it briefly, and shook her head. Carefully Helbram returned it to its chest. When he turned in his crouch, she was pointing at something spherical and metallic, two chests along.

This, too, she rejected. Another three items she spurned, ere eagerly seizing three small, glowing gems, all carefully encased in little metal cages to protect them against damage if dropped. She held the trio of gems up by their chains, gazed at them critically, and then nodded and waved lazily at the chests at her feet.

"These three I'll have," she told the three warblades. "You may keep the rest."

Veterans they might be, but the officers were unable

to keep their astonishment—and greedy joy—entirely off their faces as they plucked up the chests and departed.

Semmeira smiled and watched them go. When there was no one close to her in that corner cavern of Glowstone, she turned her back on the carnage of the watchmoot and the distant boasting of strolling Ouvahlan warriors, held up the gems, and touched a finger to her tongue and then to each stone in turn.

The incantation she murmured then was long and complicated, and she looked somehow older when she was finished.

Her smile, however, was broader than ever, though it held not a trace of mirth.

It grew even brighter when countless tiny sparks faded into existence in a ring about her forehead, an aura of silently whirling points of light that danced excitedly, flared—and then fell and faded, sinking not into oblivion but rather, it seemed, into her head.

Whereupon the dancing sparks promptly reappeared in Semmeira's eyes, causing them to glow balefully.

"I'm tired of being spied upon," she announced softly, to the empty air around her.

Her smile went mean.

"As Coldheart is now discovering."

A shriek arose from one whorl, and then another. Luelldar leaned forward to glare at them—and was hurriedly closing them and turning to peer at others even before Aloun started to gape.

Whorl after whorl was showing the two Watchers of Ouvahlor the same thing.

Each whorl held the same priestess it had held moments earlier. Back then, all of those Anointed, each alone in her chamber, had been individually scrying the distant Semmeira.

Now they were all doing the same thing, but it was a different thing. Rather than calmly spying from afar, they were now all shrieking, clutching, and clawing wildly at their heads as if to reach inside and tear out utter agony raging within—and then collapsing and falling senseless.

Priestess after priestess of Coldheart, until—

Luelldar flung up his hands and shouted a word that rocked the chamber with rolling echoes, and snatched every last whorl out of existence in an instant.

Panting in the sudden darkness, the two Watchers stared at each other as low, feeble light slowly returned, stealing hesitantly in around their ankles as if afraid to enter the room.

"You . . ." Aloun lacked breath enough to say more, but the Senior Watcher knew very well what he'd meant to ask.

"I ended all the whorls, yes. In time, it seems; before Semmeira's magic could lash out at us, and deprive Coldheart of its only trained Watchers."

"D-deprive?"

"Yes," Luelldar said simply. "That spell would have slain us."

He strode across the room and did something to a panel Aloun had seen him open only once before.

Behind it were the same drinkables it had been hiding last time. The Senior Watcher selected a decanter, unstoppered it, and took a good long swig. He was gasping when he turned and offered it to Aloun.

Who took it in a kind of wonderment, sipped tentatively, winced, and then took a longer quaff.

"We lack some of the sacred bindings of the Ice that the Consecrated enjoy," Luelldar explained. "Most of them should survive what we just witnessed. Some may never regain the ability of scrying, or even full mastery of holy spells they've hitherto hurled with ease . . . but they should live. No such kindness does the Ever-Ice show us."

"So all scryings of Semmeira . . ."

"Are abruptly and painfully ended. Even the Revered

Mother would have been mind-smacked by *that* magic. Many higher-ranking priestesses know how to work it, but all of them except Lolonmae—or someone else calling on the full power of the awakened Ever-Ice—lack the spell-might to do it. Klarandarr himself couldn't manage it."

"So *why* did Semmeira do that? It helps her not at all to make more foes among the Consecrated of Cold-heart!"

"Aloun," Luelldar replied patiently, holding out his hand for the decanter, "Semmeira can't make any more enemies at Coldheart. Every last priestess and would-be priestess within its walls hates her already. What she did was free herself from their scrying. Even Lolonmae will be able to watch over her only for short periods, now, and with intense pain."

"I *know* that," Aloun said carefully. "What I meant to ask was: what good does ending their scrutiny of her do? What does she intend to do, that she doesn't want them to see?"

"Betray Coldheart or defy her orders, obviously. Just what she intends, I know not—but I *do* know that the Revered Mother will be calling on us, very soon, to scry the wayward Exalted Daughter just as subtly and briefly as we know how, so that we can all discover what Semmeira is up to."

"Briefly and subtly," Aloun muttered, "so we can avoid being mind-blasted, right?"

"Right. Semmeira's little army has taken Glowstone with ease, slaughtering most of the Nifl there, and we saw her rejecting most of the admittedly paltry magics brought to her. Which means she's quite confident in her own power right now—given that she's alone in an army of rampants, the most capable of whom she's just relinquished all that magic to, so they just might at some point stand together and use it all against her. So she might be planning *anything,* from conquering Talon-norn to slaying Klarandarr to establish a reputation as *the* most dangerous Nifl in all the Dark, to setting up some sort of a lure for the Anointed of Coldheart, so she can slay them one by one as they arrive to investigate it. These are but three whims of conjecture I've just indulged in, mind, and should be treated as such."

Aloun nodded soberly. "Do we know the Revered Mother's plans regarding Talonnorn? Or Klarandarr's?"

"Not well enough to discuss," the Senior Watcher said firmly.

Aloun took the hint. "What of the other cities, nearby?"

"Uryrryr, Imbrae, Nrauluskh, Yarlys, and Oundrel are all arming themselves right now, preparing forces to set forth into the Dark. What those forces will be sent to do is pure conjecture, but I suspect it will depend very much on what they believe Ouvahlor is intending to accomplish. They do *not* want us—or any city—to grow as strong as Talonnorn was, and so threaten all. Nrauluskh may be intending more than that. They have long coveted Talonnorn's Rift, and the richest of its ore-veins. The strife in the Talonar temple of Olone will give them all the pretext they need to 'cleanse' decadent, fallen-from-Olone Talonnorn. By conquering it, of course."

"And Jalandral? Is *he* readying an army?"

"Full of questions, aren't you? He is, but is most concerned right now with tightening his hold on his own city, and being ready to fend off attackers hired by rival Talonar. He's no fool, mind; he'll be expecting Ouvahlor to come calling again, to test Talonnorn's weakness and his own rule, and to give their warblades more battle-tempering. To say nothing of what experiments on large numbers of screaming, fleeing Niflghar Klarandarr's next spells may involve."

"So lots of Nifl may soon be butchering each other in the Dark between here and Talonnorn. Erlingar and Faunhorn Evendoom are still out there, heading for Glowstone to hire Ravagers and not knowing it has fallen to Ouvahlor. The Ravager they most want, Blood-blade, is somewhere else in the Dark, with Taerune Evendoom and whichever Ravagers they've managed to gather around themselves. Which means the few who are too desperate to do otherwise, or who haven't heard how dangerous it is to walk the Dark with Bloodblade, these days."

Aloun frowned.

"A thought strikes me: how many Ravagers—and slave-takers in Talonnorn and other Nifl cities here-abouts—know the ways to the Blindingbright, and are daring to seek them right now? To gain slaves, or allies, or magic, or just a refuge from all of this strife, to return when the time is right?"

Luelldar smiled. "Ah. At *last* you are truly ready to begin to become a Watcher, Aloun. I have waited so long for you to truly begin to think. And see."

Orivon stifled another belch.

Sleeth-meat was greasy, and though he'd long since finished it, its aftertaste was both less than pleasant and prone to returning.

Often.

He refrained from cursing as that foul taste filled his mouth again. Glowstone was very near, so a guardpost was somewhere close by, now. Which is why the Wild Dark had fallen very quiet around him.

He tried not to fill that heavy silence with more noise than he absolutely had to, stealing forward as softly as any sneak-thief, with drawn sword reversed under his arm and the metal map held firmly against its hilt.

"There!" The voice out of the darkness was as sudden as it was harsh. "Ravager—a Hairy One, by the Ice! *Kill it!*"

That darkness fell away as if magic was banishing a curtain of clinging darkness, and Orivon saw armed and armored Nifl standing all around him. Their swords sang out—as Orivon Firefist cursed, flung the map into the face of the nearest Nifl, and drew his other sword as he bounded forward at the next warblade.

And recognized the badge of Ouvahlor, in the instant before three blades thrust at him, and the Nifl behind one of them snarled, "Welcome to Glowstone, human! Now, *die!*"

11

No Shortage of Death

Food? We've all too little to go round
Softer than stone, our beds are mere ground
Our riches and garments are all that you see
Our only plenty? No shortage of death have we.
> —old Ravager song

Orivon's best sword was met and parried, the Nifl using both hands and staggering—but his second-best blade bit deep into that Nifl neck. The warblade sagged and started to fall, head flopping loosely amid spurting blood.

The forgefist ran on, knowing that to stand and fight would mean being surrounded and swiftly hacked down.

'Ware behind! Yathla snapped, in his mind, and Orivon twisted and slashed behind him, without slowing or looking; his blade sliced into something that shrieked.

Then he was through the tightening ring of Niflghar warriors, and turning sharp left to hack the back of another neck as he ran along behind hastily turning Ouvahlan warblades.

Keep running in this direction. There's a cavern ahead where you can turn back into the Dark, away from Glow-stone.

"Been here before, have you?" Orivon grunted, smashing a Nifl sword aside with his own best blade and driving his other sword up under the warblade's chin. The Nifl staggered away, gurgling and dying, into the path of a warblade who was pursuing Orivon—which gave the forgefist time enough to hack down the last Ouvahlan in his way, and sprint into the darkness. "What if I don't *want* to turn away from Glowstone?"

A horn-call roared out into eerie echoes right behind him.

Then you'll die, here and now. Hear that horn? This patrol is summoning others. They'll be closing in around you.

Orivon spat out a few vicious curses, and added, "I threw the map away!"

So you did. Worry not. These are Ouvahlans, so they'll be heading for Talonnorn soon enough. Once you've gotten away and they've calmed down again. First things first.

"Full of trite advice, aren't you?"

Once a crone of Evendoom, man, ALWAYS a crone of Evendoom.

And running hard, stumbling and reeling on uneven stone, Orivon Firefist found himself chuckling.

"What," Nurnra asked, her voice closer to shaking than steady, "is *that*?"

Oronkh shook his head, watching great looping coils glide and undulate in the cavern ahead. Whatever it was seemed snakelike, but to have four—no, more—heads, all of them on their own long neck that branched out from the main body somewhere near the back of the cavern.

The beast was *huge*. And angry. And hungry, or looked it. He could see fangs as sharp as swords and longer than his own body, and those jaws were thrusting this way and that, as if *tasting* the air . . .

"I know not," he told the sharren grimly, scratching one of his tusks, "but I *do* know it's between us and the only way to Darkfirefalls, and *filling* the Olone-damned cavern! We're turning back."

"To greet scores of Ouvahlan warblades?"

"To lead it into their ranks, if we can. The thing has scented us already. See?"

Nurnra peered for a long moment.

"It's following us," she said softly—and then shivered, against the knife-seller's shoulder. "Get me out of here."

"As you command, Lady," the half-Nifl, half-gorkul growled, sweeping an arm around the shapely sharren and whirling them both around. Behind them, much hissing arose, sounding as if it was coming swiftly closer. "Whither shall we—"

"Manyfangs," Nurnra snarled, "just shut up and get *going.*"

Oronkh lowered his unlovely head between his broad shoulders, tightened his arm enough around Nurnra to lift the sharren off her feet, and did as he was told.

Suddenly there were Nifl in front of him, warblades with swords in their hands.

Orivon hacked at them viciously, burst through their line, and ran on.

Horns were calling in several caverns behind him; many, many Nifl seemed to be closing in around him.

Six—no, seven—patrols, at least; had Ouvahlor emptied itself, to flood to Glowstone? Well, with this sort of an army, they'd be heading for Talonnorn, for sure.

Which meant he had to get there first, and somehow find the four younglings and get them out—and then, somehow, get them home through the Wild Dark going *around* an advancing army.

And he was running out of curses.

Orivon rounded a corner into a larger cavern—and skidded to a halt. It was full of Ouvahlan warblades, all looking his way and with swords ready on their hands.

Spitting heartfelt dirty words, he ran in the other direction, down a long and curving cave that was heading around Glowstone on the far side of that moot from

Talonnorn, toward a distant, larger trading town called Darkfirefalls. A completely unfamiliar reach of the Dark to him, and—

This new cavern seemed to go on forever, and to be something of a roadway; he could see the wet, rotten fragments of old sledges here and there among the teeth of rock that studded the floor. A gentle breeze was blowing into his face, and he could hear water trickling, somewhere unseen but nearby. Water he went on hearing, as he ran and ran with Niflghar warblades flooding into the cavern far behind him. A stream, then, which would inevitably mean prowling monsters of the Dark, lurking as they awaited food to come running right down their waiting maws.

Such as a lone and winded Hairy One, a sword in either hand and—

Orivon panted out a despairing oath and skidded to a stop again. There were Nifl ahead of him, too, lots of them. An entire Thorar-damned army!

He looked back. The Nifl pursuing him were still there, of course.

Orivon drew in a deep breath, and then turned and ran toward the sound of water, up off the relatively smooth cavern floor into tumbled, rising rocks. The Nifl at both ends of the cavern were shouting now, calling to each other excitedly, amusement in their voices as they confirmed that there was only one Hairy One— and started to bargain over what they'd do to him, and who'd get to do·what bloody torment first.

Get across the water. DON'T tarry in it. Unfriendly jaws await.

"Thank you, Yathla. What's across the water?"

A little ledge a lone Hairy One with two blades and swift hands just might be able to defend. It even has a rock to get down behind, if they try arrows.

"And you know this how?"

I was young once, human, and tasted a few adventures of my own. Enjoy the swim.

The water was ink-black—and icy!

Orivon grunted involuntarily as he plunged into it, his boots finding bottom immediately. He hurried through the stream, water thick about his legs, and then was up and out of it, rolling across the ledge.

Just in time, it seemed.

Something unseen was causing the water to bulge up over a just-submerged bulk that was sliding lazily but inexorably out of the distance toward him. Orivon cursed and shrank back from the water, moving along the ledge to get behind the shoulder of rock Yathla had mentioned.

Whatever it was in the water slowed when it got to where Orivon had crossed, and then sank down, leaving only ripples behind.

Which was when the foremost Nifl who'd been chasing Orivon reached the spot where he'd turned off the cavern road, and came rushing up through the rocks, and over the ridge, down to where the stream was.

No, don't try to hide behind the rock. They need to see you.

They already had. Warblades plunged into the water, snarling, "Get the Hairy One!" and similar sentiments, and—vanished.

The water boiled briefly, Nifl swords and heads abruptly sank from view, and a few bubbles arose.

Orivon and the Nifl still on the stony bank watched those bubbles pop, and the warblades fell silent, standing wavering on the bank.

The other Ouvahlan band arrived at the bank of the stream farther down, having seen none of this. They plunged into the dark waters without pause, to wade in great numbers along the dark flow toward Orivon.

The black waters promptly roiled, and warblades started to vanish again.

This time, some reappeared, drifting lifelessly to the surface, blades fallen from hands.

One rolled over as it came up, and Orivon saw that its

throat had been bitten away. The water-monster, it seemed, had eaten all it could for the moment, and was now slaying for later dining.

Shouting in alarm, the Ouvahlans still in the water turned and tried to clamber out, falling and splashing in their haste. More than one shrieked as he was taken from behind and dragged under, but the water was soon empty of the living.

Silence fell again, as everyone stared at the drifting bodies and the waters started to calm. No one had yet really seen the slayer in the water—and no one, it seemed, really wanted to.

Orivon heard what was being shouted, and his stomach lurched. They had no spellrobe, and were led by a priestess no one wanted to disturb for anything—he smiled mirthlessly at that—but their highest-ranking officers, the commanders, had found slaying magics in Glowstone. One was being sent for.

Thorar, be with me.

He ducked down below the rock, where the Nifl couldn't see him, and muttered, "Now what? How do I fight magic?"

By doing as you're told. For now, stand up again. When this "commander" arrives, point at him with the arm you're wearing me on—point your sword—and leave the rest to me. If someone looks like they're about to send an arrow this way, first, point at them, too.

Orivon stood up. Nifl warblades stared at him. He smiled back at them and stood leaning on his swords, watching the bodies drift slowly downstream. The water looked placid again.

The bodies were all gone, and the stream was flowing mirror-smooth again, by the time the commander shouldered through the Nifl along the bank, some sort of slender metal baton in his hand. It looked something like a Talonar slave-goad scepter, and the Nifl holding it looked calm and capable and ready to use it. The warblades around him pointed at Orivon and then at the water, saying many swift things in voices too low for the man across the stream to hear.

Then the commander gave an order that sent Nifl to searching along the banks for loose stones, and hurling them into the stream. Orivon shrank down, hoping no one would decide to just bury the human in hurled rocks and be done with all of this, but the stones went on plunging into the water and sending it up in little plumes and geysers as it gulped them.

Suddenly the water bulged again—and something black and glistening and serpentine burst into view. It reared up with frightening speed, powerful coils that split into a forest of writhing snake-bodies, each ending in a snapping-fanged head. Those heads lunged for the Nifl-crowded bank, reaching angrily—

For oblivion, as the Nifl commander struck a pose, aimed the scepter in his hand, and fed the beast snarling spheres of roiling lightning.

The water-monster shuddered as those spheres burst in its jaws and along its dripping coils, unleashing snarling, clawing arcs of lightning that split and sizzled, racing and coiling in an eyesight-searing instant that left glowing steam rising from sagging, falling coils.

Point at the commander. Point at the Olone-blasted commander NOW.

Orivon pointed. The bracer on his arm quivered once, and then erupted in a racing red bolt of flame, a line of fire that spat across the water and through the sinking monster-heads, to melt through Nifl chests beyond.

Aim true, human! Strike that scepter, before he drops it into the water!

Orivon moved his arm, snarling in concentration, and aimed true.

Abruptly the little knot of stricken, staggering-back Niflghar on the bank vanished in a blinding ball of white fire that smote the ears like a forgehammer and sent shards of stone clacking and spinning past Orivon and everywhere else in the cavern.

The stones underfoot shook, the dying monster and much of the water in the stream were hurled up into the air, and dark elves in that more distant band were flung in all directions, limp and broken.

The Nifl on the bank right across from Orivon shouted in fear and turned to frantically flee, Orivon winced as his shoulders were slammed into the cavern wall behind him hard enough to drive all the breath out of him, and . . . silence fell again, the silence of temporary deafness.

Groaning on the ground, fighting for breath, the forgefist could hear nothing but the deep vibrations of his own groaning and the much fainter quiverings of shock waves dying away through the rock beneath him. He felt rather than heard the water crashing back down into the stream, and the limp carcass of the water-monster slapping down into it.

MUCH better, Yathla of Evendoom purred in his mind.

Orivon heard that well enough, and felt her satisfaction, too, but of the Dark around him—nothing.

Then, slowly, as he lay gasping, air slamming back into him and then failing again, slamming back and failing, sounds started to come back to Orivon. His own labored breathing, louder than all else.

He struggled to roll over and rise, managing to get as far as up on one elbow, to where he could see the cavern again.

There was a great scorched, blasted place on the bank of the stream where the Nifl with the scepter had been, and for quite a distance beyond, to a ring of lifeless, heaped Nifl that defined that deadly ground.

Groaning, wounded Nifl were limping, crawling, and staggering around behind that ring, and beyond them, their unharmed fellows were hastening away, fleeing down the cavern into the distance.

The dark elves who'd pursued Orivon here, however, had drawn back only as far as the road down the center of the cavern, where veteran Niflghar—more commanders, by the looks of them—had arrived and were rallying them, with much stern shouting and wavings of swords. Glowing swords.

Orivon's spirits sank again. Magic swords weren't something he could fight against, if—

Oh, stop GLOOMING, human. You're as bad as a close-cloistered Consecrated, worrying over which finger to raise in prayer-gestures! Besides, things are about to get worse. Save your despair for when it's truly appropriate.

"I . . . I'll try to remember that," Orivon muttered sarcastically. He glanced down the cavern again, and added a curse.

The distant group of Nifl had stopped fleeing. It seemed superiors had arrived there, too.

More than that, they were coming back. Slowly and warily, with swords held ready and gazes darting everywhere, the Ouvahlan warblades were coming back.

To meet with their fellow Nifl in the cavern road, and stand talking . . . before turning in slow unison to face the lone human across the stream, and striding forward.

"Oh, *dung*," Orivon said feelingly. "This is not how I wanted to—what's *that?* Thorar shield us, Lady of Evendoom, what's that?"

Something was moving, far down the cavern. Something high up in the darkness, flapping and undulating—no, several somethings, curling and banking and gliding . . .

"Raudren," he breathed, suddenly recognizing what he was seeing. Dozens of them, dark and sinister, swooping suddenly to skim along amid the Nifl.

"The Hunt!" a Nifl shouted, mistaking the raudren for darkwings. "The Hunt of Talonnorn!"

A bright beam lanced out from one of those glowing swords, to stab up at one of the raudren.

See that one, who did that? Keep your eyes on him, the voice in Orivon's head snapped, sounding very much like Taerune giving him cold, insistent orders in his years of working beside the Rift.

Raudren banked and swooped wildly as those brief-lived beams spat at them. They were the deadliest flying hunters of the Dark, not mere cruel and stupid steeds like the darkwings. Their entire bodies were one great, leathery wing, its edges lined with a razor-tail and even sharper jaws and claws.

One dived down behind a rock pinnacle, then swooped out its far side to plunge down among the nearer group of Ouvahlans. The commander with the sword spat another beam at it, enshrouding it in flames that flared purple, and trailed sparks.

The raudren shrieked, convulsed in the air, and suddenly shot away, climbing swiftly, and another beam raced after it.

Now, Yathla said firmly. *Aim me at that Nifl with the sword NOW.*

Orivon obeyed, the bracer quivered again, and red fire howled out across the cavern, to drench and immolate the Niflghar commander, very much as he was burning the raudren.

Warblades fell or scrambled away from around him as that Nifl convulsed, staggered—and was dashed to a bloody smear and tumbling severed limbs as the flaming raudren crashed into him, biting in furious agony, and slid him along the cavern floor to a shattering collision with a rock spur of the wall.

As that raudren sagged and others started to swoop down, all over the cavern, Yathla of Evendoom spoke again.

Time to get yourself across the stream and out of this cavern. Head back toward Glowstone; there are far fewer Ouvahlans in that direction. Stop and point at my command—otherwise, use your swords and do as you were doing before: keep moving, tarrying to end no fights.

"Yes," Orivon agreed gratefully, and plunged into the water. "As you command."

A bit less sarcasm, Hairy One, if you DON'T mind.

The voice in his head sounded as if it was trying not to chuckle.

Lying flat on the high ledge as raudren swooped and soared below them, Nurnra laughed aloud.

"Enjoying the carnage, Softfingers?" Oronkh growled, chin down on the cold stone beside her. The half-gorkul was busy lying very still, unsuccessfully trying to make his huge bulk look like a lump of rock.

"That's *Lady* Softfingers to you, Manyfangs," came the tart reply. "And yes, I am." She sighed happily, like a glutton anticipating a glorious feast. "So much blood . . ."

Chin down on the rock just as her longtime shady business partner was, she lifted a slender hand to point. "There goes the Hairy One; getting away clean, by the looks of it. Not too lax in butchering foes who stand in his way, is he? Wonder where he came from? He certainly wasn't in Glowstone before the Ouvahlans pounced; I'd done several survey-the-meals strolls."

The half-gorkul shrugged his massive shoulders, reaching out his long tongue to lick one of his tusks clean. "Aye. I mean 'no.' That is, I saw him not, too. A slave escaped from somewhere else, then."

He grinned, large yellow teeth gleaming as another bright bolt of magic flashed, in the battle below. "Whoever he is, he got them all gathered together nicely for us to butcher."

Nurnra gave him a sidelong look. " 'Us'? Since when are we raudren?"

"Well, 'twas *my* magic as called them, Softfingers."

Though she hadn't seemed to move at all, the sharren was suddenly pressed against Oronkh, soft and sleek, her sweet breath warm on his tusks.

"And can you call them whenever we need them?" she breathed, excitement in her eyes. "Or when *I* want them?"

"No," Oronkh replied a little sadly, not wanting to

banish that ardent eagerness in her face, but knowing he dared not deal in falsehoods when doing so could soon snatch away their lives. "That was it."

The knife-seller shifted on the ledge, to bring his far hand around to where she could see it. "I could summon them but the once. Spellrobes craft gewgaws that win but one battle."

He opened his hand, to display the formerly magical gem in his palm. Dull, now, it had cracked and was crumbling into dust.

"Thank the Ever-Ice, Olone, and whatever other gods there be for *that,*" Nurnra replied crisply, seeking to salvage something from her own disappointment. "Or the damned spellrobes would be ruling us all."

"Instead of corrupt noble lords and malicious priestesses," Oronkh said sarcastically. "Oh, yes, that'd be *much* worse."

The gathering-place was too small and too new to have a name yet. It had no handy water or sheltering side caves, which meant no traveler in the Dark would ever have bothered to tarry there at all if Glowstone hadn't become so dangerous, recently.

Yet Glowstone had, and there were more than a dozen dirty and weary traders and outlaws warily sitting there now, backs to the rock walls and keeping watchful eyes on each other.

They all looked up as someone new shuffled into view in the distance, approaching along the smaller, lesser-used of the two tunnels that met at the nameless moot. More than one of the Watchers peered idly, only to shift in obvious interest, and half rise to stare the better.

It was someone they knew, someone thought to be dead—or so the word had recently spread, through the Wild Dark. Word had been wrong before, but then, undeath had dragged the dead unpleasantly to lurching "life" again before, too. More than a few undead walked like the lone wayfarer, too. Hands felt for ready weapons out of long habit.

The newcomer saw the handful of gathered travelers, halted for a moment as if trying to decide whether or not to turn and flee, and then came on again, trudging slowly on through the Dark. Alone.

No one traveled the Wild Dark alone.

This "no one" was a Nifl rampant, and he was the perfect picture of what most Haraedra, the city-dwelling "Towered Ones" among Nifl, thought all Ravagers looked like. He wore tangled scraps of weathered, salvaged armor, and struck even a less than fastidious Nifl eye as "dirty." He looked every bit as battered as his armor; scarred, with a torn ear, and sporting an eye patch. Gaudy battle-trophies hung about his neck, and a profusion of rusty, well-used weapons hung off his body everywhere else. He bore a worn knife in his hand too broad-bladed to have begun its existence as anything less than a full-sized sword, and his face was grim and unwelcoming.

"Daruse," someone said his name as he came up to the moot. He replied with a hard stare, and kept right on walking, past them all and on down the tunnel, on toward Manyworms Cavern.

No one called his name again.

12

Why Knives and Throats Meet

Always we are ready here
A stranger fair to greet
Yet watching them for the times when
A knife and throat must meet
For forest dark and valley fair
Many a beast do hold
And smiling strangers sometimes are
A-seeking everyone's gold.
            —Orlkettle firesong

"We must *hurry*," Andralus Dounlar snapped at his kin urgently, striding through the busy throng of House warblades crowding the great hall at the heart of House Dounlar. He hoped they could hear him through the din all of these sword-louts were making.

The warblades were gathered in the vast and lofty chamber because they were loyal to the younger generation of the Blood of Dounlar. They were used to all of the family they served arrogantly thrusting their ways through anything that was happening, so they paid Andralus little heed. They were all too busy readying carry-sacks of food for the long and perilous journey through the Wild Dark; moreover, it wasn't any of them that Andralus was addressing.

"We are well aware of the need for haste, Littlest," his

eldest brother said dismissively, using the childhood name that always made Andralus pale with anger. "The High Lord won't be pleased if his intended slaves—Olone pardon, his subjects—start departing the city in droves; we *expect* him to do something to try to stop us. Yet neither are we eager to find ourselves out in the Dark without a morsel or drop to eat or dr—"

"Barrandar," Andralus burst out, "will you stop sneering at me and *listen*? There's an *army* out there trying to break down our gates, right now—and none of them are Evendoom warblades!"

That got their attention, all of them: Barrandar, Garlane, and even their three lofty sisters. Alohphea even looked alarmed, mouth falling open above her glossy, magnificent fall of hair. They stopped their arguing to stare at him.

"Well?" Barrandar snapped. "Whose army?"

"I—I know not. They're wearing all manner of weapons and armor; they look like all the malcontents of the Araed: the wildblades who go out seeking bounties!"

Garlane frowned. "Someone has hired them," he said grimly. "It could well be Jalandral, not wanting to be seen to openly storm and loot a House of the city. Andralus, back to the gates with me, and beckon the best of our blades as we go. We'd best—"

Shouts and screams deafened him. Everyone turned to face the front of the hall in time to see the reason: a spell had melted away the great front doors in a sighing instant, and the wildblades of the Araed were streaming in, hacking at every scurrying Dounlar servant and shouting House warblade they saw.

The three brothers all drew their swords and bellowed at their sisters to do various things; it was Barrandar's voice that rose like a deep war-horn over them all, snarling: "Alohphea! Raelimel! Lorneera! Get you to Father, or to the House Spellrobe Hlammaras! Let *nothing* prevent you, or House Dounlar is lost!"

The three sisters needed no urging to flee, racing through the rushing House folk as swiftly as their skirts would let them. Wincing at the shrieks of Niflghar dying behind them, they spared not a moment to look back, but departed the great hall like frightened, flitting birds, darting around and between everyone in their way.

Their brothers were already crossing swords with various of the murderous intruders, and were devoting all their attention to slaying, and all their breath to cursing.

Rorlann had been a blade-for-hire for a long time, and had a reputation for being lucky. It had been his good fortune, for example, not to have been anywhere near the infamous Bloodblade when a certain maimed lady noble of Talonnorn, in the company of a fearsome Hairy One, had encountered the Ravager leader, and brought down on Bloodblade's band the attention and long reach of Talonar nobles—and their dooms.

Wherefore Rorlann was a Ravager, yet still alive.

Alone, mostly, but alive nonetheless.

And both astonished and pleased to see someone he knew, walking up to where he'd camped in a little hollow of rocks, in the string of caves that led like a long and untidy staircase down into Manyworms Cavern.

"Daruse!" Rorlann said delightedly, setting down the hurlbow he'd raised at first sight of a visitor, right beside the drawn sword laid across his knees. "'Tis me, Rorlann! I heard you were killed!"

"You heard correctly," Daruse told him sweetly, sitting down beside Rorlann with a weary thump and smiling like a wolf—as the old knife in his hand swept up through Rorlann's throat. "How long it will be before word spreads that *you* were killed? I wonder."

Rorlann gurgled helplessly as he stared at his slayer, his chin held up on that oh-so-cold blade as his eyes slowly lost their focus and the light behind them faded.

Slowly his body slumped over.

Daruse let the dead Nifl slide wetly down the blood-ied steel, then wiped it on his supple-worn leathers and turned away.

As there was no one to see what crossed that eye patch–adorned face, the Nifl-she whose strongest spells had gone into shifting herself to exactly match Daruse the Ravager's body, so she could wear his gear and filthy garments—Olone *spit,* but they *still* made her itch like fire-fury, a dozen vermin-banishments later!—curled her lip in contemptuous disgust.

What they said back in Talonnorn was true; all Rav-agers *were* unwashed, stone-headed cave-rats. Cunning, yes, or none of them would ever last long enough to get dirty, but . . .

She shrugged. Not that she'd had much of a choice. Between the hungry jaws of beasts large and small, and swift-gnawing molds and fungi, uneaten bodies out in the Wild Dark were rare indeed.

This Daruse, whoever he was, had literally fallen into a spell as he died. He'd toppled into where a magic worked for other reasons entirely, in whatever battle had claimed his life, had been raging. Forgotten yet still flickeringly powerful, it had kept predators of the Dark at bay, and greatly slowed the corpse's decay.

Which had made the dead Ravager just what she was looking for. She very much needed to be someone other than who she was, for a time, and a Ravager was ideal.

She needed to find others, though—and better ones than idiots like the one she'd just slain.

This Rorlann had a poor knife, a poorer sword, and a slim purse; nothing she wanted. She was after someone who hadn't known Daruse by sight, who could tell her where the Ravager known as Bloodblade could be found—or someone who could confirm *his* death.

Either would do.

House Spellrobe Hlammaras was striding scowlingly toward the terrific din arising from the great hall at the front of House Dounlar, wondering what dark idiocy the rebellious younglings of the Blood Dounlar had unleashed *this* time.

Pranks and rebellious misbehavior had marked their lives as long as he could remember, but since the Ouvahlan attack they'd spewed oriad schemes and fancies so wild and fast that—

Hlammaras came out onto his favorite high balcony, overlooking the great hall, and stopped thinking.

He just stared, as horror rose to take him by the throat, as he beheld in disbelief the tumult of wild battle now filling the vast chamber. Nifl were dying bloodily everywhere, and strangers—wildblades!—beyond counting were streaming into the hall, through the great arched hole where the front doors should have been.

Hlammaras stood quivering—and then blinked, and at the last instant ducked aside from a pair of hurled daggers that came whirling up out of the fray below to seek his life.

Whirling around, the spellrobe left the balcony, darted back out into the dark upper passage he'd just come storming along, and ran faster along it than he'd ever run in his life before.

He needed a door that locked, and for privacy, a deserted chamber behind it.

He found both in an undermaid's room, after he'd snatched her shrieking and half-dressed out of it and hurled her bodily out into the passage. Pausing only as long as it took him to properly draw breath before working a certain spell, House Spellrobe Hlammaras began its casting, altering the incantation carefully as he went, to boost it into the strongest magic he knew how to craft.

All over House Dounlar, as the altered incantation took effect, every last apprentice spellrobe of the House collapsed to the floor, dark-eyed and empty, their lives snatched out of them.

With all of that bewildered life-energy raging and

crackling through his arms, and nigh-choking him, House Spellrobe Hlammaras unleashed his spell.

A breath later, the great hall fell suddenly silent. Everything in it—living or dead—had been sucked out of it to somewhere far away across the Wild Dark.

Hlammaras knew not where. He stood panting in the sudden stillness, all the energy gone from him, barely able to keep his feet.

Outside House Dounlar, he knew, the last roiling remnants of his spell would claim any Araed wildblades—or anyone else—who dared to step through the empty doorway of the great hall.

They would vanish, without any fuss at all, and their next steps would be somewhere out in the Wild Dark.

Where they would have to fend for themselves; he had no time to spare for any worrying about them. He had his own skin to see to, and the heads of the rest of House Dounlar.

High Lord Jalandral would very soon be far less than pleased with any of the Blood Dounlar, or their household. With not enough spellrobes left in all the city to restore them, the greatest spell ever worked by House Spellrobe Hlammaras had just shattered the wards of Talonnorn.

Leaving it defenseless against the Dark.

"Belorgh, *quiet!*"

Grunt Tusks lashed out hard with his heavy length of chain to take the ever-talkative Belorgh right across the tusks, and added in a roar, "Silence, all of you!"

All of his battle-band blinked at him in astonishment. He saw them shift their feet uneasily at the sight of Belorgh's blood on the chain, and Belorgh down on the ground clutching his face and rocking back and forth in silent agony.

Grunt Tusks gave them all a baleful look, and turned back to trying to hear the distant sound.

Remarkably, it was still continuing. A dying, mournful chiming, the tinklings of a thousand tiny bells that were sliding downward in pitch even as they rang.

Grunt Tusks had heard that sound only six times in his life before, and knew very well what it meant. When he turned back to his brutish band of gorkul outcasts and escaped former Nifl slaves, his savage smile was fearsome.

"The wards of Talonnorn are no more!"

His band all stared at him blankly, incomprehension as plain on their faces as if he was looking at so many slabs of stone.

Rage flared in Grunt Tusks—and just as swiftly faded. How could they know what the collapse of a Nifl city's wards meant?

He was the former Talonnorn overseer, covered with scars Niflghar of House Evendoom had casually or maliciously dealt him.

He was the longest-serving whip of House Evendoom, charged with keeping order among the slaves who worked the precious Rift.

He was the only gorkul to survive being branded and fire-scalded and whipped with chains to the point of death, thanks to the appetites of certain Evendoom crones who delighted in watching death-agonies, and then using spells to snatch their victim back to life.

He was the gorkul who intended that Talonnorn would pay him back for such cruelties in full, and repeatedly.

And he was the gorkul who would dare to charge into the great Talonar cavern and take payment, mercilessly and even brutally, rather than cowering in the shadows and daring to strike only at outlaws and caravan stragglers.

He sneered down at the bloody and broken bodies of the stragglers he and his band had just slain, and over at the five pack-snouts they had thereby managed to remove from the tail of a long and lightly guarded Nifl trading caravan, and plucked up a knife he had left in a throat that had seemed to need it. A moment ago this had been a solid triumph; now, it seemed but a waste of time.

Grunt Tusks stalked into the midst of his band of followers, and grinned into their bewildered faces.

"So it begins," he hissed. "The proudest city still, but the strongest no longer. Soon, Grunt Tusks will feed in the heart of Talonnorn—and the skulls I crack open to scoop warm brains out of will be Evendoom heads. Screaming Evendoom heads."

"I *know* the wards are down," Jalandral snapped. "You at least should know I'm not the overbold, empty-headed young idiot half Talonnorn likes to think I am! What I want to know is: *why* are the wards down? Who did this, and why haven't they been raised again?"

Klaerra was white to her very lips with fear.

"I—I know not," she whispered, her bloodless lips trembling. "All that our spellrobes have been able to learn is that the wards were almost certainly brought down by a spell that originated within the city."

" 'Almost certainly'? What good is that? Why've they wasted their time on such frippery when they could have been—*should have been*—restoring the wards?"

"I . . . High Lord Jalandral, the surviving spellrobes residing in Talonnorn now lack the might to raise the wards. Even if they all worked together, in utter trust and with the best of assistance from us all, they lack the collective power to cast the right spells."

"Whaaat?" Jalandral roared, so loudly that the echo of his shout made even him wince. He towered over Klaerra, hand raised to smite her, lifted to slam down and break her bloody neck—

Weeping silently as she stared up at him, she tore open the front of her bodice and threw her head back, to offer her throat to his fury.

—And all the anger drained out of the High Lord of

Evendoom, as suddenly as it had come, leaving him feeling weak and sick.

"Oh," he whispered, sitting down with a jolt beside Klaerra and putting his arm around her. "Oh, dung. Olone be merciful. Dung, dung, dung."

After a moment he turned to her. "*All* our most powerful spellrobes?"

"Y-yes," she whispered. "Dead or fled. You are right to feel aghast."

Jalandral shook his head, and absentmindedly reached out to caress her bared front, still shaking his head.

"Ouvahlor will be delighted," he said mockingly. "And then Yarlys, and then whoever else gets here next. Olone spit . . ."

He shook his head again. He felt weary and lost, not furious. How could matters go from the triumph of his lordship in the forecourt to this, so swiftly? So Olone-accursed *quickly*?

"Klaerra," he asked, with a calm he did not feel, "what shall I do? You live still because you stand by me when others do not, and your guidance is always good. Guide me now."

"Jalandral," she replied, taking his hands from her breast and gently shifting them up to encircle her throat, "what I am going to say now is not going to please you." She settled his fingers into a throttling grip under her chin and whispered, "So please, if your anger masters you and you slay me, remember that I loved you."

The High Lord of Talonnorn gently drew his hands back from his loyal crone's throat. Taking hold of her torn bodice, he held it up to cover her. "Go ahead. Anger me," he commanded quietly. "Speak."

Klaerra drew in a deep breath, closed her eyes for a moment—he could feel her trembling, under his hands—and then looked straight into his eyes and said, "If you want the wards of Talonnorn restored, you must go to the temple and ask what Consecrated of Olone we have left to do it. Nicely."

Jalandral glared at her, face twisting into a snarl, and then spat, "I *must*?"

"If you want the wards restored, they have power enough," Klaerra whispered. "*Just* enough. If I and some of the junior crones of our House work with them."

Jalandral's eyes narrowed.

"And I'll be able to trust all of you?"

Silent tears were streaming down Klaerra's face again. "High Lord of Talonnorn," she whispered, "you must begin to trust someone. Or—forgive me—your death will come sooner rather than later."

"Ah, here 'tis. No lurking monsters, no dung nor leavings, no fallen blades. Nothing in all the Dark comes here, look you, but us!"

The three weary, trudging Niflghar would not have been held in high regard in Talonnorn. Their lives had been long and less than easy, and it showed in their scars and wrinkled faces and hunched, limping walks.

By what bulged in the packs strapped to their six old, lean pack-snouts, they were the sort of trader known as peddlers. By the state of their clothes and condition of their boots and weapons and everything else, they were less than successful peddlers.

Yet they had come trudging through the Wild Dark with the calm certainty of veterans who know their surroundings well. The lone lurker on the ledge high above them hesitated. Guides this good might be very useful, after all . . .

The three peddlers spat into the rocks, more or less in unison, and then belched, broke wind, and started scratching themselves.

No.

Not useful enough.

"Same old cavern," the rearmost, shortest Nifl said sourly, stepping into just the right spot. "There's—"

Grinning mirthlessly, the lurker on the ledge rolled a rock as large as her head over the edge.

It crushed the shortest trader's head right down to his jaw without even slowing, smashing his body to the ground and rolling wetly away.

His two fellows cursed, finding themselves suddenly wrestling with the harnesses of bucking, eye-rolling pack-snouts who were rearing in fear—and who each no doubt outweighed both traders put together ten or more times over.

"Easy!" one of them tried to croon, his voice higher and louder than it should have been to achieve any sort of soothing. "Easy, there! I—"

He was the one who chose that moment to stare up at the ledge, to see where the rock had come from so suddenly and silently, and if any more might be ready to follow it—so he was the one whose face the lurker loosed Daruse's hurlbow into.

Grinning, she flattened herself down on the ledge to hide from the frightened, frantic stares of the last peddler.

If she awaited just the right time to strike, taking down a lone and aging Nifl who probably hadn't been rampant for years should be Olone's ease itself . . .

"Trusting others is a weakness," Jalandral murmured, "for all that Klaerra says not doing so is also a weakness. If I rely on no one but myself, no one can ever let me down. My preparations shall be done right, because I am doing them. Yet powerful magics I cannot do—so I am here. In peril, and again trammeled by the very sorts of lesser, spiteful, and unfriendly failures that brought proud Talonnorn down in the first place."

He stood alone in a room whose floor was glossy-smooth black stone, and whose walls were veiled in draperies that hid all the exits. He could see nothing else of interest; nothing on the ceiling, no furniture, nothing. Not even any cracks or discolorations to meet his eye, as he stood waiting.

Cold, and bored, and being treated like a servant. Or a prisoner.

"Olone," he asked then, raising his voice a little but keeping his tone calm and even reverent, "have you priestesses still, in Talonnorn? Or have they all left this temple and this city, leaving you unserved? I—"

"Your mockery, Jalandral Evendoom, is even less attractive than your self-assumed title."

The voice from behind him was cold, and just this side of openly menacing. Jalandral smiled, and turned to face its source leisurely.

"Now I feel properly welcome," he said pleasantly. "Being High Lord of—"

"Dispense with your airs, Firstborn of Evendoom. We Consecrated of Olone mirror the feelings of the Holy Goddess Herself, and accordingly dislike both your fanciful title and the high-handed behavior that has accompanied it. We do not see a Talonnorn made any greater, or any closer in reverence to Holy Olone, by your office or performance. Many within these walls would prefer your swift elimination. Can you give us good reason why we should not slay you, here and now, while there is still a Talonnorn to rescue?"

"Yes," Jalandral drawled.

"Well?"

"I prefer not to share my *good* reasons. When priestesses presume to involve themselves in matters of ruling and city policy, they stray far from their holy duties and their rights—and, I daresay, from the holy favor they profess to seek. I will, however, share my most brutish and immediate reasons for you not to harm me in any way."

He strolled a step closer to the priestess. "Spells cast upon my person will unleash enchanted items I am carrying, and many mightier items hidden all over the city—including within these holy walls. Their discharges will utterly destroy this temple, and all Consecrated within it, plus many of you who are elsewhere in the Talonar cavern, if I am harmed or feel displeased or upset enough to trade my life for all of yours."

He held out the hand that bore the Evendoom ring, and added, "And whether you choose to recognize me as High Lord of Talonnorn or not, I do happen to be *Lord* of Evendoom, not Firstborn."

"I see."

The priestess facing Jalandral was one he'd never seen before.

She was impossibly tall and slender, possessed a beauty both dark and deadly—and was staring at him with open hatred in her great dark eyes. "Your certainty in correcting me leads me to conclude that you are responsible for your father's death. Such an act is an affront to Olone and a crime in Talonnorn—or did you begin your office by changing that law?"

"I had no part in my father's death, not that it is any business of yours," Jalandral replied, giving her back icy words for icy words. "Or is it? When he had been absent for so long, and none of the crones of our House could find the slightest trace of him with their most powerful spells, we turned to you Consecrated to try to do so, and shortly received report of a similar failure to find any trace of Erlingar Evendoom. So we came to the sad conclusion that he was with the living no more, and House Evendoom therefore needed his heir to become Lord in his place. An ascension this temple spoke no word against. Are there things about my father's death, or perhaps his continued life, that Consecrated of this temple know, and are keeping from me? Or is your charge mere passing insult? Ruling Talonnorn is an endless series of tasks and responsibilities that consume much time, and I do not have an infinite supply of it to spare. I came here for a specific re—"

"We know why you are here, Jalandral Evendoom. You did something that shattered the wards of Talonnorn, and you need us to raise them again. Thus far I have heard nothing from you to indicate why we should aid you in this way, or even a polite request from you regarding—"

"I can interrupt rudely and make empty and false accusations, too," Jalandral drawled, clasping his hands behind his back and starting to stroll, "so why not let the coldly hostile negotiations begin?"

The priestess almost smiled. "Why not, indeed?"

13

Watching and Listening

Bellowing and brawling kill many
Overly hasty choices slay more than a few
But watching and listening never killed anyone
Unless they started too late, or kept at it too long.
—Orlkettle saying

W e're close now, Lady-lass," Bloodblade growled warningly. He was constantly peering this way and that as they skulked forward along the jutting prow of rock, both in wary crouches. "Best be quiet and careful. If the wards rise again . . ."

"They would fry our fellows," Taerune murmured, casting a look back at the handful of Ravagers Bloodblade had managed to rally to foray with him, as they'd traveled the Wild Dark, "and trap us out here on this tongue of rock."

"Arrr-uh," the infamous Ravager war captain agreed. "So *hurry*."

"I'm crawling over rocks as fast as I can," she replied good-naturedly, "with only one hand. Elbows don't grip too well."

"I can have Arthoun add claws to some harthil—harthem—err, elbow-plates," Bloodblade offered.

"No," Taerune said firmly. "Only Hairy Ones work on *my* metal-skins, I've decided."

"Heh," the fat Ravager agreed a little breathlessly, amid the clinks and clanks of a very fat Niflghar clad in a belted chaos of mismatched plates of salvaged armor and a bristling arsenal of sheathed, scabbarded, and chained-on weapons, clambering over sharp and uneven rocks. "You really mean one particular Hairy One, I'm thinking."

"I do," Taerune agreed. "Now stop crashing around. I can see all I need to see from here."

The spur of rock they'd been climbing along jutted out over one end of one of the largest Outcaverns, affording a view down its often-bustling length. They were only a few caves away from the gigantic cavern that held Talonnorn, and this long Outcavern was a main trade route.

However, it was deserted now.

No caravans, no Talonar patrols, no daring House younglings out for a thrill . . .

Good.

"Empty as the promise of a priestess," Taerune pronounced crisply. "Let's get back, and down there."

Bloodblade hastily started to scramble and lurch back over the rocks.

He'd taken to treating her as his commander, though they both knew that without him she'd be walking the Dark alone, or even having to fight off those among the other Ravagers with them whose lust for a Nifl-she—who was both noble and strikingly beautiful, even for an Olone-worshipper, despite the blade that jutted out at the world where her left forearm should be—overrode their prudence.

Supple and long-limbed, Taerune slithered after Bloodblade, moving far more quietly than he could. "Down," he commanded simply, to the waiting Ravagers. "Fast."

Without a word they turned and started down the path. A slaves' mining-walk from long, long ago, it clove the jagged rocks like a smooth ramp, snaking back and forth as it descended. As they went, Llorgar, the Ravager walking just ahead of Bloodblade, turned and asked curiously, "No caravans? And no wards? D'you think half of what we've been hearing is true?"

Old Bloodblade shrugged and turned to Taerune, who echoed his shrug and replied quietly, "I don't know what to think. My brother Jalandral risen to lord it over the entire city? Public duels among House lords, yet their Houses aren't openly warring on the streets? The Consecrated of the temple just praying to Olone and ignoring such tumult? Can you blame me for thinking it all wild lies?"

"No," Llorgar said simply. "Hrestreen is Talonar, too, and he can't believe any of it, either. Yet says he'd not be wits-smacked if one tale out of them all is true, though he doesn't want to be guessing which one."

"*Precisely*," Taerune agreed, almost fiercely, as Bloodblade's bristling arsenal of weapons stopped bobbing wildly and they came out onto the flat cavern floor.

"No, no," he grunted, waving his empty hand. His broad, well-used favorite blade was suddenly in the other. "*Away* from the walls, rampants! We're lawful traders for the moment, not sneak-thieves!"

"Oh?" Llorgar asked good-naturedly as they formed a column and trudged out along the center of the cavern, heading for Talonnorn. "And if High Lord Jalandral has some new law that makes traders unlawful?"

"Then we'll call ourselves fugitives from Talonar justice and slayers of Jalandral's guards, and improvise our suitable behavior from there," Bloodblade said jovially. "I am among the most accommodating of Niflghar."

That claim evoked chuckles, up and down the line of Ravagers, and the inevitable exchanges of "How feel you, friend?" and "Accommodating, very accommodating!" as the Ravagers made their customary mock of the airs and speech of city-dwelling Nifl.

They were still chuckling when the air all around them

shivered—and they were suddenly ringed about by many Talonar Nifl.

One moment the long cavern had been empty, and an instant later it was full of shouting, sword-swinging Nifl, viciously battling each other in a great confusion of identically clad warblades, scurrying and terrified servants, heaped sacks and packs, and motley-clad, obviously poorer Nifl who were striking at the warblades—and being struck down, more often than not.

"Take no part!" Bloodblade bellowed to his fellow Ravagers, his roar like a deep, ragged war-horn. "To me! Stand and defend, around me! Form a ring!"

Then in lower tones, he added, "Who *are* all these brawlers? Blast all Olone- and Ice-bedamned magic! As usual!"

The Ravagers scrambled to obey, crossing swords only briefly with a blundering few of the arrivals, who seemed bewildered to find themselves in their new surroundings.

The warblades had the upper hand, and were swiftly winning. By the time the Ravagers had formed their ring, the fighting was done, with one side lying dead on the cavern floor.

"Lady Evendoom? Taerune Evendoom!" a voice arose then, from among the warblades.

"Down steel, but be ready," Bloodblade snapped to the ring of Ravagers as he and Taerune shifted and peered, trying to see the speaker.

"Who . . . ?" Taerune began, and then saw the face of the grandly dressed rampant who was pushing through the warblades toward her, with similarly garbed kin at his shoulders. "Barrandar Dounlar!"

Rival Talonar Houses are not friendly, and she and Barrandar had never much liked even the look of each other, but there was clear relief and even respect on the face of the eldest surviving Dounlar heir as he hastened forward, his brothers at his shoulders as they came out from among their own warblades, and on, bloody blades in hand.

"Let them in," Bloodblade growled, a stride before the three Dounlar would have walked right into the unmoving ring of Ravagers.

"What would you, with me?" Taerune asked calmly, pitching her voice loudly enough for everyone nearby to hear.

"I . . ." Barrandar Dounlar seemed suddenly uncertain, darting glances at his brothers; Garlane, the nastiest, and the younger one . . . Andralus, that was his name. Then he spoke in a rush.

"Lady Evendoom, we would like you to lead us. Lead us all." On either side of Barrandar, who was paling in embarrassment, his two brothers nodded.

"Lead you in what?" Taerune asked warily, wondering if, a moment from now, she might have to fight all of these Dounlar to the death.

"To rally loyal Talonar, against the oriad new High Lord of the city. Your brother, Jalandral Evendoom."

Hairy Ones can flee far and fast. There was what felt like grudging admiration in Yathla Evendoom's voice, deep in his mind.

"I only hope I'm not lost forever," Orivon Firefist replied, trudging along yet another unfamiliar crevice, and watching things that looked like spear-long centipedes, with spiders at both ends, racing away from him up the rock walls. "With the map gone . . ."

You have me. I can always feel what direction Talonnorn is. More or less.

"More or less," Orivon grunted, ducking low under a narrow place where two jutting points of rock almost met. "Well, *that's* a comfort."

A little less sarcasm, swaggering human hero. I fry foes for you, remember?

"Endlessly?"

Alas, no. That's why I unleash my flame so seldom. Too much fire, and . . . no more Yathla.

So sad was the voice in his mind that Orivon found himself on the verge of tears as he came out of the narrow way into yet another dark, silent, and unfamiliar cavern. And stopped.

All he knew was that he was somewhere out in the Wild Dark, trying to circle around Glowstone and reach the ways between Glowstone and Talonnorn that Bloodblade had led his now-lost Ravager band along, before Ouvahlor had come after all Ravagers. That had been a hectic time, and Orivon's will had been bent on surviving, and getting back up to the sun, and Ashenuld. He only hoped he'd recognize the caverns Bloodblade had led them through, when he stumbled out into them.

If, that is, he hadn't crossed them already.

Oronkh rose with a grunt, the finger he'd just swiped across a darkened stone underfoot and then licked still held out in front of him.

"Aye, man-sweat. This is the way he went." He looked at Nurnra, who stood with her slender sword drawn, looking warily up and down the cavern. "You *sure* you want to tail this Hairy One as he wanders lost across all the monster-slithering, Nifl-army-roamed, Ghodal-gnawing Wild Dark?"

The sharren gave him her most alluring smile. "I'm sure, Manyfangs." She struck a pose, knowing full well how attractive she looked, even before her longtime business partner growled longingly, deep in his throat. "Aren't *you* interested? Yes, he's not a Nifl-she panting to be under you, but he's a Hairy One with darksight, he fights like a war-hero, and things *happen* around him. He's obviously down here for a reason, and I want to know what it is. Before, perhaps, it's too late. In the meantime, he's undeniably *entertaining*."

Oronkh shrugged. "Hairy Ones are always entertaining.

They stop my knives so prettily, fountaining blood and collapsing so fetchingly, they go down under slavers' whips faster and more clumsily than anyone else, making for much comedy, they—"

"Oh, *chain* that jaw of yours!" Nurnra tossed her head, magnificent hair swirling, and strode on through the rocks. "Let's be after him!"

"Let's not," Oronkh growled, staying right where he was, "until you've answered me something. 'Tis fool-haunched to travel the Dark *talking,* alerting every lurking and skulking thing of your approach and making too much noise to hear them moving to where they can best pounce. Aye?"

The sharren halted, spun to face him, and nodded. "So ask."

"So what's your *real* interest in him, Softfingers? There's something more than mere entertainment, and I'll be disappointed sure if it's just that he's a rampant and not a Nifl, and *you* want to be under *him*."

Nurnra rolled her eyes. "The half of you that's gorkul is obviously the *lower* half." She took a step nearer the half-gorkul and wrinkled her nose in distaste. "The smell, the *hair* . . . no, Oronkh, Hairy Ones are not for me. Yet I've tasted human blood before—slaves—and can drink it safely. If I can somehow control my gorge, and seduce him, I do wonder: is his blood *strong*? Will I be able to feed on him for years without killing him? What a thing that would be, freeing me from the need to seduce or convince with coin, or attack . . ."

"Whereas mine sickens you."

"*Truly* sickens me, Oronkh. Not only does it fail to sustain me, it's unsafe for me—for which I am deeply thankful to whatever gods there may be. For that keeps you safe from me."

The fat, tusked half-gorkul nodded, turned to look down the passage toward where the human was presumably somewhere ahead of them, and asked quietly, "But what if I don't want to be safe from you?"

The sharren stood like a silent statue for a long breath, and then a second one. Then she retraced her steps through the rocks, as softly and smoothly as if she'd been made of drifting smoke, and lifted a gloved hand to stroke his cheek.

"Oronkh," she whispered, "you don't have to be." She slid deft hands inside his vest, slowly drew it open, and kissed his chest.

"Softfingers," he rumbled, "this is perhaps not the best place to—"

"Be safe?" Her eyes glimmered up at him from somewhere close to his belt. Below which something was bulging to thrust insistently at her, through his worn and filthy leathers.

Glimmered, and then winked.

Oronkh shook his head, smiled, and growled, "You win. As usual."

Vlakrel stopped so abruptly that the Oszrim warblades behind him almost walked right into him.

"They've stopped moving," he snapped.

The warblades ahead of him halted and turned to hear what he'd say next, joining their fellows of the rear guard in a ring around the spellrobe. Who promptly mumbled something magical, and closed his eyes.

Vlakrel might be the most treacherous and vicious Niflghar ever to serve House Oszrim, but he was their commander, and one of the two most powerful Oszrim spellrobes. He'd returned from his private audience with High Lord Evendoom afire with zeal, almost tremblingly eager to lead them out into the Wild Dark after the Bloodsucker and the Misbegotten. Whose heads commanded high prices, whether or not their bodies were still attached.

They all knew that Vlakrel—and with him, House Oszrim—would rise greatly in the estimation of the High Lord of Talonnorn if they succeeded.

The Bloodsucker was the rampant-meltingly beautiful

sharren Nurnra, who'd seduced Nifl beyond counting—
not a few of whom had vanished forever, or had been
left longing for her return to their arms, and seeking her
out when they dared.

The Misbegotten was the half-Nifl, half-gorkul knife-
trader and sometime slayer-for-hire Oronkh, a wily and
unlovely crossbreed whose very existence was a soiling
affront to Olone, and whose swindles were legendary.

They almost always worked together, notorious crim-
inals of the Dark who had cheated Talonar merchants
for years. They seemed to know when goods were
owned by, and traders were working for, the ruling noble Houses of Talonnorn, and to seek out such prey over
other opportunities. Wherefore the bounty on their
heads—and Jalandral's eagerness to reward Vlakrel. If
things went awry, the spellrobe had told them all, he had
been given the means to summon Jalandral's flying
Hunt, to come swooping out into the Wild Dark to him
and fight on his behalf.

Which meant that this foray was the closest thing under Olone's smile to a certain success.

Vlakrel's eyes snapped open, and his sharp, ratlike
features assumed their usual gloating sneer. "They must
have decided to sleep," he said. "So we go on, as swiftly
as we can without making overmuch noise, to perhaps
take them unawares. Speak only if peril demands."

He waved at the warblades impatiently, and they
silently and impassively re-formed their line and started
walking again. Veterans all, they already had a lot of ex-
perience in creeping up on foes.

Lolonmae stared right into Luelldar's eyes through the
whorl, her gaze as deep and steady as if she could see
his every thought and memory, and correctly anticipate
what he would think of next, too. The priestesses all
around her were staring at him, too, but Luelldar paid
them no attention at all. Even if he could have torn his

eyes away from those of the Revered Mother, he had no desire to do so.

"Senior Watcher," she said politely, showing no sign of discomfort from the embrace of the solid ice that encased her from just below her throat on down, though her lips were white with cold, "your wisdom, perceptiveness, and your attentive care for the well-being of Ouvahlor have long impressed us. We appreciate that you have interrupted private and holy deliberations for good reason, because you do nothing without good reason. You have our full attention; speak."

Luelldar made a swift reverence, and lifted his head to say in humble tones, "Revered Mother, we Watchers have noticed that the wards of the city of Talonnorn are not only down, but have been down for some time now, implying that there is something preventing or at least delaying their restoration."

"Wherefore, you are suggesting—?" she asked silkily.

"As Watchers," Luelldar said flatly, "we suggest nothing unless requested to do so."

"Then I am making such a request," she informed him, just as flatly.

Luelldar blinked. He was so used to Anointed laying verbal traps with their every utterance . . .

"Then I would suggest," he said carefully, "that you use holy spells to contact Exalted Daughter of the Ice Semmeira from afar, and order her to attack Talonnorn immediately. If the force she commands can slay this new High Lord, plunder the city, and then withdraw, Talonnorn will remain a needy chaos, at war with itself, for some time."

"Probably a long time," Lolonmae agreed thoughtfully.

"This would at last free Ouvahlor, for that long time, to turn its attention to our other rivals, rather than our traditional foe," Luelldar added.

The Revered Mother smiled.

"And that can only be a good thing. Luelldar, you serve Ouvahlor as diligently as ever."

The whorl in front of the Senior Watcher winked out of existence, astonishing Aloun.

Luelldar, who was not at all surprised that the Revered Mother could casually shatter his magics from afar, merely shivered.

". . . Well, *I've* always wondered why they don't suffocate when they sleep," the familiar, harsh voice of the older Nifl overseer said, from right above her. "The stuff grows so fast."

Kalamae lay still, taking care not to change her breathing or open her eyes. She could tell from the slight quiver of Aumril's flank, pressed against hers, that she wasn't the only one who'd come awake.

"Exhausted or not, you'd think they'd lie on their backs, just to keep from *feeling* like they're going to smother," he added.

"Who knows why Hairy Ones do anything?" The other overseer—the lazy one—sounded as bored as he always did. "They don't, that's all."

Kalamae couldn't feel Reldaera or Brith, on the far side of Aumril, but she knew from the faint hitch in their breathing that they, too, were awake and just feigning sleep, now. They always slept whenever they got too exhausted to go on, at a place where they'd dug away a lot of yeldeth. It regrew around them with its usual uncanny speed, but if they got most of it off the tunnel ceiling, there was little chance enough would fall on them to crush or smother them, and that was all that mattered.

To the overseers, nothing involving slaves—aside from keeping the yeldeth yield up—seemed to matter at all.

The two were literally standing right over the four children. Kalamae felt the sudden warm wetness as the older overseer spat on her back, ere speaking again.

"I've been wondering," he said slowly, "if we should shift all the slaves back a few tunnels, to where they'll be more out of the way of the High Lord's warblades—should the sword-swingers need to move through here in a hurry, if the city comes under attack."

"Too much trouble moving them," the lazy overseer said promptly; more to stave off the effort of shifting slaves anywhere than for any other reason, Kalamae thought. "Keep the yield up, that's our job. Which means we keep the slaves here, in these outermost ways, where the yeldeth's younger and the yields are highest. That keeps *our* necks healthy. I'm not thinking the city'll be attacked by anyone—and if it does, and the warblades come charging through here, keeping Hairy One brats alive will be the *least* of our worries."

Kalamae felt the barbs of his whip just touch her behind, in the lightest of touches, and move on in the direction of Aumril. Then the lazy overseer added, "If anything happens to these, they'll just send out more raiding bands to the Blindingbright, and get more. They're only slaves."

Daruse might have known right where he was, but copying his shape and wearing his filthy clothes didn't help her recognize anything at all out in the Wild Dark. She needed a map.

Luckily, that last peddler had been a careful keep-all-things sort. Old etched metal map plates had been used to line the insides of three of his oldest, leakiest chests.

Wherefore she thought she now knew where she was. Looking up at the soft glow glimmering in the distance that was probably Lightpools, Lady Maharla Evendoom smiled.

Talonar noble crones, Eldest of Evendooms or not, always liked to know where they stood.

"You don't think we'll have fighting in Talonnorn?"

"Ah, now, I didn't say *that*. I don't think Ouvahlor will

bother to march all the way here, and everyone else is even farther off, with the worst of the Wild Dark to get through. I think if we do have warblades down here, it'll be Talonar seeking to run around behind Talonar. What with all this strife and tumult over the High Lord . . ."

The listening children cowered, and tried not to show it. Luckily, the overseers had largely forgotten them. Seeing the bared bodies of slaves was hardly a thrill when they were this young—and were Hairy Ones, to boot.

"Aye. Now that he's hiring wildblades and poisoners out of the Araed, to hurl against the noble Houses—"

"Not that they haven't long needed taking down, right and harsh, mind you!"

"—and now, I hear, against the Consecrated of Olone when they can catch them, too!"

"What?" The lazy overseer was shocked. "Holy One, that's a . . . that's another thing entirely."

"No good will come of this," the older one said grimly.

"Agreed," the lazy one said quietly, still aghast. "Oh, agreed." After a moment he added, "I need a drink."

"Ah. *Now* you're spewing sense!"

"But of course!" The overseers chuckled, and the four slaves who were not asleep heard those hoarse chucklings dwindle away down the tunnel.

Brith, Reldaera, Aumril, and Kalamae all opened their eyes and turned to look at each other, sitting up warily to do so. "We're going to *die!*" Reldaera hissed, eyes wide with fear.

"We all die," Kalamae said dismissively. "We just have to make sure we don't die *here*. And soon."

Around them, the moist, warm yeldeth grew. Visibly.

14

Trying for Talonnorn Again

Take your sword, take your sword
Your armor and your pain
Take your spells, take your spells
Your tricks and battle-brain
And for the glory and the gold
Try for Talonnorn again!
  —old Ravager trail song

*L*eave me," Semmeira ordered her four handsome bodyguards crisply. "I must renew one of the magics that shields us. To be near to me, or to spy on me, will be more than dangerous."

She strode away across the cavern without looking at them or waiting for any reply. It really didn't matter if they correctly suspected she wanted some privacy to relieve herself, so long as they stayed where they were. By the Ice, but there *were* limits.

Warblades' leathers were designed for moments such as these. Unbuckle the codpiece, swing it aside and catch it on the belt-hook provided, use the same hook to hold the end of the crotch-leathers, and—let fly.

A little bare and breezy, but no need to crouch or worry about skirts, and turning her outermost shielding to the semblance of solid stone blocked all prying eyes.

Semmeira threw back her head, let out a shuddering sigh, and relaxed.

For just long enough to gasp in alarm, as a face appeared in her head—a face that should never have been able to pierce her weakest shielding, let alone all six of them!

Including the two that had so painfully ended the scrying and spying of Coldheart in the first place . . .

Revered Mother Lolonmae was cold-eyed, taking no seeming pleasure in Semmeira's astonishment, dismay, and flaring fear. Yet they both knew there was a note of silent triumph in her mind-voice as she said crisply, *Exalted Daughter of the Ice Semmeira, before the Ever-Ice you are bound to hear and obey this my command: you are to take all of your force of war and travel with them as swiftly as possible to the city of Talonnorn, and attack that city. You are to slay its newly proclaimed High Lord, Jalandral Evendoom, do as much damage as possible to its forces of war and leadership, plunder what you can of its wealth, and withdraw, returning here to Coldheart without delay.*

"Uh . . . Of course, Revered Mother!" Semmeira stammered, trying to seem eager—and Lolonmae was gone, leaving Semmeira with a ringing headache and a deepening feeling of dread. Surely Lolonmae had some fell punishment in mind for her, but what? And when would it be visited upon her? When she stood in peril, embattled in Talonnorn, or as a humiliation before all at Coldheart, after she'd done all the bloody work for Lolonmae?

"That little bitch," Semmeira whispered. "If she can do what she just did, she has the power she needs to do *anything* to me . . ."

Semmeira stood swaying for a moment, pale with fear, and then spat out curses as fast as she could and strode briskly away, heading . . . she knew not where.

Maharla Evendoom didn't have to be a Ravager to know that the approach to any meeting-place out in the Wild

Dark would be among the most dangerous terrain in all the Dark. So while lurking monsters and outlaws may have seen only a lone Ravager leading six pack-snouts who seemed as old and lean as he was along the trade-trail to Lightpools, an invisible shielding-spell was moving with that trudging figure, and another unseen magic was darting about peering here, there, and everywhere among the rocks and deep shadows beneath and behind rocks, seeking out anyone—or anything—that might have been waiting to pounce.

There were snakes, and cave-rats, and even something like a headless, all-wings bat that marked the approach of the Ravager with interest . . . but none of them tarried to attack, and Maharla did them no harm. She needed to keep her strongest spells for when they would *really* be needed.

Because that moment of need just might be very soon.

Lightpools, she now knew—that last peddler had kept *everything,* including old guidebooks to the Dark!—was a cavern that held a cluster of glowing pools of drinkable water, where springs bubbled up from below. From the pools, streams spilled out to wander far throughout the Dark, though their waters soon lost their glows. Lightpools was also a moot where Ravagers and traveling Nifl traders alike gathered, usually in peace. There seemed to be a code among those who lived out in the Dark, involving not hurling spells or shedding blood near drinkable water . . . but then, codes did not apply to Maharla Evendoom.

She was smiling the tight smile evoked by that smug thought as she led her pack-snouts out into the Lightpools cavern, earning some swift looks and hastily-taken-up swords from the motley-clad Nifl rampants who were already sitting around the pools.

She counted eight of them, all clad in worn and dirty leathers and scraps of armor.

Every one of them was scarred, and every one of them was dirty. They all had weapons in their hands, now, one a ready hurlbow, but no one had scrambled to his feet, and no one looked to have any battle-magic, let alone showing any signs of getting ready to hurl it.

Walking warily closer, Maharla marked two traders who were probably traveling together; the other six all appeared to be loners, spaced careful distances apart around the pools. All were watching her in expression-less, not-particularly-friendly silence, but she could see that they'd relaxed. One aging Nifl rampant, clad like any other Ravager and leading six bony pack-snouts with no trace of eagerness or good humor did not measure up to "pressing threat" in their shared judgment.

Good.

Eight armed foes, raging about on all sides, just might manage to get a hurled knife or an arrow past any crone's spells.

"Have a name, do you?" one of the nearest Ravagers—or traders, or whatever they were—asked calmly.

"Daruse," she replied, trying to keep her voice low, rough, and terse. Better to be thought surly than uncertain—or too different from the Daruse someone remembered to seem "right." If Talonar had heard many tales of shapeshifting monsters and spells that did the same thing, then so had Ravagers out here, not all that far from Talonnorn.

One of the traders frowned.

"Ran with Bloodblade, didn't you?"

"Once," she sat flatly, in a tone that invited no queries. She shifted her voice to sound a lot more friendly as she added, "I don't remember your face. You had dealings with him?"

"Some," was the prompt reply, in precise mimicry of her flat "Once." She caught herself on the verge of smiling.

"Tell truth, Orlam," another trader put in. "He outbid you on those blades in Glowstone, long time back, and you cursed him, and he laughed—and that was all the 'dealings' the two of you have had."

Orlam gave the trader a cold look, and said, "That *you* know about, Veln."

Then he looked at "Daruse" and added, "Saw you once, walking with him. Never really met Bloodblade's band, out in the Dark, though."

"Never will, now," Veln grunted, and there were some dark chuckles from around the pools.

"Oh?" Maharla asked, starting to hobble her pack-snouts. "What happened?"

"Heh. Slaughtered, all of them," another trader said eagerly, from across a pool. "Every last one. 'Cept Old Bloodblade himself, paunch and all, of course. *That* one seems to have all the rival gods' own luck."

"Yes," Maharla agreed darkly, as if remembering something that didn't please her. "*No*, don't ask," she added firmly a moment later, busy knotting the hobbles. "So what's he up to, now?"

"Recruiting a new band of fools, of course," Orlam replied. "Wildblades, mostly . . . that'll be all he'll find, who want to run with him, after what happened to the last lot. He's been seen with a maimed Nifl-she from Talonnorn, who's a blade where her left hand should be."

Backside to the rest of the traders, Maharla hoped she hadn't frozen at those words long enough for any of them to notice. Keeping her voice oh-so-casual, she asked, "Seen whereabouts, hey?"

"Owes you coin, too, does he?" Veln laughed. "Well, good luck winning anything out of *his* grasp. That one tends to reply to such requests with a swift sword thrust!"

Maharla turned in time to see the trader across the pool nodding and grinning at what Veln had just said, before he offered, "*I* heard they were last seen heading for Talonnorn. Raiding, spying—with that one, who knows?"

Maharla joined in the general sour chuckling, deciding it would be best if she showed no more interest in Bloodblade.

Thankfully, the pack-snouts had to be fed, and that

meant heaving down some of the carry-sacks strapped to them.

So she attended to that, keeping silent, and the talk among the traders moved on to other things. It sounded as if they were resuming converse her arrival had interrupted.

"Can't believe they struck Glowstone *again*. It's not like there's any riches worth having, that's sprouted there since last time."

"True, and they sworded everyone who couldn't flee in time again, too! *Glowstone*, mind you! Why seize a moot in the middle of nowhere? All you win is some drinking streams, a lot of dung and broken things, and nuisance beasts used to lurking nearby and preying on lone wanderers."

"*I* think someone in Ouvahlor has decided it's a good place to train armies in attacking."

"And pillaging."

There was general dark mirth at this, and Maharla felt moved to swing around momentarily, so the traders could all see "Daruse" joining in.

"Are they trying for Talonnorn *again*?" Veln asked. "Or is it Nrauluskh's turn, do you think?"

"Talonnorn. Wanting to put down this new High Lord before he becomes *too* mighty," Orlam pronounced. "'Swhat I would do. He's been thundering about decadent nobles and useless priestesses who let the city be raided by Ouvahlor, to justify his humbling both and taking all power to himself. So he'll be building an army, and can hardly fail to use it if Ouvahlor comes calling. Why wait for him to get strong and ready, when you can smash him now?"

"Who knows why they're attacking?" another trader said sourly. "*I've* heard they're led by a priestess. Who knows why high holy Ice-lovers do anything? It could all be her wanting entertainment, or to impress the more-exalted-than-her Ice-kissers in her temple—or

something they ordered her to do, to get her killed and
so be rid of her."

Maharla looked down thoughtfully into a carry-sack
that still had a little snout-feed at the bottom of it, ignoring the pack-snout that was trying to thrust its head in
over her shoulder, to get a little extra.

She had been intending to find, slay, and impersonate
Bloodblade, but why not, instead, "become" this army-
leading priestess?

Conquering Talonnorn was certainly one way of returning to it in style, and setting things to rights.

Lolonmae was glad she'd sent all the priestesses out.
That meant none of them could see her arching and
shuddering in pain, whimpering as blood wept from her
ears, and she groaned silently, bit her lip, and writhed
like a lover lost in lust.

That thought gave her an idea.

If she did off her robes again, and threw herself bare
and yielding onto the Ice . . .

The *pain!* She reeled, alone in her chamber in Coldheart, and almost fell, scrabbling weakly at the loop-
fastenings of her robes.

She'd known that forcing her way through Semmeira's
clawing, painful wards would mean a painful mental aftermath . . . but *this!* This was . . . ohhh . . .

The familiar cold shock of the Ice, as she fell forward
onto it, was bracing and yet comforting. She slid along
it, head throbbing insistently now but no longer stabbing like fire, and gasped in relief.

She would just lie still, numbed in the icy water her
body would melt out of the Ice, and stay until it shared its
cold strength with her, and she was clearheaded again.

Lolonmae forced herself to relax, to yield against the
hard, smooth coldness in surrender, spread-eagled in
abandon.

She deserved no less.

She was, yes, proud of herself for not showing her pain while in Semmeira's mind, nor betraying any definite hint that she was aware of what the Exalted Daughter was up to, and very angry about it.

"You betray the Ever-Ice, Semmeira," she whispered, lips immersed in icy meltwater of her own making, as she slipped down the glossy black Ice, "and shall pay the price. As I watch, and smile, and *aid you not.*"

"Be *still,*" Grunt Tusks snarled, turning his head to glare along the ledge as fearsomely as he could manage. "I'm just as restless as the rest of you! Look now, though; if we go down there now, there'll be Nifl warblades in plenty waiting for us! That's a slave caravan, and you know as well as I do that they're always guarded! And *because* they're always guarded, the city has a guard of its own watching over the caravan guards, see? Nifl trust other Nifl even less'n *we* trust Nifl!"

The gorkul beside him on the ledge grunted in reluctant agreement, but not acceptance. They were simmering in their eagerness, glowering down at what they could see through the cleft in the end wall of the cavern: Talonnorn itself.

They were *just* outside the mammoth cavern that housed Talonnorn, could have hurled stones off their ledge and watched them bounce or roll inside that huge and brightly lit, bustling cave.

Where all the slaves were standing.

Hairy Ones, all full-grown, with Nifl cracking long, snakelike whips to arrange them—with thoroughly unnecessary cruelty, Grunt Tusks noticed with disdain—into long, straight columns.

Three lines of glum, weary humans, all standing with their left wrists chained to the backs of their own necks to form a v-shape, so that long, heavy line-chains could be threaded through those arm-crooks to link them all together.

The three columns, to the accompaniment of much

shouting and lashing, were being shifted forward and back to make spaces between them for pack-snouts. Pack-snouts who would stalk along with the caravan, out in the Dark, providing mounts for the overseers, and laden with baskets of food and skins of water for the slaves' journey.

In all, the sort of caravan that came and went often as Talonar slave-owners made deals with visiting slave-traders shopping for strong slaves needed elsewhere in the cities of the Nifl.

"No younglings?" Belorgh asked, because he was young himself, and foolish. Grunt Tusks humored him, this time.

"Heed, fool. Young Hairy Ones are brought down from the Blindingbright, but thereafter never forced to travel the Wild Dark until they are grown into vigorous youth, or later. The journeys are too deadly; their lives will simply be wasted. Moreover, they are so noisy, and move so slowly, and climb so poorly, that they endanger their guards and minders, out in the Dark. Foes can't be outrun, the brats shriek whenever they see any sort of beast, and hamper their handlers in any sort of battle. Just not worth it. They're just humans, after all."

"Aye," Belorgh agreed, seeing at least this most obvious point. "They're just humans."

Then he stirred and started to ask something else stupid—but this time, Grunt Tusks cuffed him to silence, pointing grimly down at the small slice of the city cavern they could see.

Silently, the gorkuls on the ledge all beheld what he'd noticed: large, dark winged things swooping through the air, to circle the towers of Talonnorn and gather together aloft, among them.

"Darkwings," Grunt Tusks growled unnecessarily, "of the Hunt." He looked along the ledge, thrusting out his tusks belligerently. "Y'see, dolts, I don't want us to be revealing ourselves if the flying Hunt is ready to swoop and slay. All of us together are a nice meal for a dark-wings, not fighting foes for one."

Angry, impatient snarls answered him; having seen the glows of Talonnorn, the gorkul were not pleased at being held back from a charge out into that great cavern, where shrieking and fleeing food, gold, weapons, and even magic lay waiting.

"*Quiet,*" Grunt Tusks growled. "We can always butcher and plunder yon caravan, and have ourselves a right good feed on Hairy Ones, when it gets a few caverns away from here—and then come right back here, bellies full, to choose a better time to attack Talonnorn."

Snarls that built into roars were his reply, and gorkul bared their teeth and thrust their tusks at him defiantly, rising on their fists to shoulder menacingly in his direction, thrusting the nervously squealing Belorgh hard into Grunt Tusks's shoulder.

Then, in an instant, silence fell. Gorkul froze right where they were, to quiver on the ledge, only their eyes moving.

Eyes that bulged in staring fear at what had just come drifting menacingly out of the Wild Dark, to glide silently overhead.

And hopefully past. Glowering, Grunt Tusks watched them with all the rest, hoping none of them would decide to veer over and down to the ledge, and casually cleanse it of gorkul.

The raudren were hunting.

Orivon Firefist was smiling. Standing tall and proud, raising both of his swords high over his head in silent exultation, he grinned from ear to ear and shook his fists, full of sword as they were, at the cavern ceiling high overhead.

He was standing in a cave he recognized, a cave that had a trail of scratches and hoof-chips and dried dung down the center of it. This was a well-used way through the Dark, one of the main caravan routes to Talonnorn. He was lost no longer!

All right, ALL right. Capering has a certain charm, BUT . . .

Orivon grinned all the more. "What's this?" he asked. "Yathla Evendoom feels a loss of dignity? Isn't it a little late for that?"

I inhabit a bracer of elegant design.

The mind-voice was actually sniffing!

It is QUITE dignified. Even when worn by large, loud, clumsy Hairy Ones.

Orivon laughed heartily, not caring who heard the echoes.

Until something dark and sleek drifted across the cavern ahead, and he fell abruptly silent and darted for the nearest crevice, to crouch down with swords out before him.

THAT'S better, Yathla told him tartly.

Orivon found her approval rather less than necessary. He was trying his best not to breathe, and to look like an uninteresting, shadowy corner of lifeless rock.

They never hunt alone.

He knew that, too, and went on trying to look like he wasn't there.

Nothing thrusts even a strong warrior into tense, fearful waiting quite like hunting raudren.

"Softfingers," Oronkh said gruffly as they clambered through a narrow crevice out into yet another cavern, "I'm having misgivings. This Hairy One of yours is getting *very* close to Talonnorn."

"Too close for us to continue following him, you mean, and still be safe?" Nurnra responded, slipping as silently as a shadow down a rocky slope to peer around the cave.

"I mean just that," the half-gorkul agreed, sliding and jogging clumsily down the loose scree after her, arms windmilling to try to keep his balance.

"Manyfangs, do you know how ridiculous that sounds, talking of safety when we're out in the Wild Dark?"

"Humor me," Oronkh growled as he came up to her. "Talonnorn is ten-and-six caverns away from here, no more, if he takes the most direct route. And he is. He's somewhere very near, perhaps around yon rock listening to us now, but more likely a cavern or two ahead of us, and we're well into the caves Talonnorn patrols. Often. I say again: this human is getting too close to the city for us to keep tailing him."

The sharren trailed gentle gloved fingers over his chest, and licked his closest tusk.

Oronkh tossed his head a little, warning her such attentions weren't going to distract him this time, but she stroked his cheek and murmured, "You are quite right, Oronkh mine. I want his blood, but throwing our lives away trying to get it is oriad-headedness. What do you think we should do?"

The half-gorkul shrugged his massive shoulders. "Hail him? Warn him, somehow, that he's about to blunder into the wards of a Nifl city? *The* city, the one that's always been the proudest and most warlike? That's humbled a bit, now, but even more in tumult?"

Nurnra shook her head. "Warn him, perhaps, but Manyfangs, *this* Hairy One knows quite well where he's going. He's *seeking* Talonnorn." She took a few idle steps, tapping her own chin thoughtfully, and then turned back to Oronkh. "I think we should now begin to move as slowly and stealthily as you see fit to keep us best hidden, but continue—for now—to try to trace this human's progress. I believe he's been to Talonnorn before, and he doesn't strike me as a fool. He just might lead us to a hidden way into Talonnorn, or meet with Talonar thieves . . . or spies who are in that city at the behest of someone else . . . or Ravagers. Who in turn just might turn out to be of great interest, and even profit to us."

Oronkh shook his head. "Your tongue, Softfingers, gets me in more trouble . . . you could charm a Nifl into digging his own grave, then slitting his throat and leaping into what he's dug—not to mention handing you all his coin as he topples. This Hairy One could speedily lead *us* to *our* waiting graves. Yet I love you, and if I get to feel your clever little tongue often, I won't care overmuch if 'often' ends soon, for both of us."

Nurnra put her fingers to her mouth and looked at him over their tips, sudden tears glimmering in her eyes. "Manyfangs mine," she said softly, "you say the *loveliest* things."

Talonnorn was only a few caverns away, now.

Orivon had slowed so that he could move as stealthily as possible, darting from one cleft or shadowed overhang to the next, peering everywhere for patrols, lurking creatures, and the faint glows and singing sounds of spells that might be waiting to warn someone in the city of an intruder's approach.

Slow, soft and quiet, now. That was the only way to save his own skin, and there was no point in hurrying, because when he got to the last cavern before the city, he would just have to hide and wait; he needed a trading caravan or slaving band to enter or depart Talonnorn for the wards to be down.

Yet one thing was puzzling him, making his frown deepen as he went on, stealing quietly and slowly. There should be Talonar warbands or even the Hunt patrolling these caverns, marching or flying or standing sentinel.

Instead, there was nothing. He was traversing empty caverns, alone, as he got closer . . . and closer . . .

Curtly the spellrobe snapped at the Oszrim warblades to halt, and waved at them to form a ring around him.

They did so in silence, keeping their heads down.

Vlakrel's temper had been sharp since they had failed to catch up to the Bloodsucker and the Misbegotten—who obviously hadn't stopped to sleep, after all—and now it was visibly slipping.

"The two we're after are getting very close to Talonnorn," Vlakrel hissed, keeping his voice low and imperiously beckoning the warblades to bend their heads close to hear him. "*We're* getting very close to the city."

Not a warblade there dared to ask, "And so?" Yet every one of them posed that question silently, by their sidelong looks at him, the stances they took, and the way they shifted their hands on their sword hilts.

"We must be very careful," the spellrobe continued testily, "and very quiet—or our own city's patrols may strike at us. The two miscreants we're after may become aware of us, too, and arrange a trap, or lure us into a meeting with a lurking beast."

Warblade heads nodded around the ring, maintaining careful silence.

Impatience suddenly overmastering him, Vlakrel pointed and waved furiously, sending them back into their advancing line once more. As they started to form it, he paced impatiently up and down beside them, hissing, "Yet we *must* catch those two up, if we can do so without their seeing us. They may be heading for some secret way into the city—I'm sure you've heard all the tales, just as I have—or meet with conspirators against Talonnorn; spies who dwell in the city but send word out through the Dark to Talonnorn's foes, from time to time. This is why—"

Behind him, there came the brief clatter of a dropped sword from the direction of the two rear-guard warblades. It was the sound of their vanishing, though no one else yet knew that.

The warrior who'd been picking his way through the rocks just ahead of the rear guard whirled around—and shouted in horror, giving everyone else time to gape at the great black bulk sliding past through the air, just above their heads.

Silent and deadly, the raudren were hunting.

15

Spitting in the Face of Olone

No place have I to hide away
In the endless deeps of cold stone
For I have scorched the Ever-Ice
And spat in the face of Olone
　　—old Niflghar drinking song

Jalandral paused for dramatic effect at the end of a particularly eloquent and telling point—if he said so himself, and he just had—and then let out his breath and broke his pose, hiding his exasperation only with some effort.

An underpriestess of some sort had parted the all-concealing draperies behind the nameless priestess he'd been negotiating with, glided gracefully up behind her, murmured something unheard into those darkly beautiful ears, and withdrawn just as deftly and swiftly as she had come.

Leaving Jalandral's adversary visibly annoyed.

Eyes flashing, she pointed an imperious finger at him and cried, "While we stand here seeking agreement, your hired wildblades are offering violence to Consecrated of this temple in the streets of the city, and your officials are publicly uttering words of vilification and rebuke against this temple and any priestess they see!

Moreover, the one of these latter we caught and questioned—"

"Gently, I presume," Jalandral murmured.

"With our spells, as is customary," the priestess snapped, "both goading with measured and temporary pain to compel cooperation, and scrying the thoughts behind the words, as has been done for generations upon generations in Talonnorn, whilst it grew to greatness and your family was elevated in the rise and participated fully in it!"

She took two long, liquid steps toward Jalandral, and then turned just as gracefully, retraced them, and turned to face him again. "To continue, the one we caught and questioned claimed—and our spells found it truth—that *you* ordered this behavior! That you *require* all who directly serve you to blacken this temple and all who dwell and worship within it, in the eyes of all Talonar! Have you no thought at all for consequences, Jalandral Evendoom? For implications? Is shattering Talonnorn around you the goal you truly seek? For that is what you are achieving, whether you claim otherwise or not!"

Jalandral smiled, waved his hand floorward in soothing dismissal. "Now, now, Tall and Terrible—"

"*What?* You *dare*—?"

"I," Jalandral interrupted firmly, "dare many things. Leading to this meeting, which will continue forever if we wrangle about such utter trifles. Empty pride is something Talonnorn can no longer afford; something we have never really been able to afford, but have—"

"Jalandral Evendoom, do not presume to lecture any Consecrated of Olone's Glory in Talonnorn on the history of this city. It is something no Talonar noble has ever troubled to examine with any amount of dispassion, and I have my doubts that, crones excepted, most of them possess the basic wits to do so, even if—"

"Tall and Terrible, this grows truly tiresome. I am aware that most Talonar hate we nobles, and sneer at us behind our backs for any number of failings. This is something endemic to the attitudes underlings have to their superiors—and betters. It is not som—"

"My *name,*" the priestess snarled, using magic to smite Jalandral's ears with her voice as if it were a lash, "is not Tall and Terrible!"

Wincing and trying not to back away—so there were spells that used a shielded one's own shieldings against them, hey? *Interesting!*—Jalandral managed an airy smile. "Well, then, Tall and Terrible, would you prefer to be addressed as Nameless Negotiator?"

"My title," the priestess said icily, "is Holyflame, and the name by which I am known before the altar of Olone is Alaedra. 'Holyflame Alaedra' is neither an overly long or complicated name. Have the basic breeding—you *are* an Evendoom, are you not? Not an impostor from the Araed, or an Ice-lover of Ouvahlor, who did something dark to the lazy fop of a Firstborn who so exasperated Lord Erlingar Evendoom, and is now impersonating him? No?—to address me so. As I so treat with you."

"Very well, Holyflame Alaedra. As High Lord of Talonnorn and Lord Evendoom, I, Jalandral, propose that we move on from name-calling and taking offense to forms of address or mere choices of words, at least as far as the trading of silken threats. I believe we have achieved enough intimacy for that now."

Surprisingly, Holyflame Alaedra smiled.

"Very well. I, too, believe the practical time available to us is not infinite. I also understand that the passage of time brings changes to any city, and your lordship is one such. However, if you are to be recognized as High Lord of Talonnorn—by all Talonar, not just by the Holy Altar of Olone and all of its Consecrated—the powers of High Lordship must be clearly defined, understood, and accepted. By all."

Jalandral nodded, but the priestess politely held up a hand requesting he let her continue, and he nodded again and did so.

"It is our observed opinion that you have been creating

these powers as you see fit, to deal with every pressing situation before you, and are seeking, consciously or merely through accumulation, to make them very close to absolute."

She raised her voice a little, and started to speak slowly and firmly.

"We can accept a secular lord over the traditionally fractious noble Houses of Talonnorn, but what defines Talonnorn is not its nobles nor Hunt nor Araed, but its worship of Olone. To speak plainly, we *cannot* accept a lord who presumes to command Consecrated as if they are slaves or warblades or House servants, because they are engaged in a holier service, and stand in Talonnorn as the instruments of Olone—and it is clear blasphemy to give commands to Olone."

She took a step closer to Jalandral.

"So we need to know, specifically, where your powers begin and where they end. That you may have exclusive jurisdiction over certain matters we can accept, just as we must have exclusive jurisdiction over matters of worship; that you must have free hands to do just as you please at all times, neither we nor the Goddess accepts. This is our thinking, and our stance—from which we shall not be shifted, lest the wrath of Olone come down on us all."

She gestured to Jalandral to respond.

Smilingly, he did so. "Ah, yes, the 'mustn't offend the deity' argument. As expected, and differing in no specifics from what I anticipated. Well enough. Yet I hold, and intend to follow, another view. Hear me well."

He took his own leisurely step in the Holyflame's direction, and started to speak slowly and clearly, each word firm and heavy. "In matters laid down in Olone's words and teachings, her Consecrated are both directed as to how they should themselves act, and are also instruments of holy will in administering how all Talonar should follow these words and teachings. However, in all matters Olone has been silent upon, I believe—as most Talonar believe, whether they dare to say so or not—the Consecrated have no jurisdiction, and should not presume to offer their opinions or extend embellished interpretations of holy will. In short, keep to the altar and leave governance of Talonnorn to me."

He took another step, and spoke more loudly, though he kept his voice level.

"Every Talonar experienced the disastrous result of a Talonnorn invaded that was a Talonnorn dominated by feuding Houses. Houses that this temple gleefully manipulated, time and again, into furtherance of those feuds, and continuously attempted to coerce in matters large and small through the House crones. That's the only reason Talonar have accepted a High Lord at all; like me or hate me, they see the clear necessity of city defense being in secular hands. As High Lord, I must command all Talonar warriors, and such priestesses as go to war among them—and there must be such priestesses. A lone secular commander, with authority recognized by *all,* is vitally necessary to avoid Talonnorn falling to another invader."

Taking a step back again, he added sadly, "And as the crones and Consecrated of this city have amply and strikingly demonstrated through generations of self-serving, feuding-among-themselves manipulations of authority, they are unfit for command and unable to see what is good for Talonnorn—as opposed to what is best for them, and conveniently purported to be Olone's desires. An effective High Lord must not be a puppet of any priestess or of this temple as a whole, and *must* sit in command—commands swiftly and carefully obeyed, not met with delay, debate, deceit in obedience, or defiance—over all Consecrated in and of Talonnorn."

Then he smiled, and added, "I do not anticipate this thinking—which is *my* budge-not-from stance—to be eagerly accepted, but in the end, accepted it must be."

"Or—?" the Holyflame Alaedra snapped, her voice trembling with rage.

"Talonnorn will leave this temple behind," Jalandral said quietly, "and its Consecrated can dwell within these walls enforcing Olone's holy will upon each other, but not upon Talonnorn *outside* these walls."

"What you propose is blasphemy," the priestess said flatly. "You show a glib ease in confusing 'I want' with 'the High Lord needs' or with 'Talonnorn demands, and will inevitably have.' You seem to think Olone is a fiction that we Consecrated invented, and now twist into justification for personal whims and a desire to dominate or rule. You forget that Olone is *real,* and speaks to us directly, and we are her slaves when she demands it. Her *willing* slaves. We serve her, and feel glory in doing so; we will not serve you. Were I you, I would go directly to the altar of this temple, abase myself, and beg Olone's forgiveness and holy guidance."

"Guidance provided—with many conditions attached—by a helpful priestess who just happens to be standing behind that altar, yes?" Jalandral asked mockingly. "I'm sorry, Alaedra, but such clumsy tricks just don't work anymore. The crones' club can still meet to spit their spite and gossip, but Talonnorn is going to be ruled by someone else now. And if Olone doesn't like that . . . well, as the old song has it: I spit in the face of Olone."

"Blasphemer!" the Holyflame cried, shaking and pale with rage. "To speak such words here, in this holy place! You *dare*—?"

Jalandral turned the Evendoom ring on his finger, to surround himself with yet another shielding—the oldest, deepest, and most powerful shielding than any he'd seen before first donning the ring. "Let's see her try to take control of *that,*" he murmured, not caring if she heard.

Then he looked up at Holyflame Alaedra, who had flung wide her hands to begin a spell and was glaring at him with eyes burning like flame, and told her smilingly, "You're about to be surprised at just what I dare to do, in this holy place."

From behind him there arose sudden deep, rolling thunder that ended in a sharp, ear-bludgeoning *crash*.

The draperies there bulged out, as the top of a riven door thrust against—and then through—them. From out of that ruin came running Nifl rampants with swords and heavy goads and axes in their hands, wearing motley armor and enthusiastic grins.

Bright, fresh blood was dripping from many of the weapons.

Consecrated blood.

They shouted in glee as they flooded into the chamber, and swept past Jalandral—who politely stood aside, indicating the priestess with a flourish—to bear down on Holyflame Alaedra.

"Endlessly arguing over irrelevancies is so, well, boring," Jalandral drawled, watching the priestess disappear elsewhere, in the shrinking heart of a frantically generated spell-rift that hurled his fastest wildblades in all directions. The Nifl who were only a running stride or two slower sprang forward and buried their swords in the brief roiling magic of her departure, but by then they were literally thrusting war-steel through empty air.

They consoled themselves by slashing aside draperies in all directions, revealing walls of white stone and doors in plenty. Doors that were flung open before they could reach them, for furious priestesses to hurl spells through—ere the doors were slammed again.

Those spells became bursts of bright flame, explosions that hurled wildblade arms and legs in all directions, axes and broken swords clanging and shrieking off walls, the floor, and the ceiling. Jalandral winced, ducked, and hastened for the door his wildblades had forced open. The severed heads of some of them bounced and rolled beside him.

To the sound of his own hissed curses, he raced out of that chamber of death, running alone.

He hadn't expected the slaughter to be *quite* this swift and efficient. Half of his force was dead behind him, and there was no sign of the other half. Had they fallen, at the gates? Surely a few upperpriestesses could be harvested before he entirely ran out of wildblades. After all, they—the best he could hire, out of the Araed—had obviously made swift work of butchering the guard-priestesses at the temple gates . . .

The long, straight passage was empty.

Jalandral sprinted down it in undignified haste, seeking to quit the Holy Altar of Olone before anything worse happened. He'd hoped to slay every Consecrated he could reach, until those left were too few and too cowed to do anything but obey him, once he apologized to Olone before her altar and said nice things to them thereafter. Thus far, however, he'd met with no one in the temple higher-ranking than the Holyflame, and his little trap seemed, in the end, to have been more dramatic than effective.

Before he could reach the end of the passage, it filled with the last of his wildblades, waving their swords and looking excited—and then astonished at the sight of the High Lord of Talonnorn running toward them like a frightened child.

"*There* you are!" Jalandral cried, skidding to a halt and forcing the widest smile he could onto his face. "Come! There is much taming of Consecrated still to be done!" He beckoned them, and then started back along the passage, striding steadily this time rather than running—and hoping something would arise to distract them all before they all reached the conclave-chamber and found their cooked, dismembered fellows strewn around a dead end walled in by all those locked metal doors.

Doors that had murderous priestesses with ready spells waiting and listening behind them.

The furious Consecrated obliged, flinging open a side door in the passage and shouting, "*Blasphemers!* You spit in the face of Olone!" before they thrust their long-fingered hands out into the passage and sent crackling lightnings racing from every fingertip, in a leaping, eye-searing bright web of snarling death.

Jalandral watched all the rest of his wildblades—every last spasming, shrieking, helplessly dying one of them—cooked where they stood, lurching and convulsing as plumes of smoke billowed from their mouths and the dark, staring pits where their eyes had sizzled, popped, and run down their faces. They toppled, swords clanging, and . . . he was truly alone.

Being well ahead of his wildblades, and being cloaked in the Evendoom shields, had saved him from that particular doom.

Yet doors were opening all around him now, up and down the passage and all around the blood-spattered conclave-chamber, and grim-faced priestesses were stepping through them.

To stand just in front of the still-open doors, burning eyes all fixed on Jalandral.

Who had swiftly darted to a place in the passage where he could put his back to the wall, and now stood there uncertainly, fear rising in him as he held up hands that were starting to tremble, and stared at the rings he wore, wondering what best to unleash next.

Or whether he'd have fingers at all, a breath or two from now . . .

"Jalandral Evendoom," a familiar voice said coldly, from a nearby door down the passage, between him and the distant temple gates. With a sigh he didn't quite manage to conceal, the High Lord of Talonnorn turned to face Holyflame Alaedra, and awaited her next words silently, putting a slight smile on his face as he gently turned another of his rings.

The tingling of its awakening magic was racing along his limbs as the Holyflame pronounced doom on him.

"Jalandral Evendoom, you are a murderer and a tyrant to your people, perhaps also among your kin, and you are a blasphemer who brings death and unholy defiance to the Altar of Olone. Heretic are you, and you shall perish on the very altar of the Goddess. Olone demands nothing less."

With a jauntiness he was very far from feeling, Jalandral widened his smile, looked around at all of the priestesses, and said pleasantly, "Honored Consecrated, I am flattered by your attentions—but I fear I must decline. As Olone will undoubtedly tell you when you begin to ask her the *right* questions, the needs of Talonnorn must come before anyone's petty revenges."

Pushing himself away from the wall, he started to stroll down the passage. Knowing as he did so that every last priestess around him—twoscore and ten, at least—were now swiftly working spells intended to accomplish his destruction.

Smiling tightly as he strode right past the first priestess, close enough that she could have touched him if she'd stretched out her arms fully instead of using them to shape sigils in the air as she hissed out an incantation and glared at him, Jalandral turned the second ring.

It worked instantly; he felt the intense chill along his spine as its rift opened, dark and bobbing and vaguely man-shaped. Ready to drink in every rending magic hurled at him from behind. As he strode on, it moved with him. Which meant, he hoped, all of the shieldings now moving with him would only have to face the spells of the score or so Consecrated in front of him.

Who promptly vanished as the world in front of him exploded in silent white flame, crashing again and again against his shields as spell after spell struck, failed, and slid away—and the next spell came crashing through it to shatter itself against his shields and slide away in its turn.

Crash, crash, crash. Blindly, he staggered on, hoping

none of the priestesses had any enspelled knives that they could simply plunge through the shields and into his ribs as he lurched past them. Perhaps it would be wiser to stop, and wait for his vision to return and their spells to be exhausted, and—

His outermost shield, the rock-hard Evendoom shield, flickered and then was gone.

Leaving him barely time to frantically awaken his second-last ring, and no time to curse at all.

"Behold your slayer," the Talonar lord snarled into the astonished Ouvahlan's face. "I am Lord Erlingar Evendoom of Talonnorn, and you are—no more!"

He jerked his deeply buried sword back out of the dying warblade, using his other hand to thrust the body back and away from him as it fountained blood, and turned to see how Faunhorn was faring in the battle. He was in time to see the most magnificent Talonar warrior he'd ever seen calmly slaying his way across the cavern that formed the heart of Glowstone, leaving most of the Ouvahlan garrison dead in his wake. Smooth and swift, Faunhorn ducked and thrust and spun, dancing his way through accomplished warriors Erlingar would have been hard-pressed to fell. Two, three; just like that.

Even as Lord Evendoom watched, another three fell, almost too fast to see the thrusts that slew them. There hadn't been much more than a dozen Ouvahlans to begin with; the rest, he feared, had already departed for Talonnorn.

Which meant . . . yes, Glowstone was now theirs. Or what little was left of it.

Erlingar stared around the ravaged trade-moot. Blood, corpses, fallen weapons, and a fire that the Ouvahlans had been feeding with the splintered remnants of old carry-chests and market stalls.

"Our new home," he announced glumly, sketching a parody of a courtly "look ye" gesture. His pleasure-shes,

Kryree and Varaeme, planted their swords and bowed to him, grinning—and so did an Evendoom warblade or two.

There were chuckles among the House warriors, and the stretchings and arm-rubbings and wearily relieved chatter that erupts in the wake of all swift victories. Someone inspected a sword cut and groaned, someone else held up some skins of wine with a crow of triumph, and—sudden silence fell.

There were Nifl in the deep shadows of the most distant reaches of the cavern, advancing slowly out of the tunnels and other caverns, beyond. Ravagers, with swords in their hands.

The Evendoom warblades caught up their swords and formed a ring around Lord Evendoom and his two shes, facing outward. Faunhorn broke off his swift inspection of Ouvahlan corpses to heft his sword and stride to confront the nearest Ravager.

And that foremost Nifl wanderer went to his knees, reversed the sword in his hand, and held it out to Faunhorn.

"All hail the new Lord of Glowstone!" he called loudly, and Ravagers echoed those words, all around the cavern.

More and more Ravagers were emerging now, a few of them kicking and spitting on dead Ouvahlans.

Faunhorn took the Ravager's sword and handed it gravely back to him. Then he turned to catch Erlingar's eye, to be sure he saw no displeasure there at the title the Ravager had given Faunhorn.

He and Erlingar exchanged disbelieving grins—and then Faunhorn peered sharply to one side, and started to frown.

Lord Evendoom looked, too, and beheld two Ravagers bending over an Ouvahlan body, busy with rope.

"What're you doing?" Faunhorn called.

"Readying this meat for a cook-spit, Lord," one of them replied hesitantly, holding up one end of a long, rusty bar of metal.

The looks Faunhorn and Erlingar exchanged this time were more aghast than triumphant.

Jalandral was heartily glad the vaults of the Houses he'd humbled had yielded so many powerful rings; right now, they were keeping him alive!

His just-awakened ring had come from his own family caches, if he remembered rightly; right now, it had opened a wide rift that was filling the passage in front of him, and devouring the spells of the Consecrated as fast as they could arrive. Leaving him to blink swimming eyes and start to be able to see things again—as the ring-rift suddenly trembled, shuddered, almost forced him to the floor, and then did what it was supposed to do.

It spat out something dark and angry and much too big for the passage, that hissed in pain and anger as its emerging wings slammed against the walls and ceiling, splintered in bony ruin in confines just too small for it, and then erupted in shrieking pain down the passage as it frantically tried to lurch and scrabble its way out, tumbling priestesses broken or crushed with it.

It was a darkwings, huge and stinking and ungainly, and Jalandral smiled at the ruin it was working down the passage—and then awakened his last ring.

It promptly grew a tiny, leaping flame that writhed vertically in midair above its band. Jalandral's smile tightened as he selected a Consecrated who'd ducked back through her door to avoid the darkwings, and was now stepping out into the passage again with a spell snarling around her hands, as she looked balefully in Jalandral's direction.

Yes, she would make a good first victim.

Jalandral bent his will, and the leaping flame spat forth a small whirlwind of flame that spun and grew into a fiery pinwheel with astonishing speed.

The fire-wheel shot down the passage and crashed into that priestess, bursting into a roaring column of flames.

She didn't even have time to shriek.

Really smiling now, Jalandral selected his next victim. The rift at his back was still protecting him against anything more than half of the priestesses might try, and in front of him, the maddened and broken darkwings had already reached the end of the passage and burst out into the chamber beyond. He could no longer see it, but he could hear it roaring horribly. It was probably slaying anything living it caught sight of.

Good.

Matters were finally beginning to unfold as he'd hoped. Roaring flames claimed another priestess, and another, and the little dancing flame showed no signs of lessening.

Jalandral stalked down the passage dealing death until he reached its end—and then spun around, turning his back for now on the way to the gates and escape from the temple, and strode back down the passage to burn the rest of the priestesses.

When he got these down to a cowering handful, he would command one or two of them to take him to the most powerful priestesses. They were the ones he needed dead. All but the minimum needed to raise the wards again, and those he would imprison.

So much for the vengeful hand of Olone, reaching out to protect her oh-so-precious Consecrated. They deluded themselves, these preening shes, that their Goddess gave any thought at all to them, cared one whit—

Then he stopped, in the midst of happily immolating his thirty-fourth priestess, and stared.

A black, glossy altar had arisen from the smooth and seamless floor where he'd stood confronting Holyflame Alaedra—and she had just risen into view behind it now, with a dagger in her hand.

"Olone, be with us! *Aid Talonnorn now!*" she cried, her voice ringing around the room.

And then, eyes exulting as she glared at Jalandral, she plunged the dagger into her own breast, even as she leaped atop the altar to spread-eagle herself, dying, over it.

The room rocked and darkened, and all of the rings on Jalandral Evendoom's hands winked out, at once.

"Oh, no," he whispered, in the last moment left to him.

16

Armies, Battles, and Revenges

*N*o wards.
No *wards.*

Orivon shook his head in disbelief.

Why?

He could see Talonnorn itself, now, a slice of towers standing tall and dark against the light of its great cavern, through the tall cleft at the far end of the cavern he'd just entered. Talonnorn was right *there* . . . and no patrols, no wards.

What had happened in the city?

Was this going to be ease itself, striding in to search for slaves at leisure, or had some disast—

There came screams, from behind him, the panting shrieks of Nifl who were running hard—and dying.

Orivon whirled around, swords up.

In time to see raudren gliding low and menacing above

many wildly fleeing Nifl. Raudren who were diving down to snatch, and feed.

Raudren who were coming right toward him, three of them converging. There was no doubt that they'd seen him, and were heading for Orivon Firefist, and no one else.

Severed Nifl hands and feet spilled from one of them as it came. "Yathla," Orivon snarled, "now would be a good time for some of your fire!"

The bracer kept silent; no voice sounded in his head.

"Yathla?" Orivon shouted, running hastily for the nearest cavern wall, and its rocks. "Yathla?"

There was no reply. The raudren loomed up, gliding swiftly.

Olone came. Not as a striding, raging cavern-tall shining female figure, all of shining bright fire, but as a great surge of force, a wave of silent, inexorable might that swept out of the altar and rolled through the temple.

As Jalandral stared helplessly at the altar, watching Holyflame Alaedra's body melt silently away, the great wave passed through him—and left him on his knees.

There was no blasting fire, no hammer stroke shattering his mind. Only rapture that left Jalandral weeping and gasping and *alive,* every inch of his body thrilled and delighted. His rifts were gone in an instant as the sensual force swept on down the passage, melting the dead and their debris as it went.

In dazed wonder he came to his feet, not quite believing he was unharmed, and staggered toward the passage. He should leave, he must go. That thought was suddenly there, and insistent, and would not leave him. He must depart the temple.

His limbs were spasming with pleasure, stretching and writhing, almost tumbling him into a fall. His fingers sought to stroke, his heart was hammering inside him . . .

Shuddering, Jalandral stumbled into the passage—and the empty air thickened before him. He'd waded a river in the Dark once, and this, barring the cold wetness, was the same; he was wading against a strong flow that now sought to sweep him back into the chamber with the altar.

The altar! He was going to be forced onto the altar, and horribly sacrificed! Torn slowly apart while Olone shrieked vengeance into his face and kept him awake to feel every last moment of agony!

He found himself driven back, the tide against him like a silent giant's hand shoving far more strongly than he could stand against. No! *No,* by Talonnorn! "Klaerra!" he called despairingly, and heard his cry muffled right in front of his lips. "Klaerra!"

She was not going to aid him, was not even going to hear him. Olone was in this passage with him, was all around him, held this temple in her titanic grasp . . .

He was going to die.

Arching and gasping in pleasure—unless Olone turned it to pain, plunging him into agony, and who was to say she would not?—he was going to die here.

Magic!

He had no spells, but he did have all of the rings and everything else he'd worn here or stuffed into his belt-pouches. The enchanted things of several proud Houses. Great magics, for all that Olone had extinguished the rings in an instant; magics meant to serve their wielders in triumphs for generations. Could they aid him?

They were meant to serve for generations longer, but what of that? If he died, they'd be melted on that altar anyway, and lost.

Jalandral bent his will—it was suddenly hard, through a storm of swirling pleasure in his mind—and called upon the endmost ring on his left hand.

It awakened, with its customary glow and tingling, and he called on its power. Not to summon Hunts or fry warblades or whatever it was intended to do, but just to pour its power into him, so that he could—

Yes! He could walk as if there was no invisible tide against him, could stride, even trot, down the passage as far as . . . a few doors down, as the ring darkened and crumbled and fell from his hand, and the tide rose against his slowing legs again, stopping him, and then—as he leaned desperately against it, to escape being arched over and flung back—dragging at him, clawing . . .

Frantically Jalandral called on the next ring, hoping it would also serve him. How many rings would it take to get a High Lord out of this temple? Had he brought enough?

"Run, Softfingers!" Oronkh roared, swinging a futile sword at the great gliding bulk. *"Run!"*

The sharren was stripping off her gloves, smiling a little smile, as a raudren turned in the air, moving as leisurely as a gloating river-snake turns to strike at trapped prey, to sweep down on her.

"Run, Nurnra!" the half-gorkul roared, starting back toward her. "You can't bleed these if you're torn to bloody ribbons and are inside them!"

Twenty-some rocks farther along the cavern, Orivon blinked. Where had these two come from?

From among those rocks, yes, but how had they come so close without his even . . . ?

He swept that thought aside rather grimly, as the raudren coming for him blotted out all sight of the Nifl-gorkul half-breed and the beautiful Nifl-she with him, as well as the running warblades, beyond.

These were wild raudren, the great scarred hunters of the Wild Dark, not the smaller raudren kept caged as last-ditch defenders by Talonnorn. As if it mattered.

Orivon set his jaw, hefted his swords, and wondered how swiftly he would die.

Jalandral Evendoom put his head down and ran, lurching grimly along as another ring yielded up its power. He was just a step or two from the end of the passage, where it turned and opened into a larger chamber. Dark streaks of darkwings' gore glistened on the walls all around him. Just a few more steps . . .

His pouches were empty of magic, and most of his fingers were bare of rings. His enchanted earring was gone, and all three of his daggers. Even the enspelled-against-rust scabbard that had held his sword—eaten away for its magic far back down the passage—was no more.

He turned the corner, hoping the tide of Olone's will would abate.

It didn't—and the ring sighed into dust and was gone, leaving another finger bare.

All that he had left was the Evendoom ring.

Jalandral gritted his teeth, kicked himself away from the wall he'd sagged against, and called on the ring.

It fought, resisting his will even as Olone's tide shoved him back toward the passage.

"I," he gasped, gritting his teeth, "am Jalandral Evendoom!" He fought for breath. "Lord of . . . Evendoom."

Olone seemed unimpressed, but the ring seemed to hear him. Suddenly it was flooding him with power, glowing bright upon his forefinger. The tide was suddenly nothing; with an ease that it seemed forever since he'd felt, Jalandral trotted through the chamber, along the forehall, and out of the temple.

He was perhaps forty swift strides away from the temple gates, heading for the nearest side alley, when the Evendoom ring flared into a flesh-searing flame, causing him to shout in pain, and—went out. His blistered finger was bare.

Memories suddenly surged through him, memories that were not his own but that had rooms he knew in them, the Eventowers. Which meant the shouting, fighting, and lovemaking people crowding through his head, who all looked at least vaguely like his father, must be Evendooms.

Must be . . .

High Lord of Talonnorn or not, Jalandral felt over-whelmed by the flood of Evendooms. Overwhelmed, staggering, and then . . . swept away.

He collapsed, or thought he did, briefly feeling the street hard under his cheek, but was snatched up and away, still lost in a flood of Evendoom pasts, by Olone's might. It slammed him against hard stone—the front of a building that was far from where he'd fallen—dragged him along it shouting in pain, and then whirled him away to smash into even harder stone.

At some point during the battering that followed he broke an arm, and then a leg, and then perhaps his other arm—though by then, even with the broken ends of his own bones slicing him across the face, he barely knew what was real and what was . . . wild memory . . .

"Are they *all* there, in that same cavern?" Aloun asked, peering hard into an array of small whorls in front of him. "I've—whoa! What's *that*?"

Whorls were suddenly on the move, gliding away from under his hands and scrutiny as if an unseen, un-felt breeze was blowing briskly at him.

Whorls everywhere in the chamber were sliding in the same direction, back behind him. When he grasped one, or tried to, it frayed and shredded under his fingers, pulling away from him anyway.

There was real fear in his face as he looked to the Senior Watcher of Ouvahlor.

Luelldar looked up from his own collapsing whorl, sweating, as he gave up his own lost mind-battle to hold it where it was, and said grimly, "Behold the faintest echo of Olone's power. Were the Ever-Ice not shielding us, in this place, 'tisn't our whorls that would be falling into nothing and being swept away, about now."

The broken-limbed and senseless High Lord of Talonnorn struck one last wall, slid bloodily down it, and lay still, a huddled, bleeding heap.

In a deep, dark doorway, the wildblades and merchants of the Araed who'd been watching his struggle out of the temple now looked at each other, shrugged—and then a few of the younger, bolder ones darted out across the street, plucked up the fallen Jalandral, and dragged him back to their refuge, peering down the deserted street at the temple fearfully and often.

They made it inside with their prize two scant breaths before a few dazed, limping Consecrated came stumbling out of the temple gates, and peered around. They were seeking Jalandral Evendoom, with knives in their hands.

"I need the Hunt *now!*"

House Spellrobe Vlakrel's snarl rose almost to a shriek, and he glared at the ring on his finger as if it were the face of a hated foe. "High Lord Jalandral Evendoom promised me the Hunt would come at my call—and I'm calling!"

The voice only he could hear replied, and Vlakrel screamed in frustration—though his cry was nothing amid the raw, desperate howls of dying, despairing Oszrim warblades, as the raudren swooped.

"I don't *care* if you can't find him; his order remains unchanged—and *I am invoking it!* Send the Hunt to me, and send them *now!* I—"

Vlakrel's terrified eyes darted wildly around the raudren-filled Outcavern, seeking some way to make this petty *dolt* in House Evendoom budge from sneeringly denying him. Then he thought of something, and spat it at the ring.

"And how strong will your neck be, when Jalandral—ah, of course, *High Lord* Evendoom to you—gets his hands on it? After the force that I'm facing, a force that's using trained or magically compelled raudren as their forefront blades, gets past me and attacks Talonnorn itself! When I might have been able to turn it back or defeat it here in the Outcaverns, if I'd had the Hunt here in time? And Jalandral learns that it was *you* who prevented that?"

Whatever response Vlakrel heard made him smile broadly, say crisply, "*That's* better. I'll see that you're properly praised," and then relax with a great sigh.

Which saved his life. The abrupt slumping of the spell-robe's body carried him *just* below the reach of a diving raudren; it swerved, ran out of cavern to fly in, and banked sharply along the cavern wall, scraping along the rock rather than slamming thunderously into it.

"He's alive," the wildblade carrying Jalandral's shoulders said, "but that's about it."

"Bring him," a merchant ordered curtly, flinging open a door to reveal steps; the usual stone ramp, leading down into darkness.

"Oh?" the wildblade asked, hefting his half of the High Lord's dangling, blood-dripping body. "And who made *you* High Lord?"

The merchant calmly drew a belt-knife and put its tip against the bulge under the front lacings of the wildblade's breeches. "I haven't time for crones' I'm-prettier games, just now," he announced calmly. "Bring him."

The wildblade nodded silently, and the merchant started down the ramp. After a moment, the two wildblades carrying what was left of the High Lord followed, bearing their burden very carefully.

The other merchants filed down the ramp in their wake. The last one paused long enough to tell the other six wildblades who'd been in the doorway, "Stay here. If any priestesses come looking for the High Lord, *don't* say he's in here. Just invent some other pretext for killing them. Try to do it without other Consecrated seeing you; you'll last longer, that way."

"We're not stone-stupid, you know," one of the six replied.

"What's in it for us?" another wildblade, who was re-splendent in a fine purple cloak, asked the merchant.

"Ah," he replied, "but it seems you *are* stone-stupid, after all. Why even ask? The answers are: obey, and you live and gain a steep salary from the High Lord's purse; and fail to obey, and we'll kill you now, with one of the many means of doing so we've bought that you are thus far obviously unaware of. Oh, and *try* not to be stupid enough to ask me what any of them are."

In the silence that followed, the merchant nodded to them all, stepped onto the ramp, and closed the door.

It was three long breaths later before the purple-cloaked wildblade asked, "Why?"

The oldest of the three wildblades broke his silence, looking scornful. "Because he'll kill you with one of them the moment you ask what they are, to show the rest of us he wasn't bluffing."

"And how do you *know* he wasn't bluffing?"

"He's a merchant of the Araed successful enough to live to be as old as he is. You can't bluff your way through half a lifetime unless you're a priestess or the lord of a House. And the times are good."

The wildblade who'd asked sighed in exasperation. "Just killing Nifl is easier."

"You're not the first to say *that*," said the oldest wildblade. "Now look innocent, everyone: Consecrated, yonder, coming through the door!"

"Can't—" Nurnra panted, running like the wind but lacking enough of her own to speak clearly, "Can't . . . hide from raudren anywhere!"

Oronkh, who was huffing and gasping like a drowning pack-snout as he pounded along in her wake, answered with only a nod.

"So might as well"—the sharren added, over her shoulder, as she dodged the last rock and sprinted out onto the open floor of the central cavern—"run to the Hairy One! You and he, fighting back to back, just might keep us all alive!"

Oronkh shot one look at the human, standing alone

with swords in both of his hands, awaiting four swooping raudren, and then put his head down and ran. There
didn't seem much point in shaking his head in disbelief;
the Hairy One was already doing so, for him.

"The High Lord is still within the Altar of Olone, treating
with the Consecrated of the Goddess," the Nifl guardlord
said icily, "and I am *not* going to interrupt him."

"But—"

"But he left *us* in charge. Doing nothing while an
army floods into the very streets of our city and starts
butchering Talonar at will—because we're waiting for
Lord Evendoom to return, utter commands that might
have saved Talonnorn had they been given much earlier,
and then pat our heads and behinds in thanks, and sit
down with us to watch our own unfolding doom—is not
my idea of 'staunchly serving Talonnorn.' Is it yours?"

"You trust an *Oszrim* spellrobe?"

"Can you not set aside the sneerings we were all taught
to perform, and do the task we were given? I believe we
cannot afford *not* to trust this Vlakrel, proud fool that he
may be. If his claims are correct, he may already be dead;
if he has deceived us, we shall see to it that he dies. Why
would he invent an attack? If he intends this as a trap, I
hardly think the Hunt can be overcome by anyone *he*
could arrange to have waiting for them!"

"Attend, all!" a new voice called from the door, sharp
and loud. "Reports from the temple! Magic is spewing
from its very gates!"

"What?"

"I knew it! Those oriad *bitches*—"

"What sort of magic?"

"Is the High Lord inside?" an undercommander's
voice cut through the rest, sounding almost eager. "Is it
treachery?"

"We know not Lord Evendoom's whereabouts," came
the cold reply, "and he may very well still be in the temple. Yet we very much doubt treason's involved; many

new-slain Consecrated are strewn about the gates and forechambers. Our warblades have just entered the temple, to learn what's befallen."

"So we're left with a dark choice. This is treachery, whereupon *we* must deal with it; the Hunt can't fly into a *temple!* Or it's not treachery, but rather an attack that seeks to slay the High Lord and the Consecrated together, at one stroke! This could very well be the work of the same foe this Vlakrel is fighting in the nearest Outcaverns, in which case the Hunt should be streaking into those caverns just as fast as they can fly!"

A general uproar arose, out of which came a chant of "The Hunt! The Hunt! The Hunt!"

"The Hunt, indeed!" the guardlord bellowed, his voice overriding all others. "Hasten, and give them these orders: they are to fly to the ring Lord Evendoom gave to the spellrobe Vlakrel, and exterminate any invaders they find! They are then to fly around the city, through the nearest Outcaverns, seeking to learn if we are encircled by a foe! Any sighting of a serious force of enemies must be reported back to us *at once,* before the circuit is complete, so that we may be ready for whatever gets past the Hunt! I want no glory-seeking, no reckless heroics; just savage any attackers as swiftly and mercilessly as possible!"

"And who made *you* High Lord?" the undercommander snarled. "I—"

Whatever else he'd been intending to say was lost forever, then, in his helpless dying gurgles. The guardlord's sword was sharp and handy, and his temper was even shorter than the distance to the undercommander's throat.

The three raudren had become four.

Large, muscular, and bare of armor, he must look like an inviting meal.

Inviting enough to lure the largest raudren he'd ever seen—a great gliding brute of a beast, almost twice the size of the smallest of the three who'd already been after him—to fly out of the darkness, undulating eagerly.

Eager for a meal, curse them!

Orivon growled and headed for the rocks on one side of the cavern—as fast as he could trot without sheathing either of his swords or turning his back on the beasts for an instant.

They were coming for him, diving down even now—no!

The latecomer, the fourth one, larger than the rest, was bumping the others aside!

With low growlings, or hummings, or whatever—so low-pitched that they set Orivon's teeth to rattling, inside his head, and the rocks around to clacking and clattering—the raudren disputed with each other, as the large one shouldered one after another aside, swinging back and forth in the air to do so.

Orivon reached the rocks and started dodging among them, trying to keep on fleeing just as fast as he'd been in the open cavern, to reach the greater protection of the deeply fissured cavern wall.

He turned, slipped—almost getting wedged between two boulders—and saw that largest raudren driving the others back in a swirl of bulk, tail, and fangs. They gave it reluctant room to circle once, over the cavern of Nifl and half-gorkul and Thorar only knew who else, to begin its deadly dive.

Silent and massive, it descended, gliding through the air with the other three raudren following.

"Thorar be with me," the forgefist snarled, turning and leaping the last little distance, up a slope of loose and rolling stones, to reach the deepest rock cleft. It looked *just* large enough to take his shoulders, and deep enough to get himself into, no deeper.

Hastily he backed himself into it, and braced himself with blade out, so a raudren seeking to bite him would have to impale itself. Not that so puny a steel fang would be much trouble to a raudren.

"Come, death," Orivon growled, "here I wait!"

The descending raudren loomed, large and dark, not hurrying.

Sudden shouts rang out, echoing from the far end of the cavern, and bright magic erupted with a roar in the air behind the last raudren.

The forgefist winced, shielding his eyes, and could just make out, in the fading glow of that dying magic, many Niflghar streaming into the cavern. Warblades of Ouvahlor!

"Thorar!" he swore in disgust. As if in reply, bright rays of magic sped from among the onrushing warblades, to—

Orivon slammed his forearm over his eyes, the bracer of Yathla's ongoing silence cold and hard against his nose.

—burst in a blinding brilliance that hurled torn and rent raudren, flanks blazing, spinning across the chamber in all directions.

Hey, now! Yathla of Evendoom's voice was sudden, loud, and peevish in Orivon's head.

Am I missing something?

17

Great Slaughtering Battle

For grand words and promises
Mean nothing at all
solemn treaties or none
If they are not backed
by vigilant war-readiness
And an utter lack of hesitation
in plunging into great slaughtering battles
                    —Orlkettle saying

Three ruined raudren spattered the rocks, but Orivon Firefist had no time to watch that, nor even to answer Yathla Evendoom—as the foremost, largest raudren blotted out everything in front of him, rushing in to crash against the stone wall.

The cavern-stone shook, and dust and pebbles rattled down around the forgefist as the great living darkness bulged almost to touch his face. Grimly he held tight to his two blades, thrusting into that reaching bulk lower down. He'd locked them together hilt to hilt, and then thrust them together point to point, to make them into one blade—and it sank deep as the huge raudren bit at him furiously, teeth shrieking on rock.

More stone crumbled away under its onslaught, and the raudren swished its tail furiously and slammed into the cavern wall again, hard enough to make the very stone around Orivon batter him.

What is GOING ON?

Cursing at the battering rather than answering the sharp voice in his head, Orivon pulled his swords back, close against his chest—and when the raudren drew back to deliver another blow, he sprang forward and thrust at it.

One blade sliced into the snout, and the raudren shuddered, flung its jaws wide, and rammed the wall again, seeking to swallow this elusive, paining prey.

Leaping back into the cleft just ahead of its stone-shaking arrival, Orivon sprang straight up this time, and then kicked off from the wall to launch himself *over* the snout.

He came down atop the raudren with all of his weight behind his swords, and his favorite blade plunged deep into the dark floor of flesh.

Yellow-black gore fountained—and the raudren went wild.

Again and again the great beast slammed into the cavern wall, trying to bite the source of maddening pain.

Not wanting to lose his favorite sword, Orivon hung on grimly to its hilt. During one of its drawing backs, between wall-slams, he leaned down and planted his other sword against the wall, point out and hilt against the stone. The raudren promptly slammed in again, nearly breaking his hand but impaling itself deeply on waiting warsteel.

Orivon had to let go of that sword, leaving it protruding from the raudren's snout, but clung with both hands to the hilt of his favorite blade atop the raudren as it writhed under him, twisted in pain, and then swerved out into the cavern, flying fast.

Halfway to the far wall it stopped racing along and started plunging and bucking in agony, spewing gore everywhere.

Almost blinded, Orivon kicked and bucked along

with the raging beast, his thighs and hips slamming into its hide again and again as he was flung, shaken, and twisted right along with the agonized raudren.

Raudren blood *stings*. Orivon cursed and blinked furiously, and in the end sought to wipe his face along the raudren's rough hide. He succeeded only in awakening Yathla's wordless mirth, to bubble in his mind, and bruising his nose hard against the raudren, thrice.

Suddenly the beast soared, arcing high across the cavern as Ouvahlan war-commanders below aimed spell-spewing scepters and fired at it, unleashing beams of fiery force that seared more cavern-stone than twisting, racing raudren.

The cavern wall loomed up, and the raudren abruptly veered aside, towing Orivon and trailing gore. Banking across the cavern as more ruby-red beams sprang at it, it was caught by some of their fire, and abruptly shuddered and slowed.

Sagging, the raudren veered toward a side passage of the cavern.

Scepter-fire seared the stone wall nearby, but the raudren plunged into that passage, flying more and more feebly. Clinging to the top of its snout, Orivon tried to peer ahead. In the distance, the passage curved toward the nearby light of Talonnorn, and as that light grew stronger, the raudren seemed to hesitate.

Sinking a little, it flew raggedly on, around a corner into greater light—and atop its gore-laced hide, Orivon Firefist suddenly found himself staring right down the throats of the Hunt of Talonnorn, who were rushing along the passage right toward him, hungry for blood!

In his head, Yathla Evendoom trilled bubbling, merciless laughter. *The Hunt! The Hunt, Hairy One! My revenge begins!*

"We're close to Talonnorn," Bloodblade rumbled as they crouched down in a hollow amid spears of jutting rock, Ravagers, and House Dounlar Talonar alike.

"I'm aware of that," Taerune muttered, trying not to sound as seething as she felt. She took out her Orb and glared at it. All of its stored spells were gone, but it could still cloak her from prying magic, boost her voice for far-hailing, glow if she needed light for some reason, help to boost silent thoughts to someone *very* close by—and not do Olone-spitting much more than that. It *might* serve to open a brief rift in the wards . . . or might not, depending on how much power it had left and exactly how the wards had been cast.

So against all the might of Talonnorn, flying Hunt and massed Consecrated and all, they were a one-armed outcast Talonar and a handful of Ravagers, armed to the teeth but—

"Foes!"

That warning hiss brought them both whirling around. The Ravagers amid the rock spears were tense, weapons out.

Farther down the cavern, some Niflghar had risen out of rocks that had hidden them, and were hesitantly approaching.

"Made it down here unseen!" Grunt Tusks snarled, glaring at the gorkul around him as they crouched in the concealment of the slope of rocks. "So here we stay until *I* say we show ourselves. I don't care how hungry you are. I don't care how tempting a Nifl-she strolling obliviously past may be, or a pack-snout heaped with trade-sacks. Just stay quiet and still, until my signal."

He waited, then, for the reluctant growls of agreement. They were short, faint, and long in coming, but they came.

He nodded. "These Outcaverns aren't the favored ones for large caravans; too many dangers. These rocks, for one, and the passages, there and yonder, that lead to other caverns of the ring immediately around the city-cave. Yet whether you can smell it or not, there are Nifl on the move all around us, close by. I can smell them; trust me."

He paused again, and then added menacingly, "And if trusting me is your problem, you won't have to wait for some fool of a Talonar to put steel through you. I can do it right now."

"Find out who they are," Bloodblade snapped. "Don't be too swift to slay!"

"Oondaunt," Taerune murmured, before the oncoming wanderers could get closer.

Bloodblade nodded; he'd caught sight of the Talon targe, too, showing for moments here and there on shoulders and breasts of dark battle-harness, as the wearers moved warily closer, picking their ways among rising rocks. "More refugees from your brother's happy rule, I'm guessing."

"You don't think they're a lure? Or dupes carrying fell magic?"

The fat Ravager grinned at her.

"*I'm* supposed to be the wary one, remember? If they are, they're crone-cursèd good actors. See the white around their mouths? That's hunger. Long and deep hunger."

"And they're terrified," Taerune agreed. "I think these are like the Dounlar were, only more desperate. Driven out, perhaps? Too fearful to stay in the city, too terrified to fare out into the Wild Dark and become lost, hiding from every patrol . . ."

"Talonnorn has fallen far," Bloodblade said quietly, looking toward the light of the city, "and it's falling yet. Things are going to get *really* bloody."

"Oh, he'll live," the oldest merchant promised, peering down at Jalandral Evendoom's bruised, still face.

"But—but what if he doesn't?" one of the youngest merchants blurted out anxiously. "Ondrar, we could be blamed! We—"

"Rethglar," the older trader said firmly, "we of the Araed have *always* been blamed. Yet for all the blustering cruelties of the Houses, there's still an Araed, and its merchants still *truly* run matters that matter in Talonnorn. If he dies, we have the means to make him stand and walk and talk until his flesh rots away from his bones—and then some."

He smiled a cold smile.

"By then, there will be plenty of blame to go around."

The hungry refugees were still fearful, but they had been more desperate than scared, and so had hailed those in the ring of rocks and been taken in—though Taerune noticed that several of the Ravagers Bloodblade trusted most always stood between Bloodblade and Taerune and the closest of the Oondaunts.

Some of those newcomers were trembling openly now, as Bloodblade led them to the edge of the slope of concealing rocks, closer to the city. Where he stopped, and turned to the one-armed Talonar lady.

"I'm not thinking that striding into Talonnorn to fight your brother and all his waiting, gleaming-armored warblades and softly sneering spellrobes is going to end well for us," he growled. "Do you truly intend to keep striding on now, if it means all our deaths?"

Taerune looked at him a little helplessly. "I'm . . . I couldn't get away from all these Talonar if I wanted to. But *you* could slip away, you and Arthoun and Llorgar . . ."

"No," Arthoun said sharply, from right behind them. "Too long have we skulked and clawed and cowered. If there's a chance—however slim—to topple a city's rulers and make our mark, I'm for it."

"As am I," Llorgar agreed, firmly.

"And I," another Ravager echoed. It was Hrestreen, and he was holding his drawn sword on high, as if to signal a charge.

Bloodblade shrugged, rolled his eyes, and grunted, "Well, let's all die prettily, then." He waved his sword at the way ahead, and the band of outcast Niflghar stepped out of the rocks together.

"Keep running," Oronkh growled, as Nurnra, a few steps ahead of him, twisted around to look back. "That's an Ouvahlan *army* back there, not just a raiding-band, and they're not looking friendly!"

Nurnra frowned. "There're other Nifl running this way, too, right behind us. House Oszrim warblades—just three—and a spellrobe."

"Being herded just as we are," the half-gorkul snarled. "With Talonnorn ahead and nothing between us and its cavern but yon slope of rocks—where *anything* could be hiding. Not that we can hide there, if all the Ouvahlans plunge right in, looking for us!"

"We don't need to hide that way," Nurnra panted. "We just need time enough, down in those rocks, for me to call on the best trick I have left. A cloak-shell."

"That's a *spellrobe,* back there," Oronkh reminded her sharply, "and the Ouvahlans probably have six or more spellrobes. Or Ever-Ice priestesses strong enough in spells to make up for the lack of spellrobes. Your cloak-shell will last just as long as it takes them to suspect its existen—"

"Manyfangs," Nurnra gasped, running harder, "just leave the tactics to me, and—"

"Play the large, stupid sword-swinger, one more time? While you get us both killed?"

"Uh . . . yes," the sharren replied, giving him a rueful smile, as she plunged into the rocks.

Shaking his head and growling, the half-gorkul followed her.

The next thing he heard was her startled shriek.

"Your family breeds darkwings!" the guardlord snapped, pointing at one of the High Lord's most recent appointments.

That Nifl undercommander blinked, swallowed, and admitted, "Yes."

"Good. Take four warblades who won't fall off the moment they're flying, and get out there!"

"W-where?"

"Window," the guardlord snapped, pointing. "Get to it *now!*"

The Nifl scrambled to obey.

"You saw where the Hunt went!"

"Yes."

"Can you see that cave mouth now?"

"Yes."

"Get yourself through it as fast as you can, find the Hunt, and report back here, sending just one of your warblades, each time! We need to know what's going on out there! For all we know, there are armies mustering for a charge in each and every Outcavern!"

Another officer watched the undercommander rush out, shook his head, and drawled, "Oh, I hardly think *that's* likely, Mlorel."

The guardlord shrugged. "It only takes one army, Hlard. If it's big enough and has magic enough, it only takes one."

With snarls of fury, gorkul rose out of the rocks all around Oronkh and Nurnra, swinging axes and swords. One of them, larger than the rest, swung a length of heavy chain like a flail—and if he'd been a stride closer, Oronkh's brains would have been dashed out right then and there.

Nurnra heard a frantic incantation hissed from somewhere behind her, and flung herself down, sweeping the feet out from under the gorkul who was trying to sword her as she did so. He struck his arm on the rocks and lost his sword—which was all the time Oronkh needed to draw his arm back and then plunge his own blade, with all his weight behind it, deep into that gorkul's belly, and viciously up under the squalling gorkul's ribs.

All around him, gorkul were wading and clambering among the rocks, to get close enough to him to hack—but behind him, the incantation ended on a rising note of triumph, and Oronkh flung himself on his face between two rocks as fast as he could, tugging on his blade as he did so, to swing the gore-spraying, dying gorkul over atop him.

The air above the rocks went suddenly bright blue, and then purple, as stabbing tongues of lightning raced and snarled everywhere, silhouetted gorkul convulsing and writhing.

Nurnra was crouched over, murmuring, as the lightning died, dead gorkul toppled wetly to the rocks all around, and the scorched few who still stood roared out their pain as they all flung their weapons at a single target.

Oronkh struggled out from under the gorkul he'd slain in time to see the spellrobe sway with three gorkul axes buried deeply in his head and neck, stagger up against a rock, and then fall dead over it with a long gurgle that might have held the cry, "*No,* I am Vlakrel of—" in its choking midst.

A dying spell raged briefly around his fingertips, and then faded away.

The warblades who'd been with the spellrobe tried to hasten back out of the rocks—but the foremost Ouvahlans were into the rocks by now, and sworded them mercilessly.

"Come *on,*" Nurnra hissed in Oronkh's ear, tugging at him ere diving right back down among the rocks again. Startled, he followed her—only to have her slap an open-fanged hand against his cheek, piercing it.

"Oww! What're you—"

"Bite me," she snapped, extending her forearm. "Draw blood."

Oronkh stared at her for a moment, then lifted an incredulous eyebrow, drew her arm to his lips, and bit down.

A moment later, the world seemed to grow hushed and misty gray.

"We're sharing the cloak-shell now," Nurnra hissed, tugging the arm he was holding so hard that his head slammed against a rock with dazing force. "But we've got to get out of these rocks, to where no one with a sword will run into us!"

Almost right overhead, a blackened and roaring gorkul sprang past, trailing wisps of smoke. He smashed aside an Ouvahlan blade with his own, drove his tusks viciously into that dark elf's neck, and kicked the war-blade away, tearing the neck open and drenching the rocks around with Nifl lifeblood.

Steel rang on steel and clanged on rocks all around as gorkul crashed into Ouvahlan Nifl, and over it all a great bellow rolled, "Die at last, cruel Olone-teat-suckers! I am Grunt Tusks, and *I will be your doom!*"

"No," Semmeira purred, "I do *not* think your place is down there hosting gorkul blades in your belly—though you may yet persuade me otherwise, Arothral, you may indeed."

She climbed on in the wake of the veteran she was chiding, up the narrow and rock-strewn passage that led to the lofty ledge she'd spotted, and added, "I would prefer to overlook this first battle, to best learn how these untried blades fare against a tough but un-numbered foe. I can hardly do that while I'm risking my own neck in the bloody heart of the fray, can I? Nor does my paramount task of improving myself as commander preclude my wanting to see and enjoy my first real battle. Glowstone was barely a dispute, but *this . . .*"

Arothral wisely said nothing at all.

Nor did the other two veteran Ouvahlan warblades, Helbram and Lorrel, as they all came out on the ledge. Clutching the enchanted items from the plunder of

Glowstone that she'd let them keep, they looked around alertly and kept their mouths shut.

They knew better than to dispute anything at all with the Exalted Daughter of the Ice by now.

The ledge was long and wide, narrowing some distance ahead as it met with a series of deep rents in the rock. It was high on the side wall of the cavern, overlooking the half of it that stretched away to Talonnorn—and the slope of waist-high rocks where gorkul were butchering scared and inexperienced Ouvahlan warblades as fast as they could.

"Aha," Semmeira said with real pleasure, gazing down on that slaughter. "This was worth the climb."

She pointed in Arothral's direction without looking at him and ordered, "Explore the ledge to its end, that way," and then turned to point at Lorrel, and commanded him to do the same in the other direction. She ignored Helbram, who stood uncertainly just where he'd stopped when she started giving orders, and strode to the lip of the ledge to watch the battle better.

A breath later, he exploded into wetness and bones as a blast of magic tore out of the nearest of those rock clefts, vaporizing Arothral in a sighing instant, causing Helbram to burst, and smashing Lorrel far out into the cavern, to plummet with a despairing cry.

It was Lorrel's screaming fall that Semmeira stared at, astonished—which gave Maharla Evendoom time enough to stroll leisurely out of that rock cleft, wearing a crooked and mirthless smile, and approach the Exalted Daughter of the Ice.

"I've always wanted to feel the cold embrace of the other holiness," she purred menacingly.

As the Ouvahlan whirled to face her, Maharla flung the crumbling holy scepter of Olone she'd just drained of magic with her slaying blast. It smashed aside Semmeira's fingers, intended to ruin any holy spell the priestess of the Ever-Ice might have tried to cast, but Semmeira

was too astonished to have been that quick—as Maharla
pounced on her, dagger drawn.

They struck the ledge together, hard, Maharla Evendoom on top, and grappled with each other. The priestess of Coldheart frantically lashed Maharla with a
spell, or tried to—but the holy magic sang and twinkled
around them both, only to be sucked into Maharla's
dagger.

A moment later, that dagger had slashed open the Exalted Daughter's throat—and a panting breath after that,
it had been plunged between Semmeira's ribs.

Then Maharla tried to spring clear, but Semmeira's
arms were locked tight around her as she spurted blood
in all directions, and her last spell awakened flames out
of the empty air all around them.

The dagger tried to snatch the fire into itself, but was
overwhelmed, and started melting. In the heart of those
lessened flames Maharla twisted in pain, gasping, as she
fought her way free of those failing arms—and almost
rolled off the ledge.

Almost. She lay there gasping, as the flames died
away beside her, and then rolled back atop her victim
and used the last of her strength and will to work the
spell that would shift her body into a duplicate of Semmeira's. Should any Ouvahlan come charging up here,
they would find a living priestess of Coldheart sprawled
atop a dead one . . .

In the throes of that thought, darkness claimed Maharla Evendoom.

Grunt Tusks was dying. A dozen Ouvahlan blades had
marked him, and he could feel his strength flowing out
of him along with his blood. Surrounded by hard-
breathing, glaring Nifl warblades intent on grimly hacking him apart, there was no one to aid him. All of his
fellow gorkul were dead already.

So the many-times-cursed Nifl were going to win, in
the end, after all.

"Niflghar enslaved me," he spat, lurching forward to rain sword blows down on the dark elf whose face he liked the least, ignoring the thrusting blades sliding home in his back and sides. "And now Niflghar have slain me!" He spat blood into the face of the Nifl he was fencing with, then bent his head to slam the dark elf's jaw with his tusks. As his foe staggered backward, fighting for balance, Grunt Tusks sliced open his throat with a mighty slash that carried his heavy sword right on and into the next Nifl along, smashing aside a parrying blade as it went.

"What price your army *now*?" he roared, choking on his own blood. "A few raiders are all you are now, with fear in your eyes and gorkul blood on your faces! Die, all of you, *die!*"

Three blades pierced him deeply during that last roar, but he had the satisfaction of sinking his teeth through a Nifl throat a moment later.

Then he was falling, red and roiling agony searing his innards like fire as swords slid into him again and again, and everything was darkening.

Yet even as another Nifl blade smashed his sword from his numbed hands, taking a finger or two with it, Grunt Tusks knew another satisfaction.

He smiled or tried to, as he crashed down among the rocks. Darkwings were diving out of the cavern overhead, with Nifl riders who were even now unleashing speeding bolts of fiery magic that slashed down among the rocks, sending screaming Nifl flying.

The flying Hunt of Talonnorn!

With battle-scepters in hand, they were cooking Ouvahlans as fast as they could, the darkwings wheeling like carrion-things.

The last thing Grunt Tusks saw, as the long cold darkness dragged him down forever, was scepter after scepter crumbling to dust, and their Nifl wielders casting them aside and drawing their whipswords.

He wasn't going to die unavenged . . .

18

Return of the Dark Warrior

One will come unlooked-for
One of us yet not of us
To dare the unthinkable
And do the impossible
And that one shall be known
As the Dark Warrior.
  —**old Niflghar prophecy**

The raudren was dying under him.

Sluggish and failing, it sank ever-lower; Orivon knew it wouldn't even try to evade or fight the swooping darkwings of the Hunt.

Which meant it was now a platter, displaying him as its tempting morsel. The high-nosed Nifl riders would probably not even try to resist spearing him, purely for sport, as they flew by.

So Orivon gathered himself into a crouch over the sword hilt he was using as a handle to keep himself on the raudren—his favorite sword, buried so deeply in its flesh that blood was still welling out in a steadily pumping flow—and watched the Hunt rush down on him.

He tried to look wounded and despairing, hunched and helpless—but in truth he was watching the oncoming Talonar alertly, to know which way he'd have to leap, and when.

The leader of the Hunt did not try to resist. Hefting his whipsword with a sneer, he guided his mount into a dive that would let him carve the raudren's unwanted rider in twain as he swept past.

The dying raudren did not even notice; it was slumping into its last glide, drifting toward a waiting stony grave.

The foremost Hunt rider was a young and handsome rampant—a standout even among the bred-for-beauty Talonar—and he struck a pose for the rest of the Hunt, leaning out from his saddle to dramatically cleave this lone Hairy One.

His whipsword swept in—and Orivon struck it aside with one bracer-clad forearm, and then moved like lightning.

The end of the blade, whipping around the obstacle that had parried it, sliced only empty air; the forgefist was already bounding up to catch hold of the Hunt leader's elbow.

Driving iron-hard fingers into that elbow and swinging himself up in a great heave, Orivon came crashing down on the Nifl's torso and legs, breaking them. The shrieking dark elf lost his blade, spasming and writhing in helpless pain—and the forgefist ruthlessly shoved him out of the saddle and took his place, hauling on the reins to bring the hissing darkwings around and up, just as the second Hunt rider came hurtling down to hack at him.

The two darkwings crashed together in midair with teeth-jarring force, becoming in an instant a tangled chaos of wings, claws, and necks.

Together the beasts and their riders tumbled into the cavern wall, Orivon snarling in pain as wild wings buffeted him and he clung grimly to the saddle's high cantle so hard he thought his fingers would sink into its metal.

The force of smiting the unyielding stone rebounded the two darkwings out into the air again, flapping and calling wildly. Still tangled together, they fell like a cavern rock—straight down, to collide with the third onrushing darkwings of the Hunt in a bone-shattering *smash*.

Orivon had a brief glimpse of a snarling Nifl face, eyes glittering with hatred. Then the bracer on his arm quivered once—and that face burst into flames and started howling in astonished agony.

Yes.

Yathla Evendoom sounded deeply satisfied as she made the bracer on Orivon's arm spit fire into the face of the other Hunt rider, who tried to scream but managed only to vocalize a loud sizzling as that tongue of flame slammed into his open mouth and out the back of his head, with force enough to drive him out of his saddle. The rider Yathla had attacked first, now a flopping corpse beheaded with fire, toppled from his saddle, too.

Shorn of their riders, two of the three entangled darkwings started to flap and claw in earnest, seeking only to win free. One was too badly broken to fly on its own, and tumbled helplessly toward the cavern floor—falling free of Orivon's struggling mount.

That darkwings suddenly soared high and far, seeking only to get far away from entanglements. Finding itself about to smash into a hard and endless rock ceiling, it panicked, frantically rolled onto its side to turn as sharply as any darkwings can, and hurled itself back toward Talonnorn, diving fast.

Which took it behind the rest of the Hunt, shielding Orivon from the sudden volley of magic that then erupted, as the fearful, shouting Ouvahlan survivors unleashed all of the plundered Glowstone magic they had.

The priestess who'd led them and her three veterans, their commanders, had borne the best magic, but even strong Nifl can wear only so many scepters—and one of the veterans, Lorrel, had fallen from on high to land dead and bloodily broken behind their ranks; some of his scepters had survived the fall that had slain him.

None of the surviving Ouvahlans believed they'd be allowed to keep any magic they'd gained if they returned to Ouvahlor—and if they didn't call on that magic now, they'd never make it home in the first place. So anything that looked as if they might be able to awaken it, and if its magic could be used as a weapon, saw use.

The cavern blazed with a dozen vivid magical fires. One hapless Ouvahlan was propelled screaming into the midst of the Hunt, riding a jet of scepter-born flame that sent him smashing into the belly of a darkwings and then tumbling, broken-limbed, to the cavern floor far below.

All the rest, however, unleashed battle-magic with passable aim, desperately sending a volley of bright-lancing spells that burned and blasted the Hunt, reducing it to spinning, flaming chunks of darkwings and Niflghar.

Not a Talonar-ridden darkwings survived.

By then, beyond that conflagration, Orivon's terrified mount was roaring out its terror of all the magic bursting in the air or racing past it in bright, deadly beams. Its dive almost brought it crashing into the cavern floor, but it soared wildly aloft at the last instant to avoid doing so—and slammed full-tilt into a very hard and jagged cave sidewall.

Headless in an instant, it sagged and then bounced brokenly down that rock face, leaving a bruised and stunned Orivon to roll free just before it crashed to rest on the jagged edge of the cavern floor.

The forgefist rolled, bounced, and then rolled again . . . right into the path of the heartened Ouvahlans, as they roared obedience to the sudden shouts of Semmeira, Exalted Daughter of the Ever-Ice, and charged forward. Heading for Talonnorn . . . and for a lone, dazed Hairy One, lying on the cavern floor a few paces closer to them than the feebly thrashing, dying remains of the darkwings he'd ridden in on.

"Onward, for glory!" the priestess cried from the ledge

above and behind them, in a grand voice that rolled into and through their heads, and echoed around the cavern like thunder.

"The Sacred Ever-Ice commands that Talonnorn be conquered, and shall shield you and enfeeble your foes, that this may happen! You shall bring glory upon yourselves and upon Ouvahlor, and win great honor and rewards from the Holy Ice itself! It has been ordained! You *shall* prevail! So onward! Let Talonnorn fall to your swords—*Talonnorn!*"

"*Talonnorn!*" the Ouvahlans roared back, waving their swords, and started running.

On the ledge, Maharla Evendoom stood with hands on hips, smiling, watching the Ouvahlan warblades running hard away from her, to Talonnorn; from up here, she could *just* see a tiny glimpse of the city in the distance.

She let herself enjoy the moment for two breaths, no more, before starting the long climb back down from the ledge.

Beautiful, just beautiful.

The enchanted belt that had broadcast her voice on high, and unleashed the spell that heartened and inflamed the minds of the few Ouvahlans she had left, had been Semmeira's. Obviously prepared beforehand by the priestesses of Coldheart, it had worked flawlessly.

It still had those useful magics, too, leaving Maharla to ponder whether she should discard it, as it could readily be used to trace her and might well contain the means to magically slay or influence her from afar—or keep it, so that she could again inspire the Ouvahlans, and cry orders to them and be heard.

Well, it wouldn't hurt to go on wearing it at least until she was safely back down on the cavern floor . . .

She clambered down a bit, skidded on loose scree, caught at projecting rock until she'd slowed herself, and clambered some more.

Slightly clumsy, but then, she was wearing a shape not her own. She looked exactly like Semmeira, of course, and the real Semmeira was now smoking ashes on the ledge behind her.

It had taken one of the most powerful spells she knew, and all the force of will she could furiously muster, to force her way into the dying mind of the priestess.

Nor had that poisonous, furious, dying mind yielded her much. She now knew Semmeira's name, that she had been an Exalted Daughter of the Ice—*the* Exalted Daughter, for a long time—of Coldheart, and that Semmeira hated and feared a younger priestess, Lolonmae, who had been named her superior, the Revered Mother. She had seen several views of Lolonmae's face as Semmeira had remembered her, before the Exalted Daughter's mind had faded entirely into darkness.

Now Maharla was mind-weary, and weighed down with the grimness of holding intimately to a mind as it darkened into death. Yet she was still physically strong, revenge just might be within her grasp, and she didn't *think* Semmeira of the Ever-Ice had managed to creep into her mind and hide there, awaiting a chance to strike and conquer.

Orivon blinked. Where—?

Oh. Aye. By Thorar, he'd best get up!

And do it now! He could hear the thunder of running Nifl feet, and knew a score or more Ouvahlan warblades were running toward him with swords in their hands and murder in their minds . . . but he just couldn't . . .

Orivon clenched his teeth, shoved feebly at the ground, and then *heaved.*

Only to find himself wavering, half up. He'd raised himself on one hand, his lower half still sprawled . . . but he wasn't facing the Ouvahlans.

He was staring into the brightness of Talonnorn—where what looked like a slaving caravan, mustering for its journey out into the Dark, were all standing staring back at him, Nifl masters and lines of chained human slaves alike.

Not that he, Orivon, was all that astonishing a sight.

They were really staring in disbelief at the battle raging just outside the city-cave, at the Hunt spell-blasted to ribbons before their eyes, gorkul fighting Nifl before that, and now a line of charging Ouvahlan warblades. Charging *their* way.

Brith, Reldaera . . . he *had* to get up, had to move before a dozen Ouvahlans gleefully carved him . . . Aumril . . . Kalamae!

Growling, Orivon shoved at the stone cavern floor, kicked, reeled, and was up, staggering toward the dark bulk of the dead darkwings. The running, shouting Ouvahlans sounded very close . . .

There was suddenly a hand right in front of him, in midair, reaching forth to him as if in greeting. As if in aid.

It was a Nifl hand, but the strongest, fattest-fingered Nifl hand Orivon had ever seen. It was . . . it was a gorkul hand, with the hue and nails of a Niflghar hand!

And it was almost touching him, reaching out for his forearm, to grasp and haul, reaching out of a thin, dark rent in the air itself!

Orivon had no sword, and no time nor stumbling balance to reach to see if he still had a knife left. He couldn't hack this hand away, nor stab its owner . . .

He shrugged, reached out, and took the hand.

A moment later, he was being tugged forward into dark and swirling chaos, as a female Nifl voice said, "—much too useful to just let him be killed. *This* Hairy One could be not just my sustenance, henceforth; he could be the slave to overmatch all slaves—or a useful ally, out in the Dark. But we've got to *move*; this cloak-shell won't last long. You'll have to carry—"

As strong arms that smelled of sweaty Nifl closed around Orivon, the darkness swallowed him—and closed behind him.

* * *

The false priestess frowned as she came down through the rocks to the cavern floor—and then stiffened, as something unfolded in her mind. For a moment she felt icy fear, thinking Semmeira *did* live on, in her mind, and was revealing herself now to doom Maharla.

Then, with a gasp of relief, she relaxed. It was merely this belt—and the belt alone, with no hint at all of any sinister sentience at work from afar, through it—attuning itself to a new wearer, and informing her of what it could do, aside from clinging flatteringly to her hips, inflaming Ouvahlan armies, and deafening everyone nearby with her orders.

Its magics could also make her invisible, and awaken short-lived, parrying shields if she was beset by sword-swinging foes.

Well, now. Better and better.

She made herself invisible and strolled on down the cavern. She would be safest among her Ouvahlan warriors, inexperienced as they were, but she wasn't going to run to keep up with them.

She was now, after all, an Exalted Daughter of the Ever-Ice.

Orivon blinked.

He was still in the cavern, yet he was not.

He was in a hushed, gray-hued place that he could see through the walls of, could see the Ouvahlans storming past—and storming *through* where he stood.

Or sagged, actually, half falling, with those strong arms firmly around him and dragging him back and away from the dead darkwings and all running Ouvahlans. He groaned, shaking his head to try to clear it. Aye, that was why he was staggering and off-balance . . . that and the fall down the rocks from the dying darkwings.

"Come *on*," that female Nifl spoke again, from behind his head, on the far side of this half-Nifl, half-gorkul's body. "Bring him."

Bouncing and jouncing in the grasp of his puffing,

staggering savior—or perhaps captor—Orivon could see the Ouvahlan warblades rush to the end of the cavern and into Talonnorn, where the chained lines of men were trying to turn and flee, and the slave-masters were shouting and cracking whips frantically, before it was too—

Late.

The Ouvahlans slammed right into the midst of the slaves, hacking and thrusting gleefully. The slaves screamed, staggered helplessly in their chains, and died.

The Ouvahlans shouted triumphantly, rushed over the line of slaves they'd butchered, and headed for the next line, as the slave-traders abandoned their doomed wares and fled, sprinting hard.

"No!" Orivon shouted. "*No!*"

He twisted in the arms that held him, and shoved hard against a vest-covered rib cage. "Murdering Nifl!" he roared, and twisted again, free of the half-gorkul's grasp.

Who was staggering—and now falling over a slender Nifl-she behind him, as she scrambled unsuccessfully in the clinging grayness to try to get out of his way. They both fell to the ground; the half-gorkul was too winded from hauling a large, strong human to do anything to stop the Hairy One as Orivon pounced on him, snatched half a dozen knives from sheaths all over the fallen half-breed, whirled around, and burst through the gray walls, out of the conjured hideaway, racing after the Ouvahlans.

Nurnra cried out in pain as her spell was torn apart, and rolled out from under Oronkh with a soft curse, wincing and clutching at her head.

"So much for keeping the Hairy One from getting himself killed," she said sharply, as she helped the gasping Oronkh to sit up.

Then she stiffened, dug slender fingers into his shoulder to get his attention, and pointed back up the cavern. "Manyfangs! I'm thinking our own necks are at risk, now—*look!*"

Oronkh looked where she was pointing, and decided it was his turn to curse softly.

The high ledge whence the priestess had so thunder-ously commanded her Ouvahlans—and where was she now?—was occupied once more.

In a twinkling of fading yet still-blossoming spell-lights, a tall Niflghar spellrobe had just appeared, and was standing staring down the cavern toward Talonnorn.

"Oh, *dung*," Oronkh added, almost in a whisper, and Nurnra nodded silent agreement.

Taerune Evendoom took one long look out into the bright cavern that held Talonnorn, then turned her head and commanded softly, "Now!"

Bloodblade rose out of his crouch beside her with the softest of growls. Then he and Arthoun and Llorgar were all running hard, out into the light.

None of them shouted or spoke; their only noise was the faint clatterings of bouncing metal as Ravagers ran in mismatched armor. Swords flashing, as silently as possi-ble, with the one-armed Talonar lady sprinting along in their midst, Taerune's little band burst out of their narrow cavern, through a bloody chaos of slaughtered human slaves, to crash into the Ouvahlan flank.

Orivon Firefist never slowed.

When he reached the fray of Nifl battling Nifl, he carved his way through it without slowing. With swift, brutal efficiency he stabbed or sliced any nightskin in his path, not really looking at them. He was heading for the surviving, fearfully staring chained slaves.

Some of whom recognized him.

"The Dark Warrior!" a cry arose.

"Dark Warrior!" another shouted, and was echoed by still more.

Orivon waved a knife at them in salute—and sprinted right past them, calling back, "Swing your chains like whips! Defend yourselves!"

Ahead, he could see the Nifl caravan-masters fleeing back to the city. He put his head down and ran faster.

The moment one of them looked back, he roared, "Come back! Free your slaves or die!"

The Nifl stared at him in terror, and ran even faster.

The most powerful spellrobe of Ouvahlor—probably the mightiest Nifl spellrobe there had ever been, let us be honest about such things—stood and watched Nifl-ghar pour out of nowhere to attack what was left of Semmeira's band of bumblers.

Defenders, of course. Talonnorn would never be undefended. Who could possibly think otherwise?

Yet there, in front of his eyes, were Ouvahlan fools aplenty who would never live to become warblades, rushing forward like children pursuing a prize.

Klarandarr shook his head. They had been dupes from the first, unwitting sacrifices to Talonnorn—but to not even defend themselves, or expect the obvious!

As the last winking lights of his arrival faded around his feet, he glanced up and down the ledge again. The charred Nifl body lay just as it had since his first sight of it. Nor had anything else moved or changed.

Good.

He looked past the distant fighting Nifl this time, to coldly survey Talonnorn and so appraise his location. It took him only a moment to announce aloud, to himself, "This will serve."

It was a bad habit, he knew, but when one is always alone, trusting no one, who else does one have to speak to?

Smiling faintly—after all, he felt only a touch of ruefulness—Klarandarr drew two palm-sized gems from separate pouches on his belt. Extending his arms up and spread before him, he let go of them.

Rather than falling to shatter or bounce on the ledge, the two gems hung in midair and commenced to glow, pulsing slightly.

Taking a step back from them, so he was almost

touching the curving cavern wall, he unhurriedly began to cast many powerful, crackling spells to link the gems.

Lines of humming golden spell-glows built in the air around him as he worked. It seemed like no time at all before he was crafting the last one.

Then, and only then, he looked beyond his work again, to where the fighting was still going on.

"The distraction has worked," he murmured in satisfaction. "The force led by the foolish priestess has drawn forth the Hunt and shattered it, and they themselves are now beset and distracted. Leaving Klarandarr, and Klarandarr alone, to humble Talonnorn utterly."

He smiled tightly, gestured—and the lines of force all turned to hungry blue-white flame.

Luelldar suddenly stiffened, above a whorl that lit his face with sudden fire.

"Klarandarr!" he announced. "Aloun, you'll be needing new whorls, three at least; play them off this one. Quickly. We need to see what he's intending to hurl his spells against."

"Why, Talonnorn, of course," Aloun exclaimed, reaching out to bring new whorls into being.

The Senior Watcher of Ouvahlor gave him a look of disgust. "So much is obvious. Our task is to observe with a little more precision. After all, if I told you to keep an eye on Ouvahlor, would you just use your whorls to stare at our walls from a distance?"

"No, I'd try to spy on Coldheart, right away," Aloun chirped.

"And what success have we had, trying to see into the altar with Olone's risen power streaming out of it?"

"Oh. Ah. I see your point."

Luelldar rolled his eyes. "Progress," he observed with a sigh. "Solid progress. I suppose."

* * *

Klarandarr smiled at the ready, risen force of his magic, and at what he could see of Talonnorn, and calmly said the single, soft word that unleashed *the* spell.

The dark towers of Talonnorn loomed taller and taller quite quickly; Orivon was in a hurry. He needed to catch these slavers before they—

Sudden blue-white flames erupted among those towers, bursting out of nowhere to roar toward the roof of the cavern. Blinding, hungry, crackling with force—if not heat—that he could feel on his face, even this far away.

The fleeing Nifl ahead skidded to various uncertain halts, aghast—and Orivon pounced on them, spun them around with ungentle hands, and snarlingly ordered them to go back and unlock the fetters of their slaves.

"B-but they'll kill us!" a slaver wailed, waving at the raging battle back at the cavern's edge.

"*I* will kill you if you don't," Orivon snarled, afire with fresh fury. "Right here and right now!"

He was suddenly trembling with rage—what if the four children he'd come for were burning right now, in those flames?—and leaned forward to slash at the one slaver who'd started to sneer and draw steel.

His swift, deft slash sliced a finger off that Nifl's sword hand.

The bracer on his arm quivered then, as Yathla silently made it spit warning beams of flame, little lines of fire that winked out menacingly right in front of each slaver's nose.

Moaning in fear, the Nifl all obeyed him, turning back toward the chained slaves.

19

Talonnorn in Peril

Yet for all their doomsaying
I cannot believe that in my lifetime
Talonnorn shall ever be in peril.
Yet given the sneering weaklings
Who lord it over Houses now
If ever I die defending my city
Then Talonnorn will be in peril.
    —legendary Talonar saying,
    attributed to Aumdryn Maulstryke

Klarandarr of Ouvahlor raised one hand to gesture, eyes on the flames roaring up out of Talonnorn.

With a flourish, he made an intricate sign in the air . . . then frowned. He repeated the gesture, with great precision this time, omitting the flourish.

His frown deepened. The distant flames hadn't moved where he'd directed them to; it was as if he was using no magic at all.

After a moment, he shrugged, and set about casting another spell, taking great care over its crafting. Done and fine.

He raised his hand and made the gesture again. Then again, irritation sharpening into anger in his eyes. There was still no response.

He let his anger spill out of his mouth in a wordless

hiss, then slowly smiled, shrugged, and murmured, "Well, getting blood on one's hands is always more satisfying."

Spell-lights blossomed around his feet—and he was gone from the ledge.

"On," Orivon snapped, pointing at the battle raging back at the edge of the cavern, "and if any of you are thinking of running off in side directions, be well aware that I can throw these. Quite well."

He waggled the knife meaningfully, and then waved both of his arms energetically, as if he could sweep the slavers back to the fray. Fearfully, they started to hasten.

Neither they nor the lone human driving them on saw the figure that suddenly appeared right behind them, on the stretch of cavern floor they'd just left, but facing in the other direction.

The moment Klarandarr's boots were on the cavern floor rather than the high ledge of another cavern, he was walking toward Talonnorn. As he strode along, he gestured again, and some of the many tongues of flame obeyed him.

With the very beginnings of a smile playing about his lips, the greatest spellrobe in all Niflheim walked on.

As suddenly and silently as he had appeared, the sinister spellrobe was gone from the ledge.

"*Come,*" Nurnra hissed fiercely, "before anyone *else* decides to appear up there, and block our retreat. We have an urgent appointment somewhere out there in the Wild Dark."

The half-gorkul beside her hastened along willingly, but did rumble, " 'Somewhere'? Where, exactly?"

"Anywhere that's far from Talonnorn," the sharren replied crisply, "and keeping it will probably also mean keeping our lives. *Hurry.*"

Trotting along beside her, Oronkh interrupted his huffing long enough to reply, "I *am* hurrying, Softfingers!"

They were most of the way back down the cavern when Nurnra slowed suddenly and pointed off to the side, among the Nifl corpses lying sprawled and silent, among much blood.

"That was a scepter, once," she said, stepping over to look down at the broken, fallen body of the Nifl hurled off the ledge by Maharla's scepter-blast. "I wonder if any magic has survived?"

"I thought we were fleeing for our lives," Oronkh growled sourly.

"We were," she replied brightly, "but perhaps this is far enough!"

"You," he said accusingly, rolling a body over to see if it had any salvageable magic, "are going to get us killed. Quite possibly soon."

Nurnra's large, liquid eyes flashed with wry mirth. "*How* long have you been saying that?" she asked tartly.

"Ho, Firefist!" Bloodblade called as Orivon and his reluctant handful of Nifl reached the fray. "Come to lend a hand? Plenty of foes for all!"

"Many hands, I hope!" Orivon shouted back, before curtly ordering the slavers, "Free them."

A few of the slavers had swords or daggers out, and all of them were now wavering uncertainly. Under the forgefist's menacing glower they burst into sudden activity, grabbing for the keys at their belts and frantically starting to unlock chains.

"Grab every weapon you can find, and fight!" Orivon barked at the slaves as they stared at him. "Strike at yon targe of Ouvahlor wherever you see it, and at others only if they strike at you! Fight to see the sun again!"

"The sun!" one slave—a man so emaciated he looked more like a skeleton draped in hairy skin than a living human—sobbed.

"The sun!" another roared exultantly, and swung the length of chain he'd just been freed from viciously, felling an Ouvahlan.

Then he dropped that improvised lash in a rattling instant, and pounced on the stunned Nifl. Snatching the dark elf's dagger from its sheath, he stabbed its former owner viciously and repeatedly.

Even before the Ouvahlan sagged onto his face, slack mouth leaking a river of gore, the freed slave sprang up with a triumphant roar, waving that bloody dagger.

Slaves around him roared back their approval and bloodlust, causing the still-unlocking slavers to cower away. Finding Orivon standing right behind them with a wide and menacing smile on his face, they fearfully stepped forward again.

Aside from the forgefist, Bloodblade and two Ravagers—one of them wounded—were the only Nifl still living who'd fought their way right through the Ouvahlans, to reach what was left of the slaves.

Which meant they and Orivon were all that stood between the Ouvahlans and outright butchery of the slaves, if the Ouvahlans decided to undertake such a slaughter. At the moment, however, what was left of the army of Ouvahlor was thinking about anything but slaves. They were worried about who had crashed into them from behind, and hadn't charged right through them, but were still hacking and thrusting at them far too energetically to be ignored for an instant: the main body of Ravagers and House Dounlar Nifl, plus a certain one-armed, outcast noble Talonar lady Orivon hadn't noticed yet.

One slaver went down with his own knife driven hard into his neck, but Orivon bellowed at the other slaves to leave the slavers alone. If the fools slew all the slavers before they were freed, Thorar knew if he'd have time and chances enough to find all the right keys and where to put them, with this battle raging and Talonar defenders likely to show up at any murderous moment.

Most of the slaves were only too happy to claw, punch, and stab at anything wearing the targe of Ouvahlor; the rest cowered. Orivon let the slavers run off again, as the last slave-chains rattled to the ground; if they spread word and fear in Talonnorn, with that fire already raging, all the better; a city in chaos was easier for one lone forgefist to invade than one armed, ready, organized, and calm.

Snarling or shrieking out their rage, the human slaves went to war, as Talonnorn burned behind them.

Jalandral Evendoom sat grimly in a cellar as breathless Talonar merchant after breathless Talonar merchant brought word to him. All babbled excited variations on the same news: magical flames "out of nowhere" were raging all over the city.

Still drenched in sweat, Jalandral's mood was dark, even though he'd just been wholly and painlessly restored to health, by means of healing stones provided by the Araed merchants who'd rescued him.

He shook his head. "What *now*? Some fool of a spellrobe is doubtless doing this, to try to seize rule over Talonnorn on behalf of his House, but I must finish off the Consecrated while—"

"No," the old merchant Ondrar snapped. "Stop the flames."

Jalandral stared at him. "But I don't even know—"

"Stop them, Lord," Ondrar ordered, several others nodding in silent unison. "*This* is why we kept you alive."

Jalandral sprang up, and started to pace. "I need Klaerra," he snarled. "I don't even know *how* to trace spellrobes, if they're not actually working a magic when I go looking for them. And what if I'm seeking the wrong villain entirely? What if the fires *are* mischief of the Consecrated? I need—"

The old merchant held up a hand to stop him, right in Jalandral's face. While the High Lord was blinking at it, he turned his head and gave a calm order to three other merchants. "Bring them."

As those traders hurried out, Ondrar turned back to Jalandral. "Sit, High Lord," he commanded, without a hint of irony. "Compose yourself. Look regal."

Jalandral barely had time to make his face calm again before the three merchants returned, dragging a trio of young, frightened priestesses who bore bruises and fresh blood; one of them was bleeding freely enough to leave a thin trail in her wake. All were tightly chained and gagged, and all were weeping with pain and fear. The merchants handled them without respect for holy rank or gender, and halted them in a line facing Jalandral, upright, holding them upright by firm grips on the backs of their necks.

Ondrar stepped up to the three young Consecrated, gave them each a glare, then waved at the seated High Lord of Talonnorn.

"Tell him what he needs to know, and answers to what he asks," he ordered, "and speak no spell nor call upon holy aid, or we will *rend* you!"

Through their gags, the priestesses could be heard to weep in fresh and energetic earnest, but they did manage to nod, one after another, and their gags were sliced off.

The old merchant gestured, and each priestess was borne to the floor by her handler, and made to kneel facing Jalandral. The merchants then sat on the lower legs of the Consecrated and bent the priestesses back over their laps, so that each frightened she was arched over backward—with their captors holding daggers to their throats.

Jalandral avoided delay, threats, and pleasantries, but merely started asking questions. "Are these flames your doing, or the work of any Consecrated of Olone?" he snapped.

Shapely throats swallowed. "N-no."

"Then who?"

There was fresh weeping, and when Jalandral roared, *"Well?"* One of the priestesses dared to whisper that she could not tell, that none of them could, without casting holy spells.

"No," Ondrar snapped.

"Yes," Jalandral snapped right back at him. *"I* am Lord here, Lord of Talonnorn—and Talonnorn stands in peril! All else must be set aside and ignored in the face of our paramount need to defend our city!"

The oldest merchant stared at him with cold, suspicious eyes for a long, long time before turning to glare at the Consecrated who'd spoken.

When he replied to her, every word was cold and hard and flat, like a stone dropped to earth.

"Cast your spell."

Orivon Firefist was ducking and twisting in the heart of a clanging, thrusting storm of deadly steel—and he was happier than he'd been in a long time.

Slaying anyone or anything didn't please or excite him, but harming Niflghar, and thwarting their causes and their arrogant rule over anywhere, *that* pleased him deeply.

Though he hated Talonnorn and all its ways with a burning, unfailing passion, he was enough of a Talonar to hate rival Ouvahlor, too—and here were Ouvahlan warblades within reach of the blades he'd forged, and standing up to him. Earlier it had seemed as if they were on the verge of fleeing, disheartened by the ruthless yet merry efficiency of the handful of attacking Ravagers, but now something—probably something magical—was making every last one of them glare with eyes that burned with zeal, and attack with an alacrity and a ferocity Orivon had never seen anywhere before.

Ravagers were dying, now, and though it seemed to the forgefist as if he'd felled far too many Ouvahlans for any still to be standing, he was beset on three sides and being forced back, step by step, toward the heaped corpses of the slaves who'd died still in their chains.

A warblade almost as tall as Orivon—now *there* was a rarity!—came leaping in at him, heedless of other darting Nifl blades, and Orivon managed to set the blade in his right hand ready against his own thigh *just* in time.

As Orivon parried the tall Ouvahlan's sword with the sword in his left hand, the charging Nifl impaled himself on the ready sword, shrieked in astonished pain, and clawed at the forgefist in agony as he started to writhe and fall. To keep at least one blade aloft to defend himself with, Orivon kicked out with his leg and twisted, swinging the dying Nifl around in front of him as a barrier whose thrashings forced the other Ouvahlans pressing Orivon into stepping back or stumbling and falling themselves.

Orivon shed the tall Ouvahlan—who was now struggling to gurgle up blood and scream at the same time, and was managing a horrible wet choking sound—from his blade with a jerk, and stepped back forcefully, to gain himself some room.

His hip bumped solidly against someone else's, and as he twisted to hack at whoever it was, his sword was caught right at the guards by another blade, and Orivon found himself staring into the face of—Taerune Evendoom.

He faltered for a moment in astonishment, during which her fierce grin at him turned to a look of alarm directed over his shoulder. Then she flung the blade in her hand, and Orivon whirled around in time to see the Nifl she'd flung it into the face of staggering backward and jostling the Ouvahlan beside him off-balance, too. Which left just the one on Orivon's extreme left to deal with in an instant, so he did.

When he turned back to Taerune, she was two or three paces away, fencing with the blade he'd made and affixed to the stump of her left forearm, a seeming lifetime ago, and snatching opportunities to peer back in his direction.

Their eyes met.

"You seem astonished to see me," she called cheerfully. "Is it so surprising to see a Nifl in the very cavern of her city?"

Orivon lunged forward, ducking under the sweeping

sword of an Ouvahlan, and drove the tip of his own blade into that warblade's throat. Even before the blood started to fountain, he'd thrust his other blade into the throat of the Ouvahlan who'd fallen underfoot. Snatching up Taerune's fallen sword, he turned and tossed it back to her, flipping it so that it spun through the air and bit deeply into the back of an Ouvahlan corpse lying right in front of her, quivering upright for her to easily snatch.

"I . . ." He groped for words, not making the mistake of stopping fighting this time. Still burning-eyed, the Ouvahlans were beginning to falter; was the magic that was driving them starting to fade?

"I did not think I would see you again," Orivon finally said, between clanging sword blows. "Alive."

Taerune did not seem pleased.

"Such confidence," she called scornfully. "And after so many Nifl died so that you could return to your precious Blindingbright, you stand here in Talonnorn *again?* Have Hairy Ones taken to raiding Nifl cities, now?"

"Something like that," Orivon snapped as a wave of Ouvahlans charged forward from behind the ones he was killing. "Something like that."

Then the Ouvahlans were surging forward on all sides, in a wave of murderous Nifl, and Orivon and Taerune were too busy frantically hacking, ducking, parrying, and dancing about to say anything at all.

The forgefist thought hazily that if he could get back to Taerune and they could make a stand back to back, that would be one less direction he'd have to defend in, so that was the direction he tried to wade in, slipping and sliding on bodies as Ouvahlans raged around him, seeking to turn him into one more corpse underfoot.

He wasn't going to make it.

There were just too many blades coming at him, too many—

The bracer on his arm quivered, and six or seven bright tongues of flame lashed out, at as many Ouvahlan faces. Their owners cried out in startled pain, blades going wide or pulling back entirely—and the bracer quivered again.

For Talonnorn! Yathla Evendoom cried, in Orivon's head. *For Evendoom! Get to her, man! Get to her!*

More fire lashed out in front of Orivon, and there was room for him to run. Run he did, barely noticing when the bracer quivered again and fire arced around behind him, to immolate a Nifl who was racing after him, and gathering for a spring and pounce. That Ouvahlan dropped his dagger and fell, howling—and Orivon raced on, bursting through a ring of Ouvahlans who'd just slain two Ravagers and were pressing in around Taerune. Flames snarled and spat from the forgefist's bracer as he came, fire that hurled back startled Ouvahlans and gave Orivon the moments and space he needed to reach Taerune's side.

As he did so, sliding on fallen blades and blood, the bracer on his arm sighed and started to crumble.

Make me proud, human! Orivon Firefist, be my champion! Fight for Yathla Evendoom!

A sudden ring of fire encircled Orivon's arm, blackened metal falling away from him like dust, and then roared away into the heart of the Ouvahlans—and burst, hurling burning bodies in all directions.

Orivon flung himself between Taerune and the blast, to shield her, and for a moment it seemed like she might collapse against him. She sighed, hunched down—and then shook her head, flung it up briskly, and announced, "We're not done yet. There are plenty of Ouvahlans left still, to—"

"Is someone going to tell me," Bloodblade shouted to them then, across the fray, "why we seem to be defending Talonnorn against Ouvahlor? Surely we can just fight our way to the side and let them swarm the city?"

Orivon frowned as he met the blade of the foremost advancing Ouvahlan, struck it aside, and then booted the Nifl, sending him staggering into the sharp embrace of Taerune's blade. Reaching for the next Ouvahlan as the outcast Nifl lady beside him slew the first, he called back, "You're right, Ravager. As usual. Shall we take ourselves yonder, toward the cavern wall?"

"Yes!" Bloodblade roared enthusiastically, and waved his hands at the Ravagers around him, to signal such a retreat.

Trying to do the same with the slaves, Orivon caught sight of a slender Nifl-she at the rear of the Ouvahlans—a she who strode about with the air of command, and who was, just now, glaring at Taerune as if her eyes could deal painful and immediate death.

"Is that their commander?"

Taerune thrust the blade he'd fashioned to replace her hand into another Ouvahlan throat, peered at the glaring Ouvahlan, and replied, "Could well be. That's a priestess, or I'm a sleeth!"

Yet the Ouvahlans were already scrambling away from the Hairy Ones and Ravagers who were slaughtering them with such ease, and shouting in relief and triumph. Bursting past the Ravagers and freed human slaves as if they feared this sudden path to Talonnorn would be snatched away from them if they tarried, they started running across the cavern toward the burning city.

The glaring female hesitated, and then trotted with them, as if reluctantly deciding she dared not tarry to fight the Ravagers and humans alone.

"Spread out," Bloodblade commanded hurriedly, eyeing the Ouvahlan as she turned to glare at them all again. "That one can hurl spells! Spread out, so she has no clear foe to smite!"

"Gethkyl," Taerune snapped at a nearby Ravager Nifl, "watch yon priestess, and call out if you see her turn back, or use magic to disappear. We don't want her back on that ledge—or anywhere else—readying magic against us!"

"She has disappeared already," Gethkyl replied grimly.

*   *   *

The cellar rocked and shuddered a second time, a deep, rolling boom that sent ceiling slabs tumbling, dust showering down, and Nifl staggering.

"What traitor of a spellrobe is hurling blasting spells?" Jalandral snapped, eyes blazing. "Is any part of the Eventowers still standing?"

The first priestess to finish a spell looked up at him with eyes that were spilling tears, and hissed, "This is no traitor spellrobe of Talonnorn, but a stranger—just one!—who is blasting down the towers that hold any Talonar spellrobe who dares to cast spells at him! *He* is the source of the flames!"

Jalandral sneered. "Come, come! *One* spellrobe is doing all this?"

There came another thunderous tremor then, followed by a crash that drowned out the tearful "Yes, but we know not who" replies of several Consecrated.

"Yes," one of the Araed merchants said firmly to Jalandral, pointing to the fading, sinking scrying eye one of the priestesses had conjured, "one spellrobe—and I know him. I have been on many caravans faring to and from Ouvahlor, and that is Klarandarr. Said by many to be the most powerful spellrobe ever."

"We are doomed," the old merchant Ondrar decreed, and there was general grim agreement—except from the caravan merchant, who took a step toward Jalandral.

"Unless our High Lord has hidden away any clever and ready stratagems, or magical tricks of the much-vaunted Houses of Talonnorn? You have another Hunt lurking up your backside, perhaps?"

"No," Jalandral snarled at him, "just magic items dozens of us would have to give our lives wielding. Klarandarr can slay most of us as we run to just try to get to the right places to blast him—while he uses magic to take himself from here to there to here again, at will. We . . ."

Then his face changed. "Another Hunt!" he repeated fiercely.

"You have *another* Hunt?" Ondrar asked, in disbelief. "*How* long were you preparing to seize pow—"

Jalandral sprang across the room, took him by the arms, and shook him. "The dung-worms! We can do as Ouvahlor did; that much the crones and priestesses *can* do for us! We can bury him in dung-worms!"

He waved at the merchants, and then pointed at the priestesses. "Free them, and bring them!"

Wary eyebrows arched. "Where?"

"To find the crone Klaerra Evendoom," Jalandral snapped. "The spell that masters many worms at once requires the caster's life—and she owes me hers, thrice over and more!"

Suddenly, everyone was on the move, and the cellar emptied in the space of two swift breaths—except for Ondrar, the eldest merchant of the Araed, who stared at the High Lord's back as it dwindled in Jalandral's haste to be elsewhere, and murmured, "Does she feel that way? I wonder. And who considers that you owe them *your* life, Jalandral O Most High Lord Evendoom? Thrice over and more?"

20

No One Lives Forever

So I said to him
Do it if you must
And I will be there with my sword
For we are nothing
If we have no principles
And no one lives forever.
　　—legendary Talonar saying,
　　attributed to Sandral Evendoom

They stood watching Talonnorn burn.

A short, slender tower somewhere in the holdings of House Oszrim shivered and then collapsed, slumping suddenly out of view, and hurling up a storm of sparks and embers. Nifl were running, now, across the open cavern floor, heading away from the city in any direction except the one where they were standing. The one from which the ragged remnants of an Ouvahlan army were charging.

"So," Bloodblade asked the outcast Nifl lady beside him softly, the flickering flames painting his face with bright reflections, "dare we go in to seek plunder, or tarry here and wait for a lot more Nifl to slay each other?"

Taerune saw the freed human slaves go pale and thin-lipped, and raise the weapons they'd seized from the fallen. They feared being made to go back into Talonnorn more than death—and she did not want to see the outnumbered House Dounlar warblades and Ravagers face so many desperate foes, even if they were ill-treated, untrained-for-war Hairy Ones.

"For now," she announced, raising her voice just enough to be heard clearly, "we draw back."

Then, quite deliberately, she turned her back on the humans, to say to the Ravagers and Dounlar Nifl, "These Hairy Ones desire to get well away from here, not return to the embrace of those who enslaved them."

A long, loud rumble made them all look again at Talonnorn; several towers were collapsing, with a sort of slow inevitability, one crashing into the next and bearing all down into a flood of tumbling stone.

"With everything burning," Taerune added, "the fighting will be wild and everywhere. There will be much butchery." She pointed at the cavern mouth they'd burst out of, earlier. "For now, we go back into the Out-caverns, to wait and watch. There will be a better time to return to Talonnorn."

"*You* go back," Orivon said grimly. "I'm going in."

Silently, many of the surviving Dounlar warblades, bloody swords in hand, walked over to stand with him.

Taerune frowned. "Why? Man, are you *still* hungry for our blood?"

The forgefist shook his head.

"I came back down into the Dark to recover four children—human younglings—who were taken by Oondaunt raiders not long ago. If they yet live, they are somewhere in there." He waved at the burning city.

"Young? If they live, they'll be picking yeldeth, in the caverns," Taerune said grimly. "*If* they live."

"And where are those caverns?"

"Beneath our feet—and under all this rock you see, from here all the way back to the towers," she replied. "Yet the ways into them are hard to find; they are guarded, and in the cellars of the great Houses. Food is power." Silence fell, and the forgefist and the Nifl-she stared at each other, not speaking, for what seemed a long, long time—until another distant tower fell, shattering all silence.

"Lady Evendoom," Orivon said quietly, then, "I don't even know which of the towers on the far side of the city belong to Oondaunt. I need you."

His onetime tormentor stared at him, and slowly and silently walked over to stand at his side.

It was Bloodblade's turn to frown. "Taerune?"

Taerune lifted her chin and gave him a steady stare. "Those who would tarry are yours to command now," she told him. "I have—"

She patted her forearm, where it became a blade, and then used that blade to point at Orivon. "—something I must do. A debt I must pay."

The House Dounlar Nifl drew back from them both, in the same silence they'd walked to them.

Garlane Dounlar, who was bleeding freely from a sword slash across his cheek, gave them both a glare and said coldly, "Rescuing Hairy Ones defends Talonnorn not at all."

"I am thinking," Orivon told him softly, with a grin that promised much death, and soon, "that there will be many Ouvahlans between here and the yeldeth caverns that our blades will have to deal with. And Nifl beyond them who stand with whoever cast you out."

"Jalandral," Barrandar Dounlar snarled. "Jalandral Evendoom, who calls himself High Lord of Talonnorn now."

Orivon's eyes blazed up in anger. "Then your fight is mine, too. My vengeance against the sister is done if she aids me in this; my vengeance against her brother demands his death."

"As it happens, *I* have a score to settle with darling Dral, too," Taerune hissed angrily. "Let's be about this!"

It was unseemly to hurry in Coldheart, but Tariskra was too worried to care overmuch about "unseemly" just now. She bowed her way past the two senior Anointed who guarded the way into the holy inner chamber, and hastened to report to Revered Mother Lolonmae.

Who lay embracing a great rearing tongue of the Ever-Ice that was jet black and yet seemed full of trapped stars—a wonder that Tariskra would ordinarily have fallen on her knees before, to whisper prayers as she studied it intently. Lolonmae was bared to the cold, as usual, and holy Meltwater was running from under her body, and being collecting in vessels by the silently kneeling priestesses clustered all around the Ever-Ice.

"Tariskra, you are more than uneasy," the young, slender Revered Mother observed. "Speak freely; why?"

"Ah—uh—Revered Mother, my magic . . . my touch to the mind of Exalted Daughter Semmeira has been broken! Several times I've tried to restore it, taking great care over the castings and in the end using some of the holy water of the Ice. Failure, always failure. I—I tried another spell, and Lolon—ah, Revered Mother!—I found that my spells are now being deliberately blocked!"

"Now why would that be? I wonder," Lolonmae asked, sounding almost amused.

Twisting away from the Ice to look over one shoulder at the priestesses bearing the holy Melt away, she commanded, "Set your vessels down, all of you, and work a magic together. All of you are to try to contact the mind of Exalted Daughter of the Ice Semmeira—right now."

She turned back to Tariskra. "Not you," she added. "You shall go now to the Watchers, and bring the Senior Watcher here to hear our will. If we are unable to see Semmeira's mind, that does not mean we should be blind as to her doings; the Watchers' whorls will show us what befalls in Talonnorn."

Tariskra bowed in deep reverence, and hurried to obey.

She was well away from that chamber, down one passage and then another, when she realized what had struck her most about the Revered Mother's voice, upon hearing her news.

It wasn't that Lolonmae had sounded amused—it was that she hadn't sounded surprised.

The younger crone balled her elegant fingers together into shaking fists and burst out, "Who *is* he?"

The two crones stood on a high balcony in Talonnorn, watching not the dying flames—now noticeably fewer and more feeble, fading as swiftly and as unheralded as they'd come—but a whorl of their own conjuring, that hovered horizontally in the air by their ankles.

They were watching a lone tall, robed stranger striding through the heart of Talonnorn, going from one great tower to another, always heading for the grandest structures. He slew all who sought to stop or harm him, again and again blasting such Talonar with contemptuous ease.

"Does it matter?" the older crone replied balefully. "We can see what he's doing—seeking magic, everywhere it's most likely to be had, and regardless of how it's defended."

They had just seen seven House spellrobes work their mightiest spells in unison, to bring their own tower down, destroying it just to try to kill the stranger while he was inside. They had also seen that Nifl, who hurled magic so much more powerful than theirs, emerge unscathed from the rubble, in shieldings of his own magical making—and slaughter the seven spellrobes without even slowing his steady walk toward the *next* grand tower.

"C-could this be the one they call Klarandarr?"

The older crone's lip curled. "Klarandarr is a myth. A tale woven by Ouvahlor to keep the more ambitious of our own House heirs and spellrobes from destroying that city—as they should have destroyed it long ago. Klarandarr—"

"What's *that*?" The younger crone pointed at a sudden white flare of light, a pulse that shone brightly and then faded just as quickly as it had come, leaving . . . the hands of the stranger empty.

"Sending his loot home," the older crone snorted. "He was carrying too much magic to keep from staggering, so he rid himself of his load. So now he can assault the Eventowers in untrammeled comfort." She leaned forward, sounding very satisfied. "So *now* we shall see some sights. Evendoom humbled, or yon stranger destroyed—or both."

Flashes of spell-light promptly appeared in the windows of the Evendoom gate-spires, and muffled explosions could be heard. House Evendoom, it seemed, stood not unguarded.

"How can one man . . ."

The younger crone's fearful whisper trailed away as the greatest tower of the sprawling and interconnected Evendoom fortress was suddenly shattered from within, as if a great but unseen fist had punched upward from its heart. Shards of stone hurtled in all directions, pattering or crashing down all over Talonnorn—and that great domed tower fell in on itself, in a titanic collapse that shook the cavern, hurled up a huge cloud of blinding dust, and caused nearby towers to crack and topple. A great cloud of dust blossomed in the wake of their falling, amid rumblings . . . and when that deep tumult and noise faded, the dust rose still, expanding in eerie silence.

The Talonar crones stood frozen on their balcony, hardly daring to hope—and then moaned in despairing unison, as the stranger came striding into view out of the dust, evidently unharmed. He was smiling, and the flickering glows of great destroying magics swirled around both of his bare and empty hands.

A relative quiet had fallen over Glowstone. The prowling beasts of the Wild Dark who'd been arriving in great numbers to see what wounded and carrion could be easily had were all dead now, or had been taught prudence by ready Nifl blades and had slunk back out into the darkness, to lurk and await better opportunities.

Yet the most respected Niflghar in Glowstone suddenly stiffened, causing Lord Erlingar Evendoom to frown in alarm and stride toward him.

Before he could reach Faunhorn, his brother turned to face Erlingar and announced grimly, "Something is happening in Talonnorn."

"What?"

Faunhorn shook his head. "I know not. But it is very bad."

Erlingar turned to face in the direction of distant Talonnorn, then threw up his hands. "There is nothing I can do, beyond trudge there and see the aftermath. Nothing."

He turned away, striding aimlessly across the cavern, and then came to a halt, and shrugged. "I am no longer of Talonnorn."

Faunhorn silently walked to his side, and put an arm around his shoulders.

"I should have stayed and died," Erlingar whispered, after a time.

"No," Faunhorn replied firmly. "That would have been the easy way. And Lords of Evendoom do not take the easy way."

The place where Jalandral had imprisoned Klaerra Evendoom "for her own safety" was a chamber deep in the cellars of the Eventowers.

Jalandral led the way to it in silence, grimly satisfied to hear all converse among the merchants of the Araed and the priestesses following him slowly die away in awe as the descent went on, and on . . . and on. Stairs after stairs, halls after passages. None of them had ever seen such extensive underways before, nor such wealth; the Eventowers went down a *long* way.

At least a dozen times during their journey, the stone rocked and rumbled all around them, shaken by great explosions or tremors from above. Once, one of the priestesses shrieked in the heart of those shakings, and more than once, as dust and small stones rained down around them, the merchants cursed.

When Jalandral finally reached the door he was seeking, it stood open, causing him to frown and quicken his stride. Keeping pace beside him, the merchant Ondrar muttered something under his breath, and a faintly glowing aura suddenly swirled around the High Lord of Talonnorn, shielding him against . . .

Nothing, as it happened.

The chamber beyond the door was comfortably furnished, with a high oval bed whose rim was set with a fringe of fine silver manacles; they were the only suggestions of confinement or compulsion in the room. A scrying-whorl floated in the air beside the bed, and a barefoot crone in light chamber robes stood before it, gazing into it. She turned to regard the Nifl now crowding into the chamber with a polite smile and a nod of greeting, and held out her hands to Jalandral.

Who stopped well short of stepping into them, and said, "Klaerra, I am here on matters of state—"

"Dral," she said gently, her soft voice causing sudden tense silence in the room, "be welcome. I know why you've come." She aimed one finger at the whorl in explanation, and then stood silent, waiting.

Silence deepened, as everyone stood staring. Jalandral stared down at his hands as if expecting to find something unusual had appeared in them, and then threw up his head almost briskly—only to say softly, "The door . . . it was open."

Klaerra shrugged. "The chamber pot became full, and as I *wasn't* a prisoner . . ."

Jalandral winced. "But the spells on that door . . ."

The Evendoom crone smiled at him, her eyes unreadable. "Mere trifles, High Lord. You really should get someone competent to work magic for you. Me, for instance."

Several of the Araed merchants and all of the priestesses took those softly spoken words as a threat, and recoiled, expecting spells to lash out at them without warning.

Klaerra's face acquired a sad smile at their reaction, but nothing else happened.

Jalandral stood his ground, kept his eyes on hers, and said quietly, "I have made several mistakes, Lady of Evendoom. Yet I do not believe any of them had anything to do with the current crisis besetting Talonnorn—a crisis that compels me to request your help."

As if it had been listening for a cue, the room rocked, rock dust falling in a light shower, and the stone walls boomed and echoed.

"Klaerra," Jalandral said unnecessarily, "Talonnorn is under attack."

The response was a nod. "From Klarandarr of Ouvahlor within our walls, and several small fighting bands approaching out of the Dark."

"So, Lady," Jalandral said gravely, "you know our need."

"Yes," Klaerra Evendoom replied, her eyes steady on his. "Yes, I do." She smiled. "Done to death by dung-worms. How . . . prosaic. All the might of Talonnorn—warblades and crones, sorcerous items and spellrobes galore, Consecrated of Olone and holy magic—and we fight for Talonnorn with *dung-worms.*"

Jalandral sighed. "I . . . fear so."

"Are you in too much haste for a last farewell between us?" Klaerra asked, flicking one finger in the direction of the bed so subtly that only he saw it.

Jalandral's eyes fell. "I fear so."

"Then we should proceed without delay. There is, I should point out, one small impediment."

"Yes?" Jalandral asked reluctantly, into a silence that had sharpened into sudden tension again.

Klaerra waved a hand at the Araed merchants who stood glaring at her, their hands on all manner of weapons. "Unless these rampants are crones cloaked in spell-guise, you're going to need a *lot* more crones. I suggest you send a trader or two back up into the Even-towers, to summon all you can find down here, in your name." She smiled wanly. "I should not like my death to be wasted."

"There is a chance that you will live—" Jalandral insisted, taking a step closer to her, but she shook her head and waved him away.

"I shall be sacrificing myself, and you know it. To serve as focus for even three skilled Consecrated—and forgive me, but these you have brought seem far from that—savages the focus. I can yet count, Dral. I will be savaged thrice over, and you will need many more than those here. To save Talonnorn, you must have a *lot* of crones and priestesses casting through me, each working to compel one dung-worm. That is *Klarandarr of Ouvahlor* toppling buildings above our heads, not a reckless young spellrobe with his first war-scepter."

Jalandral sighed heavily, and then turned, pointed at three of the younger merchants, and commanded, "Fetch all the crones you can, and lead them back here. Haste matters, as does not getting . . ." His voice trailed off.

"Getting yourself killed," Klaerra finished for him, her voice quiet and dignified. "Obey the High Lord of Talonnorn. Go."

The traders stared at her, then turned as one and rushed out of the room. One of the priestesses started to weep softly, and Jalandral shifted his feet, drew in a deep breath, and said, "Lady, I . . ." He ran out of words to say, threw up his hands helplessly, and tried again. "I—ah—"

Klaerra held up an imperious hand, commanding his silence, and he gave it.

"I do not do this for you, Jalandral," she told him. "Not out of love, nor admiration, nor obedience—for your lordship is no more than a hollow thing of words. I do this for Talonnorn."

Jalandral stared at her, mouth open to snap

something—and then closed it again, shrugged, waved at the priestesses to begin preparations for the spell, and strolled to the back of the chamber.

The Ouvahlan rear guard rose up in front of them without warning, five Nifl who snarled defiance as their swords sang out.

The forgefist never slowed. The blade in his left hand thrust deep into one Ouvahlan face, and the one in his right struck aside a thrusting sword with such force that its wielder stumbled sideways into the Ouvahlan beside him.

Orivon swung around to face them, opening both their throats even before they could regain their balances. They started to fall—leaving him room enough to reach over them and put the tip of his sword into an eye belonging to the Ouvahlan who'd just ducked behind them.

That left only one Ouvahlan for any Nifl to deal with, and it took the Dounlar brothers barely a breath to bury their three swords in him.

Garlane Dounlar regarded Orivon with an unlovely smile. "I had no idea Hairy Ones could fight!"

"Garlane, *behave*," his brother Barrandar snapped. "Such lack of honor!"

"*Honor?* When trading with a *human*?"

"Your brother means that you demean yourself by baiting anyone so," Orivon said quietly. "Lose your fury, rampant of Dounlar. We humans are just as bad as Niflghar. And just as good, of course."

As the chant rolled over him and swept him up in its rising yearning, even old Ondrar was awed. Some of the younger Araed merchants, standing back against the walls of the chamber shaking in the thrall of the rising chant, were in tears, their arms dragged involuntarily aloft, their faces working.

In the center of the room, the crones and the handful

of Consecrated the merchants had brought here were standing in a ring around the one who'd agreed to sacrifice herself. They were chanting ever-faster, arms rising and falling in a dance of mounting urgency and—and *power.*

Power.

Yes, and how was the one who'd sought so much power, and been so changed, so swiftly, by what he'd managed to grasp?

Curiously Ondrar glanced over at Jalandral, the self-proclaimed High Lord of Talonnorn.

Jalandral wasn't there.

Blinking in astonishment, the old merchant struggled to look all around the chamber. Seeing no sign of Lord Evendoom, Ondrar thrust himself away from the wall and turned to look all around, despite the tugging might of the ongoing chant.

Aye, he'd not been mistaken. Jalandral Evendoom was gone.

Ondrar thrust out a hand and slapped the merchant next to him—who blinked, struggled as if needing to fight to regain control of his body, and then turned frowningly to Ondrar—and hissed, "Jalandral's gone! *Gone!*"

At that moment, the chant rose to a high, trilling note that smote all ears painfully—and at the heart of the ring, Klaerra Evendoom rose slowly into the air. Arms spread, bare feet together, her light robe rippling around her legs as if she were caught in a gale, she threw back her head and crowned the chant with a high, climbing scream.

A moment later, both of her eyes burst into flames, that roared up to lick and then scorch the ceiling.

Half a city away, Klarandarr stopped in midstride, and turned toward a sudden sound. High and bell-like, it was the thin, clear call of a lone Nifl-she's scream.

A scream carried to him by magic, and laced around with magic.

A scream he should not have been able to hear, through the rolling crash of the building he'd just felled.

A frown came across the spellrobe's calm face. A frown that deepened into sharp-staring alarm as the sound continued, growing louder.

A moment later, he started muttering out spells just as fast as his lips could move, leveling his arms like lances at the nearest tower.

Even before it started to topple, he was blasting down the next one.

He needed to smash down every last building between him and the source of that scream—and he needed to do it fast.

In dark caverns and tumble-rock passages all across the Wild Dark, dung-worms stopped gliding, and stiffened.

Where open spaces above them permitted, they reared up, to rock back and forth, listening.

Then they started to tremble, great flanks rippling, heads quivering.

And then they started to move, turning if they needed to, starting to slither through the long stone passages, faster and ponderously faster.

All of them, every one, they came. Converging on Talonnorn.

Orivon Firefist was really sprinting now, even as some of the Nifl running behind him faltered and stared up at the cracking, falling buildings ahead.

Beside him, Taerune Evendoom was running just as fast, speeding along like the wind, matching him stride for stride.

As always, the Talonnorn before them was a walled city without walls. Breach after breach had been made in its walls, as the city spilled out farther and farther across its vast cavern, until there were no real barriers left, but only a scattered confusion of new towers being hurled up here, there, and everywhere.

Until now. When someone was busily hurling them back down.

With the House Dounlar warblades right behind them, Orivon and Taerune rushed into the first street they came to, a way flanked by buildings that were leaning and shedding falls of stone all around them as they ran.

At the first street-moot, Talonar in armor with swords in their hands came out of the side streets to block their way.

And were promptly sworded down.

Warning horns rang out from nearby windows, and more Talonar appeared.

"You!" one of those new warblades cried, charging at Taerune with his sword raised to his shoulder to slice down and cleave her.

"I know you! You're Evendoom, you are!"

"And you," Orivon said to him, striking that sword aside, against the Nifl warrior's neck, "you're in Talonnorn, you are!"

"And in Talonnorn, no one lives forever!" Taerune snarled, grinning—as she buried her blade hilt-deep in the warblade's throat.

21

The Spellrobe Gone Mad

Priestesses cruel and ruthless
I face time and time again
The Dark holds monsters many
No relief from their creepings
Know we, nor expect any
Yet there is a danger I fear
More than these common perils
One that makes high lords
And masters-of-battle alike quake.
Beware what they fear most:
The spellrobe gone mad.
        —*legendary Talonar saying,*
        attributed to Sardron Oszrim

"Follow me," Taerune murmured in Orivon's ear as they tugged their blades free of dead Nifl, bumping hip to hip in the bloody aftermath of hewing down the Talonar who'd attacked them. "I'll take you to House Oondaunt's yeldeth caverns. They're clear across Talonnorn."

Orivon's nod was the tiniest movement of his head he could manage; he knew Dounlar warblades were drawing closer around them, to listen.

"When Ouvahlor attacked last time," Taerune told him,

raising her voice just a trifle so the Dounlar Nifl could overhear but it didn't seem like she was intending them to, "they came swarming up out of a tunnel that rises into Talonnorn on the far side of the city, *there.*" She pointed across the many-towered city with her blade. "What has come out of the Dark just now is paltry enough that I believe it must be a diversion. The *real* attack will come through that tunnel again—and we must be there to meet it."

Without another word, she started running in the direction she'd pointed, and Orivon started trotting after her. A moment later, at a nod from their House heir, the Dounlar warblades all started to follow.

The flames that had raged so freely across Talonnorn, dancing high in the air without blazing on the ground or seeming to need fuel, had scorched balconies everywhere, cooking high turrets and those in them, but were gone now.

The rumblings of falling buildings, however, were still shaking the city—and they were running right toward those rumblings.

Around them, as they ran, doors were closed and windows were shuttered. Aside from plentiful sprawled corpses, the few Talonar they saw out-of-doors were skulking grimly along in small groups, keeping close to walls, swords out and suspicion in their faces. War had come to the streets of Talonnorn.

Orivon, Taerune, and the Dounlar warblades ran on. Off to their right, a strange shrill sound was rising; a high, warbling scream or shriek that went on and on without a break. It sounded as if a Nifl-she with powerful lungs and a commanding voice was trilling ceaselessly without ever needing to breathe, and it was growing ever higher and louder.

Taerune hastened on across the city with Orivon and the Dounlar Nifl hot on her heels. They came to streets where dazed Talonar were hurrying toward them with terror on their faces, offering no violence to anyone but obviously seeking to get away from something just as fast as they could hasten.

Then the streets of frightened Nifl gave way to an open area of heaped rubble and devastation that had once—a very short time ago—been most of the Araed. The crowded hovels and ramshackle warehouses the Talonar nobles had so utterly failed to eradicate in many, many attempts had been smashed down and swept aside in a seeming trice. Ahead, over heaps of broken stone, they could see the distant, riven walls of House Oondaunt. Its central towers were shattered and fallen, and amid the slumped stones small fires were raging.

They gave that shocking destruction only a moment's glance. Far off to their right, at the end of the trail of devastation, something else snatched at their attention.

A lone Nifl rampant, a spellrobe, was standing with his back to them, arms raised as he hurled a spell that sent a seething, frothing emerald-green *something* at the walled stone mansions in front of him—mansions from which arrows and spears and a few spells of stabbing lightnings spat, in his direction.

Those hurtling dooms faded away long before reaching the spellrobe, obviously encountering unseen shielding spells, but his emerald-hued magic melted through the outer walls and then the mansions inside those walls in an instant, causing the grand buildings to come crashing down.

Even before the rumblings and rolling stones had died away, the spellrobe was striding forward into their dust-shrouded midst, and starting to work the same spell again, to throw down the *next* mansion.

In shocked silence Taerune and the Dounlar warblades watched the lone spellrobe overthrow that mansion beyond the first one . . . and then the one behind that, too.

"Holy Olone preserve us," Garlane Dounlar whispered. Beside him, Taerune nodded grimly. Talonnorn was being destroyed before their eyes, and she could see

where the spellrobe was heading: the Eventowers, the
home of House Evendoom. *Her* home—and the source
of that now earsplitting, one-note scream that went on
and on . . .

Through that deafening shriek, she barely heard the
battle cry that rose around her as the House Dounlar
warblades and heirs waved their swords in the air,
shouted, and then charged.

Orivon started to sprint after them, and Taerune ran
like a scouring wind to catch up to him, to where she
could put a hand into the crook of his arm. For a few
racing breaths they ran together, hip to hip.

Then Taerune abruptly tripped in the rubble and fell,
hauling Orivon down into a crashing fall with her. Together they plunged boots-first down a slope of heaped
stone rubble.

When they slid to a coughing, dust-shrouded stop, it
was in a hollow where an unmoving Nifl arm thrust up
through the stones, reaching vainly for something it
would never touch.

"Come," Taerune hissed at the human beside her,
rolling over. "We must be away from here! *Now!*"

Orivon blinked—her fall had been no stumble, but a
ruse!—and then clambered on hands and knees, following her shapely backside. He clawed his way over a drift
of broken stone and down its far side, to where there
was bare stone under their boots, and they could run
once more—not toward the spellrobe, but in the direction of riven House Oondaunt again.

Taerune started running hard, sunk in a crouch as if trying to avoid being seen from afar, so Orivon did the same.
Yet even as he started to hunker, he couldn't resist a look
back over his shoulder at the now-distant Dounlar Nifl.

Who were now only a few running strides away from
that lone spellrobe's back.

Where something—a warding spell, by Thorar, or
he'd spent no time watching Talonar Nifl living around
him, all those years—flared at Klarandarr's back. As its

glow brightened, Orivon saw the spellrobe whirl around to face the onrushing rampants of House Dounlar.

The Nifl wizard's hands moved in deft, intricate gestures—that were over and done in less than a breath—and were suddenly cupping a welling, swirling cloud of black and gold, a roiling spell that looked deadly and somehow sickening to look upon—as it shot out from him into those snarling Dounlar faces.

And swept them away, the spellrobe's magic melting flesh from bone, so angry Nifl were no longer running toward him; he was suddenly being charged by many skeletons with swords in their hands.

They were barely a sword-length away, but faltering as their joints failed, when his magic, still at work on them, dashed them all to dust.

Staring, too aghast to swear, Orivon saw a score of swords and daggers, amid plumes of dust, clatter to the stones in front of the spellrobe.

Who calmly flexed his fingers, nodded as if in mild satisfaction, and turned back to blasting his way on through mansions of rising splendor and size, to the Eventowers.

The walls of the great cavern that housed Talonnorn bore many high ledges suitable for overlooking much of the great city—and whereas Exalted Daughter of the Ice Semmeira would have had to peer around herself in a long search to spot most of them, Maharla Evendoom, onetime Eldest of her House who would soon be Eldest again, knew them all.

She stood on the very best vantage point right now, gazing down at the tumult of fallen buildings. The destruction formed a line that had begun in the squalid, crowded heart of the Araed—no loss there—and was now proceeding, even as she watched, in a wide swath of ruin that stretched through streets of workhouses and warehouses and respectable shops . . . heading straight for the Eventowers.

Well, *that* would have to be stopped. This was doubtless the work of some cabal of ambitious House spellrobes, seeking to take advantage of Ouvahlor's feeble attack on Talonnorn to find someone else to blame for their treasonous strike against House Evendoom.

Maharla stood for a moment with half-awakened magic swirling restlessly around her wrists—a moment in which another proud mansion collapsed with a faint, distant roar—and then hit upon the right spell to use.

The casting was intricate, but went flawlessly. As she smiled in satisfaction, a bright net spun away from her, arced high above Talonnorn, and then fell, settling gently over . . . the . . .

The spell was gone, taking her smile with it in an instant.

It had faded and failed in the face of shieldings stronger than any Maharla Evendoom had ever seen before.

Ever.

Including every Holiest of Olone, Eldest of any House, and House spellrobe.

Even the mighty ones of her youth, Aundram Maulstryke and Halovarr Raskshaula.

Frowning now, Maharla Evendoom sent a very different sort of spell to the place where another mansion had just collapsed amid clouds of rising dust. A silent, drifting shadow she could see out of, and so watch just who was down there reducing home after stone home of Talonnorn to rubble in mere moments . . .

"Olone *spew!*" she swore involuntarily, a moment later. *One* spellrobe was down there! Just one! She'd looked everywhere for signs that other, hidden spellcasters were at work, found nothing, then looked hard to see if the destroyer was using some sort of magic to harness the stored might of scepters and rings and other enchanted items.

He was not. She watched the destruction of a tall, sweeping-turreted home she'd always liked from beginning to end, from the stranger—and it *was* a stranger; she sent her shadow as close as she dared to look at his face, and found herself surveying nothing more familiar than calm confidence and hauteur—first looking at the building onward. He cast a spell she did not know, other than that it produced an emerald roiling that ate through stone with melting ease. It sliced through the walls, and the thunderous collapse promptly followed, Nifl arms waving frantically from windows as their owners vainly sought to invoke Olone or awaken magic or just do *something* ere they died . . .

Then, of course, they died, amid rising dust, and the lone spellrobe strode calmly on over their broken bodies and the rubble burying them, to behold the next building in his way, and do the same things to it, all over again.

Such power!

To do that in the first place—and to have might enough to do it again and again, when he might face foes at any time! He had to be stopped . . . if he *could* be stopped.

She lacked spells enough, unless Holy Olone Herself reached out to crown Maharla Evendoom with a lot more power. Not that such a blessing was likely.

Maharla wriggled her shoulders experimentally, but felt nothing. Olone didn't seem moved to do what she did in legends, just now.

Which left the old, brutish ways. Warblades and their weapons, perhaps a spell cast by her on three of them, to get them to snatch up this spellrobe and rush him under a building he'd just caused to collapse . . .

A roiling was building in the air around the spellrobe now; his own magics, so tormenting the web of old spells that had smoothed and shaped the stones he was shattering, that a chaos of magic was forming a wave around him, and frothing in half-seen silence in his wake.

Yes, it would have to be swords now, not spells. Very few magics would be able to lance through *that*.

If she wanted to save the Eventowers, she would have to cause those old, brutish ways to descend on the spell-robe soon.

Maharla shook her head, and then murmured the magic that would take her from the ledge back into the heart of her force of Ouvahlan stoneheads, and—

Was there.

Standing in a puddle of blood on a narrow street near the edge of Talonnorn, with soaring towers on either side and the rumblings of falling buildings faint in the distance. All around her were shouting, rushing Ouvahlans who were busily swording seemingly endless Talonar who came rushing at them out of doorways and alleys.

Dead Talonar were everywhere, and the stone underfoot was slick with blood, lots of blood. Yonder, Ouvahlans were coming out of doorways with wide smiles on their faces and plundered gem-sacks and golden coffers in their hands.

Maharla shook her head sourly; such undisciplined greed.

"Rampants of Ouvahlor," she snapped, the belt around her hips sending her words hard and clear into their minds, "the Ever-Ice commands you to undertake a most sacred—and pressing—task: you are to head across the city in all haste, and slay the spellrobe gone mad! A lone Nifl who hurls down buildings with his spells! Destroy him!"

She called on the belt to send an image of the spellrobe as she remembered him, his face and then his figure from afar, arms moving in the shaping of spells, with a building falling before him, and the heaped rubble of many buildings in his wake, into the minds of her Ouvahlan warriors, so that—

Her link with their minds was gone, shattered in an instant along with her own mind-shieldings. They were falling away in dark tatters before the sheer power of a sharp, distant mind-voice that said: *Semmeira you are*

NOT! Who are you? Where is Semmeira, and what have you done to her?

Maharla Evendoom fought to thrust that probing voice away from her, to force it out of her head, to . . .

She found herself stumbling along the street, trembling and sweating, sudden exhaustion overwhelming all else.

She had done it.

She had forced them out, those Anointed of Coldheart, spurned them and turned them away . . .

The nearest Ouvahlan turned to her with cold anger in his eyes and his sword coming up to menace her, and Maharla had to duck away. He came after her, striding purposefully, boots splashing in the puddled blood . . . and was joined by another Ouvahlan. And another, all of them seeking her with their swords, all of them—

"Olone provide!" Maharla Evendoom snarled, slapping away yet another Ouvahlan, as he turned. Her fingers brushed the bare skin of his neck for the briefest of instants—and she knew, thanks to the imperious mind-voice silently shouting in his mind, what was happening. Priestesses of the Ever-Ice were reaching out from distant Coldheart to magically goad the Ouvahlan to attack the false "Semmeira."

Fear flared in Maharla Evendoom as another Ouvahlan turned to menace her, and then another.

In the end, she barely managed to teleport away in time.

Along a score of passages and linked caverns deep in the Wild Dark, gigantic dung-worms came rushing. Faster and faster, racing along through stone that was starting to shake around them.

Lesser creatures cowered, wondering if the Ghodal was rising at last.

Heedless and nigh-mindless, the dung-worms rushed on, converging on the great cavern of Talonnorn from all directions.

*   *   *

The forgefist and the Nilf-she ran on, ignoring the end-less scream behind them, and the rumbling crashes that were almost drowning it out—crashes that were be-falling almost constantly, now.

There were no gates to keep them out of House Oon-daunt any longer, and no massed guard where the gates had been. They saw no living Nifl at all as they rushed toward the riven central keep.

The heart of House Oondaunt had been torn open from battlements to threshold, and lay spilled across the central courtyard in a great flood of broken stone. Dead crones lay everywhere, some crushed in the fallen rub-ble, and some sprawled in their blood where they had been felled by Oondaunt servants and warblades spurred by hatred.

Orivon and Taerune rushed into the keep, and through lofty, ornate rooms that were for the most part deserted. A few guards appeared, from time to time as they ran on, and sought to bar passage to the one-armed Lady of Evendoom and the half-naked Hairy One who bore bared swords in both hands. Orivon and Taerune made swift work of them.

Taerune led the way deeper into the keep, and down a level, seeking pantries and kitchens. A step behind her, shaggy head peering this way and that in case someone came rushing out at them from behind, Orivon was al-most dancing with worry that the shattering of the great keep had filled the ways down into the yeldeth caverns with stone, entombing the four he'd come to find, but Taerune dismissed that fear briskly.

"Yeldeth is *food* to us, Orivon," she reminded him. "There will be many ways down, and not all of them from this building. If these are all blocked—and they won't be—we'll seek in yonder wall-tower, or that one, or—"

A guard burst out from behind a curtain then, trying to silence her forever with his sword. With a grunt of effort, before Orivon could reach past her, she parried that sword, and delivered a kick to the guard's chin that flung his head back—and let her drive home the blade that had replaced her left arm, through the gap where the bottom of his helm no longer met the top of his gorget.

His gore drenched her, but she merely laughed and led the way, dripping, on down the stairs.

Where they found death had preceded them, and there were no guards any longer. A dead Nifl who wore a belt of many keys was slumped against a metal-shod door, and Taerune and Orivon did not need to look at each other to announce in unison, "The cellars."

The stairs beyond the door were darker and damper, all trace of elegance and adornment gone from the walls, and they descended into a heavy warmth that carried a smell they both knew was yeldeth.

"Soon," Taerune promised—a moment before they reached the bottom of a stairs that opened into a little room, and found the way barred by a gate made of dark heavy metal and greenish Nifl bones.

A gate that seemed to be *moving* as they approached it. Orivon stared for a moment, and then rushed forward and started to hack at those bones, hewing furiously, trying to stop them from whirling up into . . .

"Bloodbone magic!" Taerune hissed, drawing back in revulsion. "*Strictly* forbidden by Olone!"

Orivon laughed mirthlessly. "Oh? How well have Talonar heeded Olone at the best of times?"

Taerune's reply was a heartfelt curse, as she watched four—no, five—whirling columns of flying Nifl bones coalesce in front of Orivon. Seemingly unaffected by his slashing swords, they hovered; Nifl skulls above Nifl arms and shoulders, awaiting the arrival of rusting Nifl blades into their hands.

Orivon shattered two of those blades as they drifted up from the gate that had spawned these fell guardians, but then had to draw back to avoid being surrounded.

The gate was little more than a gaping frame now, but Taerune doubted they'd have a chance to plunge through it unscathed. Cold flames were flickering in the eye sockets of the skulls looming up over her, and she knew one thing with cold certainty:

The fighting was about to *really* begin.

Klarandarr stopped walking across rubble toward the next mansion to blast, and lifted his head to listen. Yes, there *was* another rumbling aside from those he was causing—a deeper, distant, ongoing shaking that was . . . growing stronger.

Getting nearer . . . and, yes, making the great cavern of Talonnorn, all around him, shake!

Even as he felt that growing thrumming through the soles of his boots, a tower toppled, far to his right, and crashed down through other buildings. A moment later there was a similar fall in the distance behind him, right across the city.

No doing of his, this, and something even Klarandarr of Ouvahlor just might not be able to defeat, if it struck at him.

He raised his hands, but not to blast another building; his blastings were done for now. It was time to cast spells enough to surround himself with a protective shell of magic, a shielding of interwoven spells that could armor him against anything, and move with him.

His conjured destructions had wrought too much chaos all around for any simple translocation spell to work, and take him out of this peril.

If he wanted to flee by those means, he'll have to buy himself time to walk out of ruined Talonnorn, trudging until he'd left rubble far behind—and not using other magic, even if facing dozens of Talonar with swords, or spells of their own.

So a shield it would have to be . . .

The shaking was strong, now, the rumbling rising into

a constant rolling booming, as if many marching drums were being struck at enthusiastic random. Another building toppled, nearby, and then—

The cause of the shaking revealed itself, startling him almost into faltering and ruining a spell.

Dung-worms, dark and gigantic, were bursting forth into the cavern from its every entrance, rushing at full speed, converging . . .

Yes, on *him!*

Ignoring Nifl spears and a few paltry spells, slamming through carts and running Nifl rather than swinging around them, coming at him from all sides and ignoring all else in their rush to get at him.

Klarandarr finished his spell and started on another, moving now with frantic haste.

As he gabbled incantations and danced about weaving the gestures that went with those words, so fast he started to gasp amid fast-flowing sweat, a part of Klarandarr of Ouvahlor started to wonder, with calm curiosity, if he'd manage to craft his shield-shell in time.

22
Four Good Reasons

*I had four good reasons
For returning to Talonnorn
And at least two revenges
Plus the face of a certain Nifl lady.*
—words of Orivon Firefist,
as remembered in Orlkettle

"Orivon!" Taerune panted as she danced frantically away from yet another whirling blade that sought her life. "Have you any magic at all?"

"Me?" The forgefist gasped as he sprang high into the air and whirled his blade hard around his head, shattering two skulls before he fell to the floor with a grunt. The bones of those two guardians clattered to the floor around him, bouncing and breaking. A floor that had begun to shake as the rock it was carved out of awakened into thunder.

That left three bone guards, two of them without swords—but no, they'd just swooped across the chamber to catch the swords of the two he'd just destroyed!

As the thunder of vibrating rock grew louder and stronger all around them, Taerune tried the same tactic Orivon had, leaping high and slicing with all her strength, but her bone guard spun back out of reach. It plunged after her as she fell, stabbing viciously—but was parried by Orivon at the last instant as he hurled himself across the room to smash aside its blade. As that rusty sword clanged off the ceiling, Orivon landed hard on shattered bones, chest-first, and slid helplessly on, into the wall.

Taerune rolled away in the other direction, wasting no time in watching the bone guard chase the sword Orivon had struck from its control. She was too busy dodging the other two skeletal guardians and trying to scramble across the shaking floor to the gate that had spawned them.

The gate that was now an empty frame she wasn't sure if she dared to dive through.

The gate whose destruction she *knew* would destroy the bone guards, too. If only they had some *useful* magic . . .

The guardians were little more than whirling bones, remains kept together by magic, not bones still joined by the joints living Nifl possessed. Skulls floated above shoulders, that in turn floated above arms—arms that could wield swords without grasping them, somehow, swinging those blades with the cold strength of a strong Nifl rampant or whirling them like chain-flails.

Smashing the skulls destroyed them, Orivon had just shown—and if they lacked a sword to wield, they could do little more than belabor the face and body of a foe with bony arms that annoyed, and could perhaps blind, but did no greater harm.

The floor bouncing under her hard and rapidly now, Taerune rolled onto her shoulders and kicked upward, desperately, driving a blade aside and winning herself time to roll again, this time to her knees, with the gate only a temptingly small distance away, and—

Orivon came crashing down in front of her nose, both hands locked around a skull that he drove hard against the vibrating floor.

Old Nifl bone shattered satisfyingly, and the flailing

skeletal arms collapsed into mere bouncing, lifeless bones. Evidently her former slave had got to the disarmed bone guard before it had reached its errant sword.

That left two, and Taerune spun around on her knees with her blade up before her, seeking the whereabouts of those two guardians in the now thundering and shaking chamber.

They were as high above her as they could get, moving from above the gate she'd been thinking of racing for, to above Orivon. As he rolled over, they descended menacingly, their whirling blades foremost.

It was Taerune's turn to defend the human who'd so ably rescued her. Thrusting herself up from the floor, she thrust out her blade into the whirling steel of the nearest bone guard, trying to shove it sideways into its fellow guardian.

Steel rang off steel numbingly, the rusty sword disintegrated into dust and shards, and Taerune fell, offbalance, across Orivon. Who cursed as the other bone guard came down on them both, and then frantically grabbed hold of the blade he'd fitted to Taerune's missing forearm and thrust it up to defend them both, twisting her like a straw doll.

She cried out in pain—but the bone guard's rusty sword rang off that steel and exploded into shards like the other one had, and that gave Orivon time enough to fling Taerune's body up into the second bone guard, temporarily scattering the bones it was made of, and then launch himself up through the whirling heart of the other bone guard, plunge two fingers into the eyesockets of its skull, hug the skull to his chest—and crash to the floor with all his weight atop it, shattering it.

That bone guard sighed back into lifeless bones, too, leaving only one swordless guardian—a guardian still drifting back together after Taerune had slammed through the midst of it. She was groaning on the floor, holding her flank and glaring at Orivon, but he raced right past her to get his hands on the skull, before it could rejoin the rest, wrestle it to the ground, and pummel it with his fists until it broke apart.

In their sudden lack of skeletal foes, Orivon and Taerune looked at each other and managed wry grins.

"If you tell no one about throwing me right through a dancing skeleton, I'll forgive you these bruised ribs," the outcast Talonar lady told her former slave, speaking almost severely.

"We have agreement," Orivon told her, reaching for her far more gently than he'd done just a breath or three earlier. "Are they truly . . . gone?"

Taerune shrugged. "It wouldn't hurt to stomp on the biggest bones—all but one. Keep a thighbone to thrust through yon gate. I don't entirely trust it."

"Do Talonar Niflghar entirely trust anything?" Orivon teased her.

"Only the truly stupid ones," she replied tartly, taking up a bone she judged long enough and thrusting it through the open space in the gate. Nothing happened, but she tried her blade next, before daring to insert her hand and undo the latch.

The gate yawned wide, and Taerune Evendoom turned to the Hairy One she'd once flogged so often, smiled, and indicated the dark passage beyond the gate with a flourish. Warm and damp air was rising from it, and the thunder of vibrating rock that was loud everywhere else around them seemed somehow muted when wafted up to them on that air. "The yeldeth caverns await."

"Should we expect other guards? Traps?"

"No traps; they have slaves bringing *food* through here constantly, remember? Overseers, yes, but such are usually old, weak, or disfigured Nifl, armed with whips. A few have daggers, but it's discouraged."

Orivon nodded. "Ah. If a slave snatches one . . ."

Taerune nodded back.

Orivon took up his swords again and shouldered his

way through the gate. There was a strong, nose-prickling smell he remembered, faint but growing stronger with every step he took. Yeldeth.

He looked back over his shoulder. Taerune was holding her side, but was walking right behind him. She gave him a slight smile.

"Of course I'm coming," she said, before he could ask. "You, I *almost* entirely trust."

Orivon grinned. "Likewise."

He went on down into the darkness, the passage becoming a smooth, damp ramp down into the soft warmth of the yeldeth caverns. Whimpers arose ahead of him, and he stopped and peered.

The pale faces and staring eyes of young, bony, naked humans looked back at him. "Where are the overseers?" he asked them.

"You're—"

"Human? Yes. Where are the overseers?"

"Gone. Fled. When the rumblings started. They left us to die."

Orivon nodded and strode forward, picking his way carefully as he waded in the soft, deep, clinging fungus. Most of the slaves shrank back from him, whimpering in utter terror. When they saw Taerune behind him, sword-armed and sleek, every inch an elegant Nifl-she, most hid their faces, or tried to burrow into the yeldeth and hide.

Orivon went on a long way, from cavern to cavern, until he was beginning to despair. The four could be long dead, of course, or killed after they got here and fed to gorkul . . .

Then he blinked. Was that a face he knew?

"Brith?" he called, as gently as he could. "Brith?"

"Firefist?" came the disbelieving, weeping response.

Dung-worms loomed up, dark and vast, and then rushed together, striking his shieldings hard enough to make the not-quite-completed shell flicker, shrink in on itself a little, and then . . . hold.

Around him, Talonnorn had vanished, blotted out by all the vast, pressed-together maws that were so busily biting and gnawing.

Klarandarr's shieldings collapsed a little more under that hungry onslaught, but kept him—thus far, at least—from being bitten into small, bleeding fragments.

As the spellrobe sat down to think, the incomplete shell gave way a little more—and then, suddenly, it was too late for leisurely thinking, as the shell became a small sphere around him, and he was being battered and hurled about and then . . . swallowed whole.

One of the largest dung-worms had won the struggle over him, and closed its jaws over him completely.

Swirling about in the juices of its mouth and then gullet, tumbled and churned, Klarandarr of Ouvahlor pondered his situation.

When the shell failed, his flesh would begin to melt in this churning bile, even before he drowned. Yet if he freed himself by causing the shell to burst violently, destroying the dung-worm, he'd be hurled into the air, probably stunned—and defenseless against all the *other* dung-worms.

What he needed to do was craft and then cast a translocation that was linked to the destruction of the shields, so their bursting would cause him to be whisked away before harm could come to him.

Yes, that was it. Hurled and churned about in the innards of the dung-worm, the still-shielded Klarandarr allowed himself a smile, and set to work.

Klaerra Evendoom's scream ended suddenly, as her head burst.

The watching merchants had just time to see that much before the spell that had overloaded her claimed the rest of her body—and it exploded.

Spattered by the grisly wetness that had been Klaerra Evendoom, the awed merchants of the Araed saw the priestesses and crones topple over—stunned or struck unconscious—all around the room.

Awe became fear, and amid general cursing most of the traders sought the door.

"I'm getting out of this place before it becomes our tomb!" one shouted, elbowing others aside viciously to be the first out.

When he tugged on the handle of the closed door, it toppled, too, its dark shadow descending before he quite realized what was happening.

He had just time to gape up at it before it fell on him, crushing him like a rotten fruit.

"Too late," the old merchant Ondrar commented laconically, watching fresh blood—Araed merchant blood—run across the floor. "Perhaps too late for us all. Talonnorn may already have become one big tomb."

The rumbling of their haste was done, the spell that had brought them broken. Freed, the gigantic dung-worms slithered away, wandering aimlessly.

They were uncomfortable so close to so many others of their kind, nettled that they'd been used despite not really knowing how, and filled with an instinctive revulsion for staying in the spot they'd all been summoned to. So they drew back from that meeting of mouths, turned, and glided away over rubble and along streets, heading in all directions.

The largest titan, a worm longer than any caravan that had ever been seen in Talonnorn, was halfway across the great cavern when it shuddered, convulsed—and exploded with a wet roar, spewing a bright star high into the air, and sending one last rumbling across the cavern like an inexorable wave.

Close enough to the cavern ceiling to touch it, that star winked once.

Then it faded, though no one happened to be watching. The winking was the flashing translocation of Klarandarr, snatching himself safely back to Ouvahlor.

The deep, rolling wave of the explosion struck the Eventowers, proud seat of House Evendoom and the High Lord of Talonnorn, and made its grand stones shudder.

Slowly, with seeming reluctance but then with building speed, the tallest and most splendid Evendoom tower toppled over, smashing through the front wing of the mansion on its way to the ground . . . and leaving nothing of the soaring heart of the Eventowers but rubble.

Nifl and human slaves all sounded alike when shrieking in terror.

Orivon winced, flung out a hand to keep Taerune from falling—the blade he'd fashioned to replace her left forearm was closest to him, and he preferred not to be sliced open—and waited for the rumblings to die away.

Then he stretched out his other hand to Brith, and asked, "Want to see Orlkettle again?"

Brith stared back at him, and then burst into sudden tears and swarmed up that arm to bury himself against Orivon's chest, weeping uncontrollably. Orivon stroked his back—his whip-scarred, bony young back—awkwardly, and then called roughly, "Reldaera? Aumril? Kalamae?"

Someone else started crying, far down the yeldeth-shrouded tunnel, but no one came.

Taerune Evendoom leaned close. "You should take them all, Orivon. All of the human children. How can you not?"

Orivon looked at her, face stern, and then nodded slowly and echoed, "How can I not?"

It took some time to retrieve all the young Hairy Ones, for they were almost as scared of Orivon as they were of Taerune, but in the end, carrying all the yeldeth they could manage, they reluctantly allowed themselves to be led up into House Oondaunt. They came out into the great cavern weeping and staggering dazedly.

"Claz," Munthur rumbled, from the window. "Come. You should see this."

Clazlathor the spellrobe sighed and got up from his desk. He was just beginning to hope that Klarandarr of Ouvahlor—for who else could that spellrobe of such peerless, terrible power have been?—would leave *some* part of Talonnorn standing, and a few Talonar still alive . . . and now . . .

He joined his friend at the window. More than a head taller than most Nifl, Munthur could see farther, but for once what he was staring at was laid out clearly before Clazlathor's gaze, too.

Ouvahlan warriors were roaming and pillaging at will; there were seemingly no Talonar left to resist them. A handful of tall, spired homes still stood between the long line of devastation and the Eventowers, but where the tallest Evendoom tower should have stood, proud and dark against the cavern sky, there was nothing but a little dust, drifting in the air.

Nearer, just now emerging from the litter of rubble that had recently been the front gates of House Oondaunt, were a Nifl-she and . . . a straggling line of naked Hairy One younglings!

Clazlathor chuckled sourly. "So, the last doom is come. Even the slaves are getting out."

Beside him, Munthur rumbled wordless agreement—that broke off abruptly when his friend clutched at him in astonishment.

Someone else had emerged from the rubble, swords in either hand. "That's . . . the Dark Warrior," the spellrobe said in disbelief. "So he got his vengeance after all; nothing left of proud House Evendoom but corpses and dust."

Munthur blinked. "Our High Lord's dead, then?"

Clazlathor shrugged. "Who knows? Who cares? He's

High Lord of nothing, now, anyway. There's naught left for the conquering Ouvahlans to stay here for; after they plunder, they'll go back to their city, leaving this place to the eaters-of-dead, outlaw Nifl, and Ravagers."

"Another Glowstone or Lightpools," Munthur rumbled. "The Consecrated of Olone won't like that."

"They'll soon be dead, if they say so," was the grim response. "The lucky ones are dead already."

"Orivon!" Taerune said warningly. The forgefist peered over the heads of the children, seeking to see what had alarmed her.

She was facing toward one of the mansions the spell-robe hadn't blasted, that stood between the path of rubble he'd caused and the Eventowers.

Nifl rampants were emerging from a gate in the unscathed walls of that high house now, with swords in their hands.

"Run *nowhere*," Orivon told the children firmly, as he started tramping past them. "Stay here, and keep together. Lady Taerune will protect you."

Taerune turned her head sharply at those words, frowned at him, and then nodded slowly, bringing up her sword in salute.

Orivon gave her a tight, silent smile and strode past her, hefting his swords as he walked across the sea of rubble to meet the Niflghar. A dozen warblades, in dark armor, with good blades, they were, and they were already heading toward him.

"Dark Warrior," one of them called as he strode steadily nearer to them, "did you do all of this? Are you come here to throw down Talonnorn?"

"No," Orivon told him firmly. "This is none of my doing. Ouvahlor struck here, and warriors of that city are still looting in your streets. *I* came for these children, snatched from my village by raiding warblades of Oondaunt."

The warblades came to a halt, in an arc facing him, swords up.

Orivon stopped, too, raising both of his swords.

"So," he asked them calmly, "are you going to try to kill me?"

They stared back at him coolly. Then one of them—the one who'd hailed him—shook his head.

"No, Dark Warrior. We have no dispute with you. We, too, would take up sword and fare forth to rescue our children."

Silence fell. Orivon nodded. The warblades started to turn away, but another of them added, "We want none of your blood, and nothing you bear—unless you happen to have one treasure we seek most."

"Oh? And what might that be?"

"The head of Jalandral Evendoom."

Orivon smiled. "That's a treasure I'm also tempted to seek, but we Hairy Ones are generous. If you find it, know this: it's all yours."

The warblades laughed grimly, raised their swords in salute, and headed off across the rubble in another direction.

Orivon watched them go, and then turned back to Taerune. For some reason, he suddenly couldn't stop smiling.

Jalandral Evendoom was hurrying as fast as he could, slipping and sliding in dark and unfamiliar tunnels. He'd never much cared for the Outcaverns, with their lurking monsters and their utter lack of willing Nifl-shes and good wine and other Talonar to show off in front of—and he didn't think much of them now.

He was High Lord of nothing, with Talonnorn a lawless ruin behind him, and all of this magic was *heavy*.

He'd got out of the Eventowers just in time, and if it hadn't been for the back tunnels, to the Hidden Gate, he'd probably still be in there—dead, crushed under more fallen stone than all the slaves left in Talonnorn could lift away.

Instead, he was still alive—for now, at least—and wearing dozens of deadly rings that flashed and tingled restlessly as he went, with no less than six belts buckled around him, all of them hung heavily with pouches and sheaths that bore scepters and wands and all sorts of enchanted oddments. A baldric-sling across his back held more than a dozen healing stones and a talking head sculpted of smooth metal, whose true purpose he had no inkling of, but whose magic glowed more brightly than anything else he was carrying. Yes, noble Houses of Talonnorn certainly loved their magical fripperies, and the ability to blast anyone who disagreed with them.

Maybe—just maybe—all of this would keep him alive for long enough to . . .

He slowed, coming out into a cavern where he caught sight of a grimly staring Niflghar rampant, bearing a drawn sword. Then he saw another. And another—no, three more, rising from behind rocks.

As Jalandral Evendoom came to a despairing stop, feeling for one of the few scepters he knew how to wield—for his rings could best only someone he was touching; to fell a foe from afar, he needed a scepter—he saw that the cavern held many armed Nifl—including, as a slight sound from behind him made him whirl around, more than a dozen who'd silently closed ranks behind him, standing ready with drawn swords.

As more and more Niflghar arose from behind rocks and joined in a slow, silent advance on him, Jalandral saw that he stood at the heart of a closing ring. Talonar Nifl, of all Houses and of none. All of them were armed, and all were eyeing him in silent menace.

Jalandral's hand closed over the scepter, but he did not draw it forth. There were too many of them, far too many, and he could see scepters in plenty, held ready and aimed at him.

He let out a deep breath and just stood there, awaiting his death.

A tall Nifl rampant with burning eyes—a Raskshaula, by his targe—walked slowly toward Jalandral, drawn sword held out before him as if it was a banner.

When he was close enough to touch Jalandral, he stopped, knelt, laid the sword across the toes of Jalandral's boots, looked up, and murmured almost reverently, "Command us, High Lord."

23

Rise to Blindingbright

But however deep and dark I fare
Monsters horrid to fight and slay
There is no brighter moment in my faring
Than to rise to Blindingbright again.
—words of Orivon Firefist,
as remembered in Orlkettle

Since when," the most beautiful Nifl-she the Evendoom warblade had ever seen asked him, "has the way into Glowstone been barred to a pair of traders of the Dark? We are what the Haraedra have always termed 'Ravagers,' and Glowstone is the closest thing we have to a home."

As two more warblades came up to stand with him, drawn swords in hand, the warblade barring Nurnra's path spread his hands in a gesture of helplessness and told her gravely, "I have my orders."

Nurnra turned her head and regarded him sidelong, knowing well just how devastatingly fetching such a movement made her look. "Orders? So who rules Glowstone now, hmm?"

A tall, handsome Nifl rampant strode out from behind a pillar of rock, arms folded across his chest, and face stern.

"We do, sharren." He looked from Nurnra to Oronkh,

his face making it clear how suspicious he found the very existence of a half-Niflghar, half-gorkul, and added, "And our rules are good and prudent. Let me repeat the choice you were just given: surrender your magic or begone."

Faunhorn Evendoom was used to command, and was a splendid figure of a rampant as well as a proud and honorable Talonar noble; he looked like all of those things, and Oronkh drew back with an instinctive rumble of wary respect.

Nurnra felt respect, too, but she had a different way of showing it. "Who is 'we' and 'our,' Lord Polite But Nameless Commander? *Our* rules of Glowstone seem quite different from yours."

"I am Lord Faunhorn Evendoom, late of Talonnorn, and we hold Glowstone now."

"By right of arms?"

"By right of arms. I should add that as we speak, you are surrounded, and more than a few scepters are aimed at you."

"There's that 'we' again. I ask again, who rules Glowstone?"

Behind her, Oronkh gave a low, warning rumble, but Nurnra ignored him.

"As repetition is obviously a practice personally familiar to you, sharren," Faunhorn replied almost gently, "I say again: surrender your magic or begone."

Nurnra took a slow step forward, to stand toe to toe with him. "Glowstone is and has always been a trademoot, where all Ravagers meet as equals. Magic is what we two happen to have to trade. Stand aside, refugee of Talonnorn."

Anger curled up in Faunhorn's eyes, and his hand went to the hilt of his sword. "Do you defy me?"

Nurnra shrugged. "I have yet to recognize that you have any authority over me, polite and handsome Talonar lord." She surveyed him from boots to hair, licked her lips, and added lightly, "Nice. *Very* nice."

Faunhorn stiffened, truly furious now, but another, older Nifl emerged from around a corner and said heavily, "Let them pass, brother. Dangerous they may be, but what Ravager isn't? If we deny Glowstone to all, we shall pass our days in loneliness, shunned by those who travel the Dark—or end our days under their blades, as they choose to all visit us together, and refuse to be denied."

Nurnra smiled at the newcomer, but Oronkh lifted his tusks and asked carefully, "We mean no trouble to anyone, Lord, but I want no misunderstandings. You're saying we're welcome, even if we hold on to our magic, aye? You're not going to let us in and then all try to slaughter us, are you? Y'see, I'd not want you to try that. I can't trade with a huge heap of dead Talonar Nifl."

"Empty threat duly noted," Faunhorn said gravely. "Very well. Ravagers, be aware that this is Lord Erlingar Evendoom, formerly of Talonnorn, but now Lord of Glowstone."

Erlingar Evendoom nodded. "And yes, you *are* welcome, and we have no intention—just now—of offering you any violence at all. You may keep your magic, or try to trade it to us, for there are precious few Ravagers here but yourselves."

"Say you so!" Nurnra replied, smiling. "Yonder stands Old Bloodblade, greatest Ravager of them all! Ho, Fat One!"

"Ho, Sucker of Blood!" Bloodblade replied with a grin, from where he'd strolled into view behind Lord Erlingar Evendoom. "What stolen delights have you brought this time, hey?"

Nurnra put her hands on her hips. "The answer to that, as well you know, depends on what you can offer me . . . for any delights at all."

Bloodblade looked rueful. "As to that, I've fallen into lean ways, since I led a perfectly good batch of slaves up to the Blindingbright and let them go, without seeing

so much as a fingertip-gem in payment from anyone."
He spread his hands. "So I'm poor and dow—"

"Intruders! More than a handcount!" a warblade
snapped, down the tunnel that led up to the lookout cavern. As everyone stiffened, Erlingar held up a warning
hand in front of Bloodblade's mouth to silence him,
warblades looked to Faunhorn for orders and then scur-
ried wherever he pointed, and Bloodblade beckoned
Nurnra and Oronkh to join him.

They hastened to do so, ending up around a corner, in
a side niche of a much larger cavern. "Keep to whis-
pers," Bloodblade told the sharren and the half-gorkul
hoarsely, "or we'll have Lord Sternjaws Faunhorn right
on top of us—"

"You already do," Faunhorn said from behind them,
his whisper as firm as steel. There were scepters in both
of his hands, and they were aimed at Nurnra and
Oronkh.

"Now, you two, if intruders are here *right* behind you,
and you have magic, you will *tell* me what magic you
have—or die, right now!" he added fiercely.

Oronkh started to pat frantically at his vest—only to
stop cold as the tip of a scepter struck his throat.

"Tell me," Faunhorn said icily, "and do *not* reach for
anything. Now . . ."

His voice trailed away. Nurnra had torn open her
bodice, to thrust something under his nose. Or rather, two
somethings.

Almost wearily the warblade stepped out from behind
the rocks, into the passage.

"Hairy One," he said sternly to the hulking human
warrior who was striding warily closer, swords in both
hands, "halt. A dozen scepters are aimed at you now, and
every one of them can blast you down in an instant. You
are come to Glowstone, and it stands not unguarded.
What is your business here?"

Orivon Firefist stopped. "Rest, water, and safe passage onward," he replied. "I am bound for the surface, and my companions with me. So who are you? You have the look of a Talonar warblade, but . . ."

"But when last you looked, Glowstone was not part of Talonnorn?" The warblade grinned, and then added gently, "You would save us all much trouble if you take one step to the side, so we can clearly see who is hiding behind you."

"Harm them," Orivon replied softly, "and die."

And he stepped aside, to reveal a line of large-eyed, frightened human children, barefoot and shivering with cold and fear, wearing only bloodstained scraps of Nifl cloaks wrapped around themselves.

The warblade looked at them. "Escaped slaves," he said slowly. "Where have you brought them from, Hairy One?"

"They are not *escaped,*" a new voice said crisply, out of the darkness beyond the children. It was the voice of an imperious Nifl-she. "They are with me, and my human champion is guarding them, so that they are transported in safety from one place to another. Strike at me, and House Evendoom will deem you a foe forevermore."

The warblade's smile was crooked. "Oh, I hardly think so. I am of Evendoom—as are we all, here."

The response was swift and sharp. "Is the one called Jalandral among you?"

Lord Erlingar Evendoom lost patience, and stepped out into view to ask bluntly, "Lady, who *are* you?"

A slender form stepped into view around a rock pillar behind the huddled human children. Its left arm ended in a sword blade. "Once," it replied quietly, "I was your daughter."

Lord Evendoom gasped and stepped forward, voice rising. "Taerune? *Taerune?* Can it be?"

Then he was sobbing and rushing forward. Orivon stepped deftly aside and swept some of the children out of his way, as they started to cry in bewilderment and for fear of what this weeping Niflghar might do.

Warblades were crowding forward now, but their blades hung almost forgotten in their hands; they were all staring at the tall figure who rushed to embrace their lord.

The two met and clung to each other, arms around each other, crying and kissing.

Someone burst through the warblades from behind, eyes alight. "Taerune? Did I hear right?"

"Uncle Faunhorn!" the one-armed Nifl-she cried, reaching out a hand for him from her father's embrace.

That clinging promptly became threefold, rocking back and forth, as warblades converged slowly, and Orivon gathered the children aside against a wall and crouched with them, murmuring, "This is good, this will be right. See? Nightskins cry for family, too!"

There was much laughter, and it was a decidedly friendly Erlingar Evendoom who came to Orivon, with Taerune on his arm, and said, "So, Orivon—I have that right, yes?—you fashioned this blade for my daughter's arm, and kept her alive when she was cast out."

Orivon rose with a smile, and replied, "She kept me alive, too, and we made common cause with Old Blood-blade. Is she Lady Evendoom to you, once more? Or am I going to have to break some Nifl necks?"

Erlingar smiled slowly. "She is Lady Taerune Evendoom, and heir of House Evendoom, no matter what any Consecrated of Olone might say about marred Niflghar. Yet I hear Talonnorn is much changed."

"Much," Orivon agreed dryly. "I would go so far as to say that the Talonnorn you knew is no more."

"Will you tarry with us, here in Glowstone, or—?" Erlingar gestured at the children.

"They need rest, and food, and water," Orivon said firmly. "Then we press on, to the Blindingbright, where they should be."

"And I will be walking with them," Taerune told her

father, just as firmly. "I'll return here, once these humans are out of the Dark, but I made a promise, and—"

"You'll not be making it alone!" Bloodblade rumbled, lurching into view with Nurnra and Oronkh right behind him. "I'll be with you, as before!"

"We'll come, too," the sharren added. "Being as our presence seems to so unsettle these Evendooms."

Orivon lifted his head. "You're not slavers, are you?"

The half-gorkul shook his head. "No. We trade in smaller, more portable things that don't have to be fed."

"Check your pouches and sheaths, everyone," Bloodblade advised cheerfully.

Jalandral Evendoom shook his head. "Farther," he said curtly. "If there's good water at this Tumblerocks, let's take ourselves there. I want to be farther away from Talonnorn."

More than a few of the Talonar around him looked anxious.

"They say this is the most dangerous part of the Wild Dark," one of them offered, voice hushed as he gazed around with wide eyes.

Jalandral rounded on him, raising his voice so that all could hear. "Rampant, hear me well: this is indeed the most dangerous part of the Wild Dark."

He strode away for a few slow, dramatic steps, and then turned and added, "And why? Because we stand in it, and *we* are the greatest danger in all these caverns!"

His words were now falling into a tense, rapt silence. Not a Nifl was moving; all eyes were upon him.

"Oh, there are slithering and lurking things, yes, and not noticing them approaching will mean doom for anyone, but never forget this: we must become Ravagers now, at least until the time is right to retake Talonnorn— which means these wild caverns are *our home*. Our strength is all of us, working together—and together, we can defeat anything this 'Wild Dark' can hurl at us. Together, we *shall* defeat it, and our victories shall make us ever wiser and stronger, until the day comes when we can return in triumph to Talonnorn, and make it our home cavern once again."

He was pacing now, drinking in their attention, feeling the hope rising behind their cynicism. He had them.

"To those who worry that we have turned from Olone, and stand in the shadow of Her disfavor and eternal curse, hear me well: I stood in the temple of the Holy Beauty we all worship, and heard how far Her Consecrated had strayed from Her true way, and I say to you that She will be pleased with what we do, you and I, in seeking to cleanse Talonnorn and retake it renewed and changed."

Jalandral was careful not to strut. He had to sound grave and yet confident. "Yet you need not believe me. You can set aside these words of mine, and merely watch. The Dark *is* dangerous, and will hand us perils—but it will also, through the favor of Olone, provide for us." He took another slow step. "Good things will befall, and the Dark will offer us what we need, if we but persist. You'll see."

The air beside him, where the cavern floor rose into a sort of raised ramp of stone, suddenly flickered and flashed, and a smiling Nifl-she stood there, on stone that had been bare of anything a moment before.

Maharla Evendoom's smile widened as she turned slowly, so that every Nifl in the cavern might recognize her. "Lord and High Lord Jalandral, *that* sounded like as good a cue as any Eldest of Evendoom has ever heard."

Jalandral blinked, too taken aback to hide his astonishment. "Maharla!"

"Who else?" she asked, stretching languidly so that everyone could see her magnificent body. "Who else would come out of struggling so hard against corrupt Consecrated of Olone to offer her lord her magic, her knowledge . . . and her body?"

Something akin to a growl of desire arose in a dozen

throats, all over that cavern, as the Talonar rampants all stared at her.

Maharla smiled around at them all, and then bent her gaze on Jalandral, her lips parting in longing.

"You," she whispered. "You I am *so* proud of. You have passed all the tests, bested all rivals and foes, and become what Talonnorn needs . . . and what *I* need. Take me, Dral. Take me, and command me hereafter!"

Jalandral smiled—a smile that grew as he walked to her, opening his arms to embrace.

He watched her smile turn triumphant, as he lowered his mouth to hers. Then, as his arms tightened around Maharla, he triggered three of the rings he wore, all at once: the one that paralyzed, the one that froze all magic in the body it was touching, and the one that clawed flesh.

She stiffened—because that was all the first ring allowed her to do—as the last ring's power plunged into her back, but was halted by the second ring.

Jalandral stepped back from her, drew his sharpest dagger, and plunged it savagely into her. Then, holding her so that she wouldn't fall, he slashed her across her breasts, sliced away her ears, one after another, and then cut away her nose.

She stared at him in helpless horror as her spurting blood drenched him, and he snarled, "Eldest, I remember *every last one* of your cruelties. This paltry repayment is the least I can fittingly do to you!"

Eyes on hers, contempt curling his lip, he laid open her throat, and then let go, letting the force of his slash turn her body, and let it topple.

The Nifl of Talonar watched in grim silence as he drew his sword and dismembered her body.

When he was done, and her severed head was rolling slowly away across the sloping cavern floor, he looked at them all, pointed at Maharla's head with his dripping sword, and commanded, "Let that be burned, right here, with all the rest of her."

He raised his bloody sword to them in formal salute, and added, "So passes one whom the Consecrated corrupted to their cause; their instrument to enslave us all once more!"

Then he lifted his voice into a loud bellow: *"So end the old ways!"*

The watching Nifl stirred; he could see their eyes shining.

Jalandral Evendoom flung his arms wide and added what just might become his rallying cry: "The Dark Warrior will fall, and Talonnorn will rise again!"

Swords flashed, all around the cavern, as Niflghar voices thundered those same words back to him, echoing him savagely.

"What is this place?" Taerune asked, eyes narrowing. "Why are we stopping?"

"We're stopping," Orivon Firefist growled as he strode past her through the watching, wide-eyed children, "because this is far enough away from Glowstone."

Taerune frowned. "What does *that* mean?" she asked the Dark in general.

The forgefist strode to a stop in front of Nurnra. Something in his manner made Oronkh hasten to her side, reaching for some of his daggers, but Orivon held up his hand to the half-gorkul in a "stand easy" gesture, his eyes bent steadily on the beautiful sharren.

Who lifted her chin under his hard scrutiny and asked, "Yes?"

"Nurnra, I've been warned about you. By several whom I trust. So hear me: you are *not* to try to tail me everywhere and drink my blood. Find another victim."

Her answering smile was gentle and genuine. "Orivon, I had already decided so. Worry not; I am *not* daring the Blindingbright for any blood-meal. Even you."

"Good," Orivon replied. "Then there's treasure in it for you." He turned and stalked across the cavern, through a passage, across a moot of passages, and on past warning runes into another cavern, with all of them following.

It was as he had left it, all tumbled rocks strewn with dead cave-sleeth, and with cave-sleeth treasure, more glittering riches than he'd ever have been able to carry away. The rocks were strewn with coins, gems, and gleaming things of curved and shaped metal that Niflghar would know the names and uses of. He hoped.

Behind him, he heard Bloodblade, Nurnra, and Oronkh all gasp in awe.

"Where did you—?" Taerune asked, and then wrinkled her nose at a rotting chunk of butchered sleeth. "Oh."

Bloodblade already had two scepters in one hand, and was clawing up a gem the size of his fist with the other, when he looked up at Orivon and rumbled, "You mean that? You'll let us take from this?"

The forgefist shrugged.

"So long as you let all of the children take a gem and a coin, and Taerune come back for what she wants. Oh, and so long as your 'us' includes these two." He pointed at the sharren and the half-gorkul. "After all, you'll need help carrying all *you'll* want."

Bloodblade started to chuckle. "I've a better idea. I'll let these two stay to sort and gather and guard, once I've stuffed my pouches. I'm coming with you. This time, I want to *see* the Blindingbright. Properly, with its brightshield in its sky, and all, not just the stars and the dark. Before I die, you know."

Orivon looked at Nurnra and Oronkh. "Sits this right with you? You'll not greet Taerune or Bloodblade with violence, when they return?"

Nurnra looked disgusted. "Hairy One, you *really* don't trust Niflghar, do you?"

"No," Orivon replied. "No, I don't. I guess I'm slow to learn."

"No, I'd not say that," Taerune said quietly, walking to his side. "I'd say you're slow to abandon wisdom."

Bloodblade sighed. "Are you two going to stand cooing all day? Let's be on our way." He patted his now-bulging pouches, gave them a bright smile, and added slyly, "After all, I've got mine!"

"We'll stay and revel in this," the sharren said to Orivon. "Get safely home, human hero."

She turned her head to look at Bloodblade, and added, "Remember the ways he takes to the surface, in case we have need of Orivon Firefist again."

Orivon cursed, and one of the children—Kalamae—giggled. Brith joined in, a moment later.

Taerune speared the piece of rotting sleeth on her blade, and carried it with her as they started out of the cavern.

"That *stinks*," Kalamae complained. "Why are you bringing it?"

"Because, Little Noise," Bloodblade growled, from behind her, "anything that smells it will think twice about prowling up and pouncing on succulent little human morsels. Out in the Wild Dark, anyone who can slaughter a sleeth is someone to stay well away from."

Aloun stared around, while trying not to seem to do so. He had never expected to ever stand in the holiest chamber in Coldheart, with the Ever-Ice rising like a dark pillar not two paces away.

Still less had he expected to be spoken to as an equal, by a devastatingly beautiful, nude young high priestess who was lounging in a smooth hollow of the Holy Ice as if relaxing on a bed. He wouldn't have believed the Revered Mother Lolonmae would ever dismiss all her priestesses—quite sharply, too—if he hadn't heard it with his own ears.

He barely believed what he was hearing now, as Luelldar talked to Lolonmae as if they were old friends.

"The fate of Talonnorn bids fair to be grim, yes," the Senior Watcher was saying, "but I do not see it reduced to a lawless ruin—for long enough for Ouvahlor or anyone to benefit, at least. Yes, it will be plunged into savage strife now, as everyone fights for power—but the Talonar have a way of settling matters very quickly."

"Until the *next* dispute, yes," Lolonmae agreed with a grin.

"W-what," Aloun forced himself to say, hardly daring to speak but very much wanting to join the converse, "of its vanished High Lord? He's not dead, is he?"

Luelldar and Lolonmae both shook their heads. It was the high priestess who answered him, teasingly: "Surely that question is one *I* should be asking you?"

Then she lifted her hand and gestured at Luelldar, who bowed his head and told her, "The last whorl I spun, before coming here to you, showed me Jalandral trying his hand, out in the Wild Dark, at becoming a Ravager. And vowing to retake and renew Talonnorn, of course."

"It showed you something more than that, didn't it?" Lolonmae asked slyly.

Luelldar nodded. "I was going to tell you all about that," he said gently. "Please believe me. I am merely . . . feeling my way through the maze of holy discretion."

Lolonmae threw back her head and laughed merrily. "Ah, what a phrase! Luelldar, be not a stranger here in Coldheart! Come striding in whenever you feel the need; so long as you don't interrupt a chant to the Ice, you'll be right welcome. Feeling your way through the maze of holy discretion, indeed! Say on; what *of* the slayer of Semmeira?"

The Senior Watcher smiled. "You watch whorls, too, don't you?"

"Occasionally," Lolonmae replied, and lifted a slender hand to caress the Ice beside her. "More often, I gaze into the depths of the Ice, and it informs me in the same way as a whorl does. Wherefore I know every detail of Klarandarr's foray into Talonnorn, and how he fared. Yet tell me of Jalandral's meeting with . . . this slayer."

The Senior Watcher nodded. "Maharla Evendoom,

Eldest crone of her House and a most ambitious and ruthless manipulator, slew Exalted Daughter of the Ice Semmeira, took on her likeness, and led the Ouvahlan force in an attack on Talonnorn—doubtless intending to eliminate certain Talonar and make some changes in her city without Maharla Evendoom having to bear any blame for it. She translocated herself to join Jalandral, out in the Wild Dark, offering herself to him—and he slew her before all the watching Talonar Nifl, renouncing all crones, I would say, because he loudly dismissed all 'old ways.' "

Lolonmae nodded. "There is something about Jalandral Evendoom; he survives and succeeds where others would have fallen long ago. I would say he is well on the way to becoming the most dangerous Ravager leader since Bloodblade."

"You speak of Bloodblade as if he's dead," Luelldar ventured, frowning.

Lolonmae smiled slightly. "Yes," she said. "So I did. How careless of me."

The children started to cry softly when the daylight grew too strong to ignore any longer. Wordlessly Orivon led the way up through the last few caverns, his drawn swords steady in his hands.

Bloodblade winced and narrowed his eyes as they came up into the last cave. Taerune grinned at him. "Behold the Blindingbright," she said softly. "In a moment or two you'll see the brightshield itself. *Don't* look up at it; gaze instead on the green stuff that will be around our boots. They call it 'grass.' It's the least of the marvels you'll see."

"Oh? Should I be expecting lots of Hairy Ones, with spears and bows and swords?"

"Don't get your hopes up. They're rarer than Ravager tales would have you believe."

Orivon looked back over his shoulder at them and growled, "Would you two shut up?"

*   *   *

The old merchant turned from the window as they came into the room, and the younger Araed traders with him hastily drew their swords.

"Who are you?" Ondrar asked sharply, thinking he'd seen the large Nifl—darkwings and death, the rampant was perhaps the largest Niflghar he'd ever seen!—around the city before.

Munthur came to a stop, saying nothing, his large hands hanging empty at his sides.

It was Clazlathor who spoke. "We are Talonar. I am a spellrobe and Munthur here is a . . . strong Nifl who does what the strong are called upon to do."

"Break heads," Ondrar said simply.

Clazlathor nodded. "We were wondering if you needed any broken, as you try to rebuild Talonnorn."

Several of the Araed merchants raised their swords. "How did you know we were seeking to do that?" one of them asked sharply.

The spellrobe ignored him. Clazlathor's gaze was fixed on Ondrar.

Who smiled, waved at his fellow merchants to down their blades, and said, "Be welcome. Be very welcome. We have a lot to do."

Orivon looked out into the full brightness, took a few steps out of sight, and then returned to smile and wave the children past him.

They obeyed, still crying, their voices rising into shrieks of excitement.

"No one is there," the forgefist said gruffly. "You can come and look."

He took Bloodblade by the hand and led him, adding, "Shield your eyes. Look down, first. Taerune, will you hurl that sleeth away before I do it for you?"

She grinned and swung her blade, to let the rotting meat fly far across the cavern and spatter on the wall.

"I was *saving* that," Bloodblade joked, in mock-injured tones. Then he looked up at Orivon, the sunlight bringing tears to his narrowed eyes.

"Forgefist, I stand in your debt and find myself proud to be your friend. If you need me, I'll be somewhere down *there*." He pointed at the cavern floor under his boots. "Dead or alive."

Orivon chuckled, and flung his arm around Bloodblade's shoulders. "I think Taerune just might fancy you," he whispered into the Ravager's ear.

Bloodblade squirmed out of his grasp, glared at him, and growled, "I thought the *crones* were the manipulators, not the slaves!" He waved at Taerune. "Take her and go stand out there and kiss her! I'll stand here and watch!"

"Do *not*," Taerune said sharply, "dare to do anything of the sort. Or those children will be finding their ways *alone* back to their village."

She started walking out into the sunlit world.

Orivon and Bloodblade exchanged looks and shrugs, and then the forgefist followed her.

They stopped atop a little hillock, standing a few strides apart, facing each other. The children, after much glee and running and a few falls, had calmed enough to gather together again, and were a little way down the grassy hill, watching them.

"I will be back," the forgefist told the Nifl lady grimly. "I know it."

"Should I lead the raids myself?" she teased.

"If you want to die soonest," he replied coldly.

Taerune smiled, shrugged, and beckoned him. Warily he approached, swords still out, and stopped just out of blade-reach.

Taerune nodded, face unreadable. "I think we are fated to need each other, you and I," she said in low tones. "I know we will meet again."

She tossed her head, hair streaming out behind her in a sudden rising breeze, and added, "Until that day." She took a step back, kissed the palm of her hand, and raised it to him in salute.

Orivon made the same gesture back to her, and then stood like a watchful statue as she gave him the slightest of smiles, and walked back to the cavern where Blood-blade stood waiting.

Orivon watched her go, not turning his back on her, until the two Nifl disappeared into the cavern depths.

Then, and only then, he turned toward Orlkettle and said to the four who knew where it was, "Lead the way. Don't run so hard you fall and get hurt—that would be foolish, this close to a good feast and your parents and soft beds!"

The four excited Orlkettle children started to run in an instant, of course.

The other freed slave-children hesitated for a moment, and then started to run after the four, pelting down through the grassy fields and rocks.

Orivon smiled. Soon they would see Orlkettle, and parents would come running. Waving his swords for balance, he started to run, too, to catch them up.

Coda

Many cities proclaim themselves the greatest of their realm or empire or even race, and Talonnorn of the Dark Below was one such.

Long and proud was its history, yet in its ending it proved no different than the rest. Poisoned from within by feuding among its increasingly decadent nobles and strife between those haughty ones and the increasingly corrupt priestesses of Olone, it fell into a decline of heir-slayings and slothful indulgences, depending increasingly on raiding other Nifl cities, and gorkul dens, and even the Blindingbright Above to seize the infants of Hairy Ones, to gain the brawn needed to work and fulfill daily city tasks and needs.

Many a proud place declines so, and when restlessness for renewal stirs, a tyrant always arises. Always, such a one delivers tyranny that only hastens the inevitable downfall.

So it was with Talonnorn, as the feuding noble Houses so weakened that city that the rival city of Ouvahlor raided proud Talonnorn itself, Consecrated fought Consecrated in the city temple, and Talonar turned to a charismatic but self-serving leader, Jalandral Evendoom, whose cruelties and mass executions in the end plunged Talonnorn into lawless ruin.

As with all such dooms, many legends arise, to lurk and flourish in their tellings and retellings, until all truths are lost. Talonnorn's legends include tales of a deposed lord returning from the Wild Dark in rags and desperation, to try to restore order and rule in his *turn. Some legends say his daughter, maimed or out-cast or even changed into the shape of a monster, re-turned to Talonnorn with him, or instead of him, or to oppose him.*

The wildest of these foolish, exaggerated tales is the legend that a Hairy One, once enslaved in Talon-norn, actually returned to topple the city towers, or slaughter all its people, or rule them!

Such claims only serve to amply demonstrate the folly of believing such distorted fancies.

—from *Dynasties of Darkness,*
penned by Erammon the Elder,
published the Sixth Summer of
Urraul

From the Land of Light to the Dark Below, Orivon Firefist descended.

Four slaves he sought. Four human children, taken and chained as he was taken and chained, snatched by raiding Niflghar as a child.

He cared not what might fall to his swords, nor what he might have to do. He went to deliver them from enslavement and bring them safe back up to the sunlit world, and would suffer nothing and no one to thwart him. One man, alone, he went down, and did this thing, and in the doing destroyed the proud Ni-flghar city that had enslaved him.

—from *The Deeds of Orivon,*
penned by Elmaerus of
Orlkettle
(date unknown)

Voted
**#1 Science Fiction Publisher
20 Years in a Row**
by the *Locus* Readers' Poll

Please join us at the website below
for more information about this
author and other science fiction,
fantasy, and horror selections, and to
sign up for our monthly newsletter!

www.tor-forge.com